PRAISE FOR *THE LAST GIRL TO DIE*

'A stunner! *The Last Girl to Die* truly sets the standard for the psychological thriller! I guarantee you'll put everything on hold until you arrive at the shocking final scenes . . . Without a doubt, one of the best crime novels of the year!'
Jeffery Deaver

'Oh my goodness, I absolutely and totally loved this book. Outstanding and compelling, it gave me whiplash from all the twists and turns.'
Angela Marsons

'Fantastic and utterly absorbing! A beautifully crafted, roller-coaster of a thriller with compelling characters and a dark, ominous setting. I couldn't put it down.'
Simon McCleave

'*The Last Girl to Die* had me instantly gripped. Hell fire – I lost sleep and bit my nails down as the tension ramped up. If you love murder mysteries and thrillers, you have to read this book. Fabulous!'
Carla Kovach

'An isolated thriller that is tightly wound and balanced on a hair-trigger. It sweeps you up like a brutal North Sea riptide, drowning you in tension and twists. Take a deep breath because there won't be time to come up for air. Helen Fields is a leading light in the Scottish-crime scene.'
Morgan Greene

READERS LOVE *THE LAST GIRL TO DIE*

'**Helen Fields is the queen of suspense**.'
NetGalley Review, 5 stars

'**Totally absorbing from the start**, the setting is beautiful, and the characters are very well written, **a real joy to read**.'
NetGalley Review, 5 stars

'**Breath-taking. Twists and turns galore**. I couldn't put it down, I loved it.'
NetGalley Review, 5 stars

'A **tense, twisty, phenomenal** read!'
NetGalley Review, 5 stars

'**Fantastic. Excellent. Incredible. I could not put this one down for the life of me. Love, love, love this book**.'
NetGalley Review, 5 stars

'What **rollercoaster ride** this was. **I love it when a book shocks me the way this did**.'
NetGalley Review, 5 stars

'A haunting, complex psychological mystery. **Breath-taking shocks, horror, unforeseen twists, and an emotionally shattering conclusion**.'
NetGalley Review, 5 stars

THE LAST GIRL TO DIE

Helen Fields studied law at the University of East Anglia, then went on to the Inns of Court School of Law in London. She joined chambers in Middle Temple where she practised criminal and family law. After her second child was born, Helen left the Bar, and now runs a media company with her husband David. The DI Callanach series is set in Scotland, where Helen feels most at one with the world. Helen and her husband are digital nomads, moving between the Americas and Europe with their three children and looking for adventures.

Helen loves Twitter but finds it completely addictive. She can be found at @Helen_Fields.

By the same author

THE
LAST
GIRL
TO DIE

HELEN FIELDS

avon.

Published by AVON
A division of HarperCollins*Publishers* Ltd
1 London Bridge Street
London SE1 9GF

www.harpercollins.co.uk

HarperCollins*Publishers*
Macken House, 39/40 Mayor Street Upper,
Dublin 1, D01 C9W8 Ireland

A Paperback Original 2022
5

First published in Great Britain by HarperCollins*Publishers* 2022

ISBN: 978-0-00-837936-0
ISBN: 978-0-00-853888-0 (TPB)

Typeset in Bembo Std by Palimpsest Book Production Limited,
Falkirk, Stirlingshire

Printed and Bound in the UK using
100% Renewable Electricity at CPI Group (UK) Ltd

Acknowledgements

Thank you to those amazing people who have bought and read this book. It's you I think of as I write. It's you whose faces I imagine as I kill a character, or make them fall in love, or have them betray one another. I see your faces and try to capture the emotions I want you to feel then cram them into these words. Thank you for continuing to read in a world of binge watching and social media. Thank you for loving the experience of falling into a book as much as I still do. Without you, I would just be screaming my stories alone in the darkness of my imagination.

And thank you to the booksellers who put this book into your hands. From the big chains to the independent bookshops, the supermarkets to the second-hand stores. Passionate people all, those who sell books. Likewise the librarians and the educators. The bloggers and reviewers. The bookclubs and websites.

Books bind us together. They join our hands and minds around the world. They inspire and excite us, and they are not so easily forgotten as those hours staring at a screen. Because when you read a book, you make your own images in your mind. You become the actor, the set designer, the costume, hair and make-up department. The director. A reader has a vast and varied skillset, and it is awesome. Remember this with the next book you read. The work your brain does as you soak in the text from the page is utterly magical.

I had a lot of help casting my small part of the magic spell contained herein. HarperCollins and Avon books are full of dangerously, fabulously creative and technical geniuses. I have a chance here to name a few, but know that there were more people involved than I can possibly thank.

Phoebe Morgan began the edits on this book, Helen Huthwaite finished them and Thorne Ryan ran the last leg of the relay. Brilliant editors all. My gratitude to Oliver Malcolm, Becci Mansell, Lucy Frederick, Ellie Pilcher, Elisha Lundin and Eleanor Slater. Many of you, I know, love audiobooks with a passion and I owe a huge thank you to Charlotte Brown for making audio gold from these books and to the outstanding talent that is Robin Laing – the voice of all the characters in these books and who has brought Luc Callanach to life for so many people – I am constantly astounded by how beloved the audio versions are.

But there is so much more that goes into the process. The sales and marketing teams work phenomenally hard. I appreciate each and every one of you. Likewise the cover designers and typesetters, the external editors and proof readers. The printers and distributors. Thank you one and all.

To my lovely agent, Caroline Hardman and her colleagues at Hardman & Swainson who knock it out of the park every day – Joanna Swainson, Thérèse Coen and Nicole Etherington – you have the patience of angels and the kindness of saints.

So to all the readers, for the love of books, I salute you. May we all read just one more chapter before we turn out the lights . . .

Helen Fields
November 2021

To Helen Huthwaite

For always bringing the sunshine

Chapter One

Finding Adriana Clark's body was a shock, but not a surprise. I had, after all, been searching for it. The girl had been lost to her family for eleven devastating days and nights. I mention the nights because, in my experience, they outweigh the daytime in awfulness so greatly that the daylight hours become irrelevant. Families waiting for a missing loved one to return can fill their days. They can make telephone calls, put up posters, give pleading interviews to the press, bake bread or go to church. Everyone, everywhere has some sort of altar – domestic, professional or religious – at which to bend the knee in times of crisis during the day. But when I first met Adriana's family, I saw the horror of the endless nights they'd endured waiting for the phone to ring and the seconds to pass. Nighttime is not merely a lack of light; it is the darkness within each of us when we lose hope.

The facts of the initial case were not uncommon. A teenager had disappeared. Seventeen years old from a family living on the Isle of Mull, west of the Scottish mainland. An American family, which was one of only two aspects of the case that struck me as unusual. Had they been visiting Mull as tourists then that would have been one thing, but it seemed a bizarre place for a family from Southern California to have chosen to live. For one thing, save for a brief, blissful summer, there were many fewer hours of sunshine per annum, not to mention the lack of malls, coffee franchises and delivery options. Still, I thought, good for them. Personally, I was much happier in smaller communities rooted in nature and self-sufficiency than in oxygen-deprived cities, but then I'm a Canadian who hails from Banff. Much like Mull, Banff half tolerates, half welcomes the annual influx of tourists. I always managed to escape into the mountains in winter or to sit by a lake in summer when I needed peace. A call to investigate a case in Vancouver or Toronto was how I usually defined a long-distance trek. Scotland was a commute further than I'd anticipated.

So, to Adriana. One late September Saturday morning her parents awoke, assumed their daughter was sleeping in and became concerned only at lunchtime by her failure to appear. Her father put his head round her door and discovered an empty bed. No sign of her anywhere in the house. Her bike still in the garage. Wallet gone, but Adriana's passport remained in her mother's bedside table. No sign of her cell phone.

Five days later I landed at Glasgow airport and made my way overland to the ferry.

You're wondering if I'm a police officer. I'm not. Nor am I a pathologist or any sort of forensic expert. What I am is a private investigator – a title I'm not keen on – but it comes with a licence, and sometimes a piece of paper is useful when you're asking people to share information. I specialise in missing teenagers. Not the subset of work I'd had in mind when I started out, but I'm female and short – thus apparently unthreatening – and I have what's been referred to more than once as a 'cheerful, positive manner'. Also, dimples. Sadly, none of those things were ever going to bring Adriana back, or render her parents' grief less dreadful.

They let me into their home and told me everything they believed to be relevant about their daughter. Adriana was enrolled in an online educational course to complete her American high school diploma. She'd had a summer job at the local pub in Tobermory where they were renting whilst renovating a permanent home. Good student, no drug problem, no boyfriend, very social. Missing her friends in America to an appropriate extent. No red flags. She had a twin brother, Brandon, with furious eyes. That was okay. I couldn't imagine how it would feel to have a missing twin. He was suffering. Last was a little sister, Luna, four years old and the product of a union between older parents who believed that nature was taking care of contraception, only to be caught out. Cute, bouncy, with curly black hair, she was a miniature of her Latina mother, Isabella. Their father, Rob, was the American classic – tanned skin, baseball loving, avid barbecuer. They'd looked at me as if I were both the poison and the antidote: a greeting I was used to. No one wants to be in a situation where they need my help.

I'd been working as an investigator since graduating from my Criminal Justice course eight years earlier, and Adriana's corpse was the most upsetting thing I'd seen in all that time. Given that I'd found the remains from a mountain lion mauling and witnessed a bear attack in progress, that's a high bar.

It was little more than a hunch that had taken me to Mackinnon's Cave. To be fair, a guidebook and a decent understanding of teenagers had ignited my gut instinct. Not that it was inevitable that Adriana was there; it could have been any of the caves on the island. A twenty-two mile trek from Tobermory, the distance was probably the reason Mackinnon's Cave hadn't been explored by police earlier; but Adriana's peers were old enough to be driving, and at that age, the further you partied from home, the less likely you were to be discovered.

3

Mackinnon's Cave is a billion-year-old crack in the western edge of the island that invades the land mass by some 500 feet. By early October, September's previously calm seas were washing up moodier and less predictable. There'd been a storm that morning with a high tide. Mackinnon's Cave was only accessible safely when the tide was out, otherwise the pathway required a swimming costume. I'm an outdoor sports enthusiast – skier, snowboarder, hiker, mountain climber. I've camped out in arctic conditions and endured snowstorms with nothing but a tent membrane between me and the elements. But a sea swimmer . . . at night? Not so much.

The cave was impressive. As I entered, the rock wall on the right leaned in, imposing. The entrance was a tall, thin break in the rock face that made my pulse dance in my wrist. The late sunlight was no match for the darkness inside, but I'd come prepared with a climbing helmet featuring multiple lamps. Stepping in, I knew my instinct had been right. The discarded cider can I trod on produced the distinctive metal crumpling sound that says 'teenagers' the world over.

The remains of a fire were just a few metres beyond – close enough to the fresh air that the smoke would be drawn out of the cave. More than one ring of surrounding stones, more than one type of wood burned – the makeshift fireplace had been used, relaid and reused perhaps over years.

Teenagers have places.

I'd already searched many of those places on the island. Favourite beaches, deserted farmers' huts, shells of castles, car parks with sunset views and privacy. But Adriana was waiting for me at Mackinnon's Cave.

My footsteps echoed through the mouth of the cavern, the sound sharpening as I entered the throat. Then into a substantial room, with natural shelves high on the rocky walls and ditches cracked into the ground at each edge. High-ceilinged, grand, imposing. I'd have missed Adriana if not for a break in the blanket of rocks that revealed the metallic glimmer of the teal toenail varnish her mother had said she'd been wearing. As I'd walked, the light from my helmet had lit the nail lacquer, producing the wild flash of a swamp animal's eyes at night. My feet, slower than my brain, had walked another few feet, and when I turned back the teal shimmer was nowhere to be seen.

On my hands and knees, I'd cleared the rocks away, wary of rockfalls, anxious not to seal my own premature coffin. Her body had been pushed down into one of the cracks, covered by a few large boulders, then shale, pebbles, dirt.

I touched Adriana's hand first. It was icy, the skin silken but firm, digits swollen. Closing my eyes a moment, the intimacy caught me off-guard. You always hope you're wrong, but I'd sensed her family's hopelessness. There'd been an undercurrent in their side-looks and the words they weren't saying. They'd been asking me to find a corpse, not locate a runaway. I'd felt it almost immediately.

I should have walked out of the cave there and then, let go of her hand and preserved the scene. Procedure, procedure, procedure. The problem with that is that private investigators have no rights. You don't get to consult with the forensics squad or the pathologist, you never see the police file (unless you're sleeping with a detective, and I'd sworn off them years earlier) and those first impressions are everything. It's almost all the useful knowledge.

Hands gloved, keeping everything in one place so as not to lose any trace fibres from the scene, keeping my knees in a single spot on the floor, I moved rock after rock until Adriana was laid out naked before me.

I'm glad the dead cannot see themselves. There's nothing peaceful about it. Being a corpse is an endlessly intrusive process.

Adriana had no obvious injuries to gasp or gape at. Forget

bullet wounds, claw lacerations or the raging burn of rope around neck. Her skin, though mottled purple in patches, had a base tone of grey-white-green. There's no name for that colour but in my head, I've labelled it mortuary green. It's really the only place you ever see it.

Her eyes were open, whites running red, the former sparkling brown of her pupils covered by an opaque shield. Adriana's mouth was open, too. Spilling from it, like the cave's own vomit, was sand. Not the loose sand you kick up walking along a beach on a sunny afternoon, but the packed-down sand of a child about to turn over a full bucket to make a castle. Her lips stretched wide in a perpetual scream that mine threatened to copy.

It was not a feature of a drowning case. It was not a prank gone wrong. Nor had the girl stuffed her own mouth with sand in some grotesque drug-fuelled delusion. Sooner or later she'd have spat it back out and rolled onto her side. Adriana had had company at the moment of her death.

Her long black hair – her pride and joy by all accounts – was fanned out beneath her head, and wrapped into it, twined around, was seaweed. It was dark and stinking now, although the decomposing body won the competition for assaulting my senses. The seaweed was a grotesque crown: she was a dead beauty queen belonging to the sea. I took out my camera and photographed the body. I had the family's permission – carte blanche to do whatever was required. They would never have to look at those images as far as I was concerned, but I needed them as a record in the investigation. And there was one final, terrible task. Drawing the girl's legs up, I opened them to check for injuries. Adriana had been beautiful in life. She might not have reached the peak of her looks at seventeen, her body still growing into itself, but she was easily captivating enough to have attracted the attention of people whose motives were less than pure.

I hadn't wanted to look. When I did, I couldn't look away.

A large shell had been inserted into her vagina, half of it still visible. Swallowing my revulsion, the shame of witnessing such violation, I took more photos, hating myself, knowing I had no choice.

There was no blood on the ground beneath her, nor spilled down her legs. Her nails were intact, her hands free of the scratch marks of defensive wounds. Only the heels of her feet were damaged. She hadn't run across rocks barefoot, hadn't scrambled up or down a rockface, panicked.

Setting her body back the way I'd found it, leaving the rocks to one side, I searched the remainder of the deep cave. No clothes or personal possessions remained there, only the odd food packet, cigarette stubs; human debris. Someone had defiled her body then hidden her, just not well enough that she'd never be found. They'd tidied up after themselves and removed the clothes she'd been wearing, then left her in a place that felt both empty and watchful at once.

Shivering, I knew I'd taken all the time I could, but it pained me to leave Adriana alone there. It wouldn't be long until she was inhabiting a body bag instead, I told myself. Safe from predators on a morgue slab. That was cold comfort.

Emerging from the cave an hour after I'd entered it, I sat on a rock and dialled the number for the emergency services. No reception at the cave mouth. Regretfully, I moved away, leaving Adriana lying alone in the pitch black. I was halfway up the slope to the road before my call went out.

The island officer on duty overnight would be notified, I was told. They would be there as soon as they could. A scenes of crime unit would have to come from the mainland. Something about a request being put through to Glasgow. Could I remain in situ and attract attention so officers knew where the body was? I assured them that I would.

I'd said I'd found a dead body, but not the name. I owed it to the family to break that news to them myself, and on a small island word would get out the second the name was spoken aloud. I was going to be asked to give a statement, and to explain what I'd been doing there. There would be the inevitable grilling over my handling the corpse and moving the rocks. It was going to make for an uncomfortable working relationship with the police moving forward.

But that was why my services had been engaged in the first place. An unwillingness by local officers to send out search parties. A reticence by the police to believe that any foul play had been involved. The trite phrases, 'happens all the time at this age', 'she'll be back in a week, tail between her legs' and 'probably just partying in Glasgow' had been repeated to Adriana's parents ad nauseam. Also, something less irritating and more unsettling – a sense that the police were not counting the days until they really started investigating, but were in fact counting the days until the Clark family gave up and went back to where they'd come from. I'd met Mull's most senior police officer. The family hadn't been imagining the hostility.

Which was why they'd turned to the internet for help and found the name Sadie Levesque, investigator, teenager tracking specialist. Paid my ticket from Calgary International Airport. Booked me a room at a hotel. Agreed my fee.

Now their girl was dead. Mocked, hurt, violated, abandoned. I'd grown used to dead bodies, but I would never grow used to the cruelty some humans were capable of unleashing. Adriana's death was not only an assault on her, it would spread its unwelcome fingers to touch every family member, every friend, scarring them forever. There's no such thing as 'peace over time' for the loved ones of murder victims. I know that better than most.

So the police would come, they would express their standard sympathies to the family (for what little that was worth), and an investigation would – finally, too late – be officially opened. The question I had for the police was not how they planned to catch Adriana's murderer, but, in a small, island community, would they really want to know which of their own had committed such a horrific, unspeakable act?

Chapter Two

'You often find yourself in the right place at the right time to find a dead body, do you?' Sergeant Harris Eggo asked. He was six foot two, with mousy brown hair and the sort of body that would be soft and warm on a cold night but a liability chasing a semi-fit criminal uphill.

'A few times now, actually,' I told him. That was the truth. I had a policy of rarely lying to the police. 'One lie leads to another' was one of my mother's favourite sayings. Once you started, you had a way of slipping and landing in a pile of them when you weren't paying attention.

'Are those the qualifications that persuaded the Clark family to hire you? Because where I come from, we're more impressed if you bring missing persons back alive rather than dead,' he said, aiming it at the room rather than at me. A few people rewarded him with muted laughter. That's who he was – a populist point-scorer. I wasn't in the mood for it. Adriana's parents were waiting for me.

'Why hadn't you sent out a search party?' I cut the laughter off. 'Adriana's been missing eleven days. No word. She didn't have her passport. There were no sightings of her catching the ferry to the mainland. Where I come from, we prefer our police officers proactive rather than sloppy.' It was more aggressive than I generally allowed myself to be, but then Sergeant Eggo was more of a dough-head than the police officers I was used to.

'You want to watch the tone with me, girl,' Harris Eggo murmured. 'You turn up on my island and suddenly a young woman is dead? We can conduct this interview under caution if you like.'

'Would that make it faster and more professional? Because that would be an improvement.'

Eggo stood up, walked around from his side of the desk, knocking knees with one of the other officers in the room. The tiny police station on Erray Road in Tobermory was an unloved single storey unit. Grey and drab, it had seen better times. I sighed. It would have been comical if a girl weren't dead. He perched on the desk in front of me, folded his arms and scowled.

'You jumped up fuckin' Yank—'

'I'm Canadian, but carry on,' I said.

There was a knock at the door, which probably saved both Sergeant Eggo and me from losing our tempers. Earnest hazel eyes and an impressive jaw, set in smooth black skin, graced the room.

'Thought you might like my preliminary findings,' the man said. 'Was it you who found the body?'

'It was,' I confirmed. 'I'm Sadie Levesque.'

'Right, I'm the forensic pathologist. Nate Carlisle.' He held out his hand and shook mine. His hand was warm and smooth. I don't know why I'd imagined it would be cold. Perhaps because of the time it spent inside cadavers.

'We're in the middle of something here,' Harris Eggo said. 'What was it you had for me?'

11

'Adriana's been dead a minimum of eight days, more likely nine or ten. Cause of death was drowning.'

'Could we take this outside, Dr Carlisle? I'm interviewing a potential suspect here.' Eggo stood up and pulled his shoulders back, which had the unfortunate side-effect of pushing his stomach out.

'I don't think you are,' Carlisle said, his tone light, volume set to low. 'I gather Miss Levesque only arrived in Scotland five days ago.'

'We don't know that for sure . . .' Eggo said.

'You can run my passport to check my arrival date. I'd be happy to hand it over,' I said.

'The Clark family has already sent a message requesting that I share the details with Miss Levesque. They'd rather not have to deal with the forensics themselves. She's their chosen representative for now.' I liked Nate Carlisle already.

'She interfered with a crime scene,' Harris Eggo said. 'Then there's the fact that she knew exactly where to find the girl. I'd like to finish this interview, if I may.'

'I was ascertaining who the deceased was before calling the authorities. I was careful not to remove any evidence from the scene. As for knowing where Adriana was, I've been searching the island for four days now. The question isn't how I found her, it's why you didn't.' I stood up. 'Dr Carlisle, can we talk?'

'Now listen—' Harris Eggo began.

'I have a blank witness statement form,' I told Eggo. 'I'll write all the details out tonight and drop it in to you tomorrow. If you have questions after that you can call me.' Nate Carlisle exited and I followed him to the front door. 'It's late. I'm guessing you've missed the last ferry back to the mainland?'

'I'm being airlifted out with the body at first light. I've booked into a hotel,' he confirmed.

'Okay, well I'm done for the night and honestly, I could use a drink. I suspect you feel the same. I found the corpse so in my book that means you're buying.'

'You're right, I could use a drink, but I'm Scottish so no prizes for guessing that one correctly. However, you disturbed Adriana's corpse and left fingerprints all over my scene,' Nate Carlisle replied. 'So actually, Miss Levesque, you're buying.'

The bar in The Last Bay Hotel was decked out in tartan wallpaper that would have been an eyesore when new, but which thankfully had faded over time to a welcoming indistinct blur of colours and lines. The wooden flooring had seen plenty of boots over the years, and the woman running the bar was efficient but pragmatic.

'You'll be wanting the table near that window,' she directed us. 'It's curry night and a bit stinky near the kitchen.'

We took our whisky and went where she'd directed. It was a warm October evening and the breeze where the window had been propped open with an old book was welcome. Dr Nate Carlisle – he'd given me his card and the list of letters after his name was both baffling and impressive – was in his forties, lean, upright in both body and attitude.

'I had you checked out and asked the family to give me written permission to talk to you,' Nate said. 'Most of the time I limit my conversation to direct relatives only.'

'I'm a licensed investigator,' I told him. 'For what that's worth. Where are you based?'

'Glasgow. Have you visited the city?'

'Does the airport count? It's my first time in Scotland. Wish it had been for any other reason.' I sipped the liquor and it heated my throat as I swallowed. 'To Adriana.' I raised my glass and we drank together silently. I gave it a minute before I asked the question that had been waiting to tumble out. 'If she drowned, how did she get all the way back in that cave? The tide doesn't go in that far.'

Nate checked around and decided we couldn't be overheard. He leaned forward and kept his voice down in any event. Speaking of the dead was best done in hushed tones.

'She was dragged, probably under the arms. There's substantial damage to her heels, multiple linear abrasions to the skin and debris trapped in the wounds – tiny stones, some broken shell. I can't tell yet if there are the same injuries to her buttocks.'

'Why not?' I asked.

Nate took a deep sip and drained half the remaining whisky from his glass.

'So you didn't lift her body up then? That's something.' I waited for him to explain. 'How strong's your stomach?'

'I'll cope.'

'Then I'll show you the images,' he said. 'Just don't pass out. I'm less used to live patients.'

'I'll remember that.'

He took out a digital camera, sufficiently sophisticated that it read his thumb print like a cell phone before allowing access to the gallery of photos, then went into a folder labelled 'Clark' with the date after the name. Handing me the camera, he had the grace to look away as I flicked through the images. The first few were wide shots of the body in situ – the cave, the rocks, the length of her body facing upwards into the dark. Then close-ups of Adriana's face, the seaweed crown, each hand, each breast, her abdomen. Her private parts – the shell – again, from a wider perspective, then close up. I flicked through as fast as I could.

'What type of shell is it?'

'A conch,' he said. 'Seven inches long. Before you ask, it's not native to Scotland.'

The next image was a freeze-frame with a video icon on it waiting to be pressed. I tapped at it with the edge of my thumb.

The cave was fully floodlit by this point. Protective mats surrounded Adriana's body, ensuring no trace evidence was lost as she was moved to a body bag for transportation.

'Roll her on three, slowly and gently,' a voice instructed from off-screen. Gloved hands, more than I could count, took hold, making sure no additional damage was done during the manoeuvre. 'One, two, three.' They supported the body and rolled her. Beneath her corpse, the floor seemed to move.

'Capture some of those crabs,' Nate said in the video. I looked across our sticky pub table to the real-life version of him and raised my eyebrows. 'Animal life cycles related to corpses can help give us an accurate time of death. Now we need to know what damage to attribute to animal predators and what was occasioned during her murder.'

I picked up my glass and downed what remained of the peaty liquid before returning my eyes to the screen. Adriana's back was badly mutilated and patches of flesh were missing from her arms.

'The backs of her legs are still intact,' I noted.

'They were on a layer of solid rock which protected them.'

'The extent of the damage is how you knew she'd been there so long?' I asked.

'That, the colour of her skin, the bloating. The timeline can be thrown out with drownings, especially in such cold water when the body's left exposed, but it seems likely to me that she died within twenty-four hours of leaving home. Are you okay?'

'No one should be okay after watching something like that, should they?'

'I'll get another round in,' he said. 'Turn the recording off.'

I did as he suggested, hoping no member of Adriana's family ever saw the footage.

Nate sat down and pushed a refreshed glass across to me.

'Was she sexually assaulted, other than the violation with the shell?'

'Impossible to tell at this point, and with the seawater and animal destruction, we might never be able to say conclusively.'

'Okay,' I nodded, drinking as I thought about that. 'I guess she could have drowned anywhere and been moved there in a vehicle. It didn't have to be in the water at Mackinnon's Cave.'

'No, but that would be quite some feat – moving the weight of a dead body full of seawater. It would have to be done under cover of dark and it would likely take more than one person.'

'Do you know what type of seaweed is in her hair?'

'It's kelp. *Laminaria hyperborea*'s the full name. Common around here. You're looking pale.'

'I'm from Banff. We're not known for our tans,' I said. 'No other injuries?'

'Abrasions, I won't know what else until I'm able to look under the surface of the skin. Discolouration has made preliminary assessments difficult. There's nothing obvious, though. I couldn't feel any abnormalities to the skull. There could be wounds to her back that have been removed by—'

'Yeah, I get it,' I said. 'Do you believe in life after death, Dr Carlisle? I don't. I never have. But if you did believe in it, you'd have to allow for the possibility that she could see herself there, would be aware that her body was being eaten a layer at a time.'

'She was dead when those creatures got to her. Fully dead. Adriana didn't get out of the water alive, I promise you that. Those crabs were not her problem, although I suspect they will be mine.'

'The conch shell . . . the violation. While she was alive or after she died?'

'I can't be sure until I've completed the postmortem.' Nate checked his watch. I was on borrowed time.

'She was Latina. Her mother's side. You think there might be a racist motive? From what I've seen Mull doesn't have much in the way of a varied ethnic population.'

'Are you asking me because I'm black or because I'm Scottish?'

'You're both. Makes you more qualified to answer than me. But actually I'm asking because it's notable that of all the girls on the island, the one who ends up dead in a cave is neither Scottish nor white. What are the odds?'

'Adriana was pretty, young and new here, so possibly more interesting than the girls whose families have lived here for generations. The Scots, generally, are inclusive and forward thinking. Did I get called names at school in Glasgow based on my skin colour? Yes, I did. Has it stopped my career from progressing? The answer to that should be obvious.'

'But you know only too well that not all racism is about name-calling. Sometimes it's a failure to respect someone, or perceiving non-Caucasian women as more permissive. Disposable, even. You think the police will investigate that angle of this?' I was on dodgy ground. The forensic examiner worked with the police every day. Whatever my feelings about Sergeant Harris Eggo and his uniformed cronies, I couldn't expect Nate Carlisle to agree with me.

'Go easy on them,' he said. I prepared myself for a lecture. 'This is a small island. The community will be in shock. There hasn't been a murder here for years. It's a peaceful place. And this isn't just about finding Adriana's killer for one victim's sake. Harris Eggo has to reassure the whole island that its sons and daughters are safe. He's the father of a teenager himself. The man's shocked and scared. Putting on a uniform doesn't eradicate normal human failings.'

It wasn't a lecture. It was worse. I felt ashamed. I should have been less prickly and more helpful at the police station. Nate was right. Policing a small island wasn't the same as policing a city. Everything about an investigation here would be personal.

'So tell me what a private investigator from Banff is doing in Scotland. Does your work often take you so far from home?'

His voice was soft as he asked. I got the impression he'd realised I was feeling bad and was trying to distract me. Nate Carlisle was both perceptive and kind.

'I've done a few cases outside Canada, mainly in the States where kids have run away and crossed the border. I once ended up in Honduras. By the time I found the boy I was looking for, I'm not sure which of us was the more scared. Lawless places are terrifying when you realise how few rights you'll have if something goes wrong.'

'Do things often go wrong in your cases?' he asked with a gentle smile.

'Sometimes I end up dealing with unscrupulous people. There's no kind of trouble a desperate teenager won't get themselves in. Occasionally that means I've had to be unscrupulous to get them out of trouble. I'm not proud of it, but I stopped drawing lines I wouldn't cross a while back. It can be a messy business.'

'Our professions have that in common, then. Well, I should get some sleep,' he said, standing up. 'Weather permitting, I'll be up and gone early.'

'Thanks for talking with me,' I said. 'You'll call as soon as you have more information, eh?'

'Absolutely,' he said. 'You know, you haven't asked about the sand in her mouth. The shell was almost crude, broad-brush defiling. But the sand . . .'

'The sand is everything. It's the whole of her killer's anger boiled down to a single action. I don't need any help understanding it.'

'I cleared it out, to preserve it,' Nate said. 'It wasn't just in her mouth. Whoever did that to her shoved it down into her throat. Put their fingers into her mouth and pushed all the way down and back. It would have taken effort and time. It's unlike anything I've seen before.'

I took my hotel keys from my pocket, already feeling the futility of lying on a bed when sleep would elude me.

'Cold fury,' I replied. 'That's what the sand is. Fury is the weapon that killed Adriana Clark.'

Chapter Three

To the north of Tobermory, a solitary road hugged the coastline. From there, a few houses gazed out to sea. The Clark family lived in a large, double-fronted Victorian home, free of the pebbledash so many of Mull's houses wore as a shield against wind and rain. Five of them, until last night. Today, the curtains were drawn. The press hadn't made its way to the island yet. I doubted they would until the gruesome details were released. Until then, it was a teenager's body in a cave and just one of those tragedies that strikes from time to time.

The door opened a crack – someone checking who was approaching – then the space widened to allow me entry. I'd phoned the Clarks the previous night, between the arrival of the emergency services at the cave and my police interview. Realistically, a phone call from an investigator late in the evening was unlikely to be good news. The visit was about sharing select facts. Adriana's parents would dictate how much they really wanted to know.

Brandon opened the door. His dark eyes wouldn't meet mine, and his hair was tousled. He was a good-looking kid, as Adriana had been. I greeted him blandly as he slammed the door behind me. He took the stairs two at a time, then another door slammed on the upper floor of the house. That was fine with me. The conversation I was about to have wasn't for anyone other than parents.

Isabella Clark was a statue on the sofa, gripping the arm, staring off into the distance. Rob stood up and shook my hand. I offered the usual, useless platitudes as we sat down.

'Have the police been here this morning?' I asked.

Rob nodded. 'They're treating us all as suspects.' He gave a bitter smile. 'Not that they said it out loud, but there was mention of the fact that these sorts of killings are usually done by someone known to the victim. Given how little time we've been here . . .'

'It's all just standard practice. Please don't take it personally,' I reassured him. 'How much did the police tell you?'

'Too much,' Isabella said, keeping her eyes on the wall. That glazed-eyed, dilated-pupils stare was a combination of shock and medication, and a trademark in deceased children cases.

'Was Adriana a strong swimmer?' I asked, getting right to it. No point making it a longer conversation than it needed to be, and it was already too late to spare their feelings.

'She was,' Rob said. 'She swam a lot back in . . .' he paused, swallowed, '. . . back in California. Not swim-team fit, but Carlsbad is a beach town. She was there with her friends every day.'

'So she was used to tidal water then,' I said. 'But night swimming . . . Is that something she'd done before?'

'You don't get in the water in California at night,' Rob said. 'There are great whites.'

Isabella lowered her head. 'She'd have been safer with the sharks,' she said.

I let that sink in a moment. A girl who was used to the perils of the sea. Currents, rip tides, how harmless fun could transform into danger in just one wave.

'We'll know more when the forensic pathologist has completed his report. They took Adriana's body out this morning on a helicopter. She'll be in Glasgow. I'm afraid they won't release her for burial in an active murder case. The police are going to be working full time on this now. They'll have backup from the Major Investigation Team on the mainland. I wasn't sure if you wanted me to . . .'

'You should stay,' Rob said. 'We can pay you.'

'I'm not sure I can do much more than the police. They won't share their files with me, and they're pretty hostile to be honest.'

'That's why we need you. You should have heard the way they spoke to Brandon. He's an easy target. We're the outsiders here. It would help us if we felt like there was someone here to deal with it for us,' Rob said.

As concerned as I was by how little impact my involvement might have, the term 'outsiders' was no overstatement. In their position, I'd have wanted someone to be my voice. It was neither realistic nor decent to expect them to be able to handle it themselves. I already knew I would stay.

'Does Brandon have a positive alibi or was he at home in bed?' I asked.

'He was asleep,' Rob said. 'We all were. Adriana sneaked out.' He sounded angry and that was understandable. I never wanted to become a parent. The constant conflict of love and discipline that I'd seen looked exhausting. I had yet to take a case where a victim's parents hadn't warned them a hundred times about the dangers of being careless with their personal safety. Anger amidst grief was the most human mix of emotions.

'I looked in on Brandon,' Isabella said. 'I heard a noise in the night and got up, checked on him. He was definitely here and he was definitely asleep.'

Eyes steady on the fireplace, I figured out what my next

words should be. Sounding critical or accusatory would be hurtful and inflammatory, but Isabella Clark had just made a serious mistake.

'Is that what you told the police?' I asked, my voice a notch above a whisper.

'Of course,' she responded.

'Did the police speak to each of you separately?'

Rob nodded.

'And did the police ask why, if you'd heard a noise and gotten up to check on Brandon, you didn't also notice that Adriana was missing from her bed?'

Her mouth opened and shut as Rob closed his eyes and turned his face away.

'You didn't hear how they spoke to him,' Isabella gushed. 'Latino kid in a new country, sibling rivalry, doesn't like his sister getting so friendly with the islanders, lost his temper, deviant tendencies. I grew up in a world where the police pinned you to the ground first and worried about the consequences later. Burglary, robbery, rape – my people got blamed for it all. Why should it be any different here?'

She was right. I had no idea what she'd been through. Racism in America was not a historical problem. Racism in Scotland I was less familiar with. What I did know was that giving a false alibi to the police – especially one as clumsy and flawed as this – only ever made cops more suspicious. Harris Eggo had struck me as many things, but he didn't seem stupid enough to have failed to figure out that Isabella Clark did not check on Brandon that night, and now they'd have Brandon even higher on their suspect list.

'Don't worry about it,' I said. 'It was a natural reaction to tell the police that in the circumstances. I have to ask you – only because the police here will be checking the same thing – has Brandon ever been in trouble? Either with the police or

23

at school. Anything they can latch onto and use as an excuse to interview him?'

They glanced at one another and I hated myself. I'd been engaged to help find their daughter's killer, and I was asking questions about their son's prior indiscretions.

I'd have hated me too.

'He's done nothing,' Rob said. 'Brandon's a good kid. Surly sometimes, not great at getting down to his schoolwork. They're doing online classes so they don't have to swap out of the American curriculum and we can monitor how many hours they're doing – how many hours he's doing,' he corrected himself.

'How were Adriana's grades?' I asked.

'As and Bs. She was on course to go to a good university,' Rob said.

'She wasn't going back to the States for college?' I asked.

'She could have gone anywhere in the world for college,' Rob replied. 'We've taken the children abroad since they were tiny; shown them Europe, South America, Asia. We wanted them to know the possibilities were limitless.'

Another long look between Rob and Isabella. Thoughtless of me to have raised it. Who wanted to think about their daughter's bright shiny future while she was lying on a mortuary table?

'I'll get out of your way soon, but there was an . . . issue. With Adriana's body, and a shell.'

'We know,' Rob said. Isabella began to cry. It was a miracle she'd got through until now without starting.

'The police will be focusing on that, so I need to know. Did she have a boyfriend or an ex? Anyone who'd shown an interest in her, even just online?'

'No, nothing like that. She'd have told us,' Rob said. 'We've only been here a few months. She was concentrating on her schoolwork and her job at the pub, saving money. Adriana wasn't the kind of girl who would let anyone . . .'

'No, no, no,' I rushed. 'Don't think that. Absolutely no one is suggesting that anything Adriana did got her into this or could ever be sufficient motive for what's happened to her.'

'I saw Addie with a boy,' a small voice piped up from the doorway into the dining room. The double glass doors had been standing open a crack as we'd talked.

'Luna!' Isabella gasped. 'You were supposed to stay in your room.'

She strode across to the little girl and gathered her in a tight embrace. Luna was going to grow up in her mother and father's sight every minute of every day until she'd finally had enough of it. That was what parents did who'd lost another child to a violent crime. They lived every day knowing it could happen again, and believing that if they weren't vigilant enough, it would.

'Hi Luna, I'm Sadie. We met a few days ago, remember?' Her black curls bounced as she nodded. 'When did you see Adriana with a boy, sweetheart?'

'Please don't . . .' Isabella said.

'She has to,' Rob told her. 'It's okay to answer, Luna.'

'Mommy and me were walking through town. Addie was down an alley with a boy and she saw me and she smiled and she put her finger over her lips like this.' She put her forefinger over her closed lips in a shushing motion. 'So I knew not to tell. Was I bad?'

She turned huge eyes towards her mother, who forced a smile through the pain.

'No, honey, you did good. You and Addie always had your secrets, right?'

'We're besties,' Luna said, beaming at me. Still too young to comprehend that her sister was gone for good, and years away from being told the truth of what happened, Luna was possibly the only thing that would keep Isabella and Rob from swallowing too many pills late one night to dull the pain.

25

'Can you tell me about the boy you saw, Luna?' I asked.

The little girl scrunched up her face and gazed at the ceiling as she thought about it. She was adorable.

'They were kind of dancing,' she said. 'Sort of how Mommy and Daddy used to in the kitchen.'

'That's real good. Can you remember his hair colour or his skin colour?'

'Um, his skin was white like Daddy's. I don't remember his hair.'

'Did you hear anything he said?' Luna shook her head. 'Not a problem. Anything else?'

'I think he's a daddy too,' she shrugged.

'You think he's a daddy? Did he have a baby with him?'

'No, but he had a picture of a little boy. I saw it on him. Mommy, can we make Jell-O?'

'Maybe later,' Isabella said. 'Go get yourself a Reese's. I left some out on the table.' She put Luna down and the girl raced off in search of peanut butter and chocolate. The colour had drained from Isabella's face and she looked ashen, exhausted by the effort of pretending their world wasn't imploding.

'I'll go. Nate Carlisle the pathologist has promised to call me this evening with an update. Is there anyone in Tobermory that Adriana was particularly friendly with who might know the identity of the boy Luna saw?'

'She met a lot of other teenagers when she was working at the pub. There was no one in particular,' Rob said. His eyes were on his wife. Isabella looked as if she might collapse at any second.

'No close friends in the States she was in touch with on social media? Someone she might have confided in?'

'No one,' Isabella said. 'This was a new start for us all. We encourage our kids to stay off the internet.' Her tone was hard. I'd overstayed.

'I don't suppose there's any news about Adriana's cell phone? Did the police manage to triangulate its movements or locate it near the cave?'

'Nothing,' Rob said. 'It's switched off and there's no sign of it.'

'I understand. I'll touch base with you in a couple of days then,' I said. 'Call if you need me.'

Brandon was walking back down the stairs as I let myself out. The look on his face could have frozen lava.

Chapter Four

That afternoon, I could have been any other tourist. A watery sun left the air only lukewarm, but the colours of the houses arced around Tobermory Bay were candy-store bright. Oranges, reds, yellows, blues reflected in rippling water. A chocolate shop, a soap company, guest houses and cafés, art galleries and pottery sellers – it had everything you could possibly want if you were passing through. Mull's long-term inhabitants shopped elsewhere. There was a food store on the harbour as well as a post office and a bank. Life here was simple. Tourists came and went; the island needed them to leave some of their money behind. My hometown operated on the same principles. Everyone knew everyone. Each argument, every romance, new grandchild, divorce – it was the town's dirty laundry; none of it seemed to belong to the individual any more.

I'd spent almost an hour poking into the corners of Tackle & Trade. It catered for an intriguing mix of interests. Shiny things for fishermen; authors I'd never heard of and a few I had; midge machines; art supplies. It was like a sudden influx of Christmases. I'd exited with a compass, it being a tradition of mine to buy one in every country I visited: a superstition I had, to make sure I could always find my way home. I also left with a book to use as a prop, called *Letters to my Sixteen-Year-Old Self*. Seemed appropriate given that Adriana would never grow old enough to be able to look back sagely.

My cell rang as I exited. Caller ID announced my sister.

'Hey there, Becca,' I said, smiling. 'How hard's my niece-to-be kicking you these days?'

'Hey yourself. You haven't called Mom since you arrived in Scotland. She's thinks you've been kidnapped. And your niece is refusing to exit my womb until you're back here to come to the hospital with me. When's that likely to be?'

I sighed, picturing my baby sister's bulging abdomen and envisaging the military-style birth instructions already pinned to her fridge. I was to be her birthing partner, as her former fiancé had decided that becoming a parent didn't fit in with his influencer lifestyle. For the record, I'd asked Becca if I was allowed to locate him and perform certain improvements to him that would prevent him from ever impregnating another woman, but she'd refused her consent. At some point in the future, I was planning on doing it anyway. Our mom was acting in a supportive role from home, where she was looking after our dad who was battling dementia. None of that was going to stop my sister from having a natural birth: no pain killers; no unnecessary surgical intervention; no balloons or cuddly toys.

'I'm sorry, Becca. I have no idea how long this will take. It's a month until baby girl's turning up though, right? That's plenty of time. And I'll phone Mom tonight – promise.'

'Promise, promise?'

I stopped, not liking the quietness of her voice. My sister was an all-guns-blazing kind of woman. Low volume wasn't her thing.

'I just wish you weren't so far away,' she said. 'Even my bump feels a bit sadder without you.'

'It's nice to be missed,' I said. 'Listen, it'll fly by. You've got plenty of friends there to pamper you. All that nesting to do? Organic baby food to make and freeze?' I made a retching sound and she laughed.

'Okay, okay, we'll be fine. Just keep in touch. It's not too bad a case this time is it, Sadie? I don't want you getting lost in something terrible just before the birth.'

I faked a smiling voice and prepared to lie. Not a new sensation when it came to my family. The details of my worst cases were better off glossed over.

'It's nothing bad at all. I have some leads already; hoping for a successful wrap-up really soon. Piece of cake. Now go put your feet up, eat chocolate and read that bump a story from her Auntie Sadie.'

Small brass compass in my pocket, book in hand, I strolled towards a pub called The Blether that my hotel receptionist had told me was the place all the locals gathered in the evenings. It was also where Adriana had spent her summer evenings earning £6.50 per hour washing plates and glasses. It was as good a place as any to gauge the toll the murder was taking on the community and get a sense of what the islanders' theories were.

The Blether sat one road back from the world-famous photo op of Tobermory Bay, hidden from view until you passed right in front of it. Red fronted, with windows that had once been white and clean, you made a choice at the front door. Turn left into a seated restaurant area, or go right for standing room at the bar, mismatched tables and chairs, a dartboard and a pool table. I turned right into a sudden silence.

'You'll be wanting to sit and eat then,' the man behind the bar decided without asking me. 'Better off in the other room, love.'

'I'm good thanks,' I said. 'Could I get a cold one?'

The man I assumed was the landlord smirked, but he took the lid off a bottle of lager and slid it across the bar in my direction. I paid and chose a table in the far corner, giving my new book all my attention as conversation struck up once more. I gave it a full five minutes before I dared look up and take stock.

Four men were huddled around one table. I recognised one of them as a colleague of Sergeant Eggo. He'd been sitting in on my interview, although to be fair he hadn't uttered a word. Now he was studiously ignoring me. A gaggle of girls looked simultaneously bored and over-excited, false eyelashes locked and loaded, which seemed inappropriate for a trip to the local pub the day after a fellow teenager had been found dead, but it was part of a generational culture. Couples held hands and chatted, while two lone drinkers nursed hard liquor and wallowed. A few people were watching a game of darts. The landlord had been joined by a middle-aged woman and a good-looking boy who the landlord slapped on the back. His son, I guessed. The girl pack began whispering and preening. I kept my eyes down and my ears pricked. There was a sense of drama in there – the whispering that tragedy brought with it and its equal weight in intrigue.

The door opened again and Harris Eggo entered, followed by a second bout of silence. This one bore the weight of respect and expectation. I put my head down and turned a page for something to do, but my reading session was definitely over. The landlord handed Harris a measure of whisky which he took, knocked back, and pushed forward for a refill.

'Any news?' one of the darts players asked.

'Nothing good,' Sergeant Eggo replied. 'No leads yet.'

'Sarge,' the other officer said, soft-voiced, but not soft enough that I didn't catch it. As I glanced up, he gave a pointed look in my direction, and Harris Eggo's eyes followed.

'You letting anyone in now are you, Bobby?' Eggo asked the landlord.

'Ach, she's easy on the eyes. I figured it would pretty the place up a bit.' The landlord laughed at his own joke until his wife elbowed him.

'Miss Levesque,' Harris Eggo announced. 'Was there something you wanted?'

'Beer,' I said. 'It's good.'

'Is there no' a bar in your hotel?' Eggo continued.

I shrugged and returned my attention to the book I wasn't reading.

'I thought you were here to work, not for a holiday—'

'Lay off, Dad,' the boy behind the bar said quietly. Not the landlord's son then. Another teenager helping out for some spending money.

Harris Eggo turned his back on his son and decided to address the bar instead.

'We believe whoever killed the girl was a tourist. Plenty of guidebooks mention Mackinnon's Cave. Given the length of time between her death and the discovery of her body . . .' He paused. I assumed he was looking in my direction for dramatic effect and didn't grace him with a return glance. 'I'd say he's already left the island.'

As shocking as the lack of professionalism was – making a public statement about an open case, in a pub of all places – no one seemed surprised by it. Everyone was already talking about the murder, drawing baseless conclusions and speculating furiously. Eggo was putting his own community's needs first by reassuring them that the suspect was an outsider, not to mention sending me a crystal-clear signal establishing where his loyalties lay.

The landlady appeared at my table, another bottle in her hand. She put it down gently in front of me. I smiled my thanks.

'Poor wee Adriana,' she said. 'How're her parents doing?'

'Too early to tell,' I said. 'Adriana worked for you?'

'She did, just for the last two months. Gave us no trouble, turned up on time, friendly.'

'How friendly, exactly?' Harris asked over her shoulder.

I didn't like the implications, but I wasn't sure he even meant them. I was being baited. There was nothing like a pissing competition with a small-town cop to ruin an evening.

'Harris, that's not what I meant. I never saw Adriana talking to any of our customers like that. Why would she go off with a stranger to Mackinnon's Cave late at night?'

'Maybe she'd had a few drinks, smoked some weed, felt a bit lonely. Homesick maybe? Have we had many American tourists in here in the last two weeks?'

I hated that his last comment was a fair point. There was something about running into your fellow countrymen that made you yearn both for home and for the comfort of familiarity.

'We've had Americans in and out of here every day this summer. Adriana never mentioned any of them though.' She patted me on the arm. 'I'm Rachel. These boys give you any shit and they'll answer to me.'

A man tapped Harris Eggo on the shoulder.

'Harris, there's s-s-something I n-n-need to t-t-talk about,' the man said. Thirty-something with a thick head of ginger hair, skin the sort of unhealthy grey-white normally reserved for deep sea creatures and jowls that defied description, he was sweating badly enough that I could smell him from a couple of metres away.

'Tomorrow,' Eggo said. 'I'm off duty.'

'I r-r-really w-w-want to . . .' He reached out to touch Eggo's arm and the police officer stepped away.

'I'll handle it, sir,' Eggo's junior officer stepped in, pulling the man away. 'Come on Skittles. We'll talk outside.'

'Skittles?' I asked in the landlady's direction.

'All anyone ever sees him eat,' she said. 'Don't think he's consumed a vegetable since he was a kid.'

Harris Eggo pulled up a chair the wrong way round, sat on it with his legs spread and his arms leaning on the back. He'd been watching too many American detective shows.

'You saw the Clark family today then,' he said.

'They're my clients,' I reminded him. 'What CCTV coverage is there on the island?'

'Oh, you don't get to use our assets. There'll be no information sharing. I want to know what they told you about their boy.'

I closed my book slowly and leaned forward. I kept my voice as quiet as I could, given that everyone in the pub was trying to listen in on our conversation whilst simultaneously attempting to appear as if they weren't.

'"The boy" has a name. It's Brandon, and he's in mourning for his twin sister. She has a name too. It's Adriana. The family has suffered the worst loss imaginable. I know you have a job to do, but don't ask me about private conversations with the people I'm here to help.'

'You noticed it too,' Harris Eggo lifted his chin triumphantly. 'He's fuckin' weird. You knew exactly what I was asking you. Don't even bother denying it.'

The police sergeant was just bright enough to be dangerous.

'He's been by Adriana's side every day of his life. I can't imagine how it would feel to lose a twin. I'm guessing half of him feels dead too.'

'Did they teach you that psychological crap at fake cop school?' Eggo asked.

'Have you taken statements from every regular at this pub?' was my counter.

'Not necessary. I've known these people for years.'

'So all those standard questions – when did they last see Adriana, what was their relationship, had she mentioned being worried about anything or anyone – you're already satisfied that no one here can help with any of it?'

'If anyone here had any information, they'd have come to me voluntarily.'

'Unless there's something they don't want to tell you, or there's someone they're protecting. Maybe suspicions that they feel uncomfortable voicing?' I pushed him. His face was mottling scarlet.

'Every man, woman and child on this island knows they can tell me anything. And they know that if they cover something up, they'll have me to answer to.'

'Wow, so you're both the good cop and the bad? Impressive.'

'Sir,' Eggo's junior officer said. 'Could I have a word?'

Eggo stood up, forgetting his reverse chair stance, and had to back off the seat with his legs spread. Leaning towards me, hands on the table, he finally found his quiet voice.

'The boy you're protecting is hiding something. You find out what that is and fail to tell me, I'll charge you as an accomplice,' he hissed.

'I'll be sure to keep that legally unenforceable threat in mind,' I said. 'Looks like you're wanted.' The junior officer was biting his nails.

'Come on then,' Harris Eggo said. 'None of you kids walks home alone tonight,' he ordered as he headed for the exit, revealing the truth behind his bland and unproven claim that Adriana's murderer had left the island. Eggo knew there was every chance the killer was still walking among them.

I took my fresh bottle of beer and my book, and went to stand at the bar.

'Did Adriana keep any personal stuff here?' I asked Rachel.

'We have a boot room. The staff put their coats and bags

there. Some of them leave stuff, an overnight bag maybe if they're off out with friends. The girls leave makeup quite often. We tell them not to leave anything valuable there.'

'Could I see that room, do you think? I'm not looking for anything in particular. Just trying to figure out what she was into, where she might have been hanging out.'

Rachel gave a small nod, watching her husband until he turned his back.

'Follow me,' she said quietly.

The boot room was at the back of the pub, down some steps, almost a cellar. It was damp and smelled of wet clothes. The window frame was black with mould. Nothing glamorous about it, and a far cry from California. I wondered again why the family had made such a dramatic move. It was a question I had yet to ask them, and in the circumstances I doubted I'd be having that conversation any time soon.

'From what I saw she left her stuff in that corner usually,' Rachel said. 'Those are her boots. I'd best get back behind the bar. Could you let yourself out the back when you're done? My husband might not like me letting you in here.'

She didn't need to explain. 'Of course,' I said. 'Thanks for helping.'

Adriana's rain boots were bright yellow. Outgoing girl; confident colours. I rifled through the other five coats left in the room but found nothing to suggest they belonged to Adriana. No bag. Not even gloves or a scarf that might have been hers. I checked the staff toilet, where there was nothing but soap, paper towels and hand sanitiser.

Adriana's parents would want her personal effects. They might be painful to look at right now, but with the passage of time, the smallest things had meaning, and the boots had to be moved some time. I picked them up and tucked them under my arm to deliver home the next day. One was substantially heavier than the other. I slid my hand into each and brought out a small zipped silver bag from one and a velvet pouch from the other.

The silver pouch contained eyeliner, mascara, lipstick, concealer – nothing extraordinary. All the things a teenage girl would consider essentials, and keeping makeup at the pub to reapply mid-shift or as she was leaving made complete sense. The velvet sack less so. It was purple, and so light I assumed at first that it was empty. I stuck a finger inside. It came out covered in a grey powder with no discernible odour other than a mustiness that could easily have come from being stuck at the bottom of a rain boot. I considered tasting it, then decided against. Whatever it was, anything that came in powder form raised immediate issues. The problem for me was how to get it tested, and whether or not to hand it over to Harris Eggo. Both questions were resolved when my cell phone rang. I tucked the bags back inside the boots to transport them, and headed out of the back door to speak with Nate Carlisle.

Chapter Five

'Adriana had an avulsion fracture to her left ankle,' Nate said.

'Translation please.'

'One of the ligaments in the ankle pulled away from the bone. It took a small piece of bone with it, hence the fracture,' he explained.

'Can you tell if that happened while she was alive or after death?'

'Difficult to be certain. It's usually a trauma incident caused during sports or in an accident. I'd say it happened during fight or flight – for example if she was grabbed or running and her ankle got stuck or suddenly moved in an unnatural direction.'

'Okay,' I said, building a mental picture of what Adriana's final minutes must have been like. She wouldn't have gone swimming voluntarily with an injured ankle, and she died in the water. 'Could that happen if someone was holding her ankle and she was trying to get away? Too much strain on the joint?'

'If she twisted or suddenly changed direction then yes, absolutely,' Nate said.

'Even if she was in the water at the time, which would have slowed the movements down?'

Nate was quiet for a few seconds. 'I would say yes, if the person pulling her ankle was strong enough to get a firm grip. Maybe it was the murderer who did the twisting, not Adriana.'

I kept walking along the harbour front. It was fully dark now, and it occurred to me for the first time that I was taking a risk walking alone at night.

'She wasn't assaulted by some tourist who did that to her then left the island,' I said, partly to myself, partly to answer Harris Eggo's earlier claim.

'How can you be sure?' Nate asked.

'There were so many personal touches. If she'd been kidnapped, raped and killed, then I might accept the tourist theory. But she sneaked out of her house at night. She had to trust the person she was meeting to do that.'

'Maybe she was being threatened?' Nate asked. 'It's possible she didn't feel able to refuse to go.'

'Which also requires a longer-term relationship, don't you think? But the shell – that's symbolic. It's not a normal sexual assault. And it's not as if they could have picked that shell up from the beach. They took it with them to meet her and spent some time constructing her seaweed crown. A psychopathic tourist? Why would they expend so much effort if Adriana wasn't important to them?'

'I hear you,' Nate said. 'I'm afraid as far as the question of rape goes, there's no conclusive evidence. The seawater – she did drown in saltwater rather than freshwater – has cleaned her body pretty thoroughly. The damage caused by the shell masked any other possible prior vaginal injuries. Doesn't mean it can be ruled out, but it'll never be proved.'

A car drove towards me, putting its headlights up then slowing down as it drew close. I raised my hand to shield my eyes, stepped away from the edge of the pavement, pressed my back against a wall. The car beeped its horn three times then sped away. The glare in my eyes was too bright for me to get the licence plate. I picked up the pace.

'Everything okay?' Nate asked.

'I'm fine. Listen, I need a favour. I found something and I need it tested. Can you help with that?'

'Any reason why the police aren't handling this? Only it sounds like something you should be reporting. If it's evidence—'

'I don't know what it is,' I reassured him quickly. 'It's a velvet bag with a small amount of powder in it. It's not from the body, the crime scene or from her house. I'm not even sure it's Adriana's. It's just something I found in the boot room of the pub where she worked for a few weeks.' It was only a white lie, but Nate deserved better and I knew it. Still, if I went to Harris Eggo, rumours about Adriana's drug use would be flying around in a matter of hours. I hushed my conscience. 'Can I send it to you? My hotel organises a courier service. It can go on the ferry out tomorrow morning and be with you lunchtime.'

He gave a soft sigh.

'You think it might be hers?'

'It's from a staff area. Looks like plenty of people come and go, including the landlord's family. I'd just like to know what the drug scene is around here. What she might have gotten herself into, you know?'

'I'll be able to answer that better when I get the tox screen back. I can tell you she had no needle marks or scars that suggest serious drug use. Her teeth and gums were good. Septum undamaged.'

'So will you help?' I asked, arriving at the door of my hotel.

'Only touch it with gloved hands from now on. Be careful with the packaging and the labelling. Leave the powder in the original container. To be delivered to me personally with a signature. And I need a favour in return.'

My respect for Nate Carlisle grew.

'Shoot.'

'I asked Mr and Mrs Clark where I could access Adriana's medical records in the US. They signed consent forms for me to access them but the healthcare provider denies having had Adriana as a patient. There must be some sort of mix-up, but I need those details urgently. If I email you the consent forms again, could you print them out, get them signed, scan or take a photo of them and get them sent straight back?'

'Leave it with me,' I said. 'It'll have been an administrative error. Healthcare companies in America aren't known for their easy-to-navigate systems.'

My room was on the ground floor. The hotel was clean but not luxurious. The windows creaked upon opening and the toilet flush required pulling a chain that looked like a historic artefact, but it was warm, had good pillows and reliable WiFi.

It took me a while to package up the velvet powder bag in several layers of plastic and a padded envelope, then to find a staff member to sort out the courier service. By then it was after 11 p.m. in Scotland, but only 4 p.m. in Banff. I phoned my mother, made reassuring noises, then told her I was off to bed. After that I started on the only type of research possible at that hour: social media. I had fake accounts I'd spent years cultivating under pseudonyms so I could see other teenagers' profiles without raising red flags. Runaways still posted selfies for as long as their smartphone was working, and those photos and posts solved about half my cases.

My usual experience was that for every name I checked, search results came back with at least one hundred possibles. Not so for Adriana Clark. Couple of variations on the name, but no exact match. I tried a different platform: same thing. Then another. Adriana must have used a pet name, which was clever, and good security settings, which meant she was danger aware.

So the idea that she disappeared in the middle of the night to skinny-dip with a stranger, without telling anyone where she was going? No goddamned way.

Rob Clark phoned me at 9 a.m. to say he'd received my email and that I could go over. I waited until 10 a.m. before knocking on their door. We sat in the kitchen and drank coffee. Isabella was still in bed and Luna was playing in her room. He didn't mention Brandon.

'Did you get the forms I forwarded from the pathologist?' I asked.

'Sure – I've printed them out and signed them.' He went into the dining room and rustled through some paperwork before returning to slide the forms over the table. I checked them as he stacked the dishwasher.

'This might be the problem,' I said. 'The handwriting is hard to read and they normally require a full signature rather than initials. Could I be a total pain and ask you to do it once more?'

'Printer's out of both ink and paper,' he said. 'They don't sell the right ink cartridge on the island. I'll have to send for more from the mainland.'

'That's okay. I went into Tackle & Trade yesterday. They run a business service. I can get the forms printed there and drop them round to you this afternoon.'

'Sure,' he said. 'So you spoke to the pathologist last night?'

'I did. Do you want to know—'

'No,' he said quickly. 'I just want you to find who did this. I need to know that Isabella, Brandon and Luna are safe from whatever monster did this to my little girl.' The glass in his hand cracked and he stared at the falling shards as if he hadn't even realised he'd been holding it.

'Let me,' I said, taking the remnant from his hand as he went to find a dustpan and brush from another room.

'Dad, you okay?' Brandon ran into the kitchen and stopped when he saw me. 'What are you doing here?'

'Morning,' I said. 'I had to get some forms signed. Your dad just dropped a glass, that's all.' Brandon turned his back to leave. 'Actually, I need your help. I want to get an idea of Adriana's social media presence. I can often tell if someone was being trolled or stalked.'

'She didn't do social media,' Brandon said. 'None of us do. I don't think you need it to find who did this to her.'

I let that sink in for a moment. Brandon's gaze slid away from mine.

'Who do you think is responsible?' I asked quietly. No point cajoling or playing games. Brandon wasn't going to hang around long enough for that.

'One of the fucking weirdos on this fucking island,' he said.

'Brandon, watch your language,' Rob said from the doorway.

'Are you kidding? Addie's dead and I can't swear about it? This is screwed up.'

'Go to your room,' his father said.

I waited until Brandon's footsteps had faded up the stairs before speaking.

'I was asking Brandon about Adriana's social media. Is it true that neither she nor Brandon use it?'

'It is,' Rob confirmed. 'We raised our kids to play sports and be outdoors. That's one of the reasons we moved here.'

'The other reason?' I had to ask sooner or later.

'I have a major accounting client on the west coast of Scotland. They wanted me close by for meetings.'

'So how did Adriana keep in touch with her friends in America?'

He shrugged, sweeping up the splinters of glass that had spun into every corner.

43

'Could I ask what school they attended in California? Maybe she was emailing friends there and gave over some information that'll prove useful.'

'I don't want word getting out about her death, about how she died. Her killer's here somewhere. In Scotland. We want you to focus on that. There's no way Isabella will be able to deal with people contacting her to offer their condolences right now. We need our privacy.'

'Of course,' I said. 'Whatever you think is best.' I put my coffee mug in the sink and folded the medical records paperwork into my pocket, just in case it was legible enough for Nate to use. 'Was Addie the family pet name for her, or was it more widely used between her friends?'

'Just the family,' Rob said. 'How long will this take, in your experience? I know that sounds like a stupid question, but I don't know how long Isabella can keep going.'

'It's not a stupid question,' I said. 'Getting the results from all the postmortem tests can take a few weeks. It would be helpful to see Adriana's phone records.'

'Her cell phone's on my account, but the information I can get is limited to outbound calls and contract details,' he said. 'I can give you access to that. The police said they'll be applying for a court order to get more but it takes time.'

'Thank you. Could you email whatever you have to me as soon as you access it?'

'I'll do it this morning,' he said.

'Also, I was checking out the pub where Adriana worked. They still had her rain boots. I thought I'd bring them back to you. I left them by the front door. Can I ask, did you ever see Adriana with a small purple velvet bag?' Rob looked confused. 'It's nothing, forget it,' I said. Tears formed in his eyes and I headed for the hallway.

'I feel so responsible,' he said as I took hold of the door handle.

'You're not.' I was stating the obvious, but sometimes that helped.

As I walked out of the house, the mechanical whirring and chugging of the printer started up. Rob locked the door behind me.

Chapter Six

Addie. First with two *d*s then just one. With a *y* on the end, then with *ie*. Then I checked out Brandon Clark. I didn't feel good about it, but now I had two jobs to do. The first was to figure out who killed Adriana. The second was to make absolutely sure the police didn't reach the conclusion that her twin brother was responsible for her death.

School was in session in California. I had three piles of paper in front of me that I'd been avoiding looking at all day, no email from Rob Clark regarding Adriana's cell phone data, and there were too many loose ends.

Like the printer.

As a general rule, I sit on my concerns about my clients the way you learn to sit on your hand when you're trying to give up biting your nails. That was why I hadn't taken the blank medical records form I'd printed off at Tackle & Trade up to the Clarks' house yet. It was also why I hadn't yet cross-referenced the form they'd filled in for Nate Carlisle with the one they'd filled in for me. I guess I knew it was going to be a rabbit hole, and that I'd end up doing something stupid like phoning all the high schools in Carlsbad and asking their librarian to go through the yearbooks to locate the Clark twins. But I never could let a thing go. My mother always swore it'd be the death of me.

I tackled the forms first. The blank ones, ready to be delivered for signature and emailed back to Nate, had a standard release on them to any healthcare provider in the US. All that was required was the name of the company, the patient's full name, date of birth, healthcare plan number, last address as a patient and the parent or guardian's details. Simple, quick. That saying, when you'd just lost your child, especially in dreadful circumstances, just boiling a kettle became a Herculean feat.

The form the Clarks had filled in for Nate Carlisle had an address in Carlsbad that looked like 7109 Jefferson Street, with the ZIP code 92008. The numbers were a mess and ran into one another, but it was just about legible. That meant there were three public high schools the Clark kids might have gone to. I hated to do it, but my fingers were dialling numbers before I could stop them. I gave different excuses to each high school administrator, and each was as helpful as could be, but the long and the short of it was that the Clark twins hadn't attended those schools. That didn't rule out several private schools in the area, but there was no way staff at those institutions were going to share information. That part of California was home to billionaires, oligarchs, politicians and playboys. The schools their kids attended were information fortresses.

All of which still left me with this: why had Rob lied about his printer not working?

I wished I'd exited their house sixty seconds earlier. I wish I hadn't heard the whirr of the inkjet and the paper's soft whoosh into the plastic tray. Because the truth was that Sergeant Harris Eggo had left an insect bite inside my brain and it was becoming increasingly hard not to scratch it: there was something unsettling about Brandon Clark. I breathed out hard. It was a relief to let myself think that freely. That didn't mean he'd killed his twin sister. It did explain why the police had flagged him as a person of interest though, and my concern was that Rob now appeared to be avoiding giving me any information that might lead me to find out more.

Finally, I looked at the signatures. I studied them long and hard. That's when I knew I had to get the blank forms back to Rob Clark to see if he could improve his calligraphy.

Walking past the pottery shop, behind the till I noticed an elderly woman and one of the girls who'd been part of the oestrogen circle in The Blether. I'd wanted to explore the shop anyway, so I went in, keeping my eyes fixed on a painting on the far wall. It was a seascape – nothing unusual there, no matter what island you landed on across the globe – but this one featured an ancient vessel in flames against a darkening sky. It was awesome in scale and beautifully painted.

'Excuse me, is this by a local artist?' I asked.

The elderly woman waved the girl over to me. 'It is, but it's not for sale I'm afraid. Anything else is, but that's been on the wall here since my gran took over the shop, and that was—' The girl didn't get the chance to finish the sentence on her own.

'Forty-three years ago. Two husbands and one fiancé later and I'm still here,' the woman finished.

'Why didn't the fiancé convert into a husband?' I asked.

'Cold hands,' she said swiftly. I waited. This was obviously a question she'd been asked before. 'He kept needing to warm them up inside other ladies' clothing.'

I smiled and nodded. 'Sounds like a circulation problem to me.'

'Circulation indeed. Where are you from?'

'Canada,' I said.

'Gran, that's the person I told you about,' the girl whispered.

'Ah, you're the private detective. You look too young.'

'I'm older than I look. That's not a complaint,' I said. 'I'll appreciate it when I'm forty. I love this fruit bowl.' It was rustic and roughly fired, painted with acorns and oak leaves. 'Not sure it would survive the journey home in my backpack, sadly. Can I ask, did either of you know Adriana?'

'You and your girlfriends socialised with her sometimes, didn't you Lizzy?' She looked at me. 'I call those girls the nitwits, which Lizzy hates, but in my day only a certain type of young woman wore a T-shirt that didn't cover her stomach and false eyelashes that made you look like a circus performer.'

Lizzy sighed.

'Were you friends with her?' I asked the girl. 'I need to find out who she hung around with and confided in.' The girl chewed her bottom lip. 'No one's safe until the person who killed Adriana is caught. I'm here to help her family, but this is everyone's problem. Can you tell me anything?'

Tears came next. That was normal. The difficult thing about a murder in a small community is that people still go to bed and wake up the next day. Shops still have to be opened. Milk is still required for the morning cereal. Life carries on. Even when a few miles up the road a living, breathing, pretty, bright young woman has had her life brutally cut short.

'We didn't hang out with her all the time. I mean, we got to know her, but she spent a lot of time with her brother. When she started working behind the bar at The Blether she had to go home straight after her shift. And she was, like, difficult to get to know.' The girl walked closer to me, as if the pottery shop was full and she needed to keep her voice down. 'She's not even on social media. Not anything. How weird is that?'

'Weird,' I agreed. 'Was she seeing anyone?'

'Um, Sergeant Eggo said we weren't to talk to you. In case

it messes up his investigation. I don't want to do anything wrong.'

'Anything you tell me, you should also make sure to tell the police. It can't hurt to have as many people as possible try to figure out what happened, can it?'

'I s'pose. Adriana wasn't seeing anyone that I knew of. Sometimes people flirted with her if she was in the bar. She was fairly pretty.'

Fairly pretty. Teenagers giving praise was always a sliver away from an insult.

'Are there any younger men you know who have kids already? Who might have shown Adriana a picture of their son?'

Lizzy shook her head. 'Dunno what you're talking about there,' she said. 'Who wants to screw up their lives like that? Me and the others would never have a kid at this age. If you do that, you'll never get away from here.'

Her grandmother gave a long-suffering look.

'The other girls in your group – would any of them talk to me? We can meet somewhere private if they don't want to be seen with me in public.'

'I don't think so,' Lizzy said. 'They're all friendly with Sergeant Eggo's son. They won't want to piss off the police.'

'That's fine. Listen Lizzy,' I said, keeping my voice low and private, 'between us, what's the drug scene like around here? No one's going to want to tell the police the truth about that, but you can talk to me.'

'I've never done anything!' she exclaimed. 'I know some people do, but not me. I want to work with the polar bears at the Highland Park Zoo. It's literally the best place ever. I'm not messing my future up.'

'Polars bears in Scotland? That sounds amazing. And good for you. Keep your eyes on the goal. But I've got to ask . . . what about Adriana? Did you ever see her do drugs or hang around with anyone who did?'

Lizzy glanced over her shoulder at her gran, who was staring intently into a computer screen.

'Promise you won't tell anyone I said?' she whispered.

'Of course,' I whispered back. 'This is confidential.'

It wasn't, but she didn't need to know that.

'She was interested in magic mushrooms. Some people here do them because they're organic or whatever. They're natural, so it's safe, right?'

'I'm not sure about that,' I said. 'Can you get them around here?'

'I shouldn't . . .'

'You might save a life,' I reminded her. 'You might save one of your friends' lives. This is a murder case, Lizzy. If you know something you should tell an adult.'

More tears welled in her eyes. She blinked them away. Keeping secrets was stressful work.

'The landlord at The Blether can get you weed if you want it. That's what everyone says.'

'I won't tell anyone you told me, okay? You're safe. Please don't worry about this. It's not a big deal.'

'I'd better go,' she said, checking for passersby outside the shop window.

'Me too. And if I pass you in the street or see you in the pub, I'm going to act as if we've never spoken.'

Her shoulders dropped and she smiled for the first time.

'Thanks. You're not what Sergeant Eggo said you were like.'

I should have seen that coming, and I managed enough self-discipline not to ask the obvious question as I left.

Back at the Clarks' house for the second time that day, I was disheartened to see that a few members of the press had arrived, camped at the end of the driveway. They weren't allowed to knock on the door or get in the way of anyone arriving or leaving. Break the rules and an injunction would be requested immediately. The cameras started flashing as I walked up. I didn't even bother with a 'no comment' – just ignored them and kept moving. Taking the footpath around the side of the house, I opted to phone to announce my presence. Isabella opened the door.

'Can you do anything to get rid of the media?' she asked before I was even inside. 'We can't have them here.'

'They're allowed on public land as long as they don't harass you or do any damage. You don't have to talk to them but they can take your photo if they're using it for editorial purposes. I'm sorry. Have your food delivered and ask the driver to bring it to the back door.'

'Luna can't play in the garden and Brandon can't go out at all . . .'

'It'll be fine as long as he doesn't give a statement,' I said. 'There's no knowing how long this will last. Brandon has to be able to leave the house. Teenagers and confined spaces—'

'They can't take his photograph!' Isabella shouted, clapping her hand over her mouth as if to quieten her voice.

'Come on, honey,' Rob said, appearing in the kitchen. 'I told you I'd deal with this. It's too much for you. Go on upstairs and try to sleep. Sadie's doing the best she can.'

That was kind, but not strictly true. I was pretty sure there was a lot more I could be doing if I had access to better information.

Isabella disappeared into the hallway and Rob shut the kitchen door, motioning for me to take a seat at the table.

'I brought the medical release forms,' I said. 'Would it help if I filled in the boxes? It's hard to print small enough to be legible in the space they allow you.'

'No,' Rob said.

'You want to do it yourself?'

'I'm not doing it at all. I've had a chance to think about it and it's too much. The invasion into our privacy. We've suffered enough.'

I rubbed my eyes as I thought about that. He was right; yet what parent wouldn't turn any stone necessary to find their daughter's killer?

'I understand, really, but this information won't be released publicly. It's for the pathologist to compare old fractures with new ones, skin damage to old scars. Toxicology reports with prescribed medications. There's nothing here that'll make Adriana look bad, if that's what you're worried about.'

'Are you saying the police wouldn't be allowed access to those files once I've given the pathologist my consent for their release?' he asked.

'They would, yes.'

'That's when the leaks start. The insinuations and speculation. I don't want it. Not any of it. The pathologist will have to do without.'

'That's going to raise some questions.' I folded the blank forms and put them back in my pocket.

'Listen, we were having some financial problems before we left the States. Health insurance was the first thing we cancelled. It was costing five thousand dollars a month and I lost my job for a while. The reason I can't hand over the records is because there are no recent records to get. I was too embarrassed to explain that when I signed the forms before.'

That made sense. Forty-four million Americans had no health insurance – the figures were repeated in political debates with depressing regularity. Rob Clark was ashen.

'I'll explain to Dr Carlisle,' I said. 'Apologies for pursuing it. As far as Brandon leaving the house goes—'

'I'll deal with that,' Rob said, walking to open the back door.

'Sure. I didn't get the email about Adriana's cell phone records. I just want to make some progress for you.'

'Phone records,' he said. 'I'll get right on it.'

I ripped my jeans hopping over their back fence onto a footpath to avoid the reporters, thinking how awful it must be to get to a point when you don't have health care. The next question was obvious before I'd finished that thought. How could you afford private schools but not health care?

Magic mushrooms, I reminded myself. Powder in Adriana's boot. Weed being sold at the pub where she worked. Those were the questions I needed to concentrate on. Not her family who loved her. Not the cost and inequality of health care in the USA. And not Brandon. If the Clarks had any concerns at all that their son might have been involved, there was no way they'd have brought me in to investigate.

Determined to make progress, I decided to brave The Blether again. Whisky, this time. Beer suddenly didn't seem strong enough.

Chapter Seven

'Hi, Rachel,' I said, leaning against the bar. 'What's good?' I asked, gesturing at the whisky selection behind her.

'I'll get the Macallan,' she said.

'It's quieter in here tonight. Everything okay?'

There were people dotted around the pub, but they weren't talking.

'Everyone gave statements today. Some detectives came over from Glasgow and helped Harris Eggo see as many people as possible. I think it was a bit of a shock to us all that the locals hadn't automatically been discounted.'

'Those statements are just to establish a timeline and to make sure there's a proper record of the days leading up to Adriana's death. It doesn't mean anyone's a suspect.'

'It made me realise how little I'd spoken to her. She worked two or three shifts a week through the summer, and I barely knew her. I should have dropped some food up to her parents by now. We're supposed to be better than this as a community.' She handed me a glass with more whisky in it that I'd been planning on drinking. 'On the house. Will her family leave, do you think? I'm not sure I'd stay if something that awful happened to me.'

'I don't know if I could leave the last place I saw my child alive,' I said. 'Thanks for the drink.' I raised my glass to her.

Harris Eggo entered, flanked by two other officers.

'Evening,' I said.

'You a regular now, are you?' he asked.

'She's a guest,' Rachel said. 'If you're having your usual you can all sit down and I'll bring your drinks over.'

'Doesn't do any good,' an old man shouted from the far side of the pool table. There was a moment when heads swung in his direction, then the chatter resumed more quietly. He slammed an open palm down onto the table. 'None of it. Lots of talk, lots of promises. You know what it got me?'

I looked at Rachel who looked concerned but carried on wiping a glass, keeping half an eye on him.

He was drunk. The number of empty glasses on the table and the sway of his body were enough to give that away. But the man wasn't just inebriated. He was crying too.

'Time to go home, maybe, pal,' someone yelled back at him.

'Home? What's there to go home to? It's empty!' He swung a finger at no one in particular. 'You can't even start to know what it's like. You all forgot, didn't you?'

Rachel laid her cloth down gently and came out from behind the bar, walking slow, fixing a smile on her face. She sat down next to him.

'Jasper, do you need a taxi home? I can call you one.'

He grabbed her hand. She didn't try to pull away, but there was a sea change in the atmosphere. No one was pretending they weren't watching any more. The landlord and Harris Eggo's son both appeared from the other bar.

Rachel looked up and stared in her husband's direction.

'Nae fuss,' she said.

'There's no peace,' the man cried, gripping Rachel's hand harder.

'You want to let my wife go?' the landlord asked loudly.

'That's enough.' Harris Eggo stepped in. 'Come on, Jasper. One of my men'll drive you home.'

'Don't want driving anywhere,' he cried. 'I want to be with my wife and daughter. Now there's this other girl and no one's talking about what happened before. Not a one of you.'

He had to be in his seventies. Broad Scots accent, tricky for me to understand every word, but maybe that was the alcohol and the slurring. A tweed cap that looked almost worn down to the threads. A face with lines so deep around his mouth and eyes that it was like softwood scored with a knife. Tears turned the wrinkles into riverbeds.

Harris Eggo and another officer walked over, standing between the crying man and the rest of the bar, obscuring the view.

'Away you come Rachel,' I heard Eggo say. 'We've got this.'

Chairs scraped and they took an arm either side, supporting him, manoeuvring him out.

'Police were all over the island today, asking the same questions. Didn't do any good then, won't do any good now.'

'That's enough. Best leave quietly,' Eggo's fellow officer said.

'Quietly?' he shouted. 'They put sand in my girl's mouth. Was that quiet enough for you?'

Harris Eggo looked straight back at me, motioning for his officer to get the man out of the bar. I tossed back my drink and put the glass down, picking up my bag and making for the door.

'No,' Harris Eggo told me.

'Let me pass,' I said. 'You've no right to bar my exit.'

'You're to leave Jasper alone.'

'Sergeant Eggo, I'd like to leave this pub now. Step aside.' I couldn't say what I wanted to say and he knew it. Not every detail about Adriana's death was public knowledge and I wanted to keep it that way as long as possible. 'Sounds to me like that man has relevant information. Why are you not taking his details?' I asked.

'I already have his details,' he walked close to whisper in my ear. 'His daughter died a good decade before you were born. His mind was destroyed by it. It cannot possibly have any relevance to the American.' A police car went past the pub window, its siren giving a solitary whoop. The driver raised his hand to wave at Harris Eggo. I folded my arms. 'Feel free to go back to your hotel now,' he said, stepping aside.

I gritted my teeth. 'Want to try remembering we're on the same side?'

'You're the one with a client,' he replied. 'I'm a public servant.'

I left. It was a matter of personal pride for me never to swear at anyone in the course of an investigation, and I was just about to lose my temper. Giving myself a moment to take a breath, I leaned against the pub wall. Someone would be able to tell me the old man's name, but not tonight. Feelings were running high, my own included.

I zipped up my coat. Even the best whisky couldn't protect against the wind chill off the sea. The walk back wasn't long but it was a dark street back from the harbour. Footsteps echoed behind mine and I turned back instinctively. The curve of the road shielded whoever was there, and I was freaked out. The mention of the sand had made my guts shrivel. Walking again, faster now, I took an alleyway that would let me complete my journey under better street lighting. There's a difference between being able to take care of yourself and having a false sense of your own invincibility. I was never complacent about that.

Footsteps again, but not the heel-toe heel-toe pattern I should have been hearing. Whoever was approaching me from behind was trying to come at me quietly. My pulse was up. I could feel Adriana's cold fingers in mine once more, trying to pull me away. But running wouldn't get me the information I needed. I wanted to see the face of the person following me.

Stepping into a doorway around a corner, I waited. The footsteps sped up. I was panting, trying to control my fear, but my hand was on the whistle in my pocket. The figure went past me – a male: tall, hood up, determined. He paused, looking both ways up and down the street. I stepped out, keeping my distance.

'Looking for me?' I asked loudly. Be confident, stay on a public street, never turn your back. There were rules for situations like these.

He jumped visibly, then put his hand up to his mouth and shushed me, pulling down his hood to reveal his face.

'Quiet,' he said. 'If my dad finds out I've talked to you he'll kill me. I'm Lewis.'

Lewis Eggo stepped back into the alleyway from which we'd just emerged. I conceded moving a couple of steps closer so we could talk without attracting attention.

'I know following you seems creepy but I wasn't sure where you were staying and I couldn't ask anyone.'

'Okay,' I said. 'What is it you want to talk about?'

'I feel bad for how my dad's treating you. Things on Mull aren't like where you're from.'

'I don't know about that. I live in the middle of nowhere in a town that spends half the year invaded by tourists.'

'That's not it,' he said, shifting from foot to foot. 'I shouldn't be saying anything.'

'You worked with Adriana, right? How well did you know her?'

'A bit,' he said. 'She didn't like to talk about herself much. I tried asking about her life before, about America, but she'd just change the subject. Not rude or anything, just a bit closed off.'

'Did you ever see anyone in the pub taking a particular interest in her? Anyone ever ask about her when she wasn't there?'

'A couple of times, but she was new and people do that when someone new comes to live here.'

'What about Brandon? Do you know him?'

'Not at all,' Lewis said. 'I've seen him. A couple of times he met Adriana to walk her home after her shift. He didn't ever come into the bar, just waited outside. I've got to get back. I'm just on my break.'

'You came to tell me something, Lewis,' I said. 'What was it?'

'To watch your back. Things happen here that no one talks about. It's always been that way.'

'You'll need to be more specific,' I said.

'You need to talk to Jasper. He understands. Tell Adriana's family I'm sorry. I feel so bad for them.'

'Did Adriana get in some sort of trouble, Lewis? If she did, you need to tell me. Next time it could happen to someone you know a lot better, and you don't want to have to live with knowing you could have done more.'

He swallowed hard, and the streetlight across the road sparkled against the droplets forming at the corners of his eyes.

'The girls here get fucked up, that's all. They get dragged down.' He dashed a sleeve at his eyes. 'Do you need me to walk you back to your hotel?'

I smiled. 'No, I'm only a couple of minutes' walk from here, but thank you. If you want to talk some more, call me. We can find somewhere away from Tobermory if you like. I appreciate you're in a difficult position with your dad.'

I could have pushed him harder, asked him to explain what he meant by 'fucked up' and which girls he was referring to. But just as teenagers have places, they also have a pace. They set it, they stick to it, and any attempt to push faster results at best in a slowing-down and at worst in a complete refusal to communicate. Lewis had reached out to me. He wanted me to know that something was wrong. Would he open up a little more next time? If I respected his pace and proved that I could keep his trust, then yes, I was hoping he would. Because Lewis Eggo had looked me in the eyes and told me what I'd really needed to know. That this island had killed Adriana Clark. Not some random tourist; not an impetuous night visit to a complete stranger; not her own wilfulness. And I'd wait as long as was needed for Lewis Eggo to come to me again.

He was gone. The slap of his trainers on the flagstones echoed for twenty seconds before fading. I crossed the street and looked out to sea.

The moon was bright over Tobermory Bay. It rippled in and out with the gentle tide, riding the black water. As I stood there, hating the patience my job entailed, a man slipped out of the Mull Historical Emporium wrapped up in a coat and scarf. It was a little chilly but not that cold yet. The outfit was finished off with a black hat and black gloves.

He checked every direction several times before setting off, then climbed into a battered old Jeep and drove quietly away. Enough of his face had been visible for me to recognise him as the man who'd been trying to get Sergeant Eggo's attention in the pub two nights earlier. Skittles, they'd called him. He'd been nervous, bordering on twitchy, then.

I made a mental note of his licence plate, instinctively disliking the hat and the gloves. Winter clothes in autumn. I'd thought the Scots were hardier than that.

Chapter Eight

An emerald mist was blowing off the sea at 5 a.m. It infiltrated the gaps in my ancient window and brought the scents of seaweed and salt. The curtains were damp as I pulled them back, and there was no chance I would fall back to sleep. Knowing that no one else in my corridor wanted to be woken at that time, I left my room and the hotel quietly, made for the hills behind the town and headed south.

The drop away from the land to the sea was timeless. Beyond the town, the remoteness hit me. I saw only a handful of houses as I walked. Trees that had stood for generations lined my path and the heather underfoot added a scratchy cushioned layer to the earth. Seagulls eyed me suspiciously from the air, but it was the fishing boats and lobster pots they wanted. The island was a place removed from the world, and although Tobermory was a slice of civilisation, it hadn't made a dent in the wildness of the scenery. The sea breathed in and out with me as I walked.

Finally, back at The Last Bay Hotel, I showered, dressed, put on my best attitude and went to explore what the Mull Historical Emporium had to offer.

* * *

The once dark-green sign was weather faded to something less bold and more mossy, which was how the inside felt too. The dust was what I noticed first. Overhead lighting filtered into glass cabinets that should have sparkled, lighting up the debris of ages. Guidebooks and maps alongside history books with transparent plastic covers gave the Emporium the air of a dying library. Bric-a-brac sporting various clan motifs with fading price tags lined the walls and lay unloved on shelves. Portraits, landscapes, a few animal heads that made me queasy. A lock of hair in a pearl inlay box. Many of the displays offered minute handwritten information cards next to them. A ship's manifest in a language I couldn't make out. Half the items for sale, the remainder there to encourage tourists through the doors. Not quite a museum; not quite a shop.

There were several areas to wander through, each tiny and featuring a different period in Mull's history. Low oak beams, exposed inner walls and three small but beautiful open fireplaces.

'Can I h-help?' The stutter on the 'h' told me immediately who was standing behind me. He was close enough that I could feel the heat of his body against my back.

I turned my head to reply, but kept my body facing the fireplace I was admiring.

'Hi,' I said. 'I was looking for a guidebook about the island.'

'I know who you are,' he said. The sentence took time to get through, each word a trial. I waited for him to finish.

Damp with sweat, his clothes needed more care, as did his hair and nails.

'I love this building. How old is it?'

'1820,' he said. I could smell sour fruit acid on his breath and his fingers flexed and twitched as he spoke to me. 'What's your name?'

'Sadie,' I replied.

'Sadie,' he repeated back to me slowly.

63

'They call you Skittles, right?' He gave a broad grin revealing teeth that confirmed what Rachel had told me about his diet. 'Did you ever talk to Adriana? Did she ever come in here?'

His smile melted.

'She's d-d-dead,' he said, the stutter worsening as his face reddened.

I watched, recognising his limited abilities as we talked. At some point a diagnosis would surely have been made, but I was no psychologist. It seemed to me that Skittles was functioning only at a basic level. He could answer direct questions, repeat facts, ring purchases up on a till, but beyond that I had doubts.

'Do you know Mackinnon's Cave where she was found?' I asked.

'It's d-dark there at night,' was his reply. 'Don't l-like it.'

'Really?' I said. 'I thought I saw you going out late last night. You got in your car and drove somewhere.'

His eyes slid from my gaze.

'Get you a g-guidebook,' he muttered, walking off. I followed, disliking the fact that I was leaping to conclusions, but the seeds were planted in my mind and already sprouting.

'Do you live here too or just work here?' I asked as he reached up to a shelf behind the counter and took down a book.

'Live,' he said. 'Nine ninety-nine.'

I handed over a ten-pound note and watched as his fingers took their time punching each button on the old-fashioned till. I picked up my purchase and left to check out Adriana's regular haunts and retrace the steps of her final day.

I'd asked for fresh towels and bedding to be left outside my room, and by the time I returned in the evening they had been. That's standard practice for me during an investigation when I'm handling sensitive and confidential material, even more so in a small community when I need to protect a grieving family. So no one should have entered my room — except I knew immediately that someone had. The last time I'd smelled that rotting vegetation had been inside Mackinnon's Cave.

I grabbed my glass off the bedside table and gripped it firmly by the base, ready to smash the end and shove it in the neck of an intruder. I tackled the bathroom first, checking behind the door and making sure the window was locked. My search ended with the wardrobe and under my bed. I was alone, but shaken.

My laptop was where I'd left it charging. It wasn't on, and the chance of anyone getting through my three levels of pass-words and security were slim to none. My suitcase was in the bottom of the wardrobe, my clothes hung up. Aware of the frown of distaste marking my forehead, I checked the plastic bag of dirty clothes I'd left hanging on the back of the bath-room door. Still there.

Nothing missing, nothing moved. I was being paranoid, which wasn't like me at all. It had been an early morning and I'd hiked for miles alone. Was it tiredness making me overreact? I locked the door, kicked off my trainers and put the kettle on to make myself a desperation packet coffee with long-life milk, flopping on the bed to close my eyes while I waited for it to boil.

The stench slapped me as my head hit the pillow and I jerked back up to a sitting position, already gagging. It was dead fish, sea mud, trawler net slops and insects rolled into one. Scrabbling for the other end of the bed, I stared at the pillow. Beneath it a bulging shape waited for my attention. Covering my mouth with my sleeve, I reached out for the pen on my bedside table, slid the end of it under the bedding, and flipped.

The green-brown circle had leaked rust-coloured water into my sheets, and as I drew closer some unidentified bug skittered away from the light to the crack between mattress and headrest.

Someone had brought me a crown.

I looked around the room for a second time, as if I might have missed the intruder behind a curtain or curled into a ball in the corner. There was no one there now, but they might as well have been.

From my case, I took a pair of gloves and a clear plastic bag. Before I moved it, I photographed it where it lay. I was no expert, but it certainly looked to be made of the same type of seaweed as Adriana's crown.

Several pieces of seaweed were twined around each other to form a circle. It was not without a sick sort of natural beauty, but it belonged on a dead body. That was undoubtedly the message it was designed to deliver. By now, enough people would have heard rumours of the things that had been done to Adriana. The police knew, both those on the island and those who'd attended from the mainland. Then there was Nate Carlisle's team. Beyond that, a wider body of administrators. Of course, the press had arrived today too, and they would have their sources. But it wasn't as if Adriana's killer was the only person who could have fashioned me a warning crown. My presence wasn't exactly popular with the locals.

Figuring out which hotel the Canadian private investigator was staying at would have been easy; the room less so; but then the cleaners, bar staff, waiters, receptionists might all have been making free with small talk.

I looked at the key I'd left in the back of the door. A real key, not a card. There would be others around the hotel, for emergencies, cleaning and maintenance staff. I'd had to find a method of entering hotel rooms in more cities than I could count during the course of my investigations. In most cases, it was far too easy to do. With an original key that could be borrowed or copied, access would have been tricky but far from impossible.

Two things troubled me as I slipped the seaweed into the plastic bag and ran my hands over the craftwork, the leaves slippery smooth in their new packaging. The first was where I was going to sleep that night. The second was the motive of whoever had left me such a terrible gift.

Someone, or maybe more than one person, had found out where I was staying. They'd found a way into the room. They'd known I wouldn't be there — I assumed that to be the case because the alternative, that they'd been hoping I was there to hand me my crown in person, was unthinkable. That might also mean they were watching as I'd left my hotel room earlier. And that they might be watching me again now.

I raced the few metres to the window and ripped the curtains apart, half expecting a figure to be there, leering in. Beyond my room a handful of shrubs and a few trees waved in the wind, and after that there was nothing but road and sea. No one in sight at all.

Had they laid on my bed? What else had they done while they were there? I wanted a drink but I needed to stay sober. I picked up my phone instead.

'Nate Carlisle,' he answered.

'Hi, this is Sadie Levesque. Is it a bad time?'

'Always,' he said. 'No rest for the wicked. What can I do for you?'

I breathed hard to keep the emotion from my voice. 'I just wanted to explain why you hadn't had the consent forms. My clients haven't had medical insurance for a while. Financial pressure made them cancel their policy. They were too embarrassed and stressed to explain it at the time.'

'Okay,' he said. I could hear him tapping away on the keys of his computer as he spoke and knew he was busy.

'Also, any news on the powder? I wasn't sure how long that would take to process.'

'Couple more days, probably. Depends what else is in the lab queue. As it wasn't an official case exhibit, I couldn't put a rush request on it. I'll call you as soon as I have anything.'

'That's great . . . and also I was wondering what you could tell me about the seaweed around Adriana's head.'

The tapping on the computer stopped.

'You all right? Only you sound a bit frantic.'

'I was wondering if you can get fingerprints off seaweed? Or maybe other traces from it like skin cells?'

'There were no prints on anything relating to Adriana – not the seaweed, the shell or her skin – but then she'd been in the water and her body was exposed for several days.'

'Are there ever circumstances when you'd be able to lift fingerprints from seaweed?' I asked.

'Rarely. The oil from fingertips doesn't really adhere to it, unless it's old and dry. Have you found something?'

I sighed. Not telling anyone at all was stupid. 'Someone left a seaweed crown under my pillow,' I said. 'I'm trying to figure out what to do with it.'

'In your hotel room?'

'Yup.'

'Tell me you've left the room already and called the police, Sadie,' Nate said.

'They didn't steal anything, didn't damage anything. There's no sign of a break-in. Half the island must know the details of Adriana's death by now—'

'It'll be in tomorrow's papers,' he confirmed. 'I've already had three journalists call for a comment. Someone leaked it.'

'So this could be a bad taste practical joke, or a bit of harassment.'

'Or a threat,' he finished. 'Is the seaweed still wet?'

'Yeah, it's gross. It's so fresh that something crawled off it while I was watching.'

'Looking for trace evidence now will be pointless. A hotel bedroom is full of different skin cells and DNA. I'm more concerned about your immediate safety. What are you going to do?'

'See if I can move rooms,' I said. 'You shouldn't worry about me. I've had a huge amount of self-defence and weapons training.' All of which was true, not that it would help me get to sleep later. 'Can I send you this crown? It feels as if it should be with Adriana.'

'Only if I can ask Sergeant Eggo to look in on you.'

'No deal,' I said. 'You don't get to make me a witness. If that happens, I'm useless to the Clark family and they need me. Things here are strained. Brandon's still a suspect and they're stuck in their house hiding from photographers. I don't want to have to leave them to deal with this alone. Plus I finally feel like I'm making progress.'

'That's what I'm worried about,' Nate said.

'Listen, I'll be fine. I'm sending you this disgusting thing with the next outbound courier service which will probably be tomorrow morning. If I don't get rid of it to you, I'm going to throw it into the sea anyway.'

'Send it to me.' He sighed. 'But change rooms. Preferably hotels. You need to text me at 8 a.m. tomorrow to say you're okay, or I'll have the police knocking down your door whether you like it or not.'

'Sounds fair,' I said. It was funny how an atom of human concern immediately made me feel better; or perhaps it was the fact that it was coming from Nate Carlisle that made it so impactful. I liked him. It had been a while, really, since I'd liked a man as much as I was starting to like Nate, but the ethics of concerning myself with my private life whilst hunting for a dead girl's killer were just too complex. I rang off.

Pulling the plastic bag onto my lap, I wondered what it

meant. A crown was for a princess or a queen. For someone you revered, or perhaps for someone who thought themselves important. Was it mockery, or part of a bizarre fantasy?

I wasn't going to know until I found the person who'd murdered Adriana, and I wasn't going to find them without taking some risks. Moving rooms now was a step backwards. If my gift-giver could find my room the first time, they could find it again. Maybe get access to the keys again. I didn't want to be on an upper floor if that happened.

Don't be reckless, don't be stupid – those were my rules. Careful, balanced decisions. A knowledge that I could take care of myself reasonably well. Keep my cell phone charged, keep my bear spray handy. Stay alert. So did I really need to move rooms?

I'd been in danger before. I hadn't run from it then either.

Chapter Nine

I'd dragged the heavy armchair that sat in the corner of my hotel room in front of the door and sealed out every chink of light, then changed into black clothing, including the ski balaclava that I kept with me for night-time surveillance. Sitting as close to the window as I could, I waited.

Being patient is hard work. It's hard work even when less is at stake, but then most investigative work is unexciting. I'd once spent four solid days at a train station in Vancouver waiting for one particular passenger to disembark from Toronto. I'd simultaneously thought it would never end, and been panicked that I might have missed seeing the crucial face. When a young woman lies dead and there's a possibility that the murderer wants you to be next, waiting is excruciating. I could smell the rottenness that had dripped its juices into my mattress. It was difficult not to imagine my head on that pillow, the seaweed crown wormed into my blonde hair.

Movement in the bushes at one edge of my vision made my throat contract and I wheezed in a painful breath. There was just enough moonlight to show the frantic jiggling of leaves in the undergrowth. I readied my camera. Behind me, footsteps in the hotel corridor grew louder. Fighting to keep my breathing even, I knew I couldn't fog up the window and give myself away. The footsteps kept coming. Taking a deep breath in, I held it.

Waited . . .

A rabbit bolted from the base of the bush, springing forward onto the patch of grass beyond my window and triggering security lights. My stomach was a rock. I forced myself to let out the breath, and put one shaky hand against the glass, letting my head fall forward to touch the pane as I got a grip. The footsteps in the corridor faded away.

It was eleven thirty. I'd been sitting there waiting to see the face of my stalker for three hours and all I had to show for it was embarrassment and an aching back.

The rabbit carcass hit the window at the exact spot where I'd been leaning my forehead, hard enough to leave the glass vibrating. I leapt backwards, crying out. Speckles of fluffy hair were caught in the bloody outline on the pane. The poor slaughtered creature slid down and hit the ground with a dull thud. I yanked the window up, stuck my right then my left leg through, sprinted over the grass and ran between the trees. A figure took off in the distance, disappearing around the side of the hotel. I pursued, refusing to think about the consequences, close enough to a well-populated building that I'd be heard if I screamed, and fit enough to run away again if needed. All I wanted was a look at the bastard who was going after me.

Across the gravel driveway, over flowerbeds, he or she – medium build and athletic – was still a long way ahead. Jumping a low stone wall, they entered the tree line beyond the lights of the hotel and I knew I couldn't risk it. I let myself slow to a jog then stop, hands on my knees as I panted. My blood was up. It was never conducive to making rational decisions. Now I'd left my room unguarded and my window wide open. My cell phone buzzed in my pocket and I cursed as I began jogging back to my room.

'Sadie,' I answered, clambering back through bushes.

'Brandon's in trouble with the police. I can't leave Isabella. Can you go see what's happening?'

Rob Clark's voice was shaking. I checked behind me before approaching the rabbit carcass outside my room.

'Where is he now?' I asked, picking up the rabbit and inspecting the damage to its body. Its head flopped to one side, neck snapped in two.

'Mackinnon's Cave. Brandon called me first, then Sergeant Eggo got in touch and asked me to go up there, but the press are camped outside. I'm worried about Luna too.'

'I'll go,' I said. 'Let Sergeant Eggo know to expect me.'

Throwing the poor slaughtered animal back to the ground, I re-entered my room, taking a brief, furious tour. Balaclava hidden, laptop and essentials with me, I jumped in my hire car and headed south-west across the island to Mackinnon's Cave.

Twenty-two miles of backroad later, I followed the trail of flashing blue lights and headed down to the cave entrance.

Mull's handful of resident police officers were in attendance, together with the few mainland officers still on the island to assist with Adriana's murder investigation. The first police officer put one hand up and told me to stay where I was.

'There's an incident in progress, ma'am. I need you to return to your vehicle.'

'I'm here to see Sergeant Eggo,' I said. 'And to help Brandon Clark. I was asked to come by his parents.'

'This is an active situation. The suspect has a weapon. Please step back.'

'What weapon?' I asked.

'I can't discuss—'

'Sergeant Eggo!' I yelled. 'This is Sadie Levesque. Let me speak with Brandon.'

Harris Eggo appeared from the rocks at the bottom of the pathway.

'Let her through,' he instructed the police officer, sighing audibly. I walked down to meet him. 'Do I need to explain again that you have no status here?'

'Rob Clark phoned me. He's too worried about his wife and daughter to be able to leave the house and he's being harassed by the press. I'm here on his behalf. Brandon's a minor.'

'He entered a crime scene, breached the taped area and interfered with the environment. He ignored specific instructions from the officer posted here and he's carrying an offensive weapon, so he may only be seventeen but he's in serious trouble.'

'Did he use the weapon?' I asked. Eggo put his hands on his hips and didn't respond. 'Did he threaten anyone with the weapon?'

'One of the reasons I had an officer posted here was because I knew the murderer would return to the scene of the crime sooner or later. They always do.'

'Really? I thought the murderer was some long-gone faceless tourist,' I said.

'You've got a smart mouth.'

'My orthodontist was a genius,' I replied. 'Why is this an active incident? What's happening?'

'The boy's in the cave, refusing to come out. Says he'll stick the knife in his own throat if we go anywhere near him. Cave's dark, small entrance, I'm not risking one of my officers getting attacked. We're communicating with him. I phoned his parents hoping they'd come down and talk some sense into him.'

'Shit. I don't think Rob appreciated quite how bad it was. He just told me Brandon was in trouble—'

'He is,' Sergeant Eggo said.

'Oh please, the boy's grieving and he came here to be close to his sister, probably armed with a knife because he was already seriously contemplating suicide.'

'His mother lied when she gave him an alibi. Why would she have done that if she didn't already suspect him?'

'I don't know if she lied or not. I wasn't there. I'm here now, though. He's still a kid. If he sticks that knife in his femoral artery while you and I are out here sparring, how's that internal investigation going to go for you?'

'Two minutes. At your own risk. Don't touch anything.'

'Don't need to,' I said as I entered. 'I did enough of that the first time.'

It was darker than I remembered, but then during my first visit I'd been properly prepared with multiple head lamps. Tonight I was limited to the few lights the police were shining inside, and my own flashlight.

'Brandon,' I shouted. 'It's Sadie. Your dad asked me to come. I'm entering now.'

No answer.

'Your parents want me to get you home safely. I think if you hand over the knife, there's a reasonable chance I can get Sergeant Eggo to back off.' I kept talking as I moved, listening for his response. 'I know your parents aren't coping, Brandon. How could they possibly? But I'm on your—'

'Leave me alone,' he said. He was maybe two metres from where I'd found Adriana's body. Her outline remained marked by flags on the cave floor. 'I know what they did.'

I stepped the last few feet forward and looked over his shoulder. The blade he was clutching reflected the light from the cave entrance.

'People were always jealous of Addie. She was too pretty, too clever or too confident, you know?'

'Brandon, you're making the police nervous. Nervous police do stupid things. They overreact, make poor decisions. I don't have long to get you out of here.'

'They're all part of it,' Brandon said. 'Nothing's right here. They hated Addie from the start.'

'Who did?' I asked.

'They all did. They were working together.'

'Let's go outside, sort out the situation with the police. I'd like to know everything you know and help find the person who did this to Adriana – but not here.'

'Are you coming out?' Eggo shouted. 'Ms Levesque, I'm out of patience.'

'We're coming,' I shouted. 'One more minute, please!'

'Thirty seconds,' Eggo shouted back.

'Brandon,' I said. 'I'll help, I promise, but your parents need you. Your dad's trying to stay strong for your mother but he's losing the battle. Luna's big sister's gone. You have to go home to her. She's so little. She needs you.'

'Before you die on this island, you're given something cursed to mark you,' he whispered. 'That's what I heard.'

'To mark you . . . for death?' I clarified. 'Is that why you were here? To see what Addie had been given?'

He nodded.

'Okay,' I said. 'I get it.' There was a clock counting down inside my head. Any moment now Eggo's men would be storming the cave and Brandon was still holding a potentially lethal blade. 'But you need to give me the knife. They're going to arrest you, but I should be able to sort it out. Don't fight them. Let me do my job.'

'Addie just missed her old friends and she wanted new ones. They tricked her.' He handed me the knife and I slipped it in my pocket before standing up.

'Stay there, Brandon. Put your hands on your head. I'm going to look after you.'

They came quickly and quietly. I told them I had the knife. Brandon did as he was told. They put him on the floor face down and there was nothing I could do to stop any of that from happening. Then there was a procession across the island to Tobermory and the police station. A police officer drove Brandon's car back and I trailed along behind them, hoping I could make good on my promise to help.

I sat outside the police station for thirty minutes letting them do their paperwork, then I went on in and worked my magic. I handed in the knife, gave a statement detailing how Brandon was simply there looking for something he thought Adriana had lost and made clear there was no threat. I reassured Harris Eggo that I would ensure Brandon's parents got him medical help in the morning. Then I distracted the sergeant by telling him about the person outside my room who threw a dead rabbit at my window. I missed out the part about the break-in and the seaweed crown.

It was a cheap trick that paid off. Eggo insisted that an officer remain outside my window for the night, and I got to drop Brandon home with nothing more than a caution.

By the time I was back in my room, I was ready to collapse. It occurred to me that I should probably ask Rob Clark to consider a psychiatric evaluation of his son. If Brandon was more than just grief-stricken, and suffering deeper mental health problems, it could go from bad to worse very quickly. It led me to consider whether or not he might have been suffering from psychological problems for a long time. The lack of records from a Carlsbad high school was strange enough, but no medical records at all and no social media? Something wasn't right.

The dead rabbit and seaweed crown were just the icing on today's cake, all of which could only mean I was getting closer to some answers.

I dumped a blanket and the one clean pillow in the bath, locked the bathroom door and slept in the tub, dreaming of a beautiful girl wearing a dripping crown and eating a feast of sand.

Chapter Ten

'Call me when you're awake,' was the text I'd written to Nate Carlisle. That was at 5.30 a.m. My cell phone rang eight minutes later.

'You okay?' he asked without introduction.

'Honestly, I'm not even sure how to answer that one. I'm alive, which I'm taking as a win. When all this is over, I'm coming to Glasgow with a two-four and we'll drink beer late into the night and compare war stories.'

'A two-four?'

'A pack of beer. You need to learn Canadian. Before that though . . .'

'Are the next words out of your mouth going to be, "I need a favour"?'

I'd have blushed if I'd been the blushing kind of girl.

'Is this the point where I say, "You complete me"?' I laughed.

'What do you need?' I could hear a teaspoon clinking as it circled a mug, a fridge door being shut, a distant radio. The sounds of normality. They made me homesick for a single lurching moment, and I wondered what I was doing on Mull, chasing a killer at the same time I was trying to avoid them.

'I think another girl was killed on Mull. The details are sketchy. It was about forty years ago but you'd have to look a decade either side to be sure. Parents were native to the island, mother now deceased. It's another death where sand seems to have featured and it's unresolved.'

'You going to be patient while I get through secure login or will I have to listen to you sighing?'

'I'm gonna be good, I promise.' I switched my own kettle on and hoped I had enough tiny plastic pots of long-life milk left for a decent coffee.

'Okay, it's firing up. How was your evening?'

'Brandon Clark threatened to commit suicide in Mackinnon's Cave. Someone slaughtered a rabbit outside my room then threw its carcass at my window. Also, I slept in the bathtub for safety reasons. You?'

'Netflix,' he said. 'If you haven't told the police what's going on by now, I'm phoning them with or without your permission.'

'No, you're good.' I could hear him tapping on a keyboard. 'I told Sergeant Eggo all about it. So have you got anything for me?'

'Fortunately there have been very few murders on Mull in the last hundred years, so if it's here I'll find it. How did it get onto your radar?'

'Where I get all my best information – in a bar. The victim's father came in upset.'

'That would have been Jasper Kydd. I have virtually no details here as older file details were only added to the system in brief. A sixteen-year-old girl died on the island thirty-nine years ago, definitely murder. No conviction for it. I'd have to do a lot more digging to get the case details. Her name was Flora. Cause of death was suffocation.'

'Thirty-nine years.' My brain was whirring. 'So, say Flora's killer was eighteen at the time, now he'd be fifty-eight. It's feasible.'

'You'd need to know a lot more about it before you took a leap like that,' Nate said.

'On it.' I already was. The name Flora Kydd was all I needed. Cold case maybe, but the long fingers of the internet were still able to reach out into the past and grab it. 'Thanks Nate. I'll be in touch.'

There were references to Flora Kydd's disappearance but the newspaper coverage was not accessible online. I'd need to visit a library and a microfiche machine for that. What I did find was an article twenty years after Flora's untimely death asking why her murderer had never been identified, and attempting to persuade the powers that be to reopen the case in an age of better forensics. The article had been written by a journalist called Lance Proudfoot. Fortunately for me, the reporter was alive, kicking, and maintaining a news blog based in Edinburgh. If he cared enough to still be thinking about a case twenty years after it happened, there was a reasonable chance he'd recall a fair amount of the details today.

His blogsite had an email address for contacts and a cell number to report news stories in progress. I stared out of my window. The fluffy white tail of the dead rabbit was fainty visible through the early morning sea mist. Adriana's killer might or might not have been the person outside my window last night, and a girl lay on a steel table with grains of sand still adhering to parts of her mouth. That was enough of a story in progress for me.

I dialled Mr Proudfoot's number and let it ring. When it went to voicemail, I stopped the call and dialled again. The third time, he took the call.

'This'll be the story of the century, then,' he said. His voice was sleepy and soft, the accent softer and more melodic than Nate's.

'Flora Kydd,' I replied. There was a pause and the sound of a light switch being flicked.

'You got my attention.'

I explained who I was, as many details as were already public knowledge, then asked about the elderly man who'd been crying in The Blether. Lance Proudfoot sighed.

'Flora's father, Jasper, was a good man. They investigated him when she died, of course. Family are always the prime suspects. She was their only daughter. Her mother died of a heart attack twenty years later, way before her time. That's one of the reasons I wrote the follow-up piece. Losing a child in a violent attack is appalling. Never knowing why or who, never being able to turn the page that stops the grieving process. The nightmare never ends. It didn't do any good, though. The police chased their tails for a few months then seemed to give up.'

'You don't sound like much of a fan of the police force.'

'Oh, I've got some very good friends in that line of work. I've had bones broken by some of the bad ones too. The police are an odd collection of humanity, I've found. Now shall we cut to the chase? You called for a reason if you're investigating the Adriana Clark murder. What would that be?'

There wasn't much wiggle room between the rock to one side of me and the hard place at the other. To get information I was going to have to give some, but confiding in a journalist was contrary to every belief I had.

'Lance – I hope you don't mind me calling you Lance?'

'Been called worse, you go ahead.'

'Thanks. I have a request. Could you tell me about Flora's case? Every detail you can dredge up? I need the colours and flavours of it. I'd rather not say why right now. That's as honest as I can be and you sound like one of the good guys, so I'd prefer not to lie to you.'

'You had a parent who raised you right,' Lance said, leaving me homesick for the second time. 'So fine. I've a tendency to go on a bit, so cough politely when you've had enough.'

'I'll do that,' I told him. Lance Proudfoot was the nicest stranger at the end of a phone line I'd ever encountered, and I found myself wishing he lived on Mull so I could've met him over a coffee and confided in him.

'I covered this case twice. Once when it happened, and again some time later. Flora Kydd was a sweet wee girl. Everyone said so. Teachers, friends, her boss at the plant nursery where she worked at weekends. It was the only aspect of the case where there wasn't a single person who disagreed. It was a mild summer. I remember it all too well. My first year working for the *Glasgow Daily News*. I was still finding my voice, learning how to edit my own words, and taking life for granted. I don't know why they sent me to Mull – God knows they must have been short-staffed that week – but I went there a boy and came back a man. If that sounds like bullshit then disregard it, but it's the best way I have of describing the effect the case had on me. Flora Kydd didn't deserve to die. No murder victim does. But she sure as hell didn't deserve to die in the manner she did. I'm opposed to the death penalty, Sadie. Properly left of centre most of the time. But the monster who took Flora's life had no right to his existence. None at all.'

As Lance told the story, I wrote it down, his words forming pictures in my mind. I didn't hear a single page turn or the tap of a computer key. The tale of Flora Kydd's death was imprinted in his mind in dreadful technicolour, and as he spoke I understood why.

Flora left home one morning to attend church. She always did that before proceeding on to the nursery where she would water the plants, pot seedlings, shovel mulch, weed the beds and keep the crops happy in the rows of greenhouses at Kintra on the western coast. Mull was sparsely populated with little for a teenager to do, the same number of kids in her whole school year as they'd have in a single class on the mainland. But Flora Kydd wasn't the kind of girl who looked for trouble when she was bored. She sought out tasks to help people. Ironing for the elderly whose hands were being eaten by arthritis. Shopping for the ageing fishermen weakened by the sea over decades. Childminding for the few young mums who had not escaped Mull as soon as they were independent.

She didn't make it to church that day. Her parents weren't religious and had stayed at home. Flora was presumed ill or busy. No one batted an eye. She didn't arrive for work either, but she was such a good girl that the boss wasn't going to raise a fuss when she didn't turn up for once. In his statement he wrote that he'd hoped she'd finally got a date or was taking time out for herself. She deserved it. He said he would regret those sentiments for as long as he lived.

When night-time fell, Flora's parents assumed she'd stopped to see a friend after work or was doing some good deed. It didn't occur to them to be concerned.

It was Mull. Flora knew the land. The family knew everyone there. The weather was fair. It was your average June day. So they waited.

By 8 p.m. they were worried. By 9 p.m. they were looking at the clock every few minutes. At 10 p.m. they phoned the owner of the nursery to ask if Flora had said where she was going after work. At 10.03 p.m. they called the police in Tobermory, then rallied the neighbours. That in itself was a task. By then it was pitch dark and a gale was beginning to blow in. Even then, there was an underlying belief that they'd find her lying in a ditch with a broken leg, unable to walk but otherwise unharmed, having come off her bike.

They found the bike, but not the girl, halfway between her house and the church.

Mull police notified the mainland but there was little that could be done in the dark without evidence that the girl was the victim of a crime. Someone, somewhere, uttered that most damaging of phrases, the one most likely to cost a life instead of saving one: 'she's probably just run away'.

By the time the police found her body two days later, they were able to piece together this much. Flora had indeed been heading for church. Her bike was unmarked so it seemed unlikely she'd been involved in an accident. The carefully plucked stalks of the wildflowers scattered around the tyres indicated that she might have been picking flowers to take into the church as decorations. She never got back on that bike, yet there was no blood or clothing discarded in the area and no passerby had witnessed anything untoward. It was possible that someone had pulled over to ask directions, and Flora – sweet, unsuspecting Flora who'd never had to worry about 'stranger danger' or 'doubt first, trust last' – had gone close enough to be dragged into the vehicle and driven off.

Maybe she was kept in the vehicle for the next two days, or maybe her captor had taken her straight to the deserted bay where her body was found. But Flora had suffered. Deep ligature marks circled her wrists and ankles. Cuts in the flesh of her torso and back suggested she'd been flayed. Then there was the sand. Shoved into her mouth. More and more, until she could no longer breathe, and even drawing breath in through her nose dragged grains into her lungs until she was simply full of it.

The dog walker who'd found her body had been the first to vomit as she'd turned Flora's body over. The first, but not the last. Police officers had tears in their eyes. The forensics team worked in absolute silence. The community never spoke about it in public places, although they must have whispered behind shut doors, clutching their loved ones tight and wishing they'd never lived to see the day.

Sweet, innocent Flora had been suffocated with the sand of the island she had adored. Alone among her peers, she'd never wanted to leave, did not hanker after the adventure of the wider world. She'd found beauty in every landmark and the constantly changing sky. The summer had ended then for everyone on the island. Tears were shed for months. The fear echoed through every hamlet. Mull was transfixed and transformed.

And then time finally passed. Suddenly Flora's death had happened a year ago. A remembrance service was held. Then it was two years ago, and prayers were said in church. By the third anniversary it was felt better not to dredge up the terrible memories but to focus on healing. By the fourth anniversary, Flora Kydd's parents rarely left their house except to farm their land and buy provisions. The world continued to turn.

'There you have it,' Lance Proudfoot said. He'd been crying as he told the story. That was okay. I'd been crying too. 'A waste of a good life. The destruction of a community. If it happened today, with forensics so much more impressive than they were back then, with police procedures so much more concentrated, I'm sure they'd have got whoever did it. I stayed on Mull for a month reporting the story. Became obsessed with it for a while. With the need for justice for her parents, to feel safe again, to know that the person capable of so much violence and hatred wasn't walking free in the world ready to do the same again. I had to be ordered back to Glasgow by the newspaper. I only did as I was told when they said it was that or lose my job.'

I wiped the tears from my cheeks and took a deep breath.

'Could they be back, do you think? The person who did that to Flora?'

Lance was silent for a very long time.

'Why would you say that?' he asked.

'This is pretty crappy of me after you've been so helpful, but I need to say it for my clients' sake. Are we off the record?'

'Off the record,' he confirmed.

'Adriana was found with her mouth packed full of sand,' I explained. 'Cause of death was drowning. The sand was shoved into her mouth afterwards. And there was a form of postmortem sexual assault. That's why I called you.'

'Of course,' Lance said. 'Makes sense. Give me a minute.'

Footsteps, a door opening, taps being turned on, water splashing. Footsteps back, and the phone was picked up again.

'Sorry,' he said. 'Is it possible the same person did this? I suppose so. They'd be in their late fifties at least, probably older, so your Adriana would have had no reason I can think of to go off and meet them in the middle of the night. The real question is, why a gap of forty years between offences? I've spent too many years covering violent crime to think a person capable of that can hide their true personality for so long. There have been no murders of women or girls on Mull in the inter-vening years.'

'Maybe the killer travelled. Holidays in the sorts of countries where you can pay for almost anything. Road trips round Europe. How do we know they haven't struck again?'

'Pardon my French, but if this person is from Mull and killing Flora Kydd taught them not to shit where they eat, then why take the risk of murdering Adriana and reopening past wounds? It's such a small community that someone who'd left suddenly moving back would be big news there.'

'I don't know,' I said. 'I haven't had a chance to think this through. But you've got to admit, the similarities are crazy. This isn't a coincidence. It can't be. You should've seen Flora's father. He was distraught, talking about her being silenced with sand.'

'Flora's case got a lot of publicity forty years ago. Maybe you've got a copycat.'

'Murder tourism? You think someone became obsessed with how Flora was killed and visited Mull to kill another girl in roughly the same way? Jesus.'

'Doesn't necessarily have to be a tourist. Small islands have long memories,' Lance said. 'The more dreadful the memory, the longer it endures. Listen hard enough and you'll still hear its echoes.'

Chapter Eleven

Lance Proudfoot promised to email me the address of Jasper Kydd's farm. Rather than sit in my room and wait, I opted to exercise and get breakfast from the bakery on the bayfront. This time I took a path due west of the town, punishing my legs by striding up and down the hills and enjoying the view. As the mist blew away, the sky revealed itself to be clear with only a few rippling clouds adding texture. Mull was every conceivable shade of green and blue. It was a new day and I had a job to do. Buying a croissant and takeout coffee from the bakery, I returned to the hotel and got ready for the drive to Kintra. It was only when I saw the tyres of my hire car that I realised my plans for the day were going to be pushed back.

All four of them slashed. I'd been freaked out by the seaweed crown and scared by the rabbit thrower, but now I was absolutely furious. Someone didn't want me there, which made me all the more determined to stay. Of course there was no CCTV covering the carpark. The hotel receptionist looked at me as if I'd just flown in from New York wearing enormous sunglasses, a fur coat and complaining that the ice wasn't cold enough. I called the local garage who promised to fetch the car by midday. It was 6.30 p.m. when they phoned to say the tyres had been fitted, and 7 p.m. before I'd paid my bill and had the keys in hand.

The 56-mile trip to Kintra took me an hour and a half in the dark. Twice, animals dashed across the road and I had to brake to a standstill. I didn't want another rabbit on my conscience. There was one road in and out. I missed the farmhouse as I passed it, reaching an impasse at an arc of houses that looked out to sea. A forlorn fishing boat sat on what I guessed was a front yard – a mossy green patch with boulders rising from it. In Kintra, you fished or you farmed. It could have been the ends of the earth.

Windridge Farm was a two-storey with white plaster that had been attacked by too many decades of sea spray to last much longer. It sat a quarter of a mile back from the road, windows dark, as if the very building had shut its eyes to the civilisation beyond. I'd have phoned if that had been a possibility, or put a note through the door if I'd had a spare day. As it was, I left my car in the driveway and knocked on the oak door. It occurred to me that Mr Kydd might already be in bed. He had to be close to eighty years old, and what was there to do in the evening if you lived alone? The man I'd seen at The Blether certainly wasn't spending his evenings watching box sets. He'd been inconsolable. The news of Adriana's death must have dredged all his grief from where he'd shoved it and brought it up as fresh and sharp as the day his daughter failed to come home. Perhaps he wasn't sleeping. Perhaps he'd decided he couldn't relive those horrors again. Or maybe nature had finally been kind.

I looked from the house to my car. The most sensible course of action was to go back to my hotel and ask Sergeant Eggo to check up on Mr Kydd in the morning. That might be too late – I couldn't stop the voice in my brain that always spoke up at moments like those and never brought good news. What if he'd had a stroke? He could have been lying there, unable to move.

'Oh, for crying out loud,' I answered myself. 'I'll need a flashlight.'

Torch in hand, I headed first for the shed and picked up a shovel. It never ceased to amaze me how many people left the tools necessary to break into their house in a small unsecured wooden structure just a few feet away from their back door. Windridge Farm dated back at least a hundred, more likely two hundred years. Slotting the shovel into the frame and pressing down was all that was necessary to open the kitchen window a crack then slip my fingers in and slide it up.

'Mr Kydd?' I shouted. 'My name's Sadie Levesque. I just want to check you're okay.' Paused, listened. 'Hello?' Nothing. 'Mr Kydd, I'm coming in. Please don't be alarmed.' The kitchen window was too high to get a leg in. I went head-first and dragged myself across the windowsill and over the draining board.

The house was cold and silent. Only the rush of the breeze could be heard, a constant shushing in the darkness. I ran the torchlight around the walls until I located the light switch. The single orange bulb did little to illuminate the place, casting a pool of light downwards onto the red tiled floor. I called out again but my voice was met by nothing except a dull stillness, as if the house itself were dead.

'Mr Kydd?' I tried again, but as much effort as I made to sound upbeat and neighbourly, the words were swallowed by the sadness that lined every wall like woodchip paper, impossible to scrape off. My imagination on hyper-drive after too many hours today spent contemplating Lance Proudfoot's description of Flora's death.

The interior of the house was white-washed brick and bare beams. The kitchen, which doubled as a dining room, was alone worthy of an hour of weeping. A place mat was laid out on the table. One knife, one fork. A salt and pepper pot. Nothing else. I tried to conceive what it would be to live alone here: wife dead; daughter dead; every meal taken alone.

One knife, one fork.

Wondering how many more meals you'd have to endure until you too could die and find respite from the memories.

'Jasper?' I shouted, convinced he was here, that he must be swinging from a beam somewhere. Because that's where I'd have been, living this life.

A door slammed above me and I cried out, staggering backwards before rushing forwards and taking the stairs two at a time. The upper hallway was a blank. Not a picture, a photo or an ornament in sight. The doorway at the end was open and led to a bathroom. Two other doors either side of me. I took the one to my right.

The air I breathed in might not have entered lungs for thirty-nine years. My mind played tricks on me, and I could smell fresh flowers and perfume, the heavy sweetness of lip gloss and the chemicals of hairspray. Only those odours could not have been in the air, in spite of the fact that I could see their sources. A shell bracelet sat on a dressing table in front of the mirror. The bed was made, sheets tucked in, daisies on the duvet cover with a matching pillowcase. A solitary book was on the bedside table, bookmark poking out of the pages so near the end it was tantalising. Flora would never know how that story finished. A pile of laundry waited on a chair ready to be put away in the closet, and I itched – ached – to pick up those clothes and hang them up, find the right drawers for each shirt and pair of socks. Flora would have done so if she'd ever made it home.

A board creaked out in the hallway and my breath stuck like dry toast in my throat. It's just the building settling, I told myself. Stay calm.

'Is someone there?' I called out anyway, peering into the hall but seeing no one there.

If I told you I felt a presence behind me, you wouldn't believe me. I wouldn't believe me either. The dead live on in the minds of the living, but that's the limit of their earthly existence. Yet I found myself shivering as I looked around, Flora's name on the tip of my tongue. The room was empty. I stood a moment to check myself, hands on hips, staring at the ceiling. The beams were dappled. Marked. Tiny little tadpole-shaped blotches swam across the beam in Flora's room. At first it seemed they must be part of the grain, but when I stepped closer they had a different texture. I put the pile of clothes on Flora's bed, moved the chair, and stood on it to see better. Beneath my fingertips, the marks were gritty and flaky. My skin came away with the faintest of black dust on it. The smell, unmistakably, was charcoal.

Burn marks.

I photographed them, returned the chair to its proper place, put the clothes back and smoothed the top of the pile.

'I'm so sorry for what happened to you, Flora,' I told the room. Not because I believed she was in there with me. Just because it made me feel better to say it aloud.

Shutting the door gently, I looked up. The tadpole marks, now that I'd noticed them, continued along each beam. Above each doorway a tiny bouquet of greenery had been hung upside down, the stems wrapped in a hessian bag. These bags, unlike the ancient burn marks, had been recently refreshed. Cuttings of three different plants had been mixed together. A memory flexed its muscles deep in my mind. I rescheduled the recollection for later, intent on continuing and getting out.

Gripping the door handle, I forced myself to enter the last upstairs room. The window was wide open, frame rattling in the wind, explaining the earlier door slam – a lesson in disciplining my imagination.

Mr Kydd's bedroom was a shrine. A painting of his wife and daughter adorned the wall opposite the bed, the woman in her thirties, the girl in her early teens. They were hugging, laughing. Caught up in a moment of pure love. The painting must have been done from a photograph. Every other inch of wall space was taken up by photos. A girl pictured from birth to death, every month, each emotion. Sleeping, skipping, eating, studying, pointing, in a hat, in a swimsuit, wearing a fancy dress, on a bike, a plane, a boat. Him at his wife's bedside, looking pale and thin, trying to smile. Nearly succeeding. That was what heartbreak did to you. It dissolved your smile, and you never really got it back. You just forced your muscles to make the shape it used to be.

The act of intrusion I was committing became too much for me. Closing the bedroom door, satisfied for now that Jasper had come to no harm under this roof, I returned to the hallway. As I exited, the circular scorch marks seem to glare at me from their inset points in the wood. I moved faster, hurrying down the stairs, through the lounge. There they were again, and the hairs on the back of my neck stood up as I went, knowing I had to turn the lights off before I left, not relishing the thought of relying on the weak beam from my flashlight. Down here, the bouquets of greenery hung above each window, and they shifted fractionally in the moving air from the ill-fitting wooden frames. Reaching up above the kitchen sink, I took the final bouquet with me.

Chapter Twelve

The Island

Whispers rose up, tiny blossoms at first, but they entwined and fused and became a wreath of gossip, the day Adriana Clark and her brother arrived. Twins. Americans. Foreign and exotic with their tanned skin, black hair and bright white teeth. Their parents kept themselves to themselves. The baby sister would grow more interesting with the passing years. But those teenage bodies – ripe for hunting and fighting and mating – those were the focus of the real attention.

The islanders looked upon Adriana and misted the air with breathy emotions. Girls peered round corners and peeked between curtains, and knew envy and spite. Mothers watched and saw trouble, competition, imagined arrogance. And the men felt that burn that only a beautiful young woman can induce. The itch of lust.

Adriana met their gazes and smiled back, open and guileless. Brandon saw the way the island folk appraised and judged, and his own eyes filled with hatred. He wanted to lock Addie away. He wanted to wrap her up and keep her by his side. As young as he was, he knew trouble was brewing.

Long before one man could no longer bear to look upon Adriana's loveliness without needing to touch it.

Long before his sister was slain.

In human memory, Flora Kydd was the only other who had suffered so. But the island's memory is as long as time and does not fade. The land has seen too many slaughtered in the name of love and the spirit of jealousy. Evolution dealt women the cruellest blow. With one hand it bestowed a face fit for worship, then designed the body that carries it to be fragile and tender, too easily broken by the men who would dominate and control.

Flora Kydd was slaughtered at a man's hand and a woman's bidding. She was singing as she picked wild flowers to take with her to church. She was smiling when she approached the vehicle that pulled up to ask for directions. She was polite when the man driving looked her up and down, slowly, obviously, as she explained how to find his way. She was steadfast when she refused to follow his directions and get into the van.

And she was screaming as it drove away, her in the back, bound so tightly the feeling went from her hands and ankles in a matter of minutes, an oily rag stuffed into her mouth. The island screamed with her.

Birds flew from their resting places and worms squirmed from the surface of the earth. Hedgehogs folded their little bodies inwards hoping their spikes would keep out the noise. Bucks and does surrounded their fawns, pressing close to ward off the evil in the air. But no human heard. No prescient realisations were visited upon her doting parents. No witness appeared around the bend at the crucial moment.

She was driven to a quiet corner of this quiet corner of the world. The young woman who'd found a weak and vicious man to do her bidding kept Flora's mouth gagged, not so her screams would go unheard, but so the man would not be softened by the begging and pleading.

Tied between two trees, bare-skinned and shivering, they took turns lashing her with an old nylon clothesline, knots tied every few centimetres along its length to maximise the damage.

Flora cried and prayed, and cried and prayed.

Knowing she was going to die was uniquely untroubling for Flora. By then, she welcomed it. Her faith would guide her to a better place, without pain, without fear. Her parents would be wrapped in the love of friends and neighbours. And she would, she firmly believed, be able to look down on them from Heaven, to see their faces and wait for their souls to join hers.

What troubled Flora Kydd was not the afterlife. It was the hours before she died that scared her. That those would be peppered with violence and pain was inevitable. That she would be defiled seemed increasingly likely. But there were other things.

The crucifix that had been ripped from her neck.

Endless, incomprehensible, slithering words that the woman hissed in her ear.

The intestines of some poor creature laid out in patterns on the ground around.

A bowl of sand in the middle of it all. Waiting.

There is no emotion that the island does not feel. Each one springs a new bud or deadens a bough. Flora passed from a living girl into a memory, her face fading in the minds of those who knew her, swirling softly as it went, like sugar dissolving in water. Decades followed, not without losses. There were babes who never made it from their mothers' wombs. Teenagers who could find no light to head for in the storms of growing up. Adults whose lives were cut short by illnesses no medicine could treat. Pain in daily doses, some transient, plenty permanent. Each terrible in its own right. But then there was Adriana Clark.

Addie, to those who loved her. Who cast a spell so strong that she was impossible to forget, and whose laugh was a glittering jewel in the greyness of Mull's sea fog. She had secrets, too, that made her an enigma. A past no one knew very much about. Legs a shade of brown that was fresh honey and milk coffee and caramel. Adriana Clark was simply delicious.

Sea deaths bring furious tides. The waves slap the sides of boats, knocking the sailors from port to starboard, and the fish thrash so hard they break nets. Shells smash, scattering vicious fragments on beaches to slice careless feet. Salty tears form an ocean.

Adriana fought the impulse to scream, kept her mouth shut until she could reach the surface and gulp down oxygen. She kicked and twisted. Thrashed and pulled. Her clothes ripped from her as she was dragged down the beach by her hair and into the icy depths.

The island heard the screams she had no chance to issue. It washed her pain in its water. Addie regretted her own stupidity. Her desire to befriend and fit in. Her warmth and openness. She regretted the job she'd taken that had put her face on show for all to see and for some to desire.

By the time she realised she was dying, her leg was already fractured, her hands uselessly clutching seaweed. She longed only to return to the land she missed. To see her grandmother once more and sit in the shade of a palm tree waiting for the sun to set.

There is a price to pay for violence. It cannot be accounted for in the drip, drip, drip of days spent behind prison bars. That price is paid in lost childhoods and corrupted innocence. Toxic is the atmosphere on a murderous island. The poison is inhaled, absorbed, exhaled. The affliction is contagious. It wants Sadie Levesque, too.

The island feels it all.

Chapter Thirteen

As I turned off the last light in the house, the darkness pursued me to my car. I put my flashlight and the bundle of foliage down on the passenger seat and set off along the road out of Kintra, back towards the centre of Mull. The A849 was a single lane enclosed by gorse bushes for long sections, and hand-built stone walls at others. It hugged the coast past Ardchrishnish, and the vast water to my left as I drove was intimidating.

At the junction past Loch Beg a car came in my direction fast. I pulled in to a passing place, pleased to stop for a moment, concerned for Flora Kydd's father and disturbed by the watchfulness of the house. The car slowed to manoeuvre around mine then sped up again. I pulled away, needing food and rest. The previous night's broken sleep had caught up with me, and at some point during the day I'd made the decision to stop being stubborn and ask to move rooms to an upper floor. It wouldn't stop anyone who had access to the keys, but it would make me less nervous about the ground floor window.

Headlights swept from left to right in my rear-view mirror, then came full on towards me. I sped up, shifting up a gear from the tailgater. Whatever idiot was driving kept pace with me then began flashing their headlights. Blinded, I pulled in hard to the side and gave a brief flash of my right indicator to say they could pass. Instead the driver followed suit and stopped behind me.

Slamming my foot down on the accelerator I raced away. Whoever was following me was going to have to make the decision to do the same or to disappear from my back bumper. It was with me again in seconds, and I tried to focus on the road, avoiding the bumps and scanning left and right for animals about to cross. It was no good. I had miles to go and there were virtually no built-up areas between my position and Tobermory. Cursing, I pulled my car over again, rolled it to a stop and took a can of bear spray from my bag. Not quite as effective as pepper spray when dealing with an attacker, but it was still going to stop someone in their tracks if it hit their eyes or nose, and it had the benefit of being legal to transport. I held the can in my left hand and the car keys in my right, the metal of the key poking out from the crack between two of my fingers. In Canada, I'd have had a licensed gun in the car if I was travelling alone for work. In Scotland, this was the best I could do.

I wound the window down and checked behind me. The car was slowing to a stop. Exiting my vehicle, I walked slowly to the driver's side of the car that was parked twenty yards behind mine. A lone figure inhabited the driver's seat, undoubtedly a man. The window was down as I drew parallel with him, staying six feet away from the car. The man was wearing a black hoodie and gloves. I raised the bear spray can so he could see it.

'You want to explain?' I said.

'Nervous, aren't we?' he countered. I took another step forward, getting a better look at his face. It was familiar but I couldn't place him immediately. What I couldn't help but notice was the terrible scarring on the back of his right hand. 'What were you doing in Kintra tonight?'

I stiffened my grip on the bear spray.

'How long have you been following me?'

'You were told to leave Jasper Kydd alone,' he said. 'Why are we getting reports of your car in his driveway?'

The pieces slotted together. He'd been at the police station the night I'd called in Adriana's body.

'You're police. Take your hood down. I like to see who I'm talking to.' He did as I asked then swung his door open and climbed out.

'You're pretty ballsy for someone so wee.' He walked to stand less than a metre from me.

'I'm doing a job. Any reason you're neither in uniform nor in a marked car?'

'Only two marked cars on the island and they're both out tonight. I took this call when I was off duty. There are only 2,800 people on this island, Ms Levesque, and none of them like outsiders snooping around. We take care of each other.'

'Do they like murderers remaining at large?' I shouldn't have taunted him, but he was sneering and too tall to be standing so close.

'Lower the can,' he said. 'You're currently threatening a police officer.'

'Don't flatter yourself. I reserve my threats for situations where there's something to be scared of. Now unless you're accusing me of a crime and prepared to arrest me, I'm getting back in my car and heading to my hotel. I wasn't snooping around, I was working, not to mention concerned about Mr Kydd.'

'Jasper Kydd doesn't need you to look after him. You shouldn't have been down in Kintra at all. You'll upset things even more,' he said.

'Don't tell me where I can or can't go. I saw Mr Kydd in

100

The Blether. It didn't look to me as if anyone was listening to him at all. He got shoved in a police car and driven home so no one had to deal with his pain.' I thrust the bear spray in my pocket and turned my back on him. His hand hit my shoulder from behind as I was opening my car door.

'You know, I could charge you with careless driving,' he said. 'Maybe you should try being a bit nicer.'

I resisted the temptation to let him taste the bear spray. Instead, I turned around and gave the sweetest smile I could muster.

'Just how nice do you want me to be?'

'Well, there's no ring on your finger and from what Sergeant Eggo said you've been having some trouble at your hotel. Maybe you should consider the advantages of having a man there at night to keep you safe?'

So I looked like a target. It wasn't a novel situation for me. Blonde hair that I kept long but tied up in a ponytail while working. Not exactly tall, which made men want to prove how big they were compared to me. Someone once described me as 'that cheerleader-looking chick'.

'I think I'll pass,' I said, getting into the driver's seat and slamming the door. 'Don't be offended. I just prefer my men a bit more substantial on the moral and intellectual scale.'

'Fucking prick tease,' he said. 'Just like that dead girl you're so concerned about.'

I slid the keys into the ignition.

'That dead girl *we're* so concerned about,' I corrected him. 'Or are you not, given what you apparently thought of her?'

'You want to know the truth about your client? She was happy to flirt but never put out, that's what the rumour is. Girls who do that get themselves in trouble.'

'Did she get herself in trouble with you?'

I had to ask. He'd given me no choice.

'She was half my age. I prefer my women with a few years'

experience behind them.' He leaned down so our faces were level. 'Sergeant Eggo might be putting up with you, but you should watch yourself.'

'Who was spreading those rumours about Adriana?' I persisted.

'Common knowledge,' he said. 'If you'd been doing your job properly, you'd have found that out yourself by now.'

He walked away pleased with himself. I let him drive off before leaving the area. It was my own fault more than his. Of course someone was going to report a strange car in a small village at the little-toe end of an island at night. I'd been careless, but now I knew one more thing about Adriana. Someone in Tobermory hadn't liked her much at all.

The hotel couldn't help me with moving rooms that night but agreed to the next day when housekeeping were doing their rounds. I got a beer from the bar and headed back to rest, but my mind was too busy. The seaweed crown had gone via delivery service to Nate, but the memory of it lurked on my sheets. I had a bath and washed off the residual presence of my encounter with what passed as Mull's law enforcement, then fired up the laptop.

The photos I'd taken of the marks in the wooden beams got no image recognition hits. They were just vague shapes, hard to make out on the wood's surface.

I turned my attention to the small bouquet of greenery. In the confines of my warm room I could smell it. The sage and dill were easy to identify. It took me longer to figure out the mullein, mugwort and elderberry. Either found growing wild, or easy to cultivate in pots indoors, these were common enough plants, but I'd never seen them bound like that together before, nor hung upside down above doorways and fireplaces.

It was late. Too late to be phoning anyone I didn't know really well. I dialled Proudfoot's number anyway. He answered immediately.

'Hi, Lance,' I began. 'Sorry to bother you again. This is Sadie Levesque.'

'It's no bother,' he said. 'I was wondering if you'd call. Give me a second.' His voice became muffled as he turned away from the receiver and shouted at someone. 'I've got to take this. Open that other bottle of red, would you?' I heard Lance's footsteps then a door closing gently. 'So what is it I can do for you?'

'I can call back tomorrow,' I said. Not that I meant it. 'You've got company.'

'Ach, my friend here's a police officer so he understands, and he owes me enough favours that he can wait. I was worried about you today. What's happening there?'

'I went to the Kydd farm. Jasper wasn't answering the door and I was worried about him, so I went in through a kitchen window. I know I shouldn't have done that but . . .'

'No, you shouldn't. Farmers out there have shotguns. You could have ended up on the wrong end of a shell.'

'Bit late for that warning. Anyway, I'm calling because I saw some things in there I don't understand. It's a long shot but I thought you might know more about traditions here than me.'

'What did you find?' he asked.

'It'll sound stupid now . . . the house was like a time capsule. I guess I was expecting that. But above every doorway and window there were these weird little bundles of herbs wrapped in coarse cloth and hung upside down.'

'Anything else?' Lance's voice was quieter now.

I rolled onto my back on the bed. 'Yeah, all the beams have been burned with tadpole-shaped markings. Not recent, but deeply ingrained. Definitely not decoration. And I guess it all looks a bit obsessive, like Jasper Kydd really lost the plot.'

Lance sighed.

'He did lose the plot,' Lance said. 'Understandably. But I

don't think the things you're describing to me have much to do with psychological problems.'

'What then?'

'Listen, Sadie, there were rumours. There always are with killings that have any element of ritualised torture. You shouldn't get distracted by it. Adriana — and Flora for that matter — were killed by real people with real-world fantasies and psychopathy. Everything else is just myth and superstition.'

'What are you not telling me?' I asked.

'I never let myself go down that particular rabbit hole when I was reporting Flora's death, but there was talk of evil spirits, of — I don't know — something like a curse. There was some vague reference to silencing a woman with sand to stop her telling the island's secrets but this is ancient legend and none of it's real. Those things you found at the Kydd farm sound like more of the same.'

'This is crazy,' I said. 'Why would anyone revisit a historic ritual on a young girl in the 21st century?'

'First of all, whoever killed Adriana Clark is neither rational nor reasonable, so it's impossible to classify anything they did to her as normal. In terms of filling someone's mouth with sand? That resonates as well today as it ever did. The act of silencing feels complete. It stops things whispered in intimate moments from becoming gossip, and it punishes the speaker — there are other examples in history of women being silenced through implements of torture.'

'But the marks and the herbs — that's more like voodoo. Who really believes in that stuff these days?'

'The people who live on the island where you're staying can trace their families back, in some cases, hundreds of years. They know the name and the history of the clan from which they came. They worshipped different gods to the ones we recognise today. They suffered more hardships and I suppose they put more faith in nature than we have to. Tides, harvests, the moon, the rain. They survived thanks to nature, but they could also be killed by it. How could they not have elevated it to a godlike status?'

'That's a lot to think about,' I said. 'I should let you go. Your wine's waiting.'

'Call me any time,' he said, 'and take my advice. Keep a healthy regard for the island's history but don't get dragged down by it. Sometimes the past should stay in the past.'

'Thanks Lance. Have a glass for me.'

I tried the internet searches again, this time armed with new knowledge. The results came back immediately.

The herbs were a combination that had been used for centuries to ward off evil spirits. The demons disliked the scents, apparently, and the combination of them was potent enough to ensure no evil entered your home. The burn marks did the same job a different way. Permanently engraving a sign warding off evil into the very fabric of your home was done routinely in times gone by, often as a home was being built. The same marks appeared in sections of the Tower of London. These burn marks had a very specific purpose though. They'd been left there to protect the occupants of the house against the ill-effects of witchcraft.

At any other time, in any other place, I'd have laughed. But lying on my pillow, the memory of a rotting seaweed crown left where I would lay my head, the icy chill of Adriana's fingertips fresh in my mind, the idea of witchcraft didn't feel like a joke at all.

Chapter Fourteen

The police station doors were locked. A sign said it would be manned from 11 a.m. Infuriating, but hopefully Sergeant Eggo and his men were out actually following up leads in Adriana's case. With the hours I had to kill, I went back to the Mull Historical Emporium. If the complete history of Mull's myths and legends was going to be anywhere, it would be there.

The door was open but Skittles was nowhere to be seen. That was no bad thing as far as I was concerned, and I headed directly for the book section. Mull's ancient history was covered in detail. There were several books on how the British Fisheries Society built Tobermory in 1788. Nothing about murders or mysteries on Mull.

I checked the beams of the shop as I went. No taper burns there, nor herbs hung above doorways. The back room was dedicated to the sinking of a ship in Tobermory harbour. The *San Juan de Sicilia* was part of the Spanish Armada, and had been burned to the depths of Tobermory Bay in 1588. Rumours of gold and other treasures had circulated ever since. A quill pen on the shelf caught my eye, not for the quill itself but for the space in front of it. A tiny paper placard bore the legend,

'Quill from an early salvage of the wreck by the Duke of Monmouth together with shell believed to have been used as an inkwell.'

I was slipping my camera from my pocket when a couple entered. Skittles came in from another door and took his place behind the till.

Dust is not our friend, we're told throughout our lives. It comes from human skin, and a lack of hygiene and cleaning. It indicates that we're slovenly and poor housekeepers. But it also leaves evidence in its absence. Missing pieces of information that show where things were but are no longer. On the shelf, near that quill pen, was the outline of a large shell, maybe seven inches long, pretty wide too. Given how close up I'd gotten to the one that had been used to violate Adriana Clark, the space on that shelf required a serious explanation.

Engaging the camera flash to combat the darkness and hoping it wouldn't draw Skittles' attention, I took a quick snap of the space where the shell should have been. Passing him as I exited, I caught him staring blankly out of the window and sucking his thumb, an infant stuck in an adult's body.

I headed for a quiet bench on the harbourside and called Nate Carlisle.

'Sadie, I'm just headed into court to give evidence,' he said.

'I'll make it fast. I need the conch shell. I have an idea of where it came from but I'll have to put it on a shelf to compare it with a shape.'

'I can't let you touch the shell. It'll be an exhibit in the case if it ever gets prosecuted, and if I've broken the chain of evidence, it could get excluded. The best I could do is to have an officer deliver it to Sergeant Eggo and you can explain your theory for him to investigate.'

'If I do that and word gets out here, the opportunity to check the shell shape will disappear. It's already precarious.'

I thought on my feet. 'Hey, could you take a plaster cast and send it to me? Like a reconstruction. Then you wouldn't have to let the actual shell out of your possession at all.'

Silence for a few seconds. 'I guess that would work,' Nate said.

'And I'm going to text you the name of a guy who's linked to the shell. Do you have access to the police database to check it out?'

'I have contacts who would do that for me, but that's confidential information. If anything relevant comes up, all I can do is flag it to Sergeant Eggo. It'll be up to him to decide what to tell you, so it might be faster for you to ask him to run the name at the police station there.'

'Fine,' I said. I knew when I was losing a battle. 'Thanks Nate. I'll let you go.'

'Sadie, wait, I have some positive news for you. Whatever your concerns were about Adriana being involved in drugs seem to be unfounded. Her tox screens came back completely negative. Nothing in her system from the night she died and her hair shows zero long-term narcotics use.'

'Not even alcohol?' I asked.

'She was completely clean,' he said. 'And that powder you found in the velvet bag wasn't drugs either. You can reassure her parents that she hadn't got involved in anything they weren't aware of. Cold comfort now, but they'll appreciate it later.'

'Oh,' I said. That was one theory busted. Part of me was hoping Adriana had been seriously drunk when she'd died. Anything to have numbed her awareness. Sadly she'd been denied even that. 'What was the powder then?'

'Took the lab a while to figure it out, but it turned out to be bone. Crushed and very finely ground.'

My stomach lurched.

'Ground bone? Tell me it's not human.'

'Still working on that one. I should have an answer for you in the next couple of days. Sorry, I'm being called in. I'll get working on that plaster cast later today.'

Ground bone in a velvet bag, hidden in Adriana's boot in the pub where she worked. Nate might think that was good news, but it was sour in my mouth. There was no reason I could think of for Adriana to have knowingly hidden bone dust in her own boot, but the only alternative was that someone else had put it there.

I headed for the pottery shop and smiled seeing Lizzy's grandmother behind the counter.

'Morning,' I said brightly.

'Good morning, how's your car? The grapevine has it that some trouble found you yesterday.'

'It did, but it was nothing that couldn't be fixed.' I kept a smile glued on my face. I didn't like too many people knowing my business. Gossip made it harder to do my job. 'Listen, I was in the Historical Emporium earlier and I got talking to the man who works there, but I've only ever heard him called Skittles, and I can't bear the thought of referring to him by a nickname. Could you tell me what his actual name is so next time I don't have to be so rude?'

'That'll be Rhys Stewart. Keeps himself to himself. Has learning difficulties and can be prone to emotional outbursts, but his father owned the Emporium and Rhys just about manages to keep it going with help from the community here.'

'Rhys,' I said. 'I'll remember that. Lizzy not working today?'

'No, her friends wanted to go and lay down some flowers for Adriana. They're not allowed at Mackinnon's Cave for obvious reasons so they're away somewhere else to commemorate her together.'

'Would you happen to know where and when?' I asked. 'I'd like to pay my respects too.'

'I think they were planning to spend the afternoon and evening there. You know how elaborate teenagers can be. You'll find them down at Lochbuie. It's on the map.'

I walked north from the harbour to the Clark house. The family was due more information, and if anything was going to be announced regarding the relevance of Flora Kydd's death I wanted it to come from me first.

The scale of the press encampment had increased, but this time I was prepared to peel off and take the footpath to the rear of the house then hop the fence. The atmosphere felt different before I'd even knocked on the back door. There was a new stillness to the place. Usually a TV, Brandon's computer or Luna was making noise somewhere. No one responded to my knocking. I dialled Rob's number but he didn't pick up. Their car was absent from the driveway, but the house had a freestanding garage that I knew Rob kept locked because of the press invasion, and I had no way of getting in there to check it out.

Going to the plant pot where I'd seen Rob put the emergency key previously, I let myself in through the kitchen door, calling out softly as I went.

There was no one downstairs. The computer was off. The curtains to the front were all closed as they had been since Adriana's death had been discovered. No cooking smells in the kitchen, no trash in the bin. I went up the stairs, calling their names once more. Every room was deserted. A couple of dolls had been left stranded in the middle of Luna's floor, but otherwise it was neat and tidy. No signs of a break-in or a struggle. All of which begged the question – where the hell was the Clark family? Were they safe? If they'd been forcibly removed from their home I'd have expected some signs of conflict, but then again, people put up remarkably little resistance when faced with a gun or a threat to a child. My decision was to continue a quick search to see what information I could gather, then notify the authorities if it seemed necessary, keeping my fingers crossed that it wouldn't be.

From the edge of Brandon's bed, I stared at a photograph on his bedside table. He and Adriana stood hugging and grinning wildly into camera in the middle of a crowded arena, a band on stage in the distance. The twins looked delirious. I counted to ten contemplating the rights and wrongs of my next move, and hadn't changed my mind by ten, so I opened Brandon's drawers one by one.

I found a lighter and cigarettes. Homeopathic sleeping tablets but no other drugs. A girl's clothes – a sweatshirt and a woolly hat with a faux rabbit-tail bobble – I assumed they'd been Adriana's. After that I checked his wardrobe but found nothing unusual there. Finally I looked under the bed, around the wooden base. It would be difficult to explain my behaviour to the Clarks if they walked in now. The trust would be shattered. The golden rule in private investigating was never to undermine your client, yet there was no shaking the feeling that they were hiding something from me. I listened for a moment, waiting for creaks on the staircase or the whisper of footsteps on carpet, and succeeded only in hearing my own heartbeat all the more clearly. Wasting time, inviting discovery. If I was going to do this, it was time to get moving. Like magic, my hand hit a plastic bag taped to the wooden underside of the bed. Teenagers thought they were careful, but the truth was they all hid contraband in the same places.

Magic mushrooms with their pale brown shrivelled caps and skinny stalks. Lizzy had said Adriana was asking about them too. Perhaps they were Adriana's, and Brandon had taken them out of his twin's room to stop her parents finding them, or perhaps both brother and sister were planning on trying something new.

I slipped them into my pocket. Whether Brandon liked it or not, his parents wanted me to keep him safe. Given the scene at Mackinnon's Cave two nights ago, if the police did a sweep of the house, the mushrooms would only provide more damning evidence against him. The mushrooms were better off with me until any suspicion levelled at the family had passed, or until grounds for that suspicion had solidified.

I'd been in Adriana's room before when my services were first engaged, but I went in again. Knowing she was dead made everything seem sadder. She had a calendar on her wall with work shifts marked in blue, and other commitments – school, the doctor – marked in green. She had university prospectuses on her desk in a neat stack. She liked floral scents and bright lipsticks. By her bed was a photo of her and Brandon either side of Luna, the three of them lying on a picnic rug, smiling up at whoever was holding the camera. She was painfully beautiful in comparison with the bloated, ravaged girl in the cave. I checked my emotions and moved on to Rob and Isabella's room.

This was functional. Little effort had been made with soft furnishings. The duvet cover was plain white. No paintings adorned the walls. There was no makeup or jewellery on the dressing table, only paperwork. It felt unloved.

I hesitated momentarily before opening the bedside drawers. They contained the usual debris of adult life. A bundle of passports was in the third drawer down. I opened each in turn and saw familiar faces, familiar names, put them away, went to check the bathroom, then returned for a second look. The passports were genuine, I was sure of that, but each had been issued on the same date, five months earlier. It made sense for the twins. Their original passports would have been requested together and renewed together. Conceivably even Rob and Isabella might have had their first passports issued at the same

112

time if their honeymoon was the first time either of them had been abroad. But otherwise, how did five family members come to renew their passports at the same time?

Taking the hallway back to first Adriana's then Brandon's room, I began looking for the same thing I'd phoned California to locate – their high school yearbooks. Issued every year, I'd kept every yearbook I'd ever been in. I didn't know anyone who hadn't. Yearbooks were a rite of passage – a means of confirming that you were growing up.

No yearbook in either of their rooms. No photos of anyone other than family, either. No diaries or calendars from their time in America. It was as if they hadn't existed before arriving on Mull.

I was going back down the stairs when my cell phone rang. My heart was beating a little too fast when I answered.

'Hi Rob,' I said. 'Are you all okay? I'm at the house.'

'Yeah, sorry, I should have called. The press were getting invasive and after what happened with Brandon we decided we needed to get away. We left in the middle of the night with just the essentials,' Rob explained.

'Where are you now?'

'We've booked into a holiday rental just outside Tobermory for a month. I'll text you the address. Was there something you needed?'

I left through the kitchen door and locked up quietly behind me.

'Just checking in,' I said. 'There's a cold case I'm going to speak with the police about that might have some relevance, but it's a long time ago. Nothing for you to be concerned about right now. Also the tox screen results came in from the forensic pathologist. There were no drugs or alcohol in Adriana's system. Dr Carlisle wanted me to tell you. How's Brandon doing?'

A long pause at Rob's end. 'Not so good,' he said. 'None of us are. We just need some sort of resolution.'

'I know. There is progress, I promise you, but it's all separate strands of evidence that need tying together. I'm sorry.'

I rang off. There was nothing more I could say.

The only thing I was certain of as I ended the call, was that my clients were withholding more information than they were giving me. I couldn't help but wonder why.

Chapter Fifteen

My next trip was to the police station. A woman came to the desk as I entered.

'Hi,' I said. 'Could you help me? I wanted to speak with an officer but I didn't catch his name when he pulled me over. Tall, thin, mid-thirties, scar on the back of his right hand.'

'That would be Constable Bathgate.'

'That's it! Honestly, my brain. Is Constable Bathgate here at the moment?'

'He goes off shift at 5 p.m. It might be easier if I passed your query on to an officer who'll be here longer?' she suggested.

'This won't take a minute. Could you tell him Sadie Levesque is here? I just want to thank him for how helpful he was.'

The woman disappeared through the door behind her and called his name. A minute later the door opened again and Bathgate appeared.

'What do you want?' he snapped.

'That's not very friendly, Constable, given how close you seemed to think our relationship was last night. I just need a favour. I'd like to know a bit more about someone. You have access to the Police National Database. Could you take a look for me?'

He leaned over the counter and down to my ear.

'Now why the festering fuck would you be under the impression that I'd step an inch out of my way for you?' he asked.

I smiled, shook my head and wagged a finger at him.

'Such awful words coming from such a pretty mouth,' I said loudly, before whispering, 'Because if you don't help me, I'm going to play the audio recording I made with my cell phone that was in my pocket the whole time last night. I'm guessing using police powers to pressurise a member of the public into having sex with you would probably get you sacked in what . . . about twenty-four hours? Shall we find out?'

'Show me,' he demanded.

'The first time I'll play this will be in front of Sergeant Eggo and anyone else I can find here. There's also a copy on the cloud waiting to be sent to a journalist I know called Lance Proudfoot who lives in Edinburgh. Look him up by all means. Wanna play chicken?'

He glared at me as I kept a slight smile on my lips. Constable Bathgate should have negotiated, of course, but the threat of losing his job was potent.

'Who is it?' he hissed.

'Rhys Stewart from the Mull Historical Emporium.'

'Oh come on, is that all the Clarks are getting for their money? You identify the one guy in town with a learning difficulty and some developmental problems, and decide he's the culprit? Put your prejudices away.'

'You're giving *me* a moral lecture?' I laughed. 'Maybe I just want to exclude him. Are you going to help or not?'

He flashed an angry look at his watch.

'Come with me,' he said, lifting the moveable section of countertop and opening the door in the rear wall.

We walked past one office and into another that bore the legend 'Sergeant H Eggo' on the door. Sitting at the desk, Constable Bathgate began typing furiously into Eggo's computer.

'This is blackmail,' he said as he typed.

'I have no idea what you're talking about. I asked for help with an investigation. You're entitled to look anyone up on that database. As yet you've shared no information. No crime has been committed. You've given me precisely nothing so far.'

'The sergeant'll be back any minute,' he said.

'Then hurry.'

As he finished typing, the computer's internal fan whirred and the printer began chugging. I reached for the sheet.

'No you don't,' he said, pulling it from the printer. 'Me first.' His facial expression went from stubbornly bored to confused to concerned. 'What do you know that we don't?' he asked.

'Nope, you go first,' I said.

'He has a record for possession of category C indecent images. Got a year's probation.'

'He lives in your community. How did the police not know about this?'

'He wasn't put on the sex offenders register, and this offence happened on the mainland, not here. It dates back to when he was nineteen. Now he's thirty-four. We didn't have cause to check him out.'

'Well you do now. Did he provide a statement explaining his whereabouts on the night Adriana was killed?'

'Did who give a statement?' Sergeant Eggo asked from the doorway.

Constable Bathgate and I exchanged a glance, shifting gears from enemies to co-conspirators in a heartbeat.

'Miss Levesque came in asking about Rhys Stewart,' Bathgate said.

'Yes, and now Constable Bathgate appears to have found something on your system that he won't share with me,' I lied. I didn't like Bathgate but I wasn't going to betray him while I was getting what I wanted. 'I'm going to have to insist on you handing over pertinent information. My clients deserve to be party to the ongoing investigation.'

'Insist away,' Eggo said. 'Just know that you're entitled to jack shit from us. Constable, I'll deal with this from here. Your shift ended ten minutes ago.'

Bathgate walked away, his earlier anger replaced with relief. Eggo sat down and read Rhys Stewart's previous conviction. He took a deep breath in, gritted his teeth, then stared at me.

'What's on there?' I asked. Might as well continue the performance.

'Rhys Stewart didn't kill Adriana Clark,' Eggo said. 'He struggles to open and shut that shop every day. Half the towns-folk here help with his book-keeping and finances out of respect for his father. His shopping is delivered, his laundry is done for him. Skittles can barely take care of himself, let alone abduct and kill a young woman.'

'Why are you defending him?' I asked. 'There's something relevant on that piece of paper. I saw it on Bathgate's face and it's on yours too.'

'Possession of category C images – I shouldn't even be telling you that much, but you're intent on seeing the worst in people here so you should know just how ridiculous the leap is from that to a sexually motivated murder. He's not had so much as a driving conviction in the last twelve years. The indecent images offence happened while Rhys was off the island, as I recall attempting to live in a supported unit near Glasgow that gives people with mental health disabilities a chance to live semi-independently. He came back soon after and has caused no trouble since.'

'You mean he hasn't been caught for anything. Not the same thing,' I corrected him. 'How do you define category C images?'

'Non-penetrative, no torture, no animals, no force. It's more about the context the images are used in,' Eggo said.

'But they still constitute illegal porn.'

'A man who says he's never watched porn is either a liar or a saint.' Eggo folded up Rhys Stewart's paperwork and shoved it roughly into his desk drawer.

'Can I quote you on that to the press?' I asked.

'You'll not find anyone prepared to print your ridiculously far-fetched conclusions.'

'I wouldn't be so sure about that. I'm following up every lead I find and I won't apologise for it. Any decent police officer would be doing the same.'

Harris Eggo folded his arms. 'Fine. In the light of this conviction, I'll have a statement taken from him and ask for a voluntary DNA sample. I'll even check out whatever alibi he has. But I guarantee we won't find anything. I know these people, and I know my town.'

'I want his car swabbed for Adriana's DNA too. She must have been driven to Mackinnon's Cave. It's too far to hike or bike. I saw him leaving his place late the other night dressed all in black – hat, gloves, the works.'

'Is that why you're here? A pair of gloves? This is Scotland, girl. We sunbathe in bloody gloves.'

I considered telling him about the shell. Probably I should have. But Eggo had already decided Rhys wasn't capable of the sort of killing Adriana had suffered and I knew intractable when I saw it. If the shell fitted, I'd take it further. Until then, the dust in the Emporium was best left settled. I let Eggo win the battle and saved my energy for the coming war.

I headed down the island to Craignure. From there Lochbuie was south-west. My map gave me Moy Castle as the nearest point of interest. It occurred to me as I approached that I didn't know what I was looking for. Lochbuie was a few houses, and the castle was deserted, not a visitor in sight. Even so, finding the revellers was easier than I'd anticipated, mainly by following the music. Had it been uninhabited, the site of the Lochbuie stones would have been the sort of place I could have sat for hours and just looked. The landscape was stunning in every direction, and the stones themselves stood in the shadow of the mountain Ben Buie. But it was hard to look up and away from the stones. It was no Stonehenge, but the eight stones, one newer boulder and three outlying granite slabs, were impressive. In a perfect circle, some twelve feet across, they reached skywards. I hadn't had a chance to research them, but my little knowledge of other such ancient monuments was that they had to be at least 3000 years old, maybe much older. It was breathtaking. Far enough away from civilisation to feel private. Mystical enough to feel exciting. Like I said, teenagers have places. They'd excelled in choosing this one.

Running between them, dancing, singing and playing was a group of perhaps fifty teens. I recognised Lizzy from the pottery shop immediately and kept my distance under the shade of the trees nearest the stones. Not hiding exactly, but not making my presence felt. There were no other adults in sight. I wasn't going to be welcomed. There were a few other faces from Tobermory. The gaggle of girls from my first night in The Blether dancing in cutoff tops and shorter-than-short shorts. Lewis Eggo, sitting quietly in a group of boys, chatting and drinking bottled beer. A couple of people who worked at my hotel in the evenings and at weekends. No sign of Brandon Clark, even though this was his age group.

Moving backwards into the tree cover, I made certain I was out of sight, and took a seat on the twig-strewn moss. I don't know what or who I was waiting for. I took an hour to contemplate how joyful it was to be young, and how sad it was that the joy was tinged with such self-doubt and desperation. An hour to look away from gyrating bodies and young men locking social horns over the prettiest girls. Sixty whole minutes to try to remember when I'd last had that much fun or felt that free. It wasn't long enough for me to answer those questions.

As the sun began to dip, a girl stood up and began shouting for silence. Her white-blonde hair shone and her skin was glowing. Some doe-eyed boy ran over with a crate for her to stand on. She'd been in the pub, I realised. One of Lizzy's friends. Maybe one of Adriana's too.

'Speak louder, Catriona,' a boy nearest my edge of the field yelled.

Catriona – the name suited her – cupped her hands against her mouth for her words to carry.

'We're here for Adriana!' The crowd whistled and cheered. 'To party for her because she can't. To dance for her because she never will again. To live now that she won't!' She raised a bottle to her lips and drank whisky neat. I was simultaneously impressed and concerned that she might be planning on driving herself home. 'To Adriana!' Catriona held the bottle aloft and as one they stood, drinks in the air, and spoke the dead girl's name. Then the crying began.

Girls sobbed and held each other. Boys, opportunistic or otherwise, made it their purpose to reassure the weeping females. I scanned the crowd, looking for the voyeurs and the oddballs. Hoping none of the girls would allow themselves to be drawn away from the crowd into the secluded depths of the countryside where an anticipated romantic escape might turn into something deadlier. Something silent.

'I should have known you'd be here,' a man whispered behind me.

'PC Bathgate,' I said. 'I thought you were off duty. You here to join the party?'

'A concerned parent asked me to check it out, unofficially. No one wants any arrests for underage drinking. These aren't bad kids.'

'One of them might be,' I said.

A bunch of wrestling boys began rolling in our direction and the two of us instinctively moved an additional tree away from them.

'I thought your suspect was hard at work in the Emporium,' Bathgate said.

'Keeping an open mind,' I replied.

A speaker crackled into life and a young woman's voice filled the air, singing 'Died for Love'. We were silent, listening to the lyrics. A tale of lost love and death. I wondered who had chosen it and what they knew that I didn't.

The mass sobbing stopped and the crowd came together, arms over each other's shoulders, swaying from side to side in a giant circle around the stones.

'Do they do this often?' I asked.

'Only when one of them dies. A fifteen-year-old boy passed from cancer last year. Another girl came off the road driving in a lightning storm two years before. This is how they get through it.'

A figure came ambling from the trees fifty metres away, rubbing tears from his eyes, teeth bared. I saw him before he saw me.

'Listen, about earlier . . .' I said to Bathgate, 'I shouldn't have used blackmail to get what I wanted. It was heavy-handed and stupid.' I spoke fast, and louder than I should have done. Brandon Clark hesitated, then moved through the trees in the direction of the road. Constable Bathgate frowned and started to move his head in the direction of the sound of cracking twigs. 'Can we start again?'

'You'll forget about what I said to you last night?' He sounded rightly incredulous.

'Everyone's entitled to one mistake,' I said. 'And we're both on the same side here, right?'

'Right,' he said.

'I'm glad that's sorted.' I looked at my watch. 'You know what, I've been here an hour and a half. You've got this. It's good to know there's someone keeping these kids safe. I'm going to head back into town.'

'Okay. Do you want to swap numbers or something? Compare notes?'

I masked my unhappiness at the thought of giving him my number with a grateful smile.

'That's a great idea,' I said, handing him my mobile for him to punch his number in. 'I'll message you mine later.'

'Do it now, so we can both be sure it got through,' he said. 'Reception on the island isn't always great.'

I did it. His phone buzzed immediately. No problem with reception in Lochbuie, unfortunately.

I said goodbye, made it beyond the trees then ran. Brandon and I needed to talk.

Chapter Sixteen

Brandon was nowhere to be seen when I reached the road, and I had no idea which direction he'd taken. Cautioning myself that any questions I wanted to ask him were better pursued the next day when he'd had a decent night's sleep and figured out that I was a friend rather than an enemy, I set off for my hotel. It was a relief to be handed a new key as I went past reception. My belongings had been moved to the second floor and I could rest knowing no intruder had slipped their hand beneath my pillow.

At the top of my email inbox was a message from Rob Clark attaching the last three months of Adriana's phone records. I locked my door, hauled a chest of drawers a couple inches across to prevent it from being opened from the hallway, and hoped there wasn't a fire that would require speedy egress by me during the night.

Beginning with the oldest calls from Adriana's phone, I worked my way forward to the date of her death.

There were no calls made to any American numbers, that was the first thing I noticed on a superficial scan. Adriana had not called a single one of her old friends. That wouldn't be so surprising if she'd had access to social media, but without that, it appeared Adriana had left America on a clean-break basis. That would have left her lonely and vulnerable, maybe even desperate for company.

Thirty days before Adriana's killing the calls were relatively slow. I had access to numbers only, not the names she would have had in her mobile directory. All the calls were to other UK mobile numbers. The longest conversation lasted fifteen minutes; the shortest was just seconds. No middle-of-the-night, hour-long sessions murmuring sweet nothings to a lover.

I shut my laptop and switched off the light, staring through the semi-darkness at the beamed ceiling. In my mind, tadpole shapes swam across the stained wood. Girls danced provocatively for boys around stones that had at some point in history been a clock or a burial ground or an altar. Adriana fought for her life in bitterly cold water, trying to get away from the person with a death grip on her ankle. A dusty old shell that had once doubled as an inkwell went missing from a glass shelf.

The next morning I awoke naked and shivering in my bathtub.

A hot shower eased most of the aching from my body. I hadn't sleepwalked since I was a teenager, but for years I'd been prolific. I'd been found on the street, in my parents' car, in a wardrobe and in my childhood treehouse in our backyard. I'd even tried hypnosis as a cure – that hadn't worked. Then one day, I simply didn't do it any more. Was there some deep, dark trauma in my past that I'd been running away from? No. But there were dreams so vivid that my days felt pale and lifeless in comparison. I'd never been a great sleeper as a child – my mother recounted how few hours' sleep she got even now – although these days those stories were told affectionately. I never remembered how I reached those bizarre places. Last night's few steps were equally blank. The drawers remained in front of the door though, and I was grateful for that.

At 10 a.m. I was outside the Clarks' new secret address – a small holiday cottage on the westerly road out of town – armed with milk, fresh bread and questions. It was Isabella who let me in.

The accommodation was cramped. We sat in the kitchen/diner/lounge and I took out my laptop. Isabella fiddled around putting the milk in the fridge and slicing bread until Rob took charge and led her to the sofa.

'What have you found out?' he asked me.

'There was a murder forty years ago. No one was ever convicted. A sixteen-year-old girl from Mull was killed, motivation was probably sexual. She was found with sand packed into her mouth.' Isabella looked away from me. I didn't blame her. Every word I uttered would be burned into this couple's memory forever, so I kept it brief. 'It's unlikely that it's the same perpetrator, given the decades that have passed. It's more likely that it's a copy of that aspect of the crime. Something specific to the island.'

'So the killer would have to be from Mull. They'd need to be really familiar with its history, right?' Rob grabbed his wife's hand and squeezed.

The gesture was an alien one in the circumstances. It was hopeful. There was something in there that moved past desperation. I couldn't help but stare at Rob's hand. If I were Rob – if I'd brought my daughter to an island 5000 miles from her home for my new job, and she'd met her end there – I'd have wanted it to have been a tourist, the same as Sergeant Eggo did. A tourist meant an active, travelling predator. It meant Adriana could have been targeted in Scotland, San Francisco, Spain or Senegal.

'Sadie?' Rob prompted.

'Sorry, I was processing. What did you say?'

'I was asking if there are any likely suspects yet,' he said.

'I have a lead,' my heart sank to have to finish the sentence, 'that links to the shell. There's a man with a conviction that might be relevant, but I'm careful not to leap to conclusions with prior behaviour unless there's a clear link.'

Brandon walked in. 'How're you doing?' I asked quickly before he could leave again.

'Okay,' he said. 'Thanks for . . . you know . . . sorting out the cave stuff.'

The cave stuff. Like it was a passing moment. No reference at all to the state I'd seen him in yesterday.

'Brandon, you might be able to help me more than anyone else. Were you and Adriana friends with the same people in Tobermory?'

'She didn't have any friends, I told you that,' he said.

'But there were people she spoke with on her cell phone, right?'

He shrugged.

'She made a lot of calls out in the last month, all to UK numbers, so it wasn't as if she was phoning friends back home,' I said.

No one spoke.

'This might be the key to figuring out what happened to Adriana. I know it's painful. I know that suggesting her cell phone might have vital information on it can feel like victim blaming, as if maybe she'd been communicating with her killer or was behaving in a way that invited trouble. But believe me, nothing could be further from the truth. The court order could take a while, so anything you know, however small a detail, might really help.'

Isabella glared at Rob who looked away. 'Tell her,' she said.

'Bella, we agreed.'

'She said it might help,' Isabella said. 'So just do it.'

I waited.

'I found Addie's cell phone,' Rob said. I did my best to keep my face neutral. 'The police are going to get a court order anyway so they'll get what they're looking for. We weren't hiding anything.'

His face said the opposite.

'Could you tell me why you made that decision?' I asked gently.

'We're a private family. I didn't want the police invading Addie's personal space more than was necessary. There's no way she was complicit in what happened to her, so we didn't see the relevance,' Rob said. 'There are family photos on there, emails, personal stuff that's nothing to do with this.'

Isabella issued a tiny tut and turned her head to one side.

'I understand why this feels intrusive,' I said. 'But have you looked through her messages, checked if there was social media use you were unaware of?'

'I couldn't . . .' Rob said, the words choking him. He began to cry, biting down on the emotion before he carried on, '. . . I couldn't look at them. And it wouldn't have done any good anyway. I don't know her pin number to get into her cell.'

'I do,' Brandon said. 'You never even asked me! How could you not have told me you had it?'

'You've gone through enough,' Rob said. 'I made a decision that I thought was best for us all.'

'Bullshit,' Brandon said. 'I want to see it, now!'

Rob retrieved it from somewhere upstairs together with a charger. Brandon punched in the pin number to unlock it, and we had access.

There were a number of calls into her cell the day she disappeared including three from the same number, a contact Adriana had listed as 'Wicked'. I checked the rest of her contacts. There were almost no normal names.

'Addie did that,' Brandon said. 'Had her own names for everyone. She liked that no one else ever knew who was calling her. It was like her own private joke.'

The messages were varied.

'Hi, want to join us tonight? Late meeting. Usual place & time.'

Another, 'Seriously, he's not worth it.'

From someone else, 'I heard he gave his last girlfriend the clam.' I was guessing that was teen slang for chlamydia, but that needed looking up. I didn't like the shell reference though. That was too close for comfort.

A day later, 'Me and L going vegetarian tonight.'

'Sneak out. Midnight. Forest path.' That was two weeks before she disappeared.

The messages got more frequent and more coded as time progressed. Then finally, on the day her family last set eyes on her, a message that read, '1am pick up, girls only, w/ happies. Del x' That message had come from the same contact. I needed to get in touch with whoever 'Wicked' was, as soon as possible.

Adriana hadn't replied.

'Do you know anyone called Del?' I asked Brandon. 'Could be short for Delia, Delilah, Derek or it might just be a nickname.'

He gave a disgusted snort. '"Del" isn't a name, it means delete. Addie obviously didn't get round to doing it. Give me the number,' Brandon said, getting his own mobile out. He typed it into his own contacts for a match. Long pause. 'I got nothing,' he said eventually.

'I really don't want Brandon put under pressure like this,' Rob said.

'I wonder if Brandon and I could have a quick chat,' I directed at Rob and Isabella. 'It's a teenager thing. He's the most likely to understand the relevance of Adriana's personal possessions, the things she had before you moved to Mull versus the things that she might have gathered since you got here.' I stood up and walked to the doorway. 'Privately.'

Brandon scowled but stood up.

'He's fragile.' The words burst from Isabella's lips. 'And exhausted. I'm not sure this is a good idea.'

'Mom, I'm fine,' Brandon said.

She stood up, firing rapid sentences off in Spanish that I couldn't understand. Brandon stepped towards her, slipping a gentle arm around his mother's shoulders and kissing her cheek softly.

'I'm okay, Mama. Stop worrying about me,' he said, then looked at me. 'Come on. We can talk in my room.'

He took the stairs slowly and I followed. Brandon threw himself on a single bed that complained at the sudden weight.

'I'm sorry you've had to leave your home. That must be making things even worse,' I said.

'That's not my home,' he growled. 'This island, this country. None of it.'

'Do you want to go back to the States?'

'We can't . . . because of Dad's job. Did you want to talk about yesterday?'

'Yes. The man with me was a police officer. You've had one run-in with them this week. He was at Lochbuie looking for anyone suspicious or who stood out. I had to distract him so he didn't see you, Brandon.'

'I don't give a fuck,' Brandon said. 'I wasn't doing anything wrong.'

'All right.' I sat on the floor, my back against the wall. 'So what were you doing there?'

'I wanted to hear what they were saying about Addie. They're all hypocrites. None of them really liked her. They were playing games. I was pissed that suddenly it's like she was their best friend. Yesterday they used her as an excuse to get drunk and get laid.'

'I can see how you'd reach that conclusion,' I said. Couldn't disagree with that one. 'There's something else I need to ask you about. You're not going to like it.' He folded his arms and rolled his eyes at the ceiling. 'I found a bag of magic mushrooms under your bed. I was looking for anything to do with your sister so I make no apology for the intrusion. I don't care about the drugs, but someone else mentioned that Adriana was asking about mushrooms. I don't get it, because her tox screen was totally clean.'

'You shouldn't have gone in my room!' Brandon said.

'You shouldn't have gone off to Lochbuie without telling your parents,' was my slightly shitty answer.

He shrugged. 'I took them from her room. Went through everything after she disappeared. I knew the police would too, and I didn't want Mom more upset, so I put them under my bed. I should've just got rid of them.'

'I'm glad you didn't. Whoever gave them to her might have information. That last message Adriana was sent? I think the word "happies" refers to the mushrooms. It's drug slang.'

'Maybe,' he said.

'One last thing.' I stood up again. 'The other night in Mackinnon's Cave, you said something about Adriana being cursed.'

'Don't remember. I'd stolen my parents' vodka and taken painkillers with it. I want to go to sleep now.' He rolled onto his side and faced the wall.

'Brandon, is there anyone or anything you're afraid of here?'

He gave a brief, bitter laugh. 'There's no point being afraid. I've got nothing left to lose.'

Chapter Seventeen

That afternoon, I headed back to The Blether in search of teenagers to answer my questions about Adriana's social life. I'd already tried to call the cell phone number to identify who Wicked was, but no one was picking up and there was no voicemail recording either.

Rachel, the landlady, poured cold water on my plan immediately. Most of the usual teenagers had apparently missed school with some mysterious stomach bug – she'd sighed at that and raised her eyebrows meaningfully. It seemed that the Lochbuie stones wake had continued well into the night.

'Is there anyone in particular you're looking for?' Lewis Eggo asked quietly.

Rachel patted him on the shoulder and bustled off into the kitchen, leaving us alone.

'Does anyone around here go by the name Wicked?' I asked. 'Or did you ever hear Adriana using it as a name?'

'No, sorry,' he said.

'You were there last night. How come you aren't suffering an all-day hangover like the rest of them?'

'How come you saw me and I didn't see you?' he countered.

'I didn't want to intrude,' I lied softly. 'It wasn't my place.' Lewis was hesitant with me. I wasn't going to rush things.

'It wasn't really my place either. When your dad's head of island police, you learn not to mess up too publicly. Plus, I don't want to lose this job. I'm saving up for university,' he said. 'Did you want a drink?'

I didn't, but I ordered one anyway. He passed the glass across the bar and into my hand.

'Do you have any idea where Adriana might have bought magic mushrooms? Or why? The impression I got was that she wasn't silly enough to get mixed up with drugs, but the issue's come up a couple of times now.'

'Most people don't really see 'shrooms as drugs,' he said. 'They're not hard to get hold of.'

'Did she get them in here?' I persisted, but gently.

He loaded a tray of dirty glasses into the dishwasher beneath the bar and ushered me over to an old-fashioned jukebox in the corner. We stood flicking through the song selections, our backs to the bar.

'I already told you, I need this job. Don't start digging around and causing trouble for Rachel. She's kind. What her husband does . . .'

I fed a few coins into the machine and Chrissie Hynde's velvet voice sang 'Hymn to Her', covering the sounds of us talking.

'I don't care about a local pub providing illegal entertainment to a handful of people, Lewis. I'm guessing your father already has a pretty good idea.' The boy looked away at that. 'I'm only interested insofar as it affected Adriana.' I laid a hand on his arm and he stared into my eyes. Green flecked with gold. Tanned, lightly freckled skin. Tall, gentle. Not at all like his dad.

'I think Adriana was . . . getting into some stuff. The 'shrooms are supposedly a part of that. Honestly, this is stupid. It's just harmless fun,' he said.

'What stuff was she getting into?'

'You won't understand.'

'Do you know how she died, Lewis?'

He shook his head. 'Dad wouldn't give me the details. He didn't want me upset.'

I was about to break a professional confidence, so I had to be sure I could make it worthwhile.

'Someone packed sand into her mouth. They drowned her and left her dead in a cave getting chewed up by the crabs.'

One hand crept to his mouth and the other clutched his stomach.

'I only . . .' he gulped air. 'I only knew that someone had drowned her.'

'Whatever she was into, I need to know all of it. Someone has to be brave. Is that you?'

The tracks switched and I waited for him to decide as the Crash Test Dummies sang about two knights and maidens, of bright lights and potions. I'd seen them perform it live at the Deerfoot Inn in Calgary and they were three minutes of my life I'd never forget. I let myself get lost in it and wondered what music would be played at Adriana's funeral – whenever that might take place – as I waited for Lewis to make a decision.

'Talk to Father Christophe at Saints of the Tides church. I know she went there sometimes. More often just before she died. I think she had questions,' he said.

'Thank you.' I put my hand over his to stop him from walking away as I pulled a piece of paper from my pocket. 'This number. Do you recognise it?'

Lewis frowned. 'Why's that relevant?'

'Someone messaged Adriana the night she died. They arranged to meet her. Is it anyone from here?'

'Does my dad know about this?' he asked.

'If he doesn't already, he will soon. Whose number is it, Lewis?'

'I won't do this. I don't believe anyone I know would hurt someone like that. I'm not turning on my friends.'

'You seem to have your hand on my son's person,' Harris Eggo said loudly behind us.

Lewis's cheeks darkened to crimson, and I withdrew my hand.

'You caught me,' I said. 'I was trying to figure out a few of Tobermory's closely guarded secrets and your son was being thoroughly uncooperative. What's that phrase – "chip off the old block"?'

Lewis stalked away, finding something urgent to do behind the bar.

'Nate Carlisle sent this for you,' he held out a package and the ripped tape was a sure sign that it had already been opened and inspected. 'He wanted to make sure it reached you safely.'

'Kind of you to deliver it personally,' I said.

'Now what would you be planning on doing with that?' Sergeant Eggo asked.

'My job,' I said. 'You've got a nice kid. The Clarks are parents too, just like you. They deserve answers.'

I left. Pretty soon I was going to have to give the cell number to the police and let them figure out who it belonged to, but I knew they wouldn't share the resulting information with me. Rightly or wrongly, I decided to hold off another day and trace the message sender myself, not least because Rob Clark hadn't given me permission to reveal that he had the phone. I hoped it was a decision I wasn't going to regret.

Heading out, I checked the address of Tobermory's Saints of the Tides church and set off to find Father Christophe. The church was a single-storey unit I'd have expected to see in an American trailer park. Weather-worn blue on the outside, but inside it was pretty and calming. Small, with an altar at one end and a few rows of chairs, it was functional rather than grandiose, and all the better for it.

'Can I help you?' a man asked.

'Father Christophe?'

'Yes. I don't think we've met,' he said, extending a hand to shake.

'I'm Sadie Levesque, working for Adriana Clark's family.' His hand was warm, the grip firm. His eyes were the palest blue I'd ever seen, his hair albino white, but he couldn't have been older than thirty-five, and his angular face was striking.

'You're the Canadian I've been hearing about. Did you want to sit?'

'Actually, Father, can we walk? I've been inside too much today.'

'I'd like that,' he said. 'Let's go.'

He exited the building without bothering to lock the door.

'Is that safe?' I asked.

'The island has a very low crime rate and my belief is that the church should be available to anyone when they need it as far as we can accommodate them.'

'Even when there might be a murderer wandering around?'

'Especially when there's a murderer wandering around. I can't think of a time when our community has needed God's help more.'

We went south down Breadalbane Street, taking it slow. He strolled, hands in his pockets, as if he'd been expecting me all day.

'That accent's not Scottish,' I said.

'French Guiana. I come from a long line of missionaries. Grew up thinking I'd break the mould and become a Formula One racing driver, but apparently that wasn't God's plan.'

'How long have you been here?'

'Three years, and I'm still settling in.'

'I gather Adriana attended your church,' I began.

'She did, to confession more often than services.'

'Can you tell me what she talked about?'

'You know what my answer's going to be,' he said, pushing his hands into his pockets. 'The seal of the confessional is absolute. It's against canon law to violate the relationship between penitent and confessor.'

'Adriana's dead. If she can see or hear you now, I guarantee she'll forgive your indiscretion.'

'Only God can forgive, and I'm not sure he would find your argument compelling.'

'I've spoken to people who thought Adriana was getting into something she was uncomfortable with. Maybe being drawn into a circle of friends who were using drugs? It's important, Father. It might help lead us to her murderer.'

'I'm not sure what you expect from me,' he said. 'I've told you I can't share anything with you regarding information passed from Adriana to me.'

I sighed.

'Fine. Talk to me about life on Mull. What aspects of living here might a newly arrived teenager find either enticing or off-putting? All I'm after is a bit of insider knowledge.'

'Is that an attempt to find a loophole?' He smiled.

'Loopholes are for lawyers. I'm carrying a photo of a dead girl in my pocket and I won't rest until I've done her justice.'

'Scotland's an old place. This island predates recorded history. It was entirely godless for hundreds of years, and worshipped false gods for hundreds more before Christianity arrived. History has taught us that where there's a religious void, people will deify other things.'

'Such as?'

He shook his head. 'That's all I have for you.'

'You don't seem upset,' I said. His eyes widened. 'Adriana's death was brutal, yet you're more concerned with canon law than doing what's right. I don't see God in your decision, I see a desire to protect your church. What would you do if the murderer was one of your congregation and they confessed what they'd done?'

'I would do my best to persuade them to turn themselves in, to express remorse, to see the evil in what they'd done.'

'How do you sleep at night, thinking that's a good enough answer?'

'Do you think anyone would come to confession if they thought their priest might act against them? The structure of the church would collapse. We are God's ear in the confessional. We keep God's silence afterwards.'

'What purpose does your god think Adriana's death serves exactly?' My patience was at boiling point.

He stopped walking to look at me square on. 'It's already brought people back to the church. Violent deaths remind us of the fragility of our lives. A murder is an indicator of society's sickness and faith provides the medicine. Adriana's passing might be viewed as a lighthouse for the soul, stopping other young teenage girls from crashing against the same rocks of thaumaturgy.'

He was entranced by his own speech. I filed the unfamiliar word away for later research. Father Christophe looked like a man in rapture, but all I could see was the horror of using a young woman's killing as parishioner clickbait.

Rhys Stewart, aka Skittles, walked up the street towards us, and I felt the weight of the plaster-cast conch shell in my pocket.

'Do you know him?' I asked Father Christophe, breaking him out of his ghoulish evangelism.

'Only socially. He's not an active member of our church. That said, we extend our prayers to anyone . . .' he fought for a politically correct term, '. . . less able.'

Skittles crossed the street and turned off, giving me a long last look.

Father Christophe and I parted ways and I was overcome with dislike for him. He'd been nothing but honest given the confines of his faith, but he was able to see Adriana's death as having fringe benefits. His reaction had been clinical. I was reminded of a college debate panel I'd once taken part in, discussing the criminality of marital rape. The trick had been to remain calm and unflappable, yet I'd found myself hating the people who were able to do so. I was fairly confident Father Christophe would have been the star of the debate team at his own college, whatever the subject.

Striking while the iron was hot, I followed the route Skittles had taken. No point delaying. If Sergeant Eggo wasn't going to follow up on the previous conviction we'd discovered, then I'd have to take matters into my own hands.

Chapter Eighteen

The Island

Humans and animals share a remarkable number of traits. They have the capacity to parent well, but sometimes they just up and leave. They can be kind, not only to their own species, but to others. They know fear, but they can be courageous. They experience both pleasure and pain. Animals grieve just as people grieve. They squabble and play for power. Some can be cruel. Cats play for hours with half-dead mice, tigers kill for sport, humans kill for sexual pleasure and dominance.

Hypocrisy, though, is an exclusively human trait.

The day Adriana Clark arrived in Tobermory, a line of teenage girls sat along a harbour bench and declared her showy and pretentious as they clutched their fake designer bags, their makeup copied from online tutorials, so much applied that it was a challenge to see bare skin. They said she loved herself, as they tossed their hair and watched passersby for any sign of admiring glances. They said she thought she was something really special, as they ignored the square girls, the ugly girls, the not-so-skinny girls who walked on by. They said they bet Adriana was a right bitch.

The Blether was no more of a sanctuary. Young men muttered to girlfriends that the new barmaid was a cold fish after they'd spent time trying to catch her eye while ordering a pint. Older men whispered to their wives that Adriana was sure to be trouble, as they waited for the long darkness of night to imagine themselves next to her warm, youthful body. Women welcomed her to their isle, to her new job, to the community, even as they wished she hadn't come, knowing their partner's eye had strayed. Older women muttered and tutted to themselves about Americans, remembering the war, all the while wishing they'd had a chance to travel and explore new shores.

Visitors came and went, leaving a trail of destruction along with much-needed money. They patronised the islanders, consigned them to the murky depths of parochialism. Drove too fast on narrow roads, left too much rubbish, trod down tender plants. But they bought mementos and guidebooks. Paid for meals at the pubs and overnight stays at guest houses. Treated the island like a plaything, then moved on.

Perhaps that was why the foreigners had not been entirely welcomed. They had yet to prove their permanency, to show they'd come with the right attitude to island life.

The priest, Father Christophe – himself a relative newcomer in island terms – had issued requests for the Clarks to be welcomed. If he'd taken the opportunity to tell the odd tale about how he'd found Americans to be morally wanting in the past, so what? If he'd made Adriana feel uncomfortable about the length of her skirt, or the tightness of her top, in the course of a discussion in the confessional, wasn't he just doing his duty to God and the community?

Harris Eggo, the island's most senior police officer, longed for more. To have risen through the ranks in one of Scotland's cities, with crimes to solve that were so much more than joyriding, drunk driving, petty theft and closing-time violence. Yet here he was, wishing Adriana's death had fallen at the feet of some other policeman. As much as the Major Investigation

Team was overseeing the case from their comfortable mainland station, he was left with the dirty end of it. The suspicion, the anger and the rising froth of vigilantism. Here it was, his chance to shine, and all he wanted was to turn out the light and go back to bed.

The island watched and wept.

Chapter Nineteen

Skittles entered through the front door of the Emporium at 5.20 p.m. but neither turned on the lights – in spite of the failing light – nor switched the shop sign to open, even though the Emporium was usually open until six. I'd run to catch up with him, then followed silently behind at a distance until he was inside. As he disappeared behind the counter and through the rear door, I took a deep breath and crept in, pulling the conch from my pocket and heading left through one narrow room into the tinier one at the end.

Footsteps above my head allowed me to relax a little, knowing the occupier was unaware of my presence. Careful not to knock anything, I checked every corner for CCTV cameras, but saw none.

The glass shelves comprised different elements. Some sections had sliding fronts with miniature locks which, although an effort at security, wouldn't withstand much force. Other parts were open shelves where you could reach in and touch the display. The inkwell shell had been displayed on an open shelf, its local historic value obviously greater than its financial worth. I had my cell switched to silent with the camera ready to roll: if the plaster cast of the conch matched the outline in the dust then I wanted video evidence to show Sergeant Eggo. Then the shop door opened again.

I fled into a corner and ducked down behind a shelf of books, waiting for a voice to call out to Skittles for attention. The shop door closed nearly silently, and I heard the soft patter of multiple feet approaching. A whisper, a shush, a gasp. Fingers fiddling around on a shelf in the room that led into mine. I couldn't tell how many there were, but it was at least two. Instinct told me it was more. Cursing, I focused on the sounds above my head. The distant clangs were kitchen noises, which was good. He was busy and distracted, but the voices in the next room – definitely female – were getting louder and careless. Sooner or later he'd hear something.

I didn't want to reveal myself. I needed more time at the Emporium. Creeping forward, I peered out into the next room. There were four of them, hoods up, pointing at a high cabinet. I recognised Lizzy, felt a moment of disappointment on her grandmother's behalf, then pulled back into my original hiding place. Phone still clutched in my hand, I made the decision to kill two birds with one stone. Lewis Eggo had obviously recognised the cell number I'd shown him. That meant it was probably one of the local teenage crowd. I just had to figure out which one.

Blocking my number so it wouldn't show, I rang the number of the person who'd messaged Adriana the night she'd died. The buzzing from the next room was sudden and angry in the stillness.

'Cat,' someone hissed, 'turn your fucking phone off.'

'Get out!' another girl urged. 'Just move.'

They went as I'd hoped they would – light but frantic steps moving away from me – but then came the crash of an object hitting the stone floor.

'Shit, shit, shit!' one of the girls shouted.

A door above me slammed. Feet running down a staircase, the front door of the shop flying open. Me, stuck in the back room.

'L-l-leave me alone!' Skittles stuttered into the darkness. The rain began to beat down as if it felt his fury, and I sank back against the wall, head low, hardly daring to breathe. The shop door slammed. I heard a lock turn, then another. Keys jangling then deadening as they slipped into a pocket. 'My shop,' he muttered to himself, over and over. 'M-my shop.'

'Oh hell,' I whispered into the blackness.

Brushstrokes on the floor and the unmistakable chimes of broken crockery. But it was the fact that Skittles wasn't calling the police that interested me. Perhaps he was used to being targeted by local troublemakers, or maybe he was keen to avoid police attention at the moment. Skittles' footsteps faded off upstairs to his flat.

As I waited for Skittles to settle himself, and for my heart to stop beating so hard, hiding behind a bookshelf, I texted Isabella Clark to keep her updated with the most important breakthrough in the case so far.

'Last text message sent to Adriana was from a teenager called Catriona. She goes to The Blether regularly and lives in Tobermory. Brandon should know her. Could you ask him about it? Let's speak tomorrow. Sadie.'

I made my way back to the glass shelf where the shell had been, but the few beams of light stretching from the till area weren't enough for me to see clearly. I switched on the torch app on my cell phone – heart still thumping – and lowered the conch, inch by inch, into place. The length was right but the shape was off-kilter. I turned it 180 degrees. And there it was.

Every curve and spike, millimetre perfect. Lifting it again, I photographed the dust-free imprint, then filmed myself putting the plaster cast back down in place. Stepping back, I photographed it in the wider context of the shelf, which was when I realised that the information placard was missing. The only remaining evidence of the original exhibit was the photo I'd taken during my first visit, my focus having been on the dust outline only, which had left the words on the placard too blurry to read.

Cursing in my head, I retraced my steps to the front door, checking out the tall cabinet where I'd seen the girls. On the top shelf was a mess of handwoven rope strung with feathers and dried flowers. Opposite that was a dagger with an engraved blade and a wooden handle. In the centre was a large stone, labelled 'blue apatite crystal'. I had no idea which of the items they'd wanted, but the cabinet remained locked. Their trip had been an unsuccessful one.

At the door, I disengaged the secondary bolt but the main lock needed a key. The windows were sealed units. That left only one exit. I was going to have to exit through the door Skittles had taken and find the back way out.

Behind the rear door was a staircase. The options were upwards to the flat or down into what had to be a cellar. Down it was. Every step was accompanied by a crack or a groan. I took as much of my weight as I could on my hands, lifting myself on the bannisters. At the bottom I opened the door into absolute blackness.

I'd been hoping for a basement window, but saw nothing. That didn't mean there wasn't a boarded window there somewhere, just that it was going to take some finding. I didn't dare switch on the light. Instead, I fired up my cell phone torch again, painfully aware of the fading battery, and began to hunt around. There were no other doors, that was clear. Huge sections of wood and cardboard lined the walls. I shifted them to check behind, to no avail.

I opened a chest and found tools – a hacksaw, hammers, screwdrivers, blades – and stuck a craft knife in my pocket. There was nowhere to run, which only left finding somewhere to hide.

In the corner was a large wooden chest covered by a cloth. It wouldn't open. Time and old paint had formed a seal. Taking a crowbar from the tool kit I shoved it under the lid and prised it open, shining the light in to see if my plan was feasible.

Slamming my right hand over my own mouth to preventing a scream from escaping, I checked the doorway for signs of movement, before forcing myself to inspect the contents a second time. A skull lay carelessly amidst a pile of bones, definitely human in origin. I didn't need Nate Carlisle to tell me that. I wasn't going to look carefully enough to see if it was male or female, but the skeleton belonged to an adult. No clothes in there, no flesh or hair. Suddenly the small knife I was carrying didn't seem enough to prevent an attack. I closed the lid of the chest, pulled the cloth back over and went to sit with my back against the door. There was only one thing left to do.

I dialled Constable Bathgate's number.

'I wasn't expecting to hear—'

'I need help,' I snapped. 'I'm in Rhys Stewart's basement. He doesn't know I'm here, and I'm trapped.'

'What the fuck were you—'

'No time. Come now. Distract him in the flat. Make sure the shop door's left open. Do it quickly. There are human remains in his basement.'

'What are you talking about? Whose remains?'

'I have to be quiet,' I whispered. 'I have no idea what he'll do if he finds me. Please, just come.'

With that, my cell phone bleeped three times, flashed a low battery warning, and the last light I had went out.

Chapter Twenty

In the fifteen minutes I waited, I shredded five of my nails and resorted to standing with one ear to the door, knife in my hand ready to wound. When I heard knocking on the shop door, my first thought was that Skittles would come racing to the cellar to hide the bones. Hearing his footsteps coming down the staircase, and waiting for him to turn off halfway to enter the shop, I could have cried. Then Bathgate's voice, loud but calm, asking for a word, suggesting they go up to the flat, finally – brilliantly – as they took the stairs together, the constable asking if Skittles wouldn't mind making him a cup of tea. As painful as the additional sixty seconds were, I made myself wait until crockery was banging in the kitchen when the kettle would have been on, before retreating up the steps, through the shop and out of the unlocked front door.

I texted Bathgate as soon as I'd made it back to my room and connected my phone briefly to the charger. 'I'm clear. Meet me in bar of Last Bay Hotel.'

He walked in thirty minutes later, face more thunderous than Mull's sky. I pushed a glass of Laphroaig whisky towards him before he could speak.

'Give me a reason not to arrest you,' he said as he sat down.

'I didn't break in. The shop door was open. I didn't steal anything, didn't break anything.'

'Skittles said there was a problem in the shop tonight, that an object got broken and whoever was responsible ran away before he could stop them,' he said.

'Yeah, well, I wasn't the only one inside the shop. Some kids came in after me.'

'Do you know who they were?'

I thought about Lizzy and her grandmother, and that I still needed to process Catriona sending the message to Adriana the night she was killed. The last thing I wanted was those teenagers on the defensive.

'It was dark and I was in a different room.'

He picked up the glass and swirled the liquid around.

'What were you doing in there?' he asked, taking a sip.

'Shouldn't you be more worried about the bones in the chest in his basement?'

'One step at a time. I need to make sure I didn't assist you in a crime. You put me in a difficult position tonight.'

'I know. I apologise . . .' I realised I didn't even know his first name.

'Simon,' he filled in my blank.

The idea of introducing a new layer of intimacy to our relationship by using his first name stuck in my throat like days-old porridge, but I needed someone on the inside or my investigation was going to stall. It was safe to say Harris Eggo was never going to be an ally, so Simon Bathgate it was. I shoved the memory of his previous behaviour to the back of my mind, and got on with the job. 'I apologise, Simon. Sergeant Eggo delivered this to me today.' I pulled the plaster-cast conch from my pocket and placed it on the table. 'The pathologist, Dr Carlisle, made it for me from the original exhibit. Inside the Emporium there was a space for a shell – an artefact that was pulled up from a local shipwreck – and an information card. There was a dusty outline where the shell had been and I wanted to see if it was a match in terms of size and shape. It is.'

'Can you prove that?'

I pulled out my cell phone and opened the gallery, pulling up the video of me placing the fake shell in its dust-free space. He peered at it, watched it two or three times, then shook his head.

'It's not good enough quality to be used as evidence. Where's the information card about the shell?'

I sighed. 'That's gone. I guess Skittles moved it.'

'You saw him do that?' Bathgate asked.

'No,' I conceded.

'I asked him about his previous conviction. Said we'd had a tip-off and I wanted to clarify matters. He explained that he was asked to download some images by his flatmate who was taking advantage.'

'But the shell, and the bones . . .'

'I'm going to have to persuade Sergeant Eggo to investigate the bones, but there's a problem with explaining how we've come by the knowledge.'

'Anonymous source?' I suggested.

'That's not enough for a search warrant. We could ask him to allow us entry, but if he refuses, he'll have an opportunity to get rid of the bones before we get the court order.'

'This is ridiculous – he has a chest of bones in his cellar right now, and you have a dead girl lying on a slab in Glasgow. Is that not enough?'

'The bones you saw could have been fake. A Halloween prop. A former medical skeleton broken down. What else was in the box?'

'Nothing,' I said quietly. 'The bones looked old.'

I picked up my own glass and drained its contents. I may

not have been a whisky drinker before arriving in Tobermory, but I was sure as hell going to leave with a taste for the stuff.

'Do I need to be worried about you?' he asked quietly. 'You must have been scared.'

'I'm actually wondering why you don't seem more concerned about the fact that the shell found inside Adriana's body came from the Emporium. Are you even interested in that?'

He leaned forward, elbows on his knees. 'You already told me that you managed to place your replacement shell on the same patch of glass shelf. So it wasn't locked away, right?'

'Right,' I said.

'Which means that anyone – tourist, visiting fisherman, local – literally anyone who had access to the Emporium could have been in there and stolen it. Of everyone, do you not think Skittles is the least likely person to have used that in a crime, given that it could lead straight back to him? Whatever problems he has, he's bright enough to have figured that out.'

I rubbed my eyes. 'Yeah,' I said. 'But it must have had some resonance for the person who stole it then used it in that way. That wasn't a random choice.'

'I leave the psychology to the experts. That's above my pay grade. If you're still feeling shaken, I can see you back to your room.' I thought of the suggestion he'd made to me at the roadside, of my instant loathing of him then, and of how I'd still be trapped in Skittles' cellar if he hadn't rescued me tonight. 'No strings,' he said, reading my mind. 'You're too much trouble.'

'I'll be fine,' I said. 'But thank you. Really. I won't forget what you did for me this evening.'

'What I did was my job. You could make it easier by not going into places you're not supposed to be. Keep your mobile on tomorrow. The sergeant might want to talk to you about those bones.'

★ ★ ★

151

Simon Bathgate left and I retreated to my room feeling both foolish and outraged. The evidence I'd gone to the Emporium to obtain was useless and I'd had to call the police to rescue me. Double incompetence. Now I wanted them to investigate a pile of bones I couldn't admit to having found. It was a mess. Shedding my clothes, I ran a bath and let my mind run blank for half an hour. By the time I climbed out it was past nine, I was exhausted, and I still needed to call Catriona. I plugged my cell back in for a few minutes to give my battery enough life then got into bed to make the call.

When I rang Catriona's mobile that time, I allowed my number to show. She had a right to know who I was, and that meant being on the level about it. There were tough questions to be answered. There was no answer. I left it a couple of minutes and tried again. This time the line opened up.

'Hi Catriona, My name's Sadie Levesque. I'm investigating Adriana's death and her phone records show you messaged her the night—'

There was a gasp, definitely female, and a choking sound. Then the line went dead.

'Shit,' I muttered, redialling the number, but by then her phone was off. I'd taken Catriona by surprise and it was pretty clear she didn't want to talk to me, which meant I was all the more determined to speak with her.

Checking the number for the pottery gallery on the internet, I braved a telling-off and dialled Lizzy's grandmother.

'Hi, sorry to call at this hour. This is Sadie Levesque. I'm trying to get hold of Lizzy.'

'Don't apologise,' Lizzy's grandmother said. 'Give me a moment.' I could hear the rustling of pieces of paper.

'While you're on, I wonder if you could help me with something else. I'm trying to get hold of Lizzy's friend Catriona, too. Could you tell me her surname?'

'Catriona Vass. Precocious but not all bad.' She read out Lizzy's number to me.

'Thank you,' I said. 'You wouldn't happen to know the Vasses' address by any chance?'

'I'm not sure it's my place to hand over that sort of information. In-person enquiries should probably be conducted by the police.' Her voice was less friendly now, and I was aware that I'd over-stepped the mark.

'You're right, I shouldn't have asked. Apologies.' I excused myself and called Lizzy instead.

'Who's this?' Lizzy asked as she picked up.

I reintroduced myself. 'Lizzy, I need to speak with Catriona. She picked up but as I was explaining who I am she ended the call. I know this is stressful but I'm not a police officer. Nothing she says can be used in evidence, not against her or anyone else. I'm not even accusing her of doing anything wrong.'

'Then why do you want to talk to her?' Lizzy asked.

I hesitated. Lizzy was going to put the phone down on me and call Catriona immediately. If I was going to be able to judge the veracity of Catriona's answers I wanted to give her the least possible time to prepare her replies. I needed to stall.

'I know she was in the Emporium after hours tonight. I think you were there too. You're probably both scared about getting caught but Mr Stewart who runs the store hasn't made a formal complaint.'

'Wasn't me,' Lizzy said quickly.

'Lizzy, I was outside when you all ran out. I know you didn't see me, but I saw your faces. You were taking a real risk going in there and I'd like to ask about why you did it.' Silence. 'I'm not going to give your names to the police, just as long as you all agree to meet me and talk this through. It's a safety issue. Part of my job involves helping teenagers. I'd much rather

153

do that before you get in serious trouble rather than when it's too late.'

A sniffle. Tears, I suspected.

'I never wanted to go in there in the first place,' she said.

'That's okay,' I reassured her. 'There isn't a teenager I've met who didn't make a mistake at some point. These tiny things don't define you, Lizzy. They just show us where the boundaries are for what we're comfortable with.'

'I just . . .' a sob, '. . . I just want to be part of the group.'

'I get that. Can you tell me what you were looking for in the Emporium? You came out empty-handed so you obviously weren't going in there to grab any random item you could. What was so important that you broke the law?'

The hypocrisy of what I was saying made me cringe, as did the intimidation behind my gentle words. I'm going to be sweet – but remember you could get in trouble with the police. Best humour me.

'I'm not sure I should say,' she said.

Time to get tough.

'Lizzy, there are going to be rumours about what happened tonight. Skittles is bound to tell other people in Tobermory that there was an attempted theft. I think I also heard something smash inside, so that's criminal damage too. You have to trust me now. Maybe I can give you some advice.'

A few fast breaths. The poor girl wasn't just upset. She sounded terrified.

'They wanted a crystal,' she said. 'The blue one.'

'Is it valuable?'

'It was too expensive to buy,' she said quietly. I hadn't noticed the price tag, but I was going to be looking it up the second I was off the call. 'I don't want to be in trouble. My parents would be so upset.'

Time to repay her honesty with soothing words.

'You're not going to get in trouble. Don't tell anyone where you were last night. No text messages or phone conversations. Make sure no one else talks. You didn't steal anything, it was just a dumb mistake. Was the shop door open when you went in?' I knew the answer, and it was helpful.

'Yes!' Lizzy said, brightening up for the first time. 'Yes, it was open.'

'So you were just going into the shop and you didn't know it was closed. That's all you have to say. If anyone figures out it was you and your friends, just apologise for being mistaken and offer to pay for the item that got accidentally broken on the way out. I promise it'll all be fine. You did the right thing talking to me.'

'Thank you,' she said, gratitude dripping from her crackling voice. I'd have felt guilty if it hadn't been so necessary.

'No problem,' I said. 'I do still need to talk to Catriona, but I'd like to do that in person. Could you call her for me and explain that I really am here to help?'

'Do you want me to get her to phone you back?' Lizzy asked.

'It's kind of late. I think I'd rather meet her in person, so she can see my face and really feel that she can trust me. Tomorrow would be good.'

'Maybe I can persuade her,' Lizzy said slowly. 'But I can't promise.'

'I totally understand,' I said. 'But there are important things I need to talk to her about. More important than just going into a shop a bit late at night.' I let that sink in for a few moments. 'I believe Catriona and Adriana had quite a close relationship. Am I right?'

'Um . . .' Lizzy was struggling to make sure she gave the right answer.

'You know what, it's not fair of me to ask you about this stuff. It's why I need to talk to Catriona in person. I really don't want to have to ask the police to talk to her. Seems like that might be intimidating. What do you think?'

'Definitely,' Lizzy said.

'Good, we're agreed then. Have Catriona contact me so we can meet up tomorrow. Thanks for helping me with this, Lizzy. You're obviously the most sensible one of your friends.'

'I try. Sometimes they just won't listen to me,' she confided.

'I bet. Hey, could you just give me Catriona's address so I know how to find her tomorrow?'

'Sure, she lives at The Wash House on Viewpoint Drive. I'll call her now. Thanks Miss Levesque. I feel better.'

'My pleasure, Lizzy,' I said. 'I'm glad I could help.'

Chapter Twenty-One

The next morning I awoke to housekeeping knocking on my door. Groaning, I rolled over and tried to focus my eyes on the clock: 10.35 a.m.

'You're kidding,' I muttered, half falling, half jumping from the bed and running to the bathroom. 'Could you come back later?' The cleaning trolley jangled and squeaked away.

The terror of the previous night had taken its toll. Monster truck tyres had parked beneath my eyes, and even allowing for the poor lighting, my skin looked sallow. I'd planned to be up at seven thirty for breakfast and work. My alarm hadn't gone off. Checking my cell to find out why, I realised I'd fallen asleep with the phone in my hand and neglected to finish charging it. I plugged it in, swearing at myself, then left it to soak up a few precious percent of battery while I answered emails.

My sister had sent an audio recording of the baby's heartbeat, and the galloping fierceness of it made me giddy. I replied with a selfie, me blowing a kiss into camera, hoping Becca wouldn't notice the glisten in my eyes. I longed to be home but I knew that I couldn't possibly leave Mull until I'd seen my job through. That baby was going to be everything. A new life to make up for my father's slow descent into forgetfulness, someone for Becca to love to make up for the heartache of being deserted, a reason for me to stay closer to home. I couldn't wait to hold her in my arms.

Twenty minutes later I was able to look at my call log and messages, and see that Catriona hadn't contacted me. I wasn't entirely surprised. After she'd ended my call the previous night, I'd suspected she might just leave her phone off for a while. That was less of a problem now that I had her address.

Breakfast service at the hotel had long since passed, so my first port of call was the bakery on the harbour. I jogged up the lane from the hotel and onto the harbourside to see a trail of vehicles at the far end, some with blue lights flashing, and a stream of police officers, locals and press watching proceedings.

I walked more slowly past the parade of stores towards the Emporium. By the time I'd halved the distance, I saw four scenes-of-crime-suited officers carry out a large chest. Vindication mixed with guilt left an odd taste in my mouth. Not that I felt sorry for Skittles – whatever he was doing with the bones in his basement couldn't be good – but I'd discovered them in the course of my own illegality then left PC Bathgate to deal with the fallout.

Nate Carlisle called as I was just reaching the police tape.

'You had a busy night, I gather,' he said. 'No lasting effects?'

'I'm fine. How did you hear?'

'I was called to remote supervise the removal of the remains. Sergeant Eggo sounded a bit put out. The bones are going to be flown back to me in Glasgow urgently. How did you know they were in the cellar?'

Nate didn't know the whole story, which made me wonder how much PC Bathgate had explained to Harris Eggo.

'Found them by accident,' I said. 'Right place at the right time, or something like that. And the shell was a perfect match for the one taken from the Emporium. Look carefully at those bones, Nate. I'm sure there's something going on with Rhys Stewart.' A police car revved its engine next to me and began to pull forward. In the rear seat, Skittles pushed his forehead against the window and glared at me. 'Nate, I've got to go.'

I could see Sergeant Eggo inside the Emporium and waited for him to notice me. He did so after a few minutes with an eye roll he made no effort to hide. As he exited, the cameras began to record. I did my best to blend into the background.

'You,' Eggo said, pointing at me. 'In here.' I ducked under the police tape and entered the shop. 'You've got some explaining to do.'

'How did you get a search warrant so fast?' I asked.

'We tried a different method. It's called asking politely. Skittles let us in. No big drama. You, on the other hand, have been nothing but trouble since you arrived. You want to show me where this supposed evidence about the shell is?'

I ignored the barb and pointed to my left in the distant room. Walking through, I got another look at the blue apatite. About eight inches tall and two inches wide, it was an eye-catching piece of rock as was the price – £549.

In the next room, I led Eggo to the shell shelf.

'What am I supposed to be looking at here?' he asked.

The quill pen was still in place, but without the information card, there was nothing to prove what else had been on the shelf, and the outline left in the dust was now blurred and messy with a combination of my fingerprints, and having picked up and put down the shell more than once. I cursed my sloppy behaviour, angry at the carelessness, even under such strained circumstances.

'It was clearer last night,' I said. 'You should ask Skittles about the shell when you interview him.'

'Thanks for the professional advice,' Eggo said. 'I appreciate that coming from a woman who had to be rescued by one of my officers last night. Did I hear correctly that you cried?' I folded my arms and let him get it out of his system. 'Is there any other evidence you're withholding from my investigation?'

'I thought we weren't information sharing,' I said. Petulant, but he didn't deserve anything more.

'Have it your way, but don't come in here again. And leave Skittles alone. Only my officers are to deal with him from now on. Understood?'

'Believe me, that won't be a problem. Can I go now?'

'That might be the most sensible thing you've suggested since your arrival,' Eggo said.

Outside, Father Christophe was looking anxiously on. He held a hand out to me as if I needed welcoming back out into the world. I smiled and waved his hand away. I'd been rescued enough for a while. I began my retreat as Harris Eggo walked over to chat with the priest.

'I heard there were bones,' Father Christophe was saying. 'I thought it might help to perform a blessing . . .'

That was the point at which I marched away. I doubted there was anyone left in Tobermory who hadn't heard what I'd found in Skittles' cellar.

I got the Clarks on the phone straight away, answered by an exhausted-sounding Brandon who called his mother and handed over the phone. Isabella's voice was strained when she greeted me.

'This is just a heads-up. A man called Rhys Stewart is being questioned by police. They've found a chest full of bones in his cellar. They'll be examined by Dr Carlisle who'll determine if they have any relevance to Adriana's case. I wanted you to hear it from me first.'

'Is that the man from the Emporium?' Isabella asked.

'That's right. Do you know him?'

'Addie applied for a job there, same time as she applied for work at The Blether. She went in to drop off her résumé then again to chase up her application. Said she felt uncomfortable so she didn't pursue it.'

'Good to know,' I replied. 'Adriana didn't ever buy anything from the shop? No crystals or artefacts?'

'Not that I'm aware of. I don't think she was into the sort of stuff he sells there.'

'That's fine. I'll catch you tomorrow,' I said.

'Wait,' Isabella said. 'I want to ask you something.'

I waited for her to continue but the silence ran on.

'Anything,' I said.

'Is there something I could have done, should have done? I keep asking myself what I missed. You've found text messages, and Brandon confessed to me about the mushrooms Addie had. I don't understand how I didn't see it if she was in trouble.' Her voice shook with the vibrato of held-back tears. I wished she'd spoken to me in person. A phone line was no place for such conversations.

'Mrs Clark, there isn't a parent who's lost a child who doesn't ask themselves the same thing. You could never have foreseen this. Teenage deaths are lightning strikes. You get the sense that there's a storm brewing, but you never anticipate exactly what's about to happen.'

'Do you have children, Miss Levesque? I never asked.'

'I don't,' I admitted, feeling as if I was failing Isabella when she needed me most. 'But I'm about to become an aunt, and honestly it seems as if it might just change my whole world.'

'It will,' Isabella said. 'There will be this tiny part of you in that baby, and every bruise, every cruel word, every knock-back that baby takes, will crush you and scar you. And you'll think it's terrible, until one day you realise it's all over, that the love you've felt is frozen in time. It can't change or grow

161

or be damaged. And you'll long to feel that daily pain again, because that pain was life. That awful pain will turn out to be the best thing you ever felt.' She drew in a deep, rasping breath, and I wondered if I would ever want to take another case again. Quite possibly not.

I grabbed my emotions in an iron vice and said what needed to be said.

'There's nothing you could have done. Nothing. Sometimes people kill. How they choose their victims will only ever be science we can apply afterwards. Your love for your daughter is still alive, Isabella. It will never diminish or die.'

She hung up, and I promised myself I would call my sister and my mother, ask her to hold the phone to my father's ear, then contact my friends – and I would tell each and every one of them how much I loved them.

My cell phone battery was getting low again. If I called Catriona Vass there was a chance the battery would die mid-conversation and give her a chance to refuse to meet me. Face to face was the better option. I took the road out past The Blether and walked to Viewpoint Drive. Hers was one of the last houses on the road, although still within town limits. It was also one of the smallest and shabbiest. It was a far cry from the image the confident, shiny girl exuded. I knocked and waited.

It was answered by an elderly woman, bent and frazzled.

'What's this now?'

'Hello,' I tried a smile to warm her up. 'Is Catriona in?'

'No. The girl was up and out before I arrived this morning. Probably won't be back until after dark. Her father barely sees her these days. I've told him to keep a closer eye on her but my nephew doesn't want to be told anything by me.'

'Is he here?' I asked.

'No, you silly girl.' I did my best not to raise my eyebrows. 'He's a fisherman. Out at dawn, back when the nets are full. I come to clean up and cook a meal. Catriona's old enough to do it, but her head's full of nonsense so I help them out. Who are you?'

'Sadie,' I said. 'Do you know where Catriona might be?'

'Your guess is as good as mine. I can try calling her if you like?'

'That would be really kind,' I said, stepping inside.

The cottage was crumbling internally. Peeling paint on the walls betrayed the untreated damp that was ravaging the place. The floor was on a gradient, and there were open doorways with hinges showing, doors long since gone. There was a faint smell of boiled vegetables, and the wet washing stuffed onto radiators was going to take days to dry. Small wonder Catriona opted to spend her time elsewhere. Growing up in poverty was destructive for children. Seeing things you couldn't have. Your friends owning things you couldn't admit to wanting. Imagining a future that was harder for you to reach than anyone else around you.

As Catriona's great-aunt was squinting at a scrap of paper and punching numbers one by one into a phone, I put my head into the bedroom where I could see posters on the wall and a desk strewn with makeup. Photos lined the mirror of a decrepit dressing table. I recognised Lizzy, some of the other girls from the pub, then a shot of Lewis. And another one, and another. Lewis at the bar. On the beach. In a car. Sitting on a wall in the middle of a line of boys. It made me smile. Poverty or not, Catriona was still able to enjoy the normal things in life. Finding a boy you liked and whiling away your hours dreaming about him. I opened a drawer and quietly rifled through. Letters, postcards, shells, dried flowers.

'Hello?' Catriona's great-aunt called.

I returned to the hallway. 'I was just looking at Catriona's photos. It looks as if the kids around here have a wonderful time together.'

'Aye, well, it's not easy living on an island. They have to make their own fun. She's not answering, I'm afraid. If you find her, tell her dinner will be in the oven and she needs to tidy her room.'

'I'll pass that on,' I said. 'Thanks for trying to help.'

I checked every shop in town, as well as The Blether, and couldn't find Catriona. By then it was lunchtime so I returned to my hotel.

I checked out blue apatite online. A deep shade of teal when polished and lit, it was a beautiful crystal. More impressive than that were the various qualities with which it had been credited. From cleansing your aura to increasing your psychic perception and paranormal skills, and helping you solve problems in your sleep, I was starting to think I needed one too. I suspected the lure for the teenage girls was just that it was incredibly pretty.

But it wasn't the blue apatite I needed to focus on, it was the conch. If someone had gone to the trouble of stealing it from the shop, then they were sending a message. I tried searching for the details I could remember from the information card next to the quill and shell. Something about a ship that had been part of the Spanish Armada, was all I could recall. That's where the conch was supposed to have originated.

It was indeed a rabbit hole. The *San Juan de Sicilia* had docked in Tobermory Bay asking for supplies and provision. It was hard to imagine a ship from the Spanish Armada sailing into the tiny Scottish port. What must the townsfolk have made of it as it came into view, with its dark-eyed men and their lyrical speech? Historians had assessed the galleon as carrying nearly 300 soldiers, sixty mariners and more than twenty guns. She was said to have been sunk by an explosion that caused a fire, with no suggestion of survivors. It must have been a grim death. To seek help and find an enemy was a cruel ending.

Multiple salvage attempts had been made, a couple success-fully. Different legends, some drawn closely from history, others enhanced to entertain, had evolved. The most regularly repeated was the story of the Spanish princess and the Scot. The legend went that the princess had dreamed of a beautiful man on an island and fallen madly in love with her vision. She'd travelled to Scotland with the Armada on board the *San Juan de Sicilia*, and on reaching land had seen the man of her dreams on the shore. The man's wife, seeing the look in the Spanish princess's eyes, had sought the help of the Mull Witch to destroy the vessel. Down it went ablaze, and caught between the fire on deck and the freezing waves, the princess had met her end in a watery grave.

It was myth and legend, made to be retold around campfires and on long nights out at sea. But there was my connection to the shell, centuries apart. A Spanish princess and a Latina girl, both aliens on Mull. Royal blood and a seaweed crown. Lungs filled with salt water. The end of a trip to a new land. A conch shell that was believed to once have graced a desk in the Spanish princess's ship, now the subject of another mysterious death.

Witch taper marks in Flora's house. Bags of ground bone in Adriana's possession. A wake held in a circle of standing stones. And the warning that Adriana was getting into something weird, out of her depth. I wondered again exactly what Adriana had been confessing on her knees before Father Christophe. Just what had she gotten involved in that had elicited so much unbearable guilt? Finally I remembered to look up Father Christophe's chosen word – thaumaturgy – used, I suspected, to force me to ask him its meaning, but pride had stopped me.

Miracle working, the dictionary informed me, followed closely by less innocent definitions: bewitchery, conjuring, devilry, enchantment, sorcery, voodooism and witchcraft. Father Christophe, I was sure, suspected the worst of whatever Adriana had been involved in. And for all his protestations, he'd wanted me to know too.

Chapter Twenty-Two

The hammering on my door began at 2 a.m. Having taken several whiskies to get me to sleep, it also took me some time to wake up.

'All right,' I shouted. 'Wait a minute, eh?' I threw on jeans and a hoodie before engaging the safety chain and peering out into the corridor. Sergeant Eggo, face like thunder, was positioned, hands on hips, waiting for me. 'What's up?'

'Catriona Vass is missing,' he said. 'We need to talk.'

I opened the door fully and let him in. 'What can I do?' I asked.

'Nothing. I want you to do absolutely nothing. What I want to know is why you were at her house earlier today.'

'Are you serious? Am I being questioned?'

'You're damned right I'm serious. Her father didn't see her this morning because he was on the boat early and didn't want to disturb her as he left. She didn't come home this evening and no one can get in touch with her. There are search parties out looking for her now but we don't even know exactly how long she's been missing.'

It occurred to me for the first time that maybe Skittles had recognised some of the girls as they'd run away, and that maybe he hadn't phoned the police because he was intending to deal with it himself.

'I don't want anyone to get in trouble,' I said. 'Promise me they won't.'

'I'm not promising you a bloody thing. Tell me what you know immediately or I'll find something to charge you with, and the Clarks will just have to get themselves a new investigator.'

Sadly this time, Harris Eggo was completely in the right.

'Catriona was in Skittles' shop last night. Not alone, she was with friends. I disturbed them so they fled, smashing something as they ran. Skittles came down and chased them but didn't actually catch them or stop them. He obviously decided not to report it to the police at the time, just swept up the broken item and locked the shop door. That's how I came to get locked in. I went to Catriona's house today to talk to her about it.'

'Fuck's sake,' Eggo sighed. 'You didn't think to mention it to me when I saw you earlier?'

'I had no way of knowing Catriona was missing then. I didn't think it was relevant.'

'And that's it?' he asked.

'That's it,' I said. If I'd been superstitious I'd have had my fingers crossed behind my back.

'Stay here,' he said. 'I don't want you leaving the hotel. Things out there are fraught enough already. You seem to be bringing nothing but bad luck to the island.'

'Bringing bad luck? I came here because a girl was already missing. The fact that I'm the one who found her wasn't bad luck, sergeant, it was proper investigating, and while we're talking about that do you want to explain why you did virtually nothing the whole time Adriana Clark was missing, but a local girl doesn't answer her phone for a day and suddenly you've mobilised the whole town?'

'Just what are you accusing me of?'

'I don't know, sergeant, what are you guilty of? A bit of racism, maybe? Was it the fact that she was American that made her less of a priority? Or maybe the fact that Adriana was Latina? Perhaps just the fact that she was an off-islander was enough for you not to care as much.'

'You're out of order,' he shouted.

'Get out of my room,' I said. 'You've got no right to be in here yelling at me.'

'It's my island,' he said, his voice low now, and threatening. 'Stay the fuck away from my people. You're cursed.' He walked out slamming the door and I heard other doors in the corridor close slowly afterwards. Apparently we'd woken up the whole place, and everyone had taken the opportunity to listen in.

It took me about thirty seconds to realise the seriousness of my omissions, in which time I'd managed to assess both my moral obligations, my professional duties and the legal responsibility I might bear if I didn't right the situation immediately. I found my behaviour wanting.

Racing to the stairwell, I took the steps two at a time, sprinting at the bottom through reception, out of the main doors and into the gardens. No sign of Eggo. Towards the car park along a gravel path where, too late, I realised I hadn't bothered with trainers. In the car park a single vehicle was pulling away, headlights blazing. Jumping for the car, I hit the bonnet as it swung past me, connecting with it harder than I'd intended. Eggo slammed on his brakes and threw open his door.

'You're under arrest—'

'I wanted to speak with Catriona because she messaged Adriana with instructions to meet up the same night Adriana died. When I tried to speak with her about it last night, she ended the call. I haven't been able to get hold of her since. It's possible that she has information about Adriana's murder, got scared when I contacted her, and has run away.'

Eggo sighed. 'I know about the text message. We got a court order for the information and it came through yesterday. I was planning on speaking with Catriona about it myself today. But I've known Catriona Vass her whole life, and there's no way she was involved with murdering anyone. Right now, Cat's father is frantic. He has no idea why his girl might disappear like this. His wife left him years ago and he raised that child single-handedly. So what else do you know that might help?'

'Just the timing,' I said. 'It was shortly after half past nine last night when Catriona ended my call to her. That was the last contact I had.'

'Thank you for that,' Eggo said. 'Your feet are bleeding. Get inside. Lock your door. You only talk to me. There are some angry people in town. First Skittles, now Catriona. Everything's messed up.'

'Did you release him after you interviewed him?' I asked. 'Have you asked him if he saw her last night?'

'You're not entitled to any answers,' Eggo said. 'Don't go near the Emporium or to the Vasses' house, or to The Blether. You won't like the reception you'll get.'

Harris Eggo got back in his car and drove away. I waited until my heart had stopped jack-hammering in my chest and walked slowly back into the hotel. The worst of it was that I was starting to think that Eggo might just be right.

Turning off all the lights in my room, I stood at the window and looked towards the town. Each building was ablaze, lights on in every room, torches in hands as people wandered the streets, vehicle headlights illuminating the sky.

The Clarks would be wondering what was going on. Even on the outskirts of town, they would have been disturbed by the activity. I called Rob.

'What's happening?' he asked.

'Catriona Vass is missing. She's the girl who sent that last text message to Adriana. I've just spoken to Sergeant Eggo. It may be that Catriona has some information about Adriana's death.'

'You have to find her,' Rob said. 'Whatever it takes, if she has answers, you need to figure out where she's gone.'

'I've been told to remain at my hotel,' I explained. 'I was trying to get hold of Catriona earlier today and I think my presence at her house started some speculation.'

'Speculation? She might know who killed my daughter. You're here to do a job, Ms Levesque, so unless Sergeant Eggo has any legal right to require you to stay indoors then I need you to do what I'm paying you to do and get answers.' The line went dead.

'Fuck!'

I allowed myself the solitary expletive and fell back onto my bed, hands over my eyes. There was no action I could take without consequences, apparently. To make progress investigating on behalf of the Clarks, I had to push the limits of what was legal and that involved keeping secrets. To do the right thing by Catriona Vass, I'd had to break promises and confidences to both the Clarks and Lizzy.

'Why would she run?' I asked the ceiling. It didn't answer me, but the various options were clear: to protect someone she loved, from fear of someone who scared her, or because she was terrified of the consequences of her involvement in Adriana's death. Running from my enquiries was a one-way street. Catriona would've known she'd be reported missing and therefore also that the reason for running would be reported to the police. Better to have stayed and come up with an explanation.

Unless someone else didn't want her to talk.

The icy reality of that concept washed over me.

My phone call to her. She'd answered, gasped, given a choking cough. Then the call had ended.

She hadn't said a word. I'd started speaking as soon as she accepted the call.

Standing up, I stared at the door. Sergeant Eggo had cautioned me – ordered me, in fact – to stay in the hotel. No one in Tobermory wanted to see my face or answer my questions, Skittles least of all.

I dressed in black, donned my hiking boots, made sure there were gloves in my pockets and picked up my bear spray and my head torch. I headed back down to the car park as silently as I could manage, checking as I went that no one was watching. Rob Clark was right. I was there to do a job, and unless I was breaking the law Sergeant Eggo had no authority over me.

It took me an hour to get across the island. It was easily the busiest the roads had been around Tobermory, and I found myself ducking as low as I could manage behind my steering wheel as other cars passed me. Ten miles from town, the cars had all gone, and it was just me, the road and the wildlife. The police were still checking Catriona's known haunts closer to Tobermory, friends' houses and the usual town hangouts. Her family's financial situation meant she didn't have access to a car, so they were spreading the investigations out geographically in stages. That was fine – made sense, in fact – but I'd always been one for worst-case scenarios.

By the time I'd parked the car at the edge of the nearest road to the footpath to the cave, I'd completely lost track of time. I was running on the drunken adrenaline-fuelled drive and purpose that only lack of sleep, terror and desperation can combine to create. Already questioning what I was thinking, I knew it was a ridiculous place to be. It was still a crime scene, with tape fluttering in the wind. I clambered down the rocks and into the narrow stone corridor that Adriana had taken to her death.

Colder tonight than when I'd first visited, more terrifying than when I'd gone there to fetch Brandon, the wind whistled cruelly in my ears and made them ache. The waves were closer, crashing threateningly against the outer structure of the cave. Salt penetrated my nose and mouth, making my eyes run, stinging my neck and face.

Nothing in the outer section of the cave. No sign of life save for scuttling crabs furious with me for invading their space with light. I walked on in, the echo of my feet accompanying me like a drumbeat.

'Hello?' I shouted. No reply. Bear spray in hand, I went further in, aware that my cell phone would be useless to me inside, knowing I should have come better armed than with only a chemical. Feeling stupid to have gone there alone in the dark. Recognising that once my heart was set on it, no one could have stopped me if they'd tried.

I went into the next chamber, pausing as a glittering caught my eye. Bending down, I checked the source, knowing better than to touch it. An earring lay on the rock, no butterfly back attached, but I couldn't remember whether or not Adriana had been wearing earrings when she'd disappeared. Taking one of the three torches off my headband, I laid it next to the earring to ensure I could find it again as I left. That dimmed the light available to see by, but it meant the exit was pre-illuminated and that was something. Through a thinner corridor of rock and out into the main chamber, colder still that deep into the rock face.

'Is anyone in here?'

I scanned the distant cave, turning my head left then right, catching the shine of blonde hair and the profile of a girl's face as she leant against a protruding rock.

'Oh Catriona, thank God,' I shouted, starting to run. 'Don't worry, you're safe. Please don't be scared.'

Sitting upright, she had her back to me at a diagonal angle. Her right arm rested along the back of the rock that was

173

supporting her, as if she was merely taking time out to think. From that view, even a metre from her, I wouldn't have known she was dead. Except for the mess of seaweed on her head, slowly dripping saline tears down her bare back. And as I walked around the side, open eyes that could not see my face.

'Catriona,' I said softly, pointlessly, walking forward to her, wishing I'd never left my room. Wishing I could turn back time and never see this poor girl, reposing in postmortem horror.

Her clothes were nowhere to be seen. A single earring, a clear stone stud, remained to decorate one earlobe. I focused on that for as long as I could before letting my eyes go where they had to eventually.

Naked to the elements, legs splayed open, she had been spared no indignity. Mouth, jaw pulled down hard, packed full of sand that was beginning to spew down her chin. I gagged. Got control. Looked on down her body for the source of the crimson river on the ground. She was intact on the left, but her right-hand side had been mutilated. Butchered. The breast was entirely gone.

I screamed, choked back vomit, cried.

Looking around the cave in the narrow beams of light from my torches, the answer to my next question was sitting in Catriona's left hand. Her right breast, placed carefully in her palm, as if she was showing the world what she had suffered.

I forgot professionalism, abandoned control, and ran from Mackinnon's Cave.

Chapter Twenty-Three

I didn't wait outside the cave that time. Instead I sprinted back to my car and made sure there were no nasty surprises waiting for me inside, before calling the police. I should have waited there for them to arrive, and I was in no fit state to drive, but at that moment, getting far away was all I could think about.

By the time I pulled into my hotel car park, I was dialling Nate Carlisle's number.

'I heard,' he said before I could speak. 'Are you somewhere safe?'

'Hotel,' I said. 'Are you coming over?'

'I'm on my way to the helicopter now.' Checking my watch I saw that it was 5 a.m. 'I'll be out of action most of the day.'

'That's fine. I just wanted to warn you. It's bad. One of her breasts is gone. She was cut. And her mouth . . .' I breathed hard to avoid gagging, '. . . more sand.'

'I'll take care of her, Sadie,' he said. 'Just stay safe. This won't be the same as Adriana, though. Her parents gave me permission to speak with you. What I can discuss will be more limited with this victim. I would like to see you, though, if we can both make the time. Just to reassure myself that you're in one piece.'

'Yes, I'd like that,' I said. 'Travel safe, Nate.'

My next call was to the Clarks. It was brief and awkward. I could hear Isabella sobbing in the background as I explained just how extensive the press presence on the island was going to get. The killing of any young woman attracts attention. Add an additional victim and the word 'serial' to that equation, and the public interest grows exponentially. Fortunately for them, their new address had not yet been discovered so they'd remain shielded a while longer.

After that, I took out a notepad and began scribbling notes on the pages, ripping them out and laying them on my floor to form a huge, chaotic puzzle of facts, times, names and places. Once I'd finished, I had a list of names requiring further investigation. It wasn't particularly scientific, and some of it wasn't even justifiable, but instinct had found me two dead girls so I decided to trust myself.

By then it was 6.30 a.m. Sooner or later Lance Proudfoot was going to come to his senses and block my number, but until he'd done so, I figured he was fair game.

'I don't seem to need an alarm clock these days,' was his opener. I felt better just hearing the easy warmth of his voice at the end of the phone. 'Tell me how I can help, Sadie.'

It was that simple kindness that set me off. The sweetness of a stranger offering assistance with no hope of reward. I managed to keep the first few tears silent, but when I tried to breathe, the air betrayed me as a sob and it was unstoppable. I cried like that for five minutes. I no longer cared that I was working the case in a professional capacity and supposed to maintain a distance. All the while, Lance reassured me with meaningless but perfect nothings. He didn't just allow me to cry, he told

176

me to. I'd never in my life experienced so much tenderness from a stranger.

'I'm okay,' I said, breath still hitching in my chest. 'Please don't think this is who I usually am.'

'I hope it is,' Lance said. 'I hope the empathy, honesty and openness you just showed stays with you every day. Take it from an old timer: every time you attempt to harden yourself, shove that instinct down as low as you can and act like it doesn't exist. It gets easier and easier to ignore emotions. Then suddenly you're not pretending any more, and the story is just words. By the time it has no effect on you at all, you've lost yourself. So don't apologise, Sadie. When we cry, we're allowing the best version of ourselves to come to the surface.'

'Wisdom as well as an early riser. I knew I liked you.' I managed to smile through my tears.

'You're only saying that because you haven't met me yet. Why don't you tell me what's happening – and yes, we're off the record again. By the time I put the phone down, I promise I won't remember a word you've said.'

'This time, I want you to remember. In fact I need a really big favour, or at least I'm asking you to call in a really big favour. When we spoke before you had a friend there. You said he was a cop. Another girl's dead, Lance. I found her tonight in the same cave where Adriana Clark was killed. Only it was more violent. Her right breast had been sliced off, then her killer put the breast in her left hand as if she was showing it off.'

'Did you say you found her? Were you alone?'

'I did, and yes I was. But I'm back in my hotel now and getting busy so I don't have to think about it. Would you be willing to help me? Because I'm feeling kind of alone here, and more than a bit scared.'

'Stuck on an island with a serial killer, I'd say scared was the most appropriate and sensible reaction. Let me grab a notebook.' I could hear him opening drawers and scrabbling around. 'Okay, go.'

'I've got some names I need checking out. Anything you can get from other stories in the media or anything on the police radar.'

'Not a complaint, but any reason why you can't ask the police there?' Lance asked.

'That'll become clear. Write these down. Rhys Stewart, thirties, lives in the Mull Historical Emporium. I found bones in his cellar. He has a previous conviction for possession of illegal images.'

'That one should be easy enough,' Lance said.

'Here's where it gets tricky. PC Simon Bathgate.'

Lance gave a soft whistle as he wrote the name down. 'That answers the question,' he said. 'Can you tell me why?'

'He pulled me over for a fake driving issue, suggested we go back to my hotel and have sex. I blackmailed him by pretending I'd recorded it, which is how I know about Rhys Stewart's conviction. He also turned up unexpectedly at a wake the island's teenagers held for Adriana, where Catriona – the new victim – was the main attraction, only he was supposed to be off duty then.'

'Anything more on him?' Lance asked.

'Yeah, I think he dropped my name to Rhys Stewart letting him know I'd been in his cellar. Not sure if that was accidental or deliberate.'

'You're living dangerously. Anyone else?'

'I'm not proud of this one. Chalk it down to my own personal biases if you like, but it's gut instinct. There's a priest here, Father Christophe, at the Saints of the Tides church. Adriana was going to him for confession but not to services. He knows something about what she was getting into here, that's the impression he gave me, but he won't say exactly what. He was . . .' I struggled to find the right word, '. . . *evangelical* about the positive effects of her death. Increased congregations, restored faith from a scared population. But I didn't see any grief or regret. He pretty much just gave me the chills.'

'I can look,' Lance said. 'If there is anything in his past, chances are it'll have been sanitised and covered up.'

'I know,' I said. I bit my tongue. There was another name I wanted to give him, but the ethical line I was crossing was monumental.

'What is it?' Lance asked.

'Sorry, I just can't decide on another name.'

'Give it to me anyway. If there's nothing to find, then no harm done. If there's something relevant, then maybe you'll save a life.'

Lance was right, but I could barely bring myself to say it out loud.

'Brandon Clark. You can't tell anyone ever that I asked you for this.'

'Your client?' he asked.

'My clients' son; Adriana's twin brother. I can't find a social media or school history for the twins, plus no medical records even though the father is an accountant for an oil company and should have been able to afford insurance. Also, their current passports were all issued on the same date. What are the odds of that for a well-travelled family of five?'

'Low,' Lance said. 'What is it that you suspect?'

'I think maybe they left the USA under a cloud, and I just need to check that it was nothing to do with Brandon – like maybe he's been violent before and they were getting him away from the authorities.'

'Okay, but hypothetically, have you thought about what you'll do if I come back with something? You going to ask your clients about it, or go to the police? You wouldn't be able to risk asking Brandon about it.'

'Cross that bridge when I get to it, which hopefully I never will. Tell me I'm wrong and I'll buy you a great big steak dinner to go with that whisky I already owe you when I'm done here,' I promised. 'Do you think your friend will help?'

'I'm sure of it. He's one of the good guys. Stay safe, my dear. Whoever did this, they're still out there. Trust no one. I'll call you later today, but I'm keeping my phone on if you need me.'

'I will. Thanks Lance. You're one of the good guys, too. I'll call if I need you.'

If I'd been laying a bet, I'd have said I wouldn't have been able to sleep for another twenty-four hours, but shock and grief had spun my mind so fast I passed out with the G-force of it. When I awoke, there was a note under my door.

'Staying in Room 214 along the corridor. Didn't want to disturb you. I'll be awake until midnight but gone early tomorrow. Nate.'

Shaking some sense into my confused brain, I looked at my watch and for a minute couldn't figure out if it was a.m. or p.m. Turned out that the smell of food from downstairs was from dinner, not breakfast, and that it was 8 p.m. I'd slept the day away, making up for a week of insomnia and bad dreams. Dragging clothes over my head, leaving my hair unbrushed, not even bothering with shoes, I crept up the corridor to Nate's room.

The man who answered the door seemed to have aged since the first time I'd met him. Or maybe I had.

'Come in,' he said. 'You look like I feel.'

I took the small sofa below the window and curled up on it. Nate poured us both a drink and handed me a glass.

'I slept all day,' I said. 'I don't understand how that could happen.'

'Your adrenal system produced too much cortisol. It was inevitable that you'd fall asleep after a shock like that.'

180

'How do you cope? I mean, I've seen some things, but that much cruelty, the suffering, it's impossible to remain untouched by that.'

Nate sat on his bed and stretched out his legs. 'The official line is that we're the advocate for the dead and their families. We're their best hope of getting an explanation, justice, finality – whatever you want to call it. As soon as you're emotional or reactive, you're not going to do that job as well as you should.'

'And unofficially?'

'There isn't a face I can't pull to mind of a victim of violence. I never forget a single one. They're burned into my brain. There are other tragedies – car crashes, undiagnosed illnesses, drug overdoses, house fires. All terrible. All unnecessary losses. But violence leaves a sense of stress on a corpse that's hard to describe. It's like the fear is the last thing that's left, even after a heart's stopped beating. For me, the fear is another identifiable wound, no different than a bullet hole or a knife wound.'

He was wearing a white T-shirt and grey jogging bottoms, and for a second I found myself wishing I'd bumped into him in one of Banff's many après-ski bars, where we could chat in front of a log fire, laugh without consequences and plan which mountain we'd tackle in the morning. For now, it wasn't to be. There was a chasm of professionalism that had to remain between us.

'Can you talk about today?' I asked softly.

'You really want to?'

'What I want is to walk. I need to be outside. It's too hot in here and I'm feeling kind of caged. You want to come with?'

'Sure,' Nate said. 'Some shoes might be a good idea though.'

I got properly dressed and met him in the lobby. We walked slowly, avoiding chatter, towards the harbour. The roads out of town were too dark to walk at night.

The town was blanketed in a deep hush. Not that the streets were usually busy at this time of night, but no one was stepping in or out of the fish and chip shop. The convenience store lights were dimmed. Not a soul, save for Nate and myself, was walking along the harbour front. We went slowly, each suddenly alive with the sense of wrongness. Tobermory had become a silently watchful alien landscape.

I drew a breath, ready to speak, reaching for Nate's hand at exactly the moment he pushed his arm in front of me, both of us recognising the artificiality of what we'd walked into.

Two men stepped from a side road holding weapons as two others appeared behind us, all of them strangers to me. Nate relaxed his body, put his hands in his pockets and gave a friendly nod to the one closest to us.

'Evening,' he said. 'Is something wrong?'

'All the women under fifty on the island have been curfewed. Starts an hour after sundown and lasts until dawn,' the man replied. 'She shouldn't be out.'

I bristled at being referred to as 'she', but knew better than to show my indignation. Nate was likely to pay a higher price than me if there was trouble.

'I see. I'm Nate Carlisle, the forensic examiner. I'm going to do everything in my power to make sure the person who hurt Adriana and Catriona is identified and prosecuted.'

'What're you doing with her? She's been in and out of everyone's business since she got here,' another of the men asked.

Nate gave a relaxed shrug. 'Ms Levesque is doing what I'm doing. Trying to figure out what's happening here to see if we can't make your girls and women safe again.'

One of the men slapped the end of a baseball bat in his free hand, succeeding only in looking like a cartoon thug.

'What's that for?' I asked him.

'We're taking shifts, sweetheart,' he said. 'Until you and yer man here actually do your jobs, someone has to keep the place safe.'

'That's very organised,' I murmured. 'Did Sergeant Eggo come up with the idea?'

'Harris Eggo didn't stop Catriona Vass from getting butchered, did he? We don't need his permission to patrol.'

'Of course you don't,' Nate said. 'You're right about getting off the streets. We should get going.'

'Hold on a minute. We heard she was at the Vass place yesterday, same time Catriona went missing.' He spoke to Nate, nodding his head in my direction when he referred to me. 'Billy Vass is going to want a fucking word about that.'

'Is that Catriona's dad?' I asked. Nate put a cautionary hand on my arm. 'You can tell him I'd be happy to speak with him. I have nothing to hide and I'd like to help.'

'No one wants you here,' one of the men behind us said.

I turned to face him, aware that having my back to an angry man showing off a weapon carried its own risks.

'You've got better places to be than this,' I said. 'Someone somewhere has clothes hidden, both Adriana's and Catriona's. Someone took those girls in their car. Think about that for a minute. Anyone you know been cleaning out the inside of their vehicle recently, to maybe get rid of DNA?'

The men looked at one another. The least I could do for Nate was distract them enough that we could get away without things turning nasty.

'If you think of anything, talk to Sergeant Eggo or call the anonymous police line. You can even tell me if you're desperate. Thanks guys,' I said, slipping my arm through Nate's and walking around the men in the direction of our hotel.

'That's going to end in violence,' Nate said. 'Vigilantes almost always end up accusing the wrong people.'

'The town's at boiling point. It's understandable.'

'Were you really at Catriona's house yesterday?' he asked.

'I was, but I had no idea she was missing then. Were you able to establish a time of death?'

'She died the night before you found her. I can't be precise yet, but I'd say between 10 p.m. and 4 a.m.'

'Then she was already dead when I was at her house. Did police find the weapon at the scene?' I asked.

'No. We have a large team checking the rocks and foliage between the cave and the road but nothing's turned up yet.'

At the hotel, we returned to Nate's room without discussing it, automatically returning to the same seats we'd had before.

'How much can you tell me?' I asked.

'You've seen the body, so you know almost everything already.'

'I saw her back. That was the first thing, her hair catching my torchlight. If she was drowned and pulled back into the far end of the cave, how come she wasn't scratched up? Her skin was still perfect.' I realised the error in the statement. 'That side of her, at least.'

'She wasn't drowned,' Nate said. 'Same type of seaweed in her hair, same use of sand, but my preliminary finding, subject to a full postmortem, is that she died from a cardiac event caused by massive blood loss. There just wasn't enough blood left in her body to keep her heart pumping.'

'But that would mean . . .' The hairs on my arms and neck stood up.

'Yes. She was alive when he cut her breast off. If she'd been dead already there wouldn't have been the same extent of bleeding you saw.'

'How?' I wanted to come up with a more coherent question, but that was all I could get out.

'Non-scientific at this stage, but I'd say he put an arm around her neck from behind then cut with his other hand. That way he'd have been able to hold her still as she bled.'

'Why put the breast in her left hand? It's symbolic, but of what?' I asked him.

'If you figure that one out, you should let me know,' Nate said. 'I can tell you what happened, but I'm afraid the answer to why human beings are so vicious and destructive wasn't in any of the textbooks I studied.'

I left with that in my head and went back the few metres to my own room knowing Nate was right. I could leave all the mechanics of the crimes to the police, forensics and pathologist. What I really needed in order to identify Adriana's and Catriona's killer was their motive.

Chapter Twenty-Four

As I exited my hotel the next morning intending to visit the Clarks and explain more about the circumstances of Catriona's death, I encountered a steady stream of darkly dressed, sombre-faced people making their way through town in a single direction. I followed, head down, kicking my heels a little and doing my best to make my own progress look coincidental. In a matter of just a few minutes I was standing watching the mourners process into the Saints of the Tides church. Father Christophe was at his post in front of the door, greeting incomers with a firm handshake or a pat on the shoulder. It wasn't a funeral. Catriona's body wasn't going to be released for a very long time, not until the police had tried everything within their power to bring her killer to trial. This was more symbolic. An act of oneness for a grieving community and solidarity with her family. It was a good thing, the right thing to do. Only no one had thought to extend the same support to Adriana's family.

Leaning on a tree some way back from the church, I wondered how long you had to live within an island community to count as one of their own. A year? A decade? Or was nothing short of a generation good enough? The Clarks would never find out.

'What's going on?' I turned to find Brandon at my shoulder, as if my thinking of his family had caused him to materialise.

'A service for Catriona,' I explained.

Brandon's mouth twisted into a grimace. 'Do they know Catriona was responsible for my sister's death?'

'Brandon, this isn't the time or the place. Catriona's family has suffered the same loss as yours.' I kept my voice gentle but my words firm.

There were still a few stragglers joining late.

'You don't think we're entitled to an explanation as to why she was asking my sister to meet her in the middle of the night, and never bothered saying a word about it to the police? These people should know the truth before they sit in that church,' he continued loudly. We got some sharp looks from a couple crossing the road. I took Brandon by the arm and pulled him further away.

'Making enemies of these people will only make it harder to get justice for Adriana. I know this feels messed up to you but I'm asking you to go home. Please. Let me do my job.'

'Your job? Do you know how jealous Catriona was of Addie? She was the centre of attention until my sister arrived. Prettiest girl in town, on the island probably. And just as fucked up and twisted as all the other girls here. My sister didn't stand a chance.'

'But also dead,' I said. 'Brutally murdered.' He froze, the anger sliding from his face. 'Whatever Catriona got herself into, she's paid a price for it.'

Brandon said nothing. The conflict within him was over-whelming. I felt it too. I'd been looking for Catriona to answer some serious questions about Adriana's death. Now my only lead was gone.

'I'll go,' Brandon said, his voice wobbling. In spite of his adult stature and his fury, he too was still a child. He kept his face downturned as he went.

'Hey,' I walked after him, took him by the arm. 'It feels like there's something you know that I don't. Now would be the time to share.'

He pulled his arm from my hand, the action more sullen than aggressive.

'They put a spell on her,' he said. 'And every single person in that church knows it.'

I watched him go.

It should have been ridiculous; the ramblings of a grief-stricken sibling carrying so much anger that he needed some enormous conspiracy with monsters and witchcraft to do justice to his loss.

But then there was Flora's house. The herbs. The scorch marks. I'd never managed to catch up with Flora's father Jasper, and I still didn't know why Harris Eggo had been so set on warning me off. All those things, plus a crawling, spidery sensation in my guts, a shadow in my peripheral vision that disappeared whenever I turned my head.

'Coming in?' PC Bathgate called across the road. He glanced once at Brandon's disappearing figure before looking back at me. 'It'll be starting.'

'Sure,' I said. A bead of sweat trickled down my back, cold and slow.

'Are you all right? You don't look well,' Bathgate said. 'Do you need to sit down?'

For a second I couldn't get any breath into my lungs and the world began to blur as if I were seeing it from a merry-go-round. A few seconds later it came back into focus.

'I'm good,' I said, trying to shake it off. 'No breakfast,' I explained.

He motioned for me to walk in front of him into the church, closed the door behind us and someone began playing a piano. I walked to stand at the back, hiding myself in the crowd. It was packed. The few rows of chairs were taken by family and close friends. Catriona's father was at the front, being comforted by his aunt among others. Take away the smart phones and the designer trainers from the mourners, and it could have been another century.

Someone began singing a hymn, a single male voice, pure as spring water. Father Christophe waited patiently, appearing to be praying in the distant corner of the church, until the song was done. Then he stepped forward.

'Friends,' he began, 'William.' He directed his gaze at Billy, Catriona's father, and nodded. 'Many of you will be asking God how it can possibly be that we're here today. Why, if there is a God, would he allow such a terrible thing to happen in our loving community?' There were a few mumbles of agreement at that. 'And I intend to answer your questions. But first I'm going to ask that we pray together, so that through faith we may see more clearly.' He lowered his head and began a chant that roughly half the congregation muttered along with. I kept my eyes open and looked around. Harris Eggo was there, exhausted and ashen. I guessed he was having to answer some pertinent questions about his claim that Adriana's murder had been a one-off, and that her murderer was no threat to anyone else on the island. Not a viable stance any longer. There were other faces I recognised from The Blether. Catriona's girlfriends huddled together, doing their best to keep their sobs quiet. As the prayer ended, Father Christophe gave a satisfied nod.

'So here we are,' he said. 'Gathered to take strength from one another. Each of us humbled as we contemplate our mortal state, and the fragility of our own lives and those of our loved ones. Reminded, tragically, of the need to express our love daily for each other. Shown that we cannot take for granted any more than this one day. Catriona was born on this island. She lived her whole life here. She was taken from us by an act of unspeakable evil.'

Lots of agreement with that, louder voices responding.

'So why did God let this happen? How did his eye slip from this child in her hour of need? Why was she not protected?' Christophe continued. More evangelical than I'd anticipated. The crowd were waiting for the answer with bated breath. Harris Eggo turned to gauge the mood and caught my eye. His raised eyebrows gave more away than he'd intended.

'The answer is that evil is as present today as it has always been. It may have been a human hand that wielded the knife and cut Catriona's body . . .' I held Harris Eggo's gaze, waiting to see what he would do. The crowd, surely, wouldn't tolerate such a brutal sermon so soon. The policeman gritted his teeth and inspected the flagstones where he stood, 'but do you think the Lord operates in a vacuum where only he is present? No. No, he does not.'

The church was thrumming. The air was electric with emotion.

'Evil is so familiar a sight now that we are not shocked when we see its face. When pornographic images flash up on our screens, when the Lord's name is taken in vain on our streets, when young people have intercourse with no thought for morality or consequences. Evil is all around us. Once it has been let in, it takes a foothold. Evil warps the mind. It controls the senses. Evil has invaded our community.'

At that, there were actual cries of agreement, some applause. Father's Christophe's face was aglow. All eyes on him. Even the teenagers had stopped crying. They were being thrown a lifeline. Want to take your mind off one horrible, empty useless emotion? Welcome to hatred and blame, your grief beta blocker.

'This evil, this destruction, this . . . *sadism*,' he shouted the last word, 'was not born here. It travelled here. Evil constantly looks for new places to inhabit. Small acts of evil are droplets of mercury. They find each other, slink together, form a mass. Seep into the cracks, poisoning, destroying, devastating. It is a foreign element that may look shiny and beautiful on the outside – it may even reflect your own face – but it is poison nonetheless.'

The congregation let out a breath. Father Christophe let the atmosphere settle. Like every good orator, he knew that he needed to drop the tone before his crescendo.

'Let us keep Catriona in our hearts. May we see her in all the places she used to inhabit on our island. Recall her taking part in those good, clean activities that are suitable for a young woman.'

My feminist hackles rose first, closely followed by my investigative senses. It was a weird comment, in any view. Dated and patriarchal, yes, but also bizarre. What 'good, clean' activities were the townsfolk supposed to recall, and as opposed to what else that Catriona had done? The same things Adriana had been confessing to Father Christophe, perhaps?

'We must be vigilant in our communities, our homes and our consciences. We should cast out those who would invade us, disrupt our traditions and disturb our private contemplations.'

Eyes turned on me. I should have seen that coming. The foreigner, the bringer of woe. Someone whispered the word 'bitch' a few people to my left and no one bothered to tut in horror. Place of worship or not, the air had taken on a lynching feel and suddenly I very much felt the need to get out. The only door, however, was at the front, and I wasn't walking through the mourners and past Catriona's father to exit right now.

'We must reject and silence those who do not take God into their souls. Cast out and speak out against those who practise atheism and worse. Mark those who walk among us but who are not of our kind.'

My palms were sweating. Father Christophe was in his element. If I could have turned back time I would never have walked into that church at all.

'Those who set a bad example to our young women and girls. Those who enter our homes and our places of work, unbidden, unlawfully, and who judge what they do not understand.'

At that Father Christophe looked at me directly. It was a clear reference to my time in Skittles' cellar, and I wondered again how the information had come to his ears.

'We shall have justice for Catriona,' he said. No mention of Adriana at all. Not one word. By now I was as incensed as Brandon had been. 'God will deliver justice for us. He will work through us to ensure that the perpetrator is found and punished. We ask that he keeps our other young women safe. I ask that you help that work by keeping those young women and girls indoors, safe, under the watchful eyes of their fathers, brothers and husbands.'

He paused; a long, dramatic moment straight from a public speaking handbook. I gritted my teeth.

Finally, so gently it was difficult to hear, said with such sadness, reverence and grace that I might have imagined the previous minutes of spewing fire, he said, 'Let us pray.'

Heads bowed. I kept mine up. Too many bodies in the tiny space and it was beginning to reek. After the amens, Billy Vass stood first. Father Christophe went with him, and the remaining congregation stood respectfully while a private moment was held at the door.

Then they began to filter out. It was painfully slow and my position at the back meant I would be almost last to exit. I stepped forward as soon as a space in the line became clear, listening to the small talk and expressions of sympathy and shock. As I reached the door I felt a warm wetness on the back of my neck. Putting my hand there, I realised I'd been spat on. Stepping aside, I turned to see who was following me out, ready to deal with a confrontation if necessary. There were some things I just wouldn't tolerate.

It was Harris Eggo who took me by the elbow and guided me out against my wishes, muttering, 'Not now, not here,' into my ear as we moved. Well beyond the doors of the church he stopped, raising both hands into the air in surrender. 'I saw what happened but not who did it, and I'm sorry. You don't want to cause a scene right now though. Blood's running hot.'

A slap echoed from behind us and we turned together to see what had happened.

An older woman was face to face with Father Christophe, him with a hand on one cheek, PC Bathgate stepping forward to pull her away. Most of the mourners had left the area but those who remained were watching in stunned silence.

'Who is she?' I asked Harris Eggo, but he was already striding into the middle of the scene, bundling the woman off down the path in the opposite direction.

I stayed where I was and watched Simon Bathgate put a brotherly hand on Christophe's shoulder. Father Christophe gave a nod and something of a wink.

I replayed that in my mind as I walked back to my hotel. Neither man seemed surprised by the attack. No effort was made to ask Father Christophe if he knew what it related to. There had been an immediate understanding of the context. There was something conspiratorial between the two men that made me feel sick to the pit of my stomach.

Chapter Twenty-Five

The Island

To Aros Castle the girls came, as they always had, every third month. Some south from Tobermory, others had a shorter journey north from Salen. Silently they approached the ruined walls to stand in the midst of its ancient hall and look down over the Sound of Mull. Some 700 hundred years women had gathered there, while all around them the castle thrived, withstood wars, was handed from clan to clan like some minor prize, and thereafter crumbled into fragments of stone, its proud history brought low.

To some of these girls the history mattered; to others the place was simply the sum of its parts. A venue for them to be still and forget the strife of home. To put aside petty arguments, troubles, wants and desires. To simply *be*, for a short while, at night. Tourists would not take photographs, locals would not gawp. In the dark, no one but the island could bear witness.

The wind played wild music through the gaps in the stonework, and the sea added percussion with the crackle-swish of waves swirling shell across stone where brine met sand.

They built a fire against the remaining castle wall. They'd brought dry wood for this purpose, and matches, although it should have been lit with flint. Modern life couldn't help but intervene. There was no makeup on their faces, nor perfume on their bodies. Their hair was loose and unstyled. Clothes simple and plain. The bitter chill did not allow for nakedness. Not that the temperature concerned them. The fire in their blood would keep them warm. Those nights, there was dopamine and adrenaline aplenty, fuelling their bodies.

As they arrived in small groups, the girls greeted one another with long hugs, feeling their sisters' heartbeats, revelling in the sense of belonging. In flasks they brought warm, spiced, honeyed wine. All there, they began, throwing handfuls of dried herbs into the flames, standing in a semicircle, facing the architecture that had endured centuries. Breathe.

In their minds they conjured the reedy majesty of the bagpipes that would have played on the clifftop. Breathe in, breathe out.

They let the wind hit their bodies, whipping their loose clothing into frenzied wings, strands of hair beating their head, neck, back. Salt spray lashed. Skin prickled with shock and with life. Breathe in, breathe out.

An older woman appeared from behind them. She walked to the fire, knelt, passed her hand through the hottest part of the flame then retreated, arm held aloft for the air to soothe. The girls reached out to one another, joining hands as they stared into the fire. Breathe in, breathe out.

The atmosphere was thick with the scents of a different time. Charcoal, purple heather, meadowsweet, bloodroot and bog myrtle. Of the island's herbs, only St John's wort was missing, reputed to ward off witches. Nonsense, but negativity had no place at such a ceremony. Breathe in, breathe out.

The elder female took a knife from her pocket, gripped the scored stone handle, upturned her burned palm to the sky and cut. One by one, each girl approached, dipped a thumb in the pooling blood and drew a long oval on her own forehead. The circle of life, stretched to its limit but holding, deriving strength from its willingness to bend.

Then the screaming began.

A single girl first, joined by another then another. Banshees lamenting not the loss of a loved one as folklore told, but the loss of themselves into motherhood, marriage, house-keeping, subservience, traditions and stereotypes. The loss of the freedom to wear what they wanted, without being seen to have invited harm. The loss of the right to do what they wanted with their bodies without judgement, gossip, rumour and labels. The loss of the right to reject norms and remain free spirits.

As the screaming faded, the dancing began, slow movements at first, limbs watery and loose. Then faster, more urgent, their bodies weaving together until the moonlight was no longer strong enough to differentiate between them. They paused to swig wine. It ran from their mouths, down their necks, splashed their clothes. They whirled and laughed, writhed and grinned. Dropped to the ground exhausted, lay face-down on the tram-pled grass, rubbing their cheeks against mud.

'Stillness,' the elder said.

All stopped dead, not a movement, letting every muscle melt into that earthy bed.

'Now look up,' she said.

As one they rolled to lie on their backs and gaze into the limitless sky, untainted by city lights. The fire had fizzled out, the moon had the grace to allow itself to be covered by clouds, and the stars were reflected in the eyes of the island's girls. Finally they cried, letting go of slights and insults, bullying and violations, arguments and invasions.

The elder walked to the fire, adding fresh wood and relighting the flame. She pulled a red crystal from her pocket which she sat on a log in the centre and called each girl by name. They sat up, startled, as if waking in a strange place from a deep sleep, and crawled to the fire on hands and knees.

Each whispered a single name into the crystal and presented a likeness – a hand-drawn picture, a photo or a crudely modelled doll. Each had their reasons, some better than others. The island listened and heard, and knew the truth of the complaints they presented. The elder woman took each girl's hand and together they held the likeness in the flame as it burned. The ends of their fingers blistered and charred. A price had to be paid for vengeance. Nothing in the natural world is free.

Sated, they stamped out the fire, retrieved the crystal, picked up their flasks, hugged their goodbyes and left. Aros Castle stood firm, as it always has, silently welcoming ships home from fishing, explorations and sea battles, watching Mull's people, and guarding their shores.

Chapter Twenty-Six

I trod on the note that had been shoved beneath my door, crumpling the paper. Picking it up, I threw it onto my bed before opening it. At the minibar, I popped the cap from a too-small bottle of vodka and downed the contents. The liquor burned my throat whilst simultaneously tasting of nothing, but it did the job. Grabbing the note, I threw myself on the bed to read it.

> *Dear Miss Levesque, I appreciate you haven't yet come to the end of your stay with us, but I'm afraid we can no longer accommodate you. You'll understand that events on the island have overtaken our agreement to provide you with lodgings. You're welcome to stay tonight but I'd ask that you vacate your room no later than 10 a.m. tomorrow.*
> *Many thanks,*
> *Manager of The Last Bay Inn.*

It would be a lie to say the note came as a complete shock but it was certainly a reality check. Given that my room in the hotel had already been broken into once, maybe it was no bad thing to be moving on. I began checking the other accommodation on the island. The first wasn't taking new bookings. Neither was the second. By the third, I'd got the message. Mull was closed to business right now. They didn't want journalists, photographers, crime scene tourists or outsiders. And they certainly didn't want me.

Fair enough. But the Clarks did, and they needed someone fighting their corner more than ever. I had preparations to make and people to see. No time to waste.

First, I headed to an outdoor supplies store on the outskirts of town, small but well-stocked with an owner who didn't stop talking from the second I entered. I took the opportunity to explain that I was leaving Mull imminently and kitting up for a hiking trip on the mainland before returning to Canada. I left with a one-man tent, quick to pitch and camouflaged. I didn't have midwinter weather to contend with so what I needed was pretty lightweight. Nate's text message came in while I was rolling my sleeping bag into its sleeve.

'Test results in. Grey powder from Adriana's boot – crushed cat bone. Falsely sold as drugs perhaps?'

'Cutting agent maybe,' I replied.

There was no end to what drug producers used to cut drugs with. I'd seen too much of it, abusing anything from talcum powder, washing powder, caffeine and aspirin to brick dust, quartz, glucose and benzocaine. Some of it heightened the effects of the drug, and occasionally the cutting agent was more deadly than the drug itself. Mainly it was just dealers making increased profit by fooling users into putting unknown substances in their body. Crushed animal bone was a new one on me. Seemed like too much hard work to use anything that had to be cleaned then crushed to make it passable.

Another possibility was already forming a storm cloud in

my brain. To investigate that further I needed to brave The Blether again, but I was hoping I'd see at least a couple of friendly faces there.

Rachel was behind the bar and Lewis was clearing tables. Thankful for small mercies, I ordered a sandwich and sparkling water to make up for my out-of-character alcohol abuse so early in the day, and took a seat.

Rachel delivered my sandwich and gave me a concerned look.

'You all right, are you? I've heard some things.' Rachel's understatement made me smile.

'It is what it is,' I shrugged, leaning forward, elbows on the table, voice low. 'There are rumours, nothing concrete, but it seems to me that Adriana and Catriona, maybe even Flora Kydd all those years ago, were involved with some sort of – I'm not sure – a cult, maybe?'

'Ach, no, that's stories we tell wee children to get them to go to bed and to finish their dinner without a fuss. Lot of nonsense. Sure, the tourists love hearing tales of the Mull Witch. Wasn't the supernatural that killed those poor girls though, was it?'

'I agree with you there. Listen, you know you let me check out the staff area for Adriana's stuff. Did Catriona ever happen to leave anything here?'

'PC Bathgate came and collected everything on Billy Vass's behalf yesterday. Not that I could let you back there now. My husband's given instructions to lock down.' Rachel cast an eye towards the main door. 'He's on the mainland today buying stock so you're all right for a while.'

'I appreciate you serving me,' I said. 'If you can do me one last favour, then I'll stay away so you don't have to fight my battles any more. Who here knew Catriona best? Anyone I can talk to who might give me some insight other than her immediate group of girlfriends?'

She looked over her shoulder and beckoned to Lewis.

'The boy can maybe help a bit. Catriona fancied him something rotten for a while. Used to sit in here mooning over him every time he was working. Not sure what happened. It just seemed to burn out.' Lewis arrived at my table still wiping a glass.

'Sadie has some questions for you,' Rachel said quietly, handing me a menu. 'Don't sit down, and keep it quick.' She winked at me.

I gave the menu a cursory look and pointed at a random entry on it before asking a question.

'Is the cottage pie good?' I asked.

'As long as you're not a vegetarian,' he replied. 'What do you want to know?'

'If Catriona had texted Adriana asking her to go somewhere, would Adriana have gone, do you think?'

'Depends on the circumstances. I know Adriana was trying to fit in here, make some friends. Catriona always seemed to be in the middle of what was going on. I guess if she'd liked you, everyone else would accept you too. But the real question is, why would Catriona have texted Adriana in the first place?'

'How do you mean?'

'I got the impression Catriona didn't like Adriana. I told you before – it seemed like she was jealous of having another pretty girl here. Catriona didn't like competition.'

It was the second time I'd heard that.

'What if Catriona had decided she and Adriana could get more attention as friends rather than separately? The two of them together would have been eye-catching.'

'I've got to get back behind the bar,' he said. 'But Catriona wasn't much good at sharing. If she'd decided to play nice with

Adriana, it was because she wanted something. Is it true you're the one who found her?' I nodded. 'I don't understand what happened. My dad said she didn't die the same way Adriana did. Do you think they'll catch whoever did it?'

'I do,' I said. 'Sooner or later there'll be some forensic evidence or a witness. It's almost impossible to stay hidden, especially in a small community. Catriona had a bit of a thing for you for a while, right?'

'Everyone said so, but we never went out. Catriona was cool but she wasn't my type. I don't want to say anything . . .' his voice trailed off. 'It doesn't feel fair now.'

'Did she have a boyfriend?'

He looked over his shoulder. There was no one nearby.

'A few,' he said. 'Her dad was away a lot, sometimes for days at sea. I guess she got lonely. I felt sorry about that. My dad thinks maybe she got involved with the wrong person. Her friends would be more help with that than me.'

'I'll talk to them. Before you go, there was a small bag of powder in Adriana's boots. It turned out to be crushed cat bones. Does that mean anything to you?'

Simon Bathgate wandered in and took a seat at the bar.

'Shit, I've got to go. Crushed cat bones sounds like some of the stupid stuff Catriona and her mates get up to. Once they got me to drink some sort of ginger tea, only one of them blabbed to my mate later that it was supposed to have been a love potion.'

'Just a bit of fun, I guess,' I said.

'Not that much fun. Made me sick for a couple of days. God knows what they'd put in it.'

Lewis picked up the menu and returned to the bar.

PC Bathgate managed to wait three or four minutes before picking up his pint and coming to join me. He sat closer than was strictly necessary. I shifted along.

'Lewis is a good-looking boy. Like them younger, do you?'

'Does Harris Eggo know you talk about his son like that? Can't imagine he'd like it.'

'I didn't know Canadians were so lacking in humour,' he replied, finishing the last drips in his pint glass.

'Not much happening on Mull to make me laugh right now,' I said. 'You and Father Christophe obviously have a close relationship. Was it you who told him I'd been in Skittles' cellar?'

'That was for professional reasons. The bones you found will need to be properly buried once a formal identification has been made.'

'Provided they're not evidence in a criminal investigation, and even so it didn't require my name to be given.' No answer to that one. 'Who was the woman throwing the well-aimed slap?'

'Nothing for you there. Personal grievances. Father Christophe was clear no charges should be pressed. He's a good man. An inspiration to the community.'

'Yeah, I'm not sure he isn't a little too keen on locking up the women and handing all the authority back to the men here.'

He moved in close and whispered in my ear.

'If Catriona Vass had been at home, being looked after, she'd still be alive now. If Adriana Clark hadn't sneaked out in the middle of the night, she'd be serving pints behind that bar. Maybe a little bit of locking up our girls wouldn't go amiss.'

I pushed the remains of my sandwich away and stood up.

'And yet you're sitting here breathing hops over me instead of looking for their killer. Have you asked Father Christophe what he knows about Adriana? She was going to confession with him.'

Bathgate's widening eyes told me he'd been ignorant of that fact.

'I hear you're planning on leaving the island tomorrow,' he said. Mull's whisper network was reliable, then. I wondered how many minutes after I'd bought my tent the shop owner had waited before calling to pass the gossip on. 'That's a shame. You and I could have become friends.'

'My loss,' I said. 'But I'm sure you'll soon find a sweet island girl who'll do as she's told.'

My next port of call was the pottery shop, seeking out Lizzy. The poor girl was red-eyed behind the counter, her grandmother vacuuming an already spotless floor. There was no point pretending I was there for any reason other than to obtain information.

'I don't want to talk,' Lizzy said, before I'd had the chance to speak.

'Of course you don't Elizabeth,' her grandmother said. 'But I'm afraid you must. No one will be safe until this murderer is caught. What is it you need, Miss Levesque?'

'It's about Catriona,' I said. 'Her private life. Can we talk somewhere with fewer windows?'

Within five minutes the shop was shut, the sign on the door turned, and we were sitting in the accommodation above – a humble but cosy set of rooms that felt as safe and idyllic as the outside world did savage. I waited for coffee to be poured before beginning.

'Lizzy, did Catriona have a boyfriend?'

'No. Well, like, a few, but not a special one. There were boys she saw sometimes.'

'Anyone new? Anyone from off-island, or older than her?'

'Nope, just the local boys. Idiots mostly. It was just a bit of fun,' Lizzy explained.

'She hadn't met anyone on social media that she'd mentioned?'

'Naw, who's going to come all the way to Mull? That's why

we talked about leaving the whole time. It's not like you're going to want to marry anyone from this lot.'

'What about Lewis?' I asked, snapping a biscuit in half. 'Did Catriona not like him?'

'Aye, everyone fancies him a bit. They never went out though.'

'His choice or hers?' Lizzy shrugged but didn't answer. 'Was he given some sort of love potion once? Something that went wrong, made him sick?'

'It was just a bunch of herbs, and Cat only meant it as a joke. He takes himself too seriously, that one.' She rolled her eyes.

'Who gave it to him?' I asked.

'I forget, but it was Catriona's idea. What's he been saying about her? He shouldn't be saying bad stuff now she's—'

'He wasn't saying anything bad. I asked how well he knew her. He was just telling me the stories he could recall. Did you know Catriona texted Adriana to meet her, the same night Adriana died?'

'She never did that. I don't believe it,' Lizzy said, looking me straight in the eyes now, adamant.

'How can you be so sure?' I asked.

'It wouldn't have been just the two of them. We were Cat's closest friends. Catriona was properly upset about what happened to Adriana. If she'd seen her that night, or agreed to meet her, she'd have told us.'

'The message was from Catriona's mobile. I've seen the records. I even dialled the number to check and she answered it.'

'Bullshit,' Lizzy said. 'You might think Catriona did something but I'm telling you, no bloody way.'

'Did Catriona's mobile have security on it that you knew of? A code or a fingerprint reading, anything like that?'

'It has a face scanner. No one else could have got into it. Her phone was in her pocket all the time unless it was charging.

205

It's an Android, same as mine, bit older. We've tried to unlock each other's with our own faces before for a laugh and it never works. Maybe someone hacked it?' she suggested.

'Difficult to do,' I said. 'I'm sorry, there's just one more thing. You're probably exhausted.' The girl gave a sad nod. 'The night you went into the Emporium – the blue apatite stone you were after – how was that going to be used, exactly?'

A long pause. Lizzy bit her nails.

'I don't remember. Catriona wanted it for something. I feel ill. Nana, can I go and lie down please?'

Her grandmother looked at me first.

'I'm done,' I said. 'I appreciate you talking to me.'

Lizzy disappeared off and I finished my coffee.

'There are words being spoken,' her grandmother said. 'They say you're always in the wrong place at the wrong time, and that you seem to know too much. We've been warned not to let you near the girls.'

'So why did you?'

'Scotland breeds strong women. I'm not a fool. My granddaughter shouldn't go out in the evening while this maniac remains at large. But I control my own house. No man tells me what to do. The majority of the women I know feel the same, even if they're too grief-stricken to pick a fight right now. I hope you're not letting the men here chase you away.'

'It's easier if they think I'm leaving,' I said. 'For now, at least.'

'Catch him, please. For all our sakes. I cannot stand walking through this town, wondering if one of the men I've known for forty or fifty years might be capable of such atrocities.'

'I'll do my best,' I said. 'Lock your doors. Keep Lizzy safe. Trust no one.'

I should have been wise enough to take my own advice.

Chapter Twenty-Seven

I made the most of my final night of indoor accommodation, eating a hot meal in the restaurant, taking a bath, and getting as much sleep as possible. I woke early, packing my belongings and slipping out of the hotel unseen. I'd already let the Clarks know I was leaving the hotel, and as they were the ones settling the bill, I had nothing to do other than leave my key on the unmanned front desk. It was 7.30 a.m. and still dark. A chill fog had blown in from the sea, and I knew the coming days or weeks – however long I was destined to remain on Mull – would be neither easy nor comfortable. That didn't bother me too much. There was a fire in my belly that had nothing to do with the partially consumed bottle of Lagavulin in my rucksack.

At 8 a.m. when the convenience store opened, I shopped for supplies – basic food that was long-lasting and easy to carry, including rice, powdered milk and porridge oats. Next I returned my car to the hire company, telling them I no longer needed it, asking for ferry times, reinforcing the impression I was quitting the island. The ruse wouldn't last long, but I needed some headspace. The Clarks were the only ones to whom I'd told the truth. For the next couple of days I planned to answer calls from them, Nate Carlisle, and my new journalist friend Lance Proudfoot only.

The library was situated to the rear of Tobermory High School. A solitary librarian dusted tables that didn't need the attention and gave me a nod as I entered that doubled as an instruction not to speak. I wasn't sure why. There was no one else in there.

I passed some time in the fiction section while eyeing the local history shelves. The librarian gave me the odd glance as she began wheeling an ancient trolley between shelves and replacing a handful of books in the assigned spaces. Obtaining a library card was out of the question and sitting there all day reading wasn't an option when I had several miles of hiking ahead of me.

I slipped a book under my hoodie as I walked past and dealt with the flush of guilt that followed. Stealing wasn't my thing. If I'd had the option to go into the Emporium and purchase a book on Mull's folklore history then that's what I'd have done. Desperate times call for desperate measures, but even so I vowed I'd return the book when I passed back through Tobermory. Crossing the road, I headed for a bench in the Memorial Park as a quiet spot for a telephone call. Lance Proudfoot, in true form, answered after just one ring.

'If you're calling to tell me you've found yet another body, I'm getting on a ferry to get you out of there,' Lance said.

I laughed. The thought of someone prepared to swoop in and rescue me was just what I needed to hear.

'Not necessary,' I told him. 'I'm tougher than I sound.'

'I don't doubt that, but I heard some more about what's going on there. Vigilante curfews, men roaming the streets with weapons – how are you supposed to know who's good and who's bad?'

'I'm just figuring that out,' I said. 'I've been kicked out of my hotel, Lance. If you need me, it's cell phone only from now on, bearing in mind I may not have a charged battery, not to mention reception. Don't panic if it takes me a day to return your call.'

'Where will you go?' he asked.

'I'll be camping. I'm used to much more severe conditions than this, and I've spent more nights in tents than I can count. This way I can be certain no one'll know where I am. Honestly, I'm kind of looking forward to it. Nature's the best cure for stress and overthinking that I know.'

'You wouldn't rather have solid walls around you?' Lance asked.

'I've survived snowstorms halfway up mountains after I've dropped all my provisions. I've got this,' I told him. Mother nature, whilst cruel, was not a man wielding a knife looking to write their kicks in blood.

'All right then. I guess you want to know what I've found. The answer to that is remarkably little. On your police officer – Simon Bathgate – the only reports are on those arrests or incidents he's participated in. Mull's crime rate is low. Bathgate's made a few arrests, the usual stuff. My friend did find one prior report about a domestic incident. An ex-girlfriend of his dialled 999 for a disturbance when they were living in Glasgow. By the time officers arrived, the scene was quiet and the girl said she'd over-reacted. No findings, no arrests. Put down to a storm in a teacup. That was nine years ago.'

'What about Father Christophe?'

'Moved from French Guiana to Scotland for university. Obtained a first-class degree in psychology before going to seminary school. As a priest, he's moved around between multiple parishes, but without attending in person and digging, I won't know if he left under any sort of cloud. He did seem to be on his way up the ranks, though.'

'So a move to minister to a tiny congregation on Mull is not what you'd expect,' I commented.

'Maybe he just wanted to be closer to God and spend more time in contemplation,' Lance offered.

'Yeah, and maybe he just likes being king of his own tiny castle,' I said before moving the conversation on. 'I'm still interested in Brandon Clark. Anything there?'

'I failed on that one,' Lance said. 'There's nothing, and I mean nothing at all. We even checked Interpol listings in case they'd fled another country attempting to avoid legal proceedings.'

'I was worried you might say that. I should have found some record of them in California but came up blank.'

'You asked me before about their passports – them all having been issued on the same day. That almost never happens. Even just the husband and wife – most adults have passports before they meet their partner, which means they'll need renewing at different times. Often different years, rather than just months.'

'Go on,' I said.

'Unless you've changed some fundamental detail about yourself. Like a family that's obtained citizenship of a new country, and all the passports have been issued together. Or when a house has burned down and all the passports have been destroyed so they need to be reapplied for in one go. Something dramatic.'

'Dramatic enough that there ought to be a record of it somewhere, or that they'd have told me about it,' I said. Lance remained quiet. 'I'll do some more digging.'

'I would,' he said quietly. 'Adriana was the first victim. She's more likely to lead you to the killer than anything that happens afterwards. If there's something in her past you don't know about, then you've currently only got half the picture.'

'Thanks Lance. Will you keep looking, just in case? If you can't get hold of me and it's important, contact Nate Carlisle from the pathologist's team based at the Queen Elizabeth

University in Glasgow. He'll want to hear anything you have to tell him.'

'Would it be too paternalistic of me to ask you to call or message once a day, just so I know you haven't eaten any poisonous berries or got stuck in a peat bog?'

'Not paternalistic, but unnecessary. I can deal with pretty much anything, and I'm as happy in a tent as I am in a house. First stop when I leave Mull is going to be your door though. We'll go for that drink.'

'Done,' Lance said. 'And as my father used to say, be brave until it's stupidity, then run like hell.'

'I'll remember that. Thanks Lance. Take care.'

Tucking the book inside my rucksack, I stood up and checked the sky. It was cloudy but not threatening rain, and the temperature was mild. I had one more stop to make before heading out of town. It was time to do what I should have done when I first realised my clients were not all they were pretending to be.

Chapter Twenty-Eight

Isabella Clark was comforting a crying Luna when she answered the door. She was a shadow of the woman I'd first met, so thin she appeared to be a slice of herself, no colour in her face or clothes.

'Is there news?' she asked.

'No,' I said, stepping through the doorway even though she hadn't invited me in yet. It was going to be that sort of visit. 'Is Rob here?'

'Out hiking with Brandon. They needed some space. It gets a bit . . .' She waved a vague hand around in the atmosphere. Dead, I thought. Everyone in that family had died a little when Addie was taken from them. Luna wriggled in her mother's arms, bottom lip a platform of unhappiness. 'I'm sorry, it's not good timing.'

'Isabella, I'm looking for anything that linked Adriana with Catriona. I need to go through her possessions again. Do you mind if I take the key and go back to your house?'

Isabella frowned and sighed.

'I guess, but try not to disturb anything.'

'Of course, I understand. By the way, did you know Adriana

was going to Father Christophe at the Catholic church for confession? Not to the services, he says, but there were obviously things weighing on her.'

'What did she tell him?' Isabella asked. She snapped the words and I did a double take. Grief isn't an emotion, it's a state. In my experience, it was an assault course of different emotions changing with each obstacle – from sorrow to anger, confusion to loneliness, hatred to resignation. The look on Isabella's face now was somewhere between fury and terror. Lance's unspoken suspicions were bang on.

'He wouldn't say,' I said. 'You know the confessional carries an absolute confidentiality. Forever.'

She nodded and walked towards the kitchen, taking a set of keys off a hook. She held them out to me, withdrawing her hand as I reached out to take them.

'You would tell me if you'd found something out, wouldn't you?' she asked.

I didn't hesitate. 'Of course, you're my client, any information I receive is relayed to you—'

'Not just your pro forma answer,' she insisted, stepping into my space and staring intensely into my eyes. 'Is there some sort of, I don't know, some law that says you have to tell me everything?'

'Not a criminal law, no, but we have a contract and full disclosure is part of what you're paying me for.'

Isabella swore in Spanish under her breath – some phrases you can translate whether or not you can speak a language.

'Was there something specific you were concerned about? I certainly don't have any current information that I haven't relayed to you.'

Her shoulders dropped and she retreated.

'No, no,' Isabella said. 'I was worried that maybe you were giving Rob information that he kept from me. He doesn't want to upset me.' She picked at a frayed sleeve and frowned. 'You have to tell us both, right?'

'Right,' I said, wondering at what point I would agree not to impart information if it seemed that I might create danger by sharing it.

'I don't need protecting,' she said softly, as if she'd read my mind. She held out the keys once more and this time allowed me to take them.

'I'll return them through this letterbox later.' I let myself out.

Fifteen minutes later I was in their home. The press had long since figured out that the Clarks had quit the property and so had disappeared from their doorstep vigil. Entering, grateful for the drawn curtains and blinds, I double-locked the front door then checked that the kitchen door was equally secure, pushing a chair in front of it so that even a key-bearer couldn't enter without my being alerted.

I took the stairs to Adriana's bedroom and sat on her bed awhile. Not that I believed there was anything to find there, but to get a feel for her again. I wished I could have met her. Of course, people often say that about the dead. Our descriptions are rose tinted and coated in glossy respect. If we really told the truth about the dead, there would be chaos. My grandfather was a case in point. A high-ranking military official by career, selfless in the service of his country, and a man who gave regularly to charity and fathered four children with his dedicated and loyal wife. The sort of man who told good stories, was popular with the boys, and who played a mean round of golf. What no one said at his funeral was that when he lost at golf, or his stocks took a tumble, or when he'd had too many with the boys, he became vicious, first with his tongue, and if pushed, also with an open palm to his wife's face. Never a fist – give the man some credit. Never a kick. He never picked up a weapon. But he could slap with the best of them. At his

214

funeral we stood dutifully, there were some tears, grand words were spoken. And then my grandma went home and burned every item of his clothing, every photograph, every trinket, and she drank white wine by the bonfire and toasted. No one tells the whole truth about the dead.

What secrets hadn't been told about Adriana, I wondered?

I wandered out into the hallway. Brandon's room wasn't going to yield any more clues. Instead, I headed for Rob and Isabella's master bedroom. It was neat and clean. Nothing unexpected in the bathroom cabinet. I didn't even know what I was looking for, which made it harder. Under their bed, inside their shoes, pockets of hung trousers, slipped into book covers. Everything came up empty. Time to look downstairs, but I'd been in those rooms plenty of times. The kitchen was no more than functional, there was a small study with a bare desk and bookshelves, and the lounge.

They'd left this house so quickly and yet it was immaculate. Sparse, in fact. Isabella wasn't happy that I was here. I determined to do something to make up with her. In the dead of night, they hadn't been able to pack much. There were still toys left on Luna's bed with some puzzles and shape sets. I ran downstairs and grabbed a bin bag from under the sink to put the items in, racing back up and packing what I could, imagining the smile on Luna's face when she reclaimed her possessions. Nearly done. As I was leaving, a large teddy in flowery cotton print on a high shelf caught my eye, a huge smile on its face and open, welcoming arms. It made me feel better just looking at it. I put a foot on Luna's bed, testing my weight before reaching my hand up, knocking the toy down rather than managing to grab it first time. It fell onto the girl's pillow.

I picked it up and gave it a hug. There was something about cuddly toys, a comfort you never forgot when you held them tight. My three childhood favourites were still sitting on a shelf in my wardrobe. Try as I might, I'd never been able to let them go. Sometimes I'd imagined giving them to my own son or daughter when I settled down long enough to have a lasting relationship.

Turning the teddy to place it into the top of the bag, I noticed the label on its back. The sort a nursery school might provide parents with so that each child's belongings could be easily identified.

'This is the property of . . .' I leaned closer to read the fading handwriting on the dotted line '. . . Luna Wilde.'

Pulling the bear back out of the bag, I perched on the edge of the bed. Luna Wilde. It was an unusual first name, Luna. What were the odds that the bear had previously been owned by another child named Luna?

None at all, my brain replied. There was literally no chance that the bear belonged to anyone except my clients' daughter. Only now I had absolutely no idea who I was really working for, and why they'd failed to give me their real name. I took the stairs down two at a time and made my way back to their temporary home.

Rob and Brandon were back by the time I arrived. Smiling at Luna, I held up the bin bag.

'I have some things here you might have missed,' I told her. Her eyes glowed as she held out her arms.

'That was kind of you,' Rob said, stretching out a hand to take the set of house keys.

'Going to my room,' Brandon said. That wasn't how I needed the meeting to pan out.

'I think we should all chat together once Luna's busy with her toys,' I said. 'Why don't you stay down here?' It wasn't really a question.

'Squishies!' Luna squealed, delighted.

'Better than that,' I said. I'd kept the teddy until last and pulled it dramatically from the bottom of the bag. 'I think this teddy has been missing you!'

'Blossom!' she shouted, reaching out her arms.

'You sure it's yours? It has someone's name written on the back. I have to make sure I'm giving it to the right little girl.'

'She's mine, she is!' Luna yelled. I handed it over and she ran out of the room clambering up the stairs.

Rob and Isabella were staring at each other. Brandon fixed his gaze out of the window.

'Told you she'd find out,' the boy said blankly.

I walked across the lounge and took a seat. 'So you're Mr and Mrs Wilde?'

'It doesn't have anything to do with Addie's death,' Rob said. 'It wasn't relevant.'

'We brought Sadie in to make sure it wasn't relevant, that was the point,' Isabella corrected him. 'Until Catriona died, we weren't sure.'

'I need to know everything. If there was some threat to Adriana you didn't tell me about—'

'The threat wasn't to her,' Rob said, sinking into an armchair. Isabella leaned against the wall, arms crossed. 'It was about me. All of it was my fault.'

'You ruined our lives,' Brandon said. 'Addie and I lost everything.'

'We all did,' Isabella said gently.

'You could have left him,' Brandon said. 'We didn't have to come with him to this stupid fucking place. Addie would still be alive.'

'You think I don't know that already?' Rob asked.

'Calmly, slowly, every detail, so I can do my job for you, if you still want me to,' I said.

217

'It might be better if you just leave,' Rob said. 'You pieced together as much as we need.'

'That's not true,' Isabella said. 'Whoever killed Catriona must have been involved in Addie's death too. I want them in prison for what they did!'

'Addie's dead!' Rob shouted. 'Nothing will make that better.'

'No, it won't, but I need to know, Rob. I need all the facts. I want to know why it happened,' Isabella said. Rob put his head in his hands and she went to his side, cradling him, kissing his forehead. 'Tell Sadie everything, please. I can't go on like this. We need some certainty.'

He nodded, wiped his face, cleared his throat.

'Fine. But this is confidential, like your life depends on it. Ours do. We're not from California. For the last ten years we've lived in Las Vegas. Before that, New York. I was a young accountant, keen to make money and get to the top. When I was offered a job as lead in-house accountant for a large casino, it seemed to be everything I'd dreamed of. A huge salary and, without the expense of living in New York, we'd be able to afford a really nice place, great car, foreign vacations, the works.'

'My sister's dead,' Brandon said. 'And you're still talking about all the things we could afford?'

I watched Brandon carefully. The fury I'd seen in his face that I'd thought was reserved for his sister's murderer was back, only it was his father he held responsible. The poor kid had been torn apart. So much anger and nowhere to put it.

'I was good at my job. Maybe too good. I knew where to funnel the money, how to eradicate profit through expenses. I thought I was being clever, only I was stepping over the lines of legality. The casino was part of a larger group and the other owners also wanted my services. I became an accountant for hire specialising in laundering.'

Isabella was rubbing her eyes. She was exhausted, anyone

218

could see it, but now I was putting together a picture of a woman who'd been exhausted for a very long time – years maybe – before her daughter had been brutally murdered.

'It was never going to last forever. I thought it would be the Inland Revenue Service that asked for the books, but in the end it was the FBI. One casino owner had been caught trafficking women across state lines to provide what he called "entertainment" for the high rollers. I knew nothing about it and I would never have helped with that. But it gave them a reason to look into everything.'

'Oh for Christ's sake,' Brandon interjected. 'He did a deal. Gave the Feds everything they wanted on all the casino owners and avoided prosecution.'

'You gave evidence at trial?' I asked.

'Didn't need to. I gave them enough of a paper trail that all the defendants negotiated pleas. They all went to jail anyway, just not for as long as they otherwise would've done. The problem was, the FBI wouldn't give me a full witness protection deal. New passports, time to disappear. They negotiated with the UK government to allow us to live here. I have enough money put by in foreign accounts that we can live without working. Not in luxury, but we'll survive.'

'Addie didn't,' Brandon said.

His father glared at him.

'You were worried Adriana's death might have been revenge for you giving the casino owners up to the Feds?' I asked. 'Is that why you called me in rather than trusting the police?'

Isabella and Rob both nodded.

'I need to make sure that neither of our other children are at risk,' Isabella said.

'I can take care of myself,' Brandon mumbled.

'Was there ever a specific threat to Adriana or to the rest of you?' I asked.

219

'Plenty, before we left Vegas. We deleted the kids' social media accounts, cell phone records, and changed our surname, although for the children's sake we let them keep their first names. Isabella and I dropped our first names – before we moved here we were Dennis and Alma Wilde – and opted to use our middle names instead.'

'Is that why you hid Adriana's cell phone from the police and from me?' Things were falling into place fast.

Rob nodded. 'I couldn't be sure what was on there. It was always possible Addie might have made some reference to our past lives or contacted old friends.'

'Has anyone threatened you since you arrived in Scotland?'

'Not that we've been aware of. We kept our heads down, no photos ever, avoided tourists. We've pretty much just stayed at home since arriving. Adriana wouldn't listen, though. She wanted friends, a social life,' Isabella said.

'But it was a local who did this to Addie, right? It had nothing to do with my screwup?' Rob's eyes were streaming tears. The burden of the guilt he was carrying was too much, and the dam had burst. He'd broken the law, put his family in danger, made them move from everything they'd known and loved. Then his daughter had died, and either way it was still his fault. A hit from unscrupulous men with too much money and a thirst for vengeance, or a psychopath who'd been entranced by the beautiful, exotic Latina girl with the American accent and who'd drowned her as some part of his own sick fiction. Either way, Rob had brought them here and now Addie would never leave.

'It doesn't seem like a hit to me,' I said, not that I'd ever had a case with mob connections. 'Surely they'd want you to know Adriana's death had been revenge and that you'd been discovered. And killing Catriona too? Why stay and do that? It's risky and unnecessary.'

'I still want to know who her killer was,' Isabella said. 'Addie needs to be laid to rest.'

'I'll do my best,' I said. 'We obviously can't tell the police about your history. As soon as the details go into the national database, they're no longer secure. It would put all your lives at risk. The guys you gave evidence against, they have deep pockets, right? Deep enough that even from behind bars they could still pay people to do terrible things?'

Rob hung his head. 'Easily,' he said.

'Okay.' There was nothing else I could say. I had to go back and reassess everything I knew about Adriana's death to see what, if anything, I'd missed. For that, I needed time, peace and a clear head. 'I'll be camping, but not too far from Tobermory. No more than an hour's hike. You can call me and I'll come straight back. For now, the fewer people who think I'm still involved, the better.'

'Sure,' Rob said. He stood up and walked me to the door. 'Sadie, I'm sorry. We thought it was best not to tell you, to just let you investigate and see where it led.'

'I get it,' I said.

He shut the door softly. I was worried about him – about all of them. In the midst of all that concern I didn't think to take care of myself. The simple act of checking I wasn't being watched or followed didn't even occur to me. That's how I failed to notice the set of eyes marking my route out of town. As I began my hike, I didn't once think that someone might be watching me go.

Chapter Twenty-Nine

I took the south westerly road out of Tobermory and headed for the hills. As the houses tailed off, I kept my head down and aimed my feet in the direction of the Tobermory Campsite. There was nothing wrong with it. In fact it boasted hot showers and flushing toilets, facilities I knew I'd be missing twelve hours from now. When I reached it, with a single longing look down its gravel track, I kept going. Early afternoon and the day wasn't going to get hotter than this. Cloud cover was filtering the weak sun, but it was dry and forecast to remain so for a few days. The roadside was brown grass but further back from the tarmac to the north was dense forest. I kept walking.

An hour later, maintaining a steady pace, I reached the tip of Loch Peallach. There I veered off the road, following a small stream up beyond the tree line, over a barbed wire fence and into the woodland. From there I was hiking with only my compass to guide me, but a little way in I reached a clearing that suited my purposes.

Constructing a circle of large stones, I made a fire pit then went off to collect wood. With running water from the stream and enough space to pitch my tent, it was all I could have asked. The low land and tree cover meant that the smoke wouldn't give my position away easily. Even so, I was planning on keeping it small and only burning for long enough to heat food and water.

Setting up camp cost me a total of two hours, but I realised as I worked that it was the first time I'd felt properly safe since finding the seaweed crown beneath my pillow. Even out in the open, there was something reassuring about the woods. Here, the worst thing I was likely to encounter was the odd adder. The sun was due to set at half past six which gave me a final hour of daylight for cooking. I threw some sausages into a pan with a chopped onion and powdered gravy, realising just how ravenous I was. Taking the pilfered library book from the ruck-sack, I settled with my back against a large tree to pass the time until the food was ready.

I flicked through the book from the beginning, not sure what I was looking for. The author had painstakingly researched the history of the island which, given the stone circles, the Viking invasion, and the various kingdoms that had laid claim to it over the years, made it a substantial work. Myths and legends was covered a little over halfway through, and I was amazed at the size of the chapter. Tin plate on my lap, steaming black coffee in my mug, I began to read.

Mackinnon's Cave came up early on. I'd read up on its history whilst looking for places teenagers might be drawn to, but missed the mythical aspects. Deep inside the cave, a large flat stone known as Fingal's Table was supposed to have been used as an altar. Another legend had it that a piper had entered the cave with a band of explorers to establish the depth of the cavity. A witch, enraged by their entry into the hallowed cave, had slain the explorers but allowed the piper to live so long as he did not cease playing until he reached the light of the rising sun outside. He accepted the challenge and began his return to the cave entrance, but became exhausted and ran out of breath. As he ceased to play, the witch attacked. His broken body was later found at the cave mouth.

Mull had been something of a Mecca for witches over the ages, spawning not just a single legend but endless tales, many mentioning not a single sorceress but a race of them living for century upon century on the isle.

Stomach full, wood smoke heavy in my head, a muddle of information fogged my thoughts – from Rob Clark's revelations to Catriona Vass's memorial service. My eyes began to close and I didn't fight it. The tree's broad trunk was comfortable enough and the earth was warm beneath me. A gentle breeze shushed away my attempts to remain awake, and the book fell shut in my lap.

There was an insect on my face when I awoke and I brushed at its many legs, the book falling off my lap as I groped blindly in the dark with my other hand. The campfire had long since burned through its fuel and left nothing more than hot ashes and a wisp of smoke. Shoulders aching, I stretched, ready to climb into my tent and give in to the night. Then a thump-thump-thump-thump echoed through the woods. I stood still, one hand out holding a tree to orient myself, turning my head left and right to catch the sound again.

Bang-bang-bang-bang.

Initially it seemed directionless, a pinball bouncing between the trees, but if I turned ninety degrees there was a definite increase in the volume. Leaving camp wasn't the cleverest idea but the sound felt close enough that I'd be able to locate the source fairly quickly. I could identify the trailing off of each beat's vibration, and tell when it was being hit harder or softer. It wasn't so far away that it was just senseless noise.

I waited until the rhythm came again, faster this time and

more insistent. It wasn't mechanical in nature – there was nothing about it that said engine or machinery. This was human-made noise, a drumming. If someone wanted me to reveal myself then they'd been clever about it. I certainly wasn't going to crawl into my tent with someone out there in the forest.

Sickened by my careless lack of foresight, I realised I hadn't downloaded the map of the area in advance, so there was going to be no pinpointing my position on GPS. Still, that was what compasses were for. Torch in hand, grey beanie hat covering my hair, black gloves and dark clothes on, the last thing I did was kick earth over the remnants of the fire before setting off to discover the source of the noise, making first for the road then the northernmost point of Loch Peallach.

I stopped whenever the sound came. It was deceptive, some-times muted, sometimes sounding nearby, depending on the thickness of the trees around me. A bright half moon made my progress easier, lighting the way as I passed along the edge of the tree line, a wire fence a metre away, then scrubland to the road. I checked in each direction, the bear spray a comfortable presence in my jacket pocket. I'd brought my mobile in case I suddenly got a signal or needed to take photos, too, but other than that, I was woefully unarmed. This was what I was good at though. Not diplomacy – I hadn't made myself popular in Tobermory – but hiking, tracking, hunting were things I knew.

Keeping low as I moved onto open ground, I waited for the noise to repeat. When it hit me again it was lighter and more musical. I headed for the edge of the loch, realising I'd misjudged the sound's proximity badly. The flat water was acting like a speaker. The sound was hitting it and travelling across, losing no volume. What I'd thought was a noise from just beyond the edge of my section of forest was originating from the other side of the loch completely. How far away was anyone's guess. I knew from the maps that the hill to the south was Meall

Doire nan Damh, and before that was more woodland. There was nothing to be done but walk.

I crossed the road at a sprint and ran round the head of the loch where I was still exposed, stopping only once inside the tree line again. The water was silent blackness. I checked my compass again. I'd moved south-south-east from my encampment.

When the sound next came, it was accompanied by a human cry. A woman's voice, not a scream but a calling. Wordless and guttural. My ears caught the direction better without the water between me and the source, so I set off more purposefully and the land began a slow ascent. That made sense. The sound would travel down the hillside and across the loch. I'd been hearing what amounted to an echo of it on the other side.

With a hefty dose of regret, I pocketed my torch; the slash of light through the dark would alert anyone that I was coming. Under the dense canopy the moon was of limited use to me. I moved through the darkness awkwardly, hoping not to disturb the forest's many creatures or trip over a log. The result was a forward shuffle, reaching for trees, finding clear footings with the tips of my toes. Twice I began to fall, only stopping myself by grabbing branches. The next cry that echoed through the woodland was feral. No drumbeat now. The night was alive, above me uphill on a clear plateau.

'Come!' The call so clear I jolted into stillness, certain I'd been seen.

'Home!' another voice shouted.

'Live!' This was a younger voice, higher pitched.

'In!'

'Us!' The triumphant ending, and now the drum began again but fast, a racing pulse.

I ducked and edged forward, my heart thumping to match the beat, just as loud to my ears.

There was no central fire, no dancing, none of the clichés my brain had told me to expect. This was not a site with standing stones or an ancient altar. It was simply an area where no trees grew within the forest, with a single pathway out of it that I could identify, the opposite side from my hiding place.

The women were naked but covered with a red-brown sticky clay-like substance. Even their faces and hair had been masked with the mineral. I counted nine of them in total, their slim waists and firm bodies providing the best evidence of their relative youth. I raised my head, risking a better look at what they were doing. Each female brought a dead creature to the centre of the clearing, knelt down and began to dig with their bare hands. At that, an older woman, grey hair not entirely covered by the clay, stepped forward with a hollow rock in her hand that must have contained a flammable oil. The effect of the flames was mesmerising.

'Catriona, sister, you will live in each of us and in the spirit of every creature on this island. Nothing has been taken from us, nothing is lost to us, nothing is in the past, nothing is forever.'

The girls dug frantically. When the holes were large enough, each deposited their dead beast into the earth. The woman walked to each small grave and tipped a few drops of the burning oil inside. They sat back, lifting their faces to the sky, smoke drifting over them.

I looked from one girl to the next, trying to identify their features, but the darkness, smoke and clay conspired to mask them, and I couldn't risk raising my head above the foliage. Charred fur wafted on the breeze and I turned my face away from the stench.

That was the only warning I had. Not long enough to act. I couldn't have moved, run or avoided the blow, no matter how fast I'd reacted. By the time my eyes registered the figure behind me, he was already swinging the branch with a combination of force and precision that closed me down in a fraction of a second.

Within the slow-motion horror of realising what was coming, I had time to think, in this order: that I would not survive the night, that no one knew where to look for my body, and that I would never return the library book I'd taken earlier that day.

I was only partially correct.

Chapter Thirty

Swaying, a floating sensation, jolting, dropping. Then I landed, my buttocks hitting something hard and rough, my back following suit. Inside my skull an orchestra was tuning up, discordant and too loud. Pain throbbed in time with the noise. Breathing was hard and I tried to raise a hand to find the cause, but inexplicably my arms were stuck behind my back.

With that, I was fully awake, my memory an express train rushing into the station, showing me those final blurry seconds as the branch swung hard, my temple its target. The aim was good. I gasped, froze, took smaller breaths to get air as I fought with the binding around my wrists, sliding to my right, and finding nothing there to grasp, slipping until I used my legs to stop the fall.

Pitch black. No sound except my own panic. Nothing made sense. I forced a shutdown. It was all I could do. Stay still, calm down, figure out where I was and what was happening, reset. Even in the darkness, I closed my eyes, stopped fighting my windpipe, breathed thin relaxed breaths through my nose. I knew I was in trouble. Probably the worst trouble of my life. I also knew that panicking wasn't going to get me out of it.

Moving my legs gently, I got my bearings. I was on a cylinder, one leg either side, high enough up that neither foot could touch the ground. Hands tied behind my back, I reached out and felt for the detail in the texture around me, the answer dawning – too slow – as the bark scraped my fingertips. I clenched my core for stability, my ankles wrapped beneath the bough on which I'd been placed and opened my eyes once more.

This time my eyes began to adjust to the low light. In spite of the thick canopy and my aching skull, I could see that the ground was maybe seven feet below the branch. Turning my neck to scope out my surroundings, I registered the bristling against my skin.

Rope.

Loose enough not to cut off my airways completely but tight enough to send me into a new round of shock. I had to get it off my head. No way I was going to manage that with my hands behind my back, so I'd have to get my arms under myself and bring them back up the front. Only, if I misjudged that and slipped sideways . . .

'You'll hang,' a man said from below me. He walked out from the base of the tree where he'd obviously been waiting for me to regain consciousness. 'If you f-f-fall off the branch, the rope isn't long enough to get you to the floor.' It took only that many words for me to recognise his voice. Rhys Stewart, also known as Skittles, was standing below me and holding my life in his hands. 'Are you listening?' He gave a tug on the rope he was holding and as one my wrists were pulled to the side, taking me with them.

Gripping with my thighs as hard as I could, I fought to stay on the branch. The noose around my neck would be tied to the branch in front of me, of course. A second rope went from my hands down to Skittles so he could play with me then pull me from the branch to my death. I was breathing too fast. It was impossible to form coherent words as I tried to second-guess my would-be killer. No cave for me, then, unless this was simply the start of what he had planned.

'S-s-say something!' he raged, tugging again, harder this time.

A war of two different kinds of panic was being waged within me. The panic of knowing what would happen if I said the wrong thing, and the certainty that if I continued to say nothing he was going to lose his temper and murder me anyway.

'What do you want me to say?' I asked.

'I want you to say sorry!' he yelled. 'You came into my house. I never said you could come into my house!'

His agitation was going to end me, punctuating his words with little tugs on the rope.

'You're right,' I said softly. 'Rhys, I'm sorry. When I got to the shop the door was open, and I got locked in after the girls ran out.'

'But you hid,' he ranted. 'You sneaked around. You went down my stairs.'

I leaned my body forward onto the branch trying to stabilise my position as he began pacing to and fro. Screaming was only going to invite him to silence me. The drumbeats and chants of the women and girls had ceased now, and I had no idea how far he had dragged me, nor how long I'd been unconscious.

'You had no r-right,' he said, his voice quieter. He put one foot up on the lowest branch and took a step up in my direction.

His movement made me wonder how he'd got me into the tree in the first place, but the boughs wound round the tree forming a natural staircase. Even so, he was strong. Not that tall, but stocky, and judging by the lack of give in the rope around my wrists, he also knew how to tie a knot. That didn't bode well for my chances of slipping the hangman's noose.

'I was scared,' I told him truthfully. 'I was scared when I got stuck in the shop. I didn't know you and I wasn't sure what would happen if I admitted I was in there. That doesn't make what I did okay.'

'Why did you go into the cellar?' he demanded.

He was another branch closer now, and the rope between him and my wrists was slackening.

'The only reason I went into the cellar was to see if there was a back door. All I wanted was to get out. Please, Rhys, if you'll let me down I'll tell you everything that happened. I wasn't trying to get you into any trouble. It was a misunderstanding.'

'Do you know what you did?' he cried.

One more step up. He disappeared briefly around the back of the tree trunk and emerged the other side. His head was level with my thigh and I wasn't sure if I should meet his eyes or not. It seemed safest to keep staring directly down at the forest floor. My breath was hot and sour, and the rope around my neck was scratching my skin raw. The little calm I'd managed to gather was evaporating into the night air.

'I called the police. Please understand, when I saw the bones I just freaked out. I'm sure there's a good explanation. I didn't accuse you of anything at all.'

'You think I killed those girls,' Skittles said, clambering onto one final branch to bring us face to face. 'Don't you?'

His voice was venomous. At that moment, I didn't want to know. The details of their pain and terror were too much for me, balanced there on that branch, gripping on for dear life, stripping the skin from my wrists as I tried to free my hands.

'I know what the girls in town think of me. They giggle and point.'

'Please . . . please don't hurt me.'

There was a pain in my chest that felt like a trowel digging into earth, cold and insistent.

232

'Those girls were cruel,' he continued. 'They looked at me like I was nothing.'

'Teenagers don't understand how much they hurt people,' I said. 'They can be mean because they don't think about consequences. If they knew how much pain they were causing you—'

'I'm glad they're dead!' He shouted the last word, reached out to grab my face, squeezing my cheeks hard and pulling me towards him.

I fought to stay back, but my legs were running out of the energy to keep me still, and I rolled to the side to rest against him, my shoulder against his chest, my face no more than an inch from his.

'Do you think they were scared?' he asked.

'Of course,' I said.

'Are you scared?'

My sob hit the air, childlike, desperate.

'You should be,' he said. 'All the pretty girls together.'

'You don't have to do this,' I said. 'I'm so sorry.'

He squeezed harder, and I tasted blood as my teeth cut into my cheeks.

'You took my dad from me.' He was crying too, our tears running together down our cheeks, his nose streaming onto my chin, his breath in my mouth. 'I need him.'

My head was fuzzy, oxygen depleted, muscles quivering. He wasn't making sense any more.

'What?' was all I could respond with.

'My daddy!' he yelled. 'They took him away. You told them and they came and took him away.'

He was shaking me as he shouted, my legs jelly, no grip left. I slid left and right across the branch, no more resistance than a rag doll.

'I don't understand,' I told him.

233

'I wasn't h-hurting anyone, and because of you they took him away.'

My head finally processed what he was saying.

'The skeleton . . .' I rasped, '. . . was your father?'

'He l-loved me!' he screeched.

He slapped me hard and as my head flew towards the tree trunk, I caught the flaxen ivory glint of moonlight on his teeth as he grinned.

Clenching my stomach muscles, I tensed to stop myself falling, kicking my heels against the tree and pushing back towards him, cracking my forehead against his, forcing my own eyes to stay open so I could aim my blow directly between his.

Skittles reeled backwards, my bound wrists flying out with him, his end of the rope bound around his hand. I fell against his body as he clutched branches to stop his own fall.

'Bitch!' he screamed. 'You fucking bitch!' No stuttering now.

There was no other way down from that tree branch than by falling. That had always been his plan. I had time to hope that my body weight would be enough to snap my neck with a single clean break. I didn't want him climbing down to hang off my legs as I struggled and kicked, fighting for breath. Didn't want him watching me during the minutes it might take for me to fade.

I spat in his face as he braced to pull the rope, staring him down. If I was going to die then he could see the look on my face as I went, and it could haunt him for the rest of his days. Part of me hadn't really accepted he would do it. The reality of our own deaths is almost impossible to comprehend.

Then the wrench came, wrists first, furthest shoulder taking the brunt of the force, my neck whipping in the other direction, tumbling to one side, legs scraping rough bark even through my jeans, tearing, catching. Not enough to stop me. Or save me.

I tipped beyond the point of return, Skittles letting go of the rope as I flew past him. My ankles left the tree branch last, still trying to grip together, proving weak and useless as they parted.

The jolt as the noose fastened was the last thing I knew, and my legs were flying up in front of me as if on a swing. I heard screaming as the light faded. And so much pain, such terrible agony, that I was glad to go.

Chapter Thirty-One

I fell a second time, aware of it only as I hit the ground. There were raised voices above my head, one man and one woman. The rope was tight around my neck but there was a whistle of air getting into my lungs. And I was blind. With the world sluggish around me, I laid still waiting for whatever was going to happen next. Terror had turned to resignation. My hands remained bound, my legs were useless, and my tongue was a swollen mass protruding from my lips. I took what little air I could in through my nose. Unconsciousness, however brief, had been preferable.

A cool hand landed on my forehead, holding me still as the rope around my neck loosened.

'You're okay,' a woman said. 'Just lie still.'

As if I had any choice.

'She deserved it!' Skittles shouted.

'You go home now,' the woman said. 'I'll look after her.'

'She should have died,' Skittles replied.

'You're upset,' the woman said. The ropes at my wrist were tugged then suddenly my arms were free. Still I didn't try to move. 'I understand, but this isn't the way to deal with your grief. Your father wouldn't have wanted you in a prison cell for the rest of your life.'

Skittles let out a furious scream, simultaneously stamping his feet just inches from my head.

The woman's hands were gone from me. If I'd had the strength remaining I'd have been scared again, but I had nothing left. Absolutely nothing. I turned my face into the leaves and waited for the blow.

'Touch her again, and I'll be the one going to the police. Do as you're told. Leave and let me tend to her. You should never have been here in the first place. It's not right, you watching.'

'I hate you,' Skittles said, but his voice was a whine not an objection.

'I'm sure you do, you've got cause. But I won't tell you to leave again. Don't make me cross.'

A pause. The rustle of feet, twigs snapping close to my head, moving further away. Movement by my head. Fingers feeling my neck gently.

'He's gone. I'm going to sit you up,' she said. Sliding one arm beneath my shoulders and taking hold of my hand, she pulled me into an upright position.

'I can't see,' I whispered, the words leaving a burning trail through my throat.

'There's been a lot of pressure on your neck causing your eyes to bulge and the blood vessels in them to burst,' she said. 'Give the swelling some time to go down. Can you walk?'

I concentrated on my legs. They were weak and wobbly, but nothing was broken. I nodded. Moving her arm to my waist, she brought my body close to hers, and we got off the ground together. That one act, the sheer effort of getting up, exhausted me. I allowed my head to fall onto her shoulder.

'Who are you?' I asked.

'A friend. For now, just worry about putting one foot in front of the other.'

'Dizzy,' I muttered.

'Aye, you will be. We need to walk to my place. I can take proper care of you there.'

'Police . . . ambulance,' I said, the effort to form full sentences too much.

'Can't do that, I'm afraid. We need to talk first. I'd like to explain why my son did what he did to you.'

Summoning what little residual strength I had, I lifted my head, pushed her away from me, and took a stumbling step backwards.

'Your son?'

She put a hand on my shoulder. 'It's complicated. Let me help you.'

I pulled away again. 'Call the police.'

'I won't do that to him. I'm already responsible for the state he's in.'

I reached out my hands, feeling for a nearby tree to lean against while I figured out what to do. Skittles might not be an immediate threat, but the woman supposedly helping me could have been anyone. I wanted a doctor, painkillers, a comfortable bed, someone to tell me why my eyes had stopped working. For the police to come and take a statement, to arrest Skittles and lock him up where he could never get near me again.

Fumbling through my pockets, I hunted for my cell phone.

'I've got it,' the woman said. 'That and the spray you had in there.'

I held out my hand in the direction of her voice.

'I'm sorry,' she said. 'I can't give you your phone.'

I wanted to scream at her. To grab her and shake her, to show her how it felt to be truly terrified. Instead I began to cry, and hated myself for it.

'Sadie,' she said. 'It is Sadie, right? I've heard enough people talking about you. I jumped into the branches of that tree, and I cut the rope with the knife I always carry. I stopped Rhys from hurting you, and I will keep you safe, I promise. I know you're still scared but I'm good at healing people. I just want a chance to talk. If tomorrow you decide you still need to go to the police then I won't – I can't – stop you. You have nothing to fear from me. Quite the opposite.'

She took a firm hold of my right hand and placed the can of bear spray into it.

'Why?' I whispered.

'I'm going to guide you back to my house. Now you're armed. If you feel scared or threatened, you can use that. The alternative is that I guide you to the roadside and you wait out the night until a passing car picks you up in the morning. If that's what you want, that's what I'll do.'

I considered it. This woman owed me nothing, but she had undoubtedly already saved my life. And Skittles had done what she'd told him. If I spent the night at the side of the road waiting for help, there was no guarantee I wouldn't find myself in more trouble.

'Okay,' I whispered, my throat a hard, throbbing mess. I needed water and rest.

'Good,' she said. 'My name's Hilda. Put your arm over my shoulder so I can guide you. It'll take about fifteen minutes as you can't see. Will you manage?'

I nodded again and gave myself up to her. There was nothing else to do. I had no idea which direction we were walking or what ground we were covering. She took me without incident, no trips or crashes, only the odd spiderweb brushing my face, and I was beyond caring about that. There wasn't a part of me that didn't hurt, nothing above my chest that wasn't swollen. Before my eyes a grey–black swimming mass was forming, as

239

if I'd spent too long staring at noise on a TV screen, but it was an improvement on the complete darkness from when I'd first fallen. A bruise at the back of my neck made its presence felt whenever I tried moving my head left or right. I didn't dare touch the egg on my skull where Skittles had knocked me out with the branch.

And now what? His mother was going to try to persuade me that he was some misunderstood vulnerable man who really meant me no harm.

'A few steps here,' she said. 'Go slow.'

There was the metal jangle of keys and the sound of a protesting lock, but then a door squeaked and I could smell bread, herbs, spices and soap. She led me in and sat me down on a low chair. The comfort was immediate. It wasn't luxurious, but just the knowledge that I was inside, somewhere with walls and a door between me and the world, was enough. I leaned back and kept my eyes shut.

A match was struck. I smelled the sulphur and heard the crackle as the flame took to the kindling. The gentle warmth was good.

'I'm going to give you something to drink,' she said. 'It's just a tea but I'll sweeten it with honey. It'll soothe your throat. You'll be needing some ice, too.'

I could hear her working away – pots, doors, mixing, movement. She handed me two linen pouches with crushed ice inside, and I put one on the back of my neck and the other on the top of my head. The tea she gave me was bittersweet, and I grimaced as I tasted it, but the effect on my throat was immediate. The soreness began to abate and a numbness took over, but that was welcome. It occurred to me that I could have been drinking poison, but there didn't seem to be any point to that. If she planned to kill me, why not just leave Skittles to it the first time?

'I'm going to apply a salve to your neck,' she said as I continued drinking. 'The skin's red and you're going to have some bad bruising, but this will get it healing faster. Are you allergic to lanolin?'

'No,' I said. 'Thank you.'

She patted my hand. Finishing the tea, I sat back and let her layer a cream onto my skin where the rope had burned it. Then she took off my shoes and socks, put a blanket over me and lit some candles around the place. With each one, I could see a small pool of blurred light erupt. My vision was returning.

'Suck some ice,' she said. I opened my mouth and she put one on my tongue. 'For the swelling.'

I dreaded to think how I looked. I'd seen hanging victims before, the whites of their eyes red with haemorrhaging, and bulging, tongue protruding, blackened marks around their neck, fingernails broken from scratching at their own throat. I'd been saved most of that by the speed at which Hilda had cut me down, but I could feel it all, the consequences of my near miss.

The woman hummed as she moved around the house, tidying up and cleaning. She was burning applewood. I could smell the fruit in the smoke.

'You were with the girls?' I asked, enunciating each word slowly, knowing my voice was unclear.

Hilda stopped whatever she was doing and appeared at my side, pulling up a small stool to sit in front of the fire with me.

'I was,' she said. 'We were commemorating Catriona.'

'Why kill all those animals?' I asked.

'Oh,' she gasped. 'Oh no, that's not what you were seeing. That was all carrion, already dead. Found at the roadside, or in hunters' traps. We return their bodies to the earth to be part of the process of fertility and rebirth.'

I picked up another piece of ice from the bowl she'd left on my lap and sucked it as I thought about it.

'Did your son kill Catriona?' I asked. 'And Adriana?'

Hilda leaned forward and added more logs to the fire. Now I could make out her dim outline against the flickering light.

'If I believed he'd done that, I'd take matters into my own hands,' she said. I wanted to ask her what that meant, but it was getting warmer now, and I was so tired. The tea she had given me was strong and the herbs it contained were heady.

'Tried to kill me,' I said, unsure as to whether or not she could understand my words, or if I was simply imagining myself saying that to her.

'I know, but there was a trigger for that. Catriona and Adriana, hurtful though they could be, were never really a threat to him and Rhys knew it. He's had a hard life, Sadie. I failed him. That's what he thinks. I'm sure it's what his father always told him.'

'How?' I asked.

'By rejecting what the traditional role of a woman is here and in most places in the world. I had a meeting of bodies with Rhys's father. No relationship, no marriage. Just a physical arrangement from time to time. When I fell pregnant, he thought I should marry him. I didn't. Then when I had the baby, everyone assumed I would move into town for us to raise him together. I didn't do that either.'

'Why not?' I asked.

My head was a lead weight, and I was losing the fight to stay awake.

'Because women don't always have to be what we're told to be. Becoming a mother does not make us maternal. Having a child doesn't mean we must comply with the standards men unilaterally impose on us. The women of my family have lived their own way for hundreds of years. The boy had a father, with a house and extended family around him. They had a shop, a trade, routines. I wanted none of it. And why should I?

242

Men get to spread their seed and run away. Why do women never feel entitled to make the same decision?'

That question lingered there in my head as I disappeared into sleep, unable to fight it any longer. Hilda was right. My sister's fiancé had turned tail and run without a second thought when Becca had found out she was pregnant. We'd all been disgusted by his choice and his behaviour, but not shocked, not astounded by it. That, occasionally, was simply how men behaved. A woman following the same course would be judged not just by different standards, but by an almost medieval type of damnation.

Here, the Mull Witches had lived by their own rules. Generations of women, living in the middle of nowhere, burying the rotting flesh of animals in the ground. Rejecting societal norms. Refusing to comply.

Women throughout history had been called witches for so much less than that.

Chapter Thirty-Two

The sun was already cruising over the treetops when I awoke. Hilda had lifted my feet onto a stool and added a further blanket, as well as a slim pillow to cushion my head. The length of the sleep, though, I put down to the herbal draught she'd given me. Moving slowly, conscious that at some point my injuries were going to make themselves felt, I set my feet on the floor and leaned forward. Apart from some slight reddening around my wrists, everything below my neck was remarkably okay.

Looking around in search of a mirror, it occurred to me that my vision had returned to normal. It was lucky the rope hadn't been around my neck for longer. If Hilda had been even just a few seconds slower in cutting me down, the damage to my brain and eyes from the pressure and lack of oxygen would have been overwhelming, if I'd survived at all.

My surroundings were comfortable but basic. The fire was obviously the main source of heat and light. There was nothing electrical in sight. The wooden cabin was tidy, with clean windows and a sturdy front door, and the entire far wall was covered in shelves, each one packed with bottles and pots, all carefully labelled, nothing ramshackle about it. A freestanding fireplace, open front and back, indicated a bedroom on the other side. As I leaned down to catch a glimpse, I became aware of the pain in my neck. I might have been lucky, but I certainly hadn't escaped without damage.

Time to attempt to stand. I gripped the chair back and took my time, but I was steady enough as I got up. Running my hands through my hair, I found the bump and pressed it gingerly. Sore and tender, but with no open wound. Hilda had, as promised, taken remarkably good care of me.

'Hello?' I called. 'Hilda?' No reply. My voice was stronger, too. I wandered over to the shelves of bottles and picked up one after another. Spices I'd heard of, herbs I hadn't, leaves, bark, moss, powders.

'Tea?' she asked, appearing from the back room.

'Is it going to put me back to sleep?'

'You sound strong enough today that I'd say it wasn't necessary. Do you have any pain?'

'A little in my neck and throat. I was expecting worse.'

'Let me see,' she said, putting down some logs by the fire and washing her hands in an enormous sink. I waited until she was ready then allowed her to feel around my neck with gentle fingertips. 'Not bad,' she said. 'You heal fast. Soft food only for a while though. I'll make porridge.'

Watching her was fascinating. She had a cold storeroom dug down a couple of feet into the earth, and there was a huge bucket of ice in there which obviously never melted. Hilda was proficiently self-reliant, but it looked time-consuming and hard. As she began boiling milk and pouring oats, I went to check the views. The cabin was in the upper woodland. I could see a loch in the distance and hear the bleat of a goat nearby.

'I know who you are,' I said, turning faster than I should have and straining my stiff neck.

'Do you indeed?' she smiled.

'You slapped Father Christophe after Catriona's memorial service.'

'Aye, well, he deserved that and more. "Cast out and speak out against those who practise atheism and worse." He'd like every female on the island back in long skirts and in their place at the kitchen sink, that one. Sees the devil in those of us who reject his ways.' Hilda put a large, heavy pan over a low flame and stirred gently. 'Did you not feel his power over the towns-folk during that service?'

'I did,' I said. 'And I disagreed with what he said, but taking your palm to the local priest isn't going to help.'

'You think it's just words? That there's no impact from his sermons and his judgements? You don't strike me as that naive.'

I noticed my cell phone on the windowsill and reached my hand out to take it.

'Don't bother. Your battery's all used up,' she said without turning round.

'Damn, do you have a . . .'

I realised the utter stupidity of what I'd been about to say halfway through the sentence. This woman's existence was a rejection of chargers, the internet, media, and 24-hour communication.

Hilda heaped steaming portions of porridge into a bowl. 'Come and sit with me.' Patting the chair next to her, she blew softly to cool the breakfast. I was reminded of my own mother doing the same for my sister when we were young and felt a rush of regret that I wasn't at home with them where I was needed, keeping my promises, waiting for the baby to arrive. Soon, I promised myself.

I took a seat, then the bowl, and she handed me honey to sweeten the dish.

'Father Christophe knows something about both Adriana and Catriona,' I said, nibbling a little porridge from the end of the spoon, wondering just how bruised my throat was internally.

246

'I'm not sure what Adriana's relationship with him was like,' Hilda said. 'But Catriona wasn't a fan of the priest. I'm fairly confident that any confessions she made would have been limited to taking God's name in vain and having impure thoughts, maybe stealing the odd dram of whisky. He'll have heard rumours though. People love to gossip to priests. I suppose it feels both a little wicked and a little cleansing, all at once. That's quite the cocktail.'

'Rumours about what? The sort of thing I saw last night?'

'What is it you thought you saw?' she asked.

'Some sort of ceremony, I guess, all young women. It looked kind of . . .'

'Don't mince your words. I cut you down from the business end of a rope last night. We can be honest with each other.'

'I was going to say pagan,' I said. 'This porridge is good.'

'Pagan is a fair description,' Hilda replied. 'But it sounds more dramatic than it really is. Paganism is about believing in nature, in the circle of life and the equal importance of everything around us – the trees, rocks, weather and dirt. Usually also a rejection of mainstream religions, but not exclusively.'

'Father Christophe thinks it's something worse than that,' I said.

'He sees the devil where we see mother nature. He hears stories of young women dancing naked under the moon and imagines orgies and depravity. I know he asked Catriona for the details on more than one occasion and she refused to tell him what he wanted to hear.'

I put my spoon down, resting my throat a moment.

'Did you know Adriana?'

'I did, but not well. She'd only just begun attending our meetings. It was Catriona who first suggested that she should come along. Someone in the group has to vouch for new-comers.'

'So Catriona and Adriana were friends? I got the impression that Catriona was rather jealous of Addie when she first arrived.'

Hilda shrugged. 'Teenage girls. Aren't they best defined by their inconsistency and changeability?'

I took another spoonful of porridge but found myself full. Setting the bowl down on the hearth, I asked the question I'd been building up to.

'Last night your son must have been watching your ceremony. I'm guessing that's how he found me. Are you not concerned that he was hiding in the bushes with all those girls naked, even given the clay or whatever it was on their bodies?'

'Ask the question you really want to ask and be done with it,' Hilda said.

'All right. Given everything – his interest in watching those young women, his violence towards me, his dislike of Catriona and Adriana – how can you be so sure he didn't kill them?'

She picked up my bowl and carried it to the sink with her own.

'During the period Adriana was killed, Rhys was with me. Two days and nights. I was ill and he was caring for me. Do you think Adriana, that beautiful girl, would have gone anywhere with my son?'

That was a fair point, and one I'd already been asking myself. Adriana's body had shown no sign of being manhandled before her drowning, so how could Skittles have persuaded her into a car and driven her all the way to Mackinnon's Cave?

'I know what he is,' Hilda continued. 'He's never been formally diagnosed – his father was too proud to allow it – but he's odd. Childlike, emotionally speaking. Prone to outbursts and temper tantrums. He reached a point where he seemed not to develop further emotionally. He was utterly dependent on his father, not just for the day-to-day, but to guide him, support him. Personally I think he did Rhys a disfavour, wrapping him up, shielding him. He was never prepared for life in such a harsh world. That's why having his father's bones removed from the cellar was so painful for him.'

'What were his father's remains doing there in the first place?'

'A few months after the burial, which was a little over four years ago now, police found the grave disturbed. The coffin was empty. Harris Eggo called me – they had their suspicions about Rhys. I asked them to leave it alone. If it was Rhys that had done it, then he was simply fulfilling a need. If it was anyone else, I didn't want Rhys upset by the idea that his father had gone missing. Eggo and I agreed that no one else needed to know. No official police report was ever filed, no investigation took place. Rhys had been in a very dark place, but he seemed calmer after that. He's not really dangerous.'

'That's not true. He tried to kill me,' I reminded her. 'He'd have succeeded if you hadn't been there.'

'You took away the only bit of comfort he has in this world. Knowing his father was still in that building with him kept him able to function. Harris Eggo and I always suspected Rhys was keeping the bones there, so it came as no surprise when you reported it. Rhys was bailed while Eggo investigates. It's not as if he wants to leave the island. I'm told the bones are being checked to make sure they belong to his father, but he had a notable leg fracture a couple of years before his death so that won't take long.'

'It's all just going to be brushed over, eh?'

Hilda shrugged gently. 'No good will be done by charging Rhys with any offences. He didn't intend any harm. The only person who could have been upset when that grave was disturbed was Rhys himself. Harris Eggo agreed to stay quiet about it all when it first happened, so why make a song and dance now? This community looks after its own, Sadie, for better or worse. This is one of the better times.'

'If your son is so unstable that he's keeping his father's skeleton in his cellar, do you not think he needs professional help? He's clearly dangerous.'

'Dangerous to you, I accept, but then he also believes you want to put him in prison for those girls' deaths, a not unreasonable assumption given this conversation.'

'Doesn't it concern you that he was willing to kill me for that?'

'He's a child,' she said. 'Children stamp on insects and pull the legs off spiders. They're not thinking about pain, death or consequences. They're expressing their own selfish little emotion the only way that makes sense to them. Rhys is still grieving and feeling lost. He doesn't have the ability to express himself clearly, and certainly not to work through strong emotions and resolve psychological issues.'

'Then he needs some sort of supervision.'

'You may be right about that, and I'll talk to the people in the town who keep an eye on him for me. But it was a perfect storm, Sadie. The bones, the girls, everyone suspicious. He's not like this all the time. He just snapped. I promise you, I'll get him the assistance he needs. I couldn't live with myself if he hurt anyone else.'

'And you're a hundred percent certain he wasn't involved with Addie or Catriona?'

'I am. But tell me,' Hilda said, 'you found poor Catriona's body in the cave, am I right?' I nodded. 'I've heard something that has made me concerned, something that has its roots in our history. Was the body cut?'

I closed my eyes, barely strong enough to relive that scene.

'Yes,' I said. 'Her killer took her breast.'

'Before he killed her. It would have been her right breast, yes?'

I opened my eyes again to study Hilda's face.

'That's correct,' I replied.

She brought a cup of hot water over to me. I could smell the sprig of mint and lemon juice in it. Sitting down again, she looked deep into the embers of the fire.

'Have you heard about the Spanish galleon at the bottom of the harbour?' Hilda asked.

'Yes, the myth of the Spanish princess who came looking for her true love. It came up in relation to Adriana's body. Why?'

'The remainder of the legend is less well documented, having been confined to folklore rather than the more respected history books. The King of Spain was devastated by the loss of his beloved daughter and vowed revenge. He sent another ship to Mull. It landed secretly in the dead of night, and having heard that it was the witch who'd caused the galleon to sink, the King had given instructions to his men to ensure that the witch was punished by maiming every woman they could find on the island.'

'What did they do?' I asked.

'They took the right breast of every woman they found here,' she said. 'Just like Catriona's killer did to her.'

I followed Hilda's eyeline to the blinking embers and smoking ashes, the porridge suddenly hard to digest.

'Did they kill the witch?' I asked. It was a ridiculous question, but I wanted to know the end of the story.

'No,' Hilda said. 'She's supposed to have survived.'

'None of it makes any sense. Why revisit a myth from hundreds of years ago? Even if Catriona was involved in . . .'

'Witchcraft? You can say it. It's inaccurate, but the word isn't offensive to me.'

'If someone thought Catriona was involved in witchcraft it still doesn't explain why they would cut off her breast.'

'Particularly my own son, who in spite of all my failings does not perceive me or my practices to be evil. He didn't do it, but someone from this island did. Someone who knows our legends and our ways, even the most secret of them.'

'Someone knows the legend – but not many people, if this is ancient folklore, right?'

'Agreed. These tales used to be passed down through families as they sat together at the fireside. Nowadays it hardly seems that families spend any time together at all, or care about the past that delivered them here,' Hilda said.

'What do you know about Flora Kydd?' I asked.

'Another tragedy. It destroyed both her parents. The whole community, really.'

'The Kydd farm building still has symbols warding off witches.'

'Doesn't surprise me,' Hilda said. 'There's a lot of ignorance, to this day, about who and what we are.'

'What are you? If you know what people say, why keep doing this? Witchcraft isn't real, magic isn't real. What's the point?'

'How's the skin around your neck?' she asked.

It hadn't occurred to me to check. I did so then. It was practically healed.

'It's fine,' I said.

'Yes, the mixture of herbs and charcoal I put on it would have helped it heal faster than anything you'd have got from a chemist. It also contained natural painkillers from tree roots which I regularly put in salves and remedies. All manner of things we ignore in favour of tablets and surgery. But that's not why those girls come to me. They've lost their sense of who they are. They take photos of themselves and wait for other people to approve of them. They see worlds that are beyond their reach and become dissatisfied with their own. They're drowning in social media, which is as much myth and legend as any tale of witchcraft you'll hear. It's not real, but it is damaging. It hurts them. It undermines them. I bring them back to reality for a while. I make them understand that the world around them is a vibrant, living thing of which they're a part. They switch off their damned phones and they get their hands dirty. They communicate and share and are thankful for the planet that gives them life. This is all witchcraft has ever been. Women offering a hand to other women. Healing bruises from rough fathers and husbands. Making childbirth bearable. Making their losses tolerable. Men fear us because we speak the truth to one another.'

'Isn't it dangerous, making the girls believe in otherworldly power? I saw them trying to steal a blue apatite crystal from your son's store. That's not harmless fun. They could have ended up in real trouble.'

Hilda gave a small shake of her head.

'They shouldn't have done that. Apatite is credited with a great deal of power, not the least of which is increasing your psychic abilities, so legends say. Want to know if your lover is being true? This is your stone. And blue apatite has long since been said to assist with weight loss by suppressing your desire to eat. My theory is that a group of girls who constantly see modified images of skinny young girls and want to replicate that look thought the crystal was the fastest way to shed some pounds. It makes me feel sad.' Hilda sat back in her chair and contemplated the ceiling.

'Isn't it dangerous, getting them to put so much store in mysticism and old wives' tales?'

'It felt more dangerous to me to have them believe in nothing but makeup, song lyrics, selfies and boyfriends.'

'But now two girls are dead,' I said. 'With seaweed crowns in their hair and ground-up cat bone secreted in a boot.'

Hilda laughed. It was a sharp, outrageous bellow of laughter that made me jump.

'Ground-up cat bone, is it now? Was there a broomstick, too?'

'I don't understand,' I said, my eyes meandering involuntarily to the multitude of bottles on her shelves.

'What you see here is plants and minerals. Not the hocus pocus of films and books. We don't grind up bones,' she said, patting me on the knee. 'Did you think we could turn ourselves into bats?'

'The girls were dabbling in magic mushrooms. Is that something you encouraged?'

'It's better than alcohol, if you ask me. Fewer chemicals and additives. I didn't encourage them, exactly. I suppose I could have done a better job of discouraging.'

'Catriona is supposed to have given Lewis Eggo a potion that made him sick. Did you know about that?'

'I didn't, but I'm not entirely surprised. Put together the wrong herbs and spices and it'll turn the strongest of stomachs. But cat bone? Seems to me that someone was trying a little too hard to lay a path to our door.'

'You have enemies,' I said.

'We always have had,' Hilda agreed. 'Normally they stop at spitting on us and calling us names. Once every hundred years or so, someone comes intending to cleanse the world of us. Will you be able to find the culprit, Sadie Levesque? Is that why you were sent to us?'

'I don't know,' I told her honestly. 'But I'll do all I can to prevent more murders here. No one should die like that.'

'It's you I'm worried about,' Hilda said. 'You're chasing evil and expecting that you'll somehow recognise its face. That's rarely the way of it.'

'I'm chasing the evidence,' I said. 'But thank you for your

concern, and for saving me last night. I'm grateful you found me in time.'

'You'll return the favour,' she said. 'Or you'll do your best, at least. Sometimes no matter how hard we try, evil gets the better of us.'

Chapter Thirty-Three

Hilda walked me back to my tent, moving quietly through the trees, disturbing rabbits and deer from time to time. She trod with a lightness I hadn't mastered in all my years of hiking and exploring. It might have been my memory of the ritual the previous night, or perhaps the herbal mixture she'd given me still in my body, but her oneness with nature, her immersion in the natural world, seemed entirely believable here. She touched the trees with a fondness, brushed strands of spiders' webs from her face as if they were a gift, and kept a sweet smile on her face as if she were walking through the door of a beloved homestead. I admired and was intrigued by her. It wasn't easy to reject traditional notions of mother-hood, or to face the judgements such decisions brought with them. In many ways, leaving the island and settling elsewhere would have been easier, but then she'd have been giving up her child completely.

'You feel it too,' Hilda said, looking over her shoulder at the loch. 'I can see it in your face.'

I shrugged and breathed the chill October air, all pine needles, heather and peat.

'I like being outdoors if that's what you mean. The simplicity of it is addictive. You have to come to terms with the voice inside your head. It's a tough place to be if you don't like yourself though. You can't escape when it's just you and a mountain.'

Hilda stopped and took my hand. I let her take it, returning her long stare.

'Are you at peace with yourself, Sadie? Truly? Nothing left unsaid to those you love?'

My instinct was to pull my hand from hers, but she was a magnet and the force of her was too great to resist. Not that I felt any threat. It was that she seemed to see too much of me, as if I were walking naked with all the hidden secrets of my life tattooed across my skin. The moments of shame, those itchy humiliations that inflame with the slightest scratch to their surface, secret hopes and deeply buried desires.

'I am at peace,' I replied. 'As much as any flawed human can ever be.'

'So be it,' she nodded.

She hugged me as my tent came into view. The gesture, hard and swift, took me so much by surprise that I didn't have time to return it.

'We'll be seeing one another again soon,' she said, disappearing quietly, the twigs choosing not to crack beneath her feet, the dry leaves allowing her soft passage.

I'd fitted a spare battery to my cell phone and was about halfway to Tobermory when my phone began notifying me of the voicemails stacked on it. My mother first, wondering why it had been so long since she'd heard from me, telling me my sister was tired and experiencing Braxton Hicks contractions. I made a mental note to call them both that evening, allowing for the time difference between Scotland and Banff.

The second call was from PC Bathgate asking me to confirm my whereabouts. I deleted that one immediately. Bathgate had no right to know anything about me. My imagination conjured his face at the standing stones at Lochbuie, watching Catriona holding court, dancing, all eyes on her. To be fair, it had been hard not to notice Catriona. There was a wildness to her, a sexual confidence that set her apart from her group of friends. Small towns accentuated big personalities.

The final call was from Nate Carlisle.

'Sadie,' his voice wavered in and out, losing connection. I put the volume up. 'I'm coming back to Mull. Harris Eggo has asked me to speak at a town meeting. I wouldn't normally, but small island communities are disproportionately affected by murders, and Eggo thinks it'd be better to release limited facts rather than letting everyone keep speculating. I'm going to see both families first to explain my conclusions in the case to date. Hoping I'll see you at either the Clarks' or the hotel later. Call me.'

'Shit,' I chastised myself for not moving faster. My watch told me I'd already wasted half the day.

Picking up the pace, I headed directly for the Clarks'. Nate's cell phone was going straight to voicemail. I tried jogging, but the bruising to my throat and the lump on my head weren't going to let that happen. Outside Rob and Isabella's house, the shiny black car let me know I was late.

If I'd walked past a mirror, I wouldn't have gone in. If I'd thought about my unchanged clothes and the fact that I hadn't showered, I wouldn't have gone in. But my feet just kept going, hand on door handle with nothing but the briefest of knocks, dropping my backpack and kit in the hallway and going straight in.

'Hi, sorry I'm so late. Nate, I didn't get your—'

'*Madre de Dios*,' Isabella said, getting up from her chair and taking hold of Rob's arm.

258

'What the fuck?' Brandon said from his chair in the corner.

Nate strode towards me and turned my face towards the window. 'I need to get you to a hospital,' he said. 'Tell me what happened.'

'Uh, could I use your washroom?' Ducking out into the hallway without waiting for a reply, I knew I needed a mirror. What I saw in it wasn't pretty.

Neck mottled purple, red and black like a summer pudding, blood crusted into my hair, and several tiny blood vessels in my eyes having burst under pressure, I looked horrific. Little wonder the reactions to my appearance had been so extreme. I splashed water onto my face and gave my hands a proper clean with soap, running my fingertips through my hair to tidy it. An explanation was going to be required. Strange how I could look so badly injured when inside I already felt as if I was healing. Nate was waiting for me outside the door.

'I want you to see a doctor,' he said quietly. 'Right now.'

'It's all just bruising. Some swelling. Nothing permanent.'

'Really? Because it looks to me as if someone put a noose around your neck, and I've seen enough of those signs post-mortem to know. Only I don't understand who would've done that, or why. Or even if you did it yourself.'

'Oh come on, Nate, we haven't known each other very long but I don't think you believe I'd do that.'

'Then who did?'

'I'm going to tell you everything, but I really need to be part of whatever you're telling the Clarks.' Nate folded his arms and gave that look – scepticism mixed with annoyance driven by concern. 'You can check me out yourself. I'll see a doctor if you insist.'

'Do you need anything?' Isabella asked, appearing in the hallway.

'No, we're good to go,' I said, stepping around Nate and re-entering the lounge. 'Before Nate starts talking again, I owe you all an explanation. I was in the woods last night camping and I came across a . . .' I hadn't planned what I was going to say, and now that I was trying to put it into words it sounded both too sinister and too melodramatic to be real. '. . . a sort of meeting between some islanders, young women, performing a ceremony in Catriona's memory. I was attacked by someone else while I was watching it but I managed to escape. This looks worse than it is. One of the women found me and took care of me. There's nothing for any of you to be concerned about.'

'The ceremony was for Catriona?' Brandon asked. 'So the rumours are true? You saw it with your own eyes. She must have been one of them.'

'I'm sorry, one of what?' Isabella asked. 'I don't understand what either of you are talking about.'

'They're witches,' Brandon said. 'It's all any of the girls here can talk about. They go to the stones at night, do weird shit and put curses on people. I told you there was stuff going on here.' He aimed the last part at me, his tone furious and accusatory.

I sat down.

'It's really not witchcraft,' I said quietly. 'At least, not the way it's portrayed in horror movies and myths. I think it's meant to get young women back in touch with the world around them. The rumours have turned it into something it isn't intended to be.'

'How do you know so much about it?' Rob asked.

'The woman who saved me last night, Hilda, is sort of their mentor if you could call it that. She's really very gentle and genuine.'

'I have no idea what the relevance of this—' Rob began.

'She knew Adriana,' I cut him off. 'They met shortly before her disappearance, but it's another link between Catriona and Addie that we should be aware of as we try to figure out who killed them.'

'Sadie,' Nate said quietly. 'We should talk.'

'Is that how Catriona lured Addie out?' Brandon asked. 'Inviting her to go to some perverted ceremony together in the middle of the night? Did they brainwash my sister?'

'I'm sure that wasn't the case,' I reassured him. 'Hilda lives a simple life in a cabin in the woods north of Loch Peallach. She's no monster, Brandon.'

'Addie was raped with a shell, or have you forgotten that? Catriona sent her messages that led to her sneaking out at night and getting killed. Why are you defending her?' Rob asked.

'Because Catriona's dead too. Whatever involvement she had in Addie's death, they are now both the victims of a serial killer.'

'Mommy, why is everyone shouting?' Luna appeared in the doorway.

Her tiny mouth was wobbling with the effort of holding back tears. Isabella ran to her. My head swam with it all. Too many possibilities, so much pain and grief.

'Sadie!' I heard Nate shout, then he was rushing forward and the room tilted ninety degrees. My right knee hit something hard as arms grabbed me. The voices faded out and the last sound I heard was a girl crying. It seemed like a very long time until the world was normal again, and by then I was on the back seat of Nate's car and we were driving.

'Nate?' I said.

'Stay lying down. I'm getting you to the doctor.'

'Please don't. I'm fine. It was just all too much. Take me to the campsite?' I asked him.

'Here's what we're going to do,' he said, pulling up to a junction and giving a quick glance over his shoulder at where I lay. 'I'm going to check you out. If I have no clinical concerns, I'll agree not to take you to a hospital but you will have to stay at my hotel tonight – I checked in somewhere different.

It turns out you're not the only person out of favour here right now. You can rest before the town meeting tonight.'

I complied. Nate drove silently for a few more minutes then turned into a car park on the outskirts of town at The Turning Tide Bed & Breakfast. He checked in. I stood behind him staring at the floor, feeling guilty for being there, more to do with the looks the owner was giving us than my actual conscience. The room was spacious and comfortable, with an enormous bed and views over the fields beyond. Nate wasn't talking, but his thoughts were loud enough to fill the silence. He ordered me to sit on the bed then bent down and unlaced my hiking boots, before disappearing into the en suite from where the sound of water gushing into the bath was a blissful distraction.

He checked my eyes, pulse, breathing, felt my neck, looked in my mouth and ears.

'You need anti-inflammatories and some strong pain killers. An X-ray of your neck would be in order too. It'll be about a week before your tongue and throat recover.'

'Hilda gave me some sort of herbal drink last night. It definitely helped me sleep, and my throat really wasn't that sore this morning.'

'You didn't ask what you were being given – you just drank it? What were you thinking?'

'Well, she'd just saved my life, cut the noose that was around my neck, got rid of my attacker, and taken me to her home without further incident. By then I was feeling pretty trusting.'

'And the attacker was?'

I rubbed my temples. My head was throbbing and the thought of sleeping on a proper bed was too appealing for me to argue.

'Her son,' I told him.

'Sadie, if you know exactly who attacked you, we have to call it in. You were a minute from death. The person who did this to you—'

'Rhys Stewart, aka Skittles. I entered his premises pretty much illegally save for a technicality, hid in his basement, went through his stuff, found his father's bones and had them taken away, then also had him detained and questioned for an ancient offence that he was probably manipulated into by a flatmate.'

'None of that matters. If he attacked you, he could attack again.'

'I don't believe he will. He's a child in a man's body and I took the most precious thing in the world from him. It was his trigger. He's vulnerable and developmentally challenged, but he does what his mother tells him. The town knows what he is and isn't capable of, and they rally around him. I've hurt him enough already, not that I'm going to be writing him a letter of apology, but what he did to me was a reaction to the pain I'd caused him. Nothing more. And for the record, I don't think he killed Adriana, either.'

Nate put a gentle hand on my neck and ran his thumb along the raw red line the rope had burned into me.

'Stop taking risks,' he said quietly. 'I'd like a chance to have a conversation with you one day that isn't about death.'

I nodded, standing up so I could turn away and cover the blush creeping across my cheeks. As the bath filled, he made coffee and picked up the plate of sandwiches that had been delivered and left outside our door.

'Drink the coffee, eat as much as you can, then get in the bath,' he said, kicking off his own shoes and pulling a thick file from his bag.

'The staff here will think we're lovers,' I smiled, injecting more lightness than I felt as I sipped the coffee.

'Given the state of you, they're much more likely to think I'm an abusive partner holding you hostage.'

'Oh crap, I hadn't thought of that. Sorry.'

The hot coffee hurt my throat and I didn't care. Nate read as I ate and drank, looking up only as I entered the bathroom.

'Leave the door open an inch,' he said. 'I want to be able to get in without obstruction if you pass out again.'

I toyed with the idea of issuing a comedic flirtatious response but the words dried on my lips as I caught sight of myself in another mirror. If there was ever going to be a woman Nate wouldn't be attracted to, it had to be me right then. Second only to a corpse, given my injuries.

'I want you to stay alert until I'm sure there's no concussion. Explain exactly what happened last night from start to finish.'

As I soaked in the bath, I told him everything. He managed to let me tell it without commenting, but even with the distance between us I could still hear his occasional tuts and sighs.

'How did you know where to find the women?' he asked.

'I didn't. It was geography and physics. The sound they were making carried downhill and bounced over the loch which acted like a speaker. It was some distance from where I'd set up camp.'

'And she just happened to find you in the nick of time, and cut you down? Have you considered that she might be part of all this?'

I dipped my head under the water, buying time as I thought about it.

'She seemed . . . I don't know . . . kind. Real. I suppose I felt sorry for her too. It can't have been easy for her living here.' It sounded lame as I was saying it.

'I still think you should tell Sergeant Eggo what happened.'

'Nate, please, I'm not sure that's the right thing to do.' I stood up, knowing as I rose that the dizziness was coming again, and groaning.

He was on his feet in a second, towel in his hands, wrapping me up and lifting my legs over the bath edge then supporting me to the bed. I laid down, relishing the softness of the pillow.

'You nearly died. I'd have been here collecting your body and making preparations to perform a postmortem. Phoning your loved ones. You need to be realistic about how close you came to that fate.'

'Will you stay while I sleep?' I asked, taking his hand. Mine felt small in his. Small and safe.

'I will,' he said. 'You've got four hours, then we'll have to go to the meeting. I'm not leaving you alone.'

'S'okay,' I said. 'I want to go anyway.' He tucked the duvet over me and I closed my eyes. 'Hey, Nate, earlier at the Clarks' you said we needed to talk. What about?'

'It can keep,' he said, taking a seat in the armchair across the room.

'Come on. No more secrets.' I was falling asleep, wanting the comfort of hearing his voice a little longer.

'All right. It's about the killer. I've put together everything I have, and there's something missing. Aside from the seaweed crown, the location and the sand in the mouth, there's nothing at all that links the two corpses.'

'What are you talking about?' I muttered, spiralling fast.

'Right now, I have no evidence at all to confirm both girls were killed by the same person,' he said. 'Nothing that would stand up in court.'

His words were distant, and they made no sense. I fell asleep disoriented and confused, wondering how it could be that such a tiny place could have been consumed by such great evil.

Chapter Thirty-Four

The Island

The pathologist is a breed apart. He sees our world as a multi-cellular organism, each part sustaining another. He's visited the Isle of Mull before, casting a careful eye over the bodies of the unexpected dead – a 20-year-old heart-attack victim, a woman who poisoned herself for no discernible reason, a child with cancer that no one ever diagnosed. Dr Nate Carlisle, gentle hands upon bodies, gentle voice to the families, knows that life and death are a spectrum, not individual events. He brings a sadness with him to the island. A regret for what he is about to see and a desire to conquer the beast that has taken a life. On each and every occasion he arrives too late to do the good he wishes he could. Sometimes he dreams he chose to practise medicine on the living, thereby reserving some success stories for family get-togethers, but he's good at what he does – the dead like him, and he knows it.

The part of his world he most longs to change is his own home. It's empty and cold. He's a talented chef, but there's no joy in cooking for one. His carpets are vacuumed and his surfaces are dusted, but he desires chaos and mess, the disruption of another life clashing, colliding and intertwining with his. The comfort of a warm body at his side during those long, dark Glasgow nights.

There have been women before, a few of them. They all stayed for a decent period of time, but found themselves drifting away before any commitment was made. None of them could give a cogent reason for their parting, but Nate Carlisle understood.

He knew that he could shower away the smell of death, wash the postmortem chemicals from his hands, make a rule never to talk about his work unless a specific question was asked, and then to sanitise the details to keep the horrors at bay. But he sensed the train of ghosts who walked in his shadow. The unresolved cases. Those deaths where fully formed conclusions had eluded him. The women in his life had seen those shadows following him after a while. He'd catch them staring, and know they were wondering why he'd chosen to live his life with one hand inside a corpse. Too often, the ghosts of the dead had lain between him and a lover in bed, and it had made him wary.

The Canadian sees the ghosts that haunt him and it draws her to him. His mind is sharp and moves in an orderly fashion around problems, and she likes that. His eyes are kind, and she has already lost herself in them more than once. Nate Carlisle is a translator between the passed and the living, and his work feels like an extension of her own vocation.

Nate worries about her. He has since the first moment he laid eyes on her. She has a burning magnesium-ribbon brightness to her that terrifies him. It is too easy to imagine it dimming or dying, and he wants to know her better, and to allow himself to be better known.

As Sadie sleeps, Nate sets his work aside and rises from his chair, hesitating before reaching out tender fingers to stroke the hair back from where it has fallen over her eyes, silken strands in his fingertips. He likes that she is untamable and untellable.

That she is more at home outdoors than in. Her fierceness is tempered with extraordinary empathy, and a desire to break down whatever barriers stand between her and the truth. When she looks at him, he feels the ignition of an engine, the rumble that marks the beginning of a journey.

He kneels at her bedside, inspecting the freckles on her face up close, noticing how golden her eyelashes are, before turning his attention to the rope mark around her neck. His breath catches in his throat. Sadie mumbles something incomprehensible and stretches before falling into a deeper sleep. For half a second he's concerned she'll wake and find him there, over her. More than that, he hopes she will. That he'll have to explain how he can't take his eyes off her, and the excitement that rises from his belly to his chest when she talks about visiting Glasgow when the case is resolved.

In his mind, they are walking a Highland path, the wind whistling cold around them, and he takes her hand on the heather carpet. They'll find a cottage to stay in, build a fire, succumb to every cliché. Talk and talk. Hide nothing, sugar-coat nothing. Empty themselves so they can fill each other up again.

He stands and walks to the window, hoping he isn't imagining the growing bond. Sadie Levesque is a force to be reckoned with and he cannot wait to begin.

The island feels it all. The ignition of love is the opposite of death. It is an emerging bud, fragile but charged with energy. It is the antidote to the horror that has fouled Mull's atmosphere. Nate Carlisle and Sadie Levesque begin to balance the scales for the taking of Adriana and Catriona.

Chapter Thirty-Five

Falling from that branch again, I awoke jolting upright, breaking free before the noose could tighten in my dream. Nate was sitting on the end of the bed, shaking my ankle gently.

'Easy,' he said. 'You're safe.'

I raised a hand involuntarily to my neck, checking for rope.

'What's the time?' Then I remembered the last thing he'd said to me. It had followed me down into the darkness like an eel, elusive, slippery. I knew I should have roused myself to deal with it, to question Nate further, but exhaustion had taken me. 'You think there are two murderers?' I asked before he could answer my first question.

'That's not what I said,' was his reply. He walked to his bag and took out a deep blue tie and began knotting it. 'It's just that assumptions are being made. The phrase "serial killer" is being bandied around. But what I have is two young women—'

'Who knew each other and moved in the same circles,' I interjected.

'I'm talking direct rather than circumstantial evidence,' Nate said. 'So, two young women, one of whom drowned, the other who died when her heart stopped pumping after massive traumatic blood loss. One was sexually assaulted with a shell. The other shows no sign of any such assault.'

'The seaweed crowns,' I reminded him.

'Yes, made from the same seaweed but it's common around here. Adriana's was carefully constructed. Someone took their time over it. Catriona's was a mess, hastily thrown together.'

'And the one left in my hotel room?'

'More closely resembled Adriana's,' he said. 'You're going to tell me about the sand in their mouths, and you're right to. It's the aspect of the killings that's identical. But think about it, Sadie. How could that not be identical? You open a mouth, pack in as much sand as you can, and you're done. Word about this stuff gets around in close communities. I doubt there's anyone left on Mull who hasn't heard that particular detail, which would make it easy for a copycat.'

'That's speculation, not a conclusion,' I said, pulling the sheet around my body and taking clean clothes from my backpack, then going into the bathroom to get dressed.

'The point I'm making is that I have strands, points of reference, similarities between the two deaths, but I'm not at a point where I can conclude it's the same killer.'

Underwear on, I pulled the door open a crack to look at his face.

'What are you really trying to tell me, Nate?'

'That if the motives for the two killings are different, maybe the girls attracted different killers. It's not unknown. Very convenient for Catriona's murderer to be able to replicate a couple of features of Adriana's death to deflect attention from him or herself. Sergeant Eggo hasn't exactly run a tight ship in terms of controlling the crime scene information. Every officer on the island lives within the same community that's demanding answers: what are the odds that not one of them has discussed the details with friends and family? So I wanted to ask you if there have been any developments in your investigation of Adriana's death. Anything specific to her only. She has to be the starting point for figuring out what's going on here.'

I pulled a brush through my hair, trying to work out how much to tell him, knowing I couldn't keep the information to myself much longer.

'All right,' I said, taking barely used makeup from my bag to smear concealer over the bruises on my face and neck. 'The Clarks had some trouble back in the States. The sort of trouble that makes you up and move country overnight. Nothing illegal. Rob gave evidence in a trial, fell short of being provided with witness protection, but there are some people who might have the motive and the means to want revenge. I don't need to tell you, that's highly confidential.'

'Understood.' Nate slipped on his shoes and tied the laces. 'So Adriana's murder could have been a vengeance killing, or a message to Rob to say he's been found.'

'It could,' I agreed. 'But it's kind of elaborate. Not least because Adriana was fully aware of what they were running from and would have been suspicious of any American approaching her – any stranger at all, in fact – asking her to go out on a midnight rendezvous. Then there's the use of the shell from the Emporium, references to local folklore, the use of the cave to hide her body. Why go to so much more trouble than was necessary?'

'You're assuming someone travelled here, a foreigner ignorant of local ways and the layout of the island. What if they made it simpler than that, and paid someone already here to kill Adriana? Sounds as if whoever Rob Clark is in trouble with is capable of that.'

'How would you go about identifying who to approach?' I asked myself in the bathroom mirror.

Nate answered me anyway. 'Hire a hacker. Find anyone with

271

a relevant criminal record. Offer them enough money. Or look at credit scores, figure out who's already in trouble. Pay Bitcoin and get someone from mainland Scotland to do it, who would stand out less here. Enough money always gets the job done.'

The Aros Hall, an unpretentious, functional building on Main Street, had been chosen as the venue for Nate to address anyone from the island who wanted to attend. The press, save for one local paper, had been excluded. Harris Eggo and his men were on the door to ensure that no one entered who didn't have a valid reason to be there. Even Rob and Brandon Clark had decided they would attend, leaving Isabella at home looking after Luna. Wearing a scarf to hide the injuries to my neck, and a hat to reduce the visibility of my face, I arrived early with Nate and took a seat halfway down the length of the hall and to the side.

It filled up fast. Fifteen rows of ten chairs with a central aisle. Nate and Harris Eggo were on the stage. The front row to the left had been reserved for the Clarks, and to the right sat Catriona's father and his extended family.

I watched the door as people filed in. No sign of Skittles. Simon Bathgate had already caught my eye and given me a curious look, but then I'd been at pains to give the impression that I was leaving the island. Not any more though – having not been attacked. It was safer for my presence to be public knowledge so anyone else planning to hurt me could be held accountable.

There were a few other faces I recognised. Rachel, the landlady from The Blether with her husband and Lewis Eggo in tow, presumably as the boy couldn't be seated with his father. Lizzy's grandmother from the pottery shop, but no sign of Lizzy. The men who approached Nate and me the night the town had decided on its unofficial curfew. Father Christophe and every other person who'd been at the church service for Catriona, save for Hilda, as far as I could make out. Not a seat remained empty and the stragglers stood at the sides.

It was Harris Eggo who stood up to get the evening underway. He looked like I felt. Not quite as if he'd been pushed from a tree with a noose around his neck, but still. He took the microphone and gave it a tap, producing a feedback squawk that reverberated around the room.

'Sorry about that,' he said. There was a combination of laughter and murmuring at his expense. 'Right, you know why we're here. This gentleman,' he motioned to Nate, 'is the pathologist from Glasgow who's come to answer our questions about Adriana and Catriona's deaths. Raise your hand if you want to say something, and keep your voice loud or we won't be able to hear. Also, we'll watch our language when we're all gathered together.' Harris Eggo sat down.

Nate took his time, a sheet of papers clutched in one hand, glasses I hadn't previously seen him wear in the other. He was imposing on the stage, professional and respectful, but relaxed. He'd shed his jacket and turned up his sleeves, a look which managed to say: I'm here to work, I'm not so different to anyone in this room, but let's have some boundaries.

'Good evening,' he said. 'I'm sorry that such terrible events bring me here to speak with you. My job is not the same as that of the police, although one of my roles is to work with them during an investigation and also to help build a solid and sustainable case once an arrest is made. The most important aspect of my work, though, is communicating with the family and loved ones of the deceased, to ensure that they're kept aware of the facts of the case, and so that we can make as much progress as quickly as possible, gathering all relevant information.'

Rob Clark reached out to put an arm across his son's shoulder, but Brandon shifted away. Even so, I was pleased they'd attended.

They needed the islanders' support, not gossip and suspicion. Hiding themselves away hadn't helped the investigation, or the attitude of the police.

I took the opportunity to glance around the hall. Nate's words were still echoing in my head. Of course an assassin wouldn't have appeared on Mull sporting a ten-gallon hat, but the thought that the Clarks' rich and powerful enemies from Las Vegas might have engaged the services of someone more local was intriguing and worrying. It was a fair bet that half the people in the Aros Hall had money worries. Income based on tourism was seasonal and subject to wider economic influences. Even in the best of times, it was clear that no one on Mull was getting rich. It wouldn't have been a challenge to find someone who'd break some laws for some extra income. But this wasn't drug running and fraud. It wasn't turning a blind eye to a robbery or growing marijuana in your garage. Murder wasn't just a skillset; it was a whole elevator ride up to psychopathy.

Now Nate was running through a brief description of each crime scene, keeping it vague. Locations, times, a single phrase summarising cause of death. Most of it was about his processes, his team's attention to detail, reassurance that everything was being done appropriately and carefully. A few scientific terms thrown in for good measure. Much of it was bland, but I saw the purpose. This community was not reacting well to being kept in the dark. Better to attempt to control the narrative.

He didn't mention the conch, nor the excised breast, and he wasn't specific about the level of violence. Nate was probably right that word had already got out, but he wasn't going to fuel the flames.

Thinking about the conch made me uncomfortable, as if I'd left a door unlocked or failed to turn the gas off. The shell that only I could attest to having been the same size as the dust

274

silhouette left in the Emporium, surrounded by the crystals and paraphernalia of the island's history and mythology. All of it was a jumble in my head.

'When can we bury our dead?' someone shouted.

'It's difficult when we can't release the bodies for burial. It causes distress and makes the process longer and harder. We're fiercely aware of that. However, the priority has to be to ensure that we have the bodies at hand for additional tests, to double-check evidence and in case of any complaint about procedure. It benefits no one if the perpetrator is able to go free from trial on the basis of a dispute over the forensics. Rest assured, we're moving with all speed. Adriana and Catriona are being looked after with dignity and care. I can't yet give you a date when we can release the bodies.'

'Do you have any fingerprints?' was the next question.

'We do not,' Nate said. 'Adriana's body was in the sea for a period of time and then subject to long-term exposure in the cave. Catriona was found faster and had not been in the water. I'd have expected fingerprints or skin cells in those circumstances, but none have been found, leading me to conclude that her attacker probably wore gloves.'

Footsteps echoed on the stairs at the back that led down to the foyer. Not just one or two, I realised, as other heads began to turn, but many feet, stepping firmly and deliberately. Nate found my eyes across the room and I shrugged my confusion at him.

The girls entered one by one, including Lizzy who was pale and stony faced. I checked her grandmother's expression and found no shock. If she hadn't known what her granddaughter had been planning, she had at least suspected that something was happening. Others among them, I was sure, had been at the ceremony in the forest. Some I'd seen in The Blether. Several were strangers, possibly from other villages. Bringing up the rear was Hilda, stern and purposeful. They made their way up the central aisle, two by two, each wearing shades of grey – not robes exactly, but an arrangement of clothing cobbled together to make the point. They were unified, organised. They were a body. When they came to a halt, Hilda continued to walk between them to the front. Save for her footsteps there was a silence worthy of the ocean floor in the hall. Tobermory held its breath.

'Our condolences to those who grieve for Adriana,' Hilda raised a hand in Rob's direction, 'and those who grieve for Catriona.' She put one hand over her heart as she looked at Catriona's father. 'We keep those young women in our thoughts, in our memories and in the island's consciousness.'

'You shouldn't be here!' a man yelled from across the room.

'There's a curfew over those girls,' someone else added.

'That curfew has no basis in law,' Hilda said. 'It was imposed by Tobermory's men – not the police – without reference to the womenfolk. Without asking us what we thought of it, or what we needed from it. Does anyone here believe that either Adriana or Catriona died at a woman's hand? Why should women's movements be restricted when the perpetrator of these crimes is a man?'

'We don't know that yet,' Nate said.

Hilda gazed up at him.

'Do you not?' she asked. 'Tell me, Dr Carlisle, how many violent deaths have you seen perpetrated by a woman against another woman?'

'Not many at all,' Nate responded. 'But it has happened, it's possible, and it would be wrong to draw any conclusions based on statistics.'

'But these girls didn't submit to their deaths, did they? They were handled, subdued, restrained. That took strength and the application of fear.'

'True,' Nate replied. 'But compliance can be achieved with threats or the brandishing of a weapon.'

'What does your instinct tell you, Dr Carlisle?' Hilda asked. 'Was the perpetrator a man or a woman? I know what my gut tells me. That a man took those young women.' She whirled round and held out an accusatory finger towards the audience. 'A man, like those who judge us here. Like those who set curfews and create rules to control us.'

The young women with her began nodding, staring wide-eyed at her. She struck an exceptional figure, both authoritarian and bohemian.

That was when Father Christophe stood up, which of course was what Hilda had been waiting for.

'You are leading these impressionable girls down a dangerous path,' he said. 'Away from God, away from goodness, away from the natural order of things.'

'You'd have us on our knees, Father. Not just you. There are plenty here who'd prefer the old ways. Women on the floor scrubbing the flagstones. Women on the floor asking God's forgiveness. Women on the floor servicing their husbands at night.' There were some gasps at that, but they weren't real. It wasn't as if you couldn't have seen that one coming. 'And now you're using these tragedies, these aberrations, as a way to hide your wives and daughters and sisters away again. Condemn him, Father. Condemn the man who's slaughtering our lambs. Let's hear it.'

'All sin is condemned by the Lord,' Father Christophe said. 'I should not need to spell it out.'

'But you do need to. There are men in here who hit their wives. I know who they are.' She walked back down the aisle looking left and right. Several men averted their gaze from hers. 'Some of these people confess their sins to you, Father, and they're forgiven. The following week they do the same again.

277

They drink, use their fists, say their prayers and on it goes. It's not just you. Other religions turn an equally blind eye to the reprehensible. There are men here who have sex with their wives knowing that their partners are unwilling, or ill, or too scared to say no. There are men here who refuse to allow their wives access to contraception.' Hilda waved an arm across the crowd. 'Men who tell their wives what they can wear, what they can have, who they can see, how much they can eat. And now you have the perfect excuse to control what the young women of this island do. Where they go, when they can go there. We're here tonight to say *enough*.'

Nate picked up his notes and took a step back, arms crossed, waiting to see how it would play out. I had a fair idea of how it would go, and it wasn't going to be good.

'Witch!' a woman yelled. 'You're perverting them. You couldn't raise your own son and you shouldn't be anywhere near our girls.'

'This isn't witchcraft,' Hilda shouted in reply. It occurred to me that the accusation was exactly what she'd been waiting for. 'This is empowerment. We respect each other. We care for our environment. Why are we not allowed to be the masters of our own bodies, of our own destinies?'

'How come you didn't manage to keep those other girls safe, then?' Simon Bathgate asked her.

Hilda narrowed her eyes at him. 'That's right, Constable. Make us responsible for the rapes, for the violence, for the bullying, for the up-skirting, the breast grazes. Ask why we have not prevented the assaults on our own bodies and each other's.'

'My sister got killed because Catriona sent her messages to get her to leave our house that night,' Brandon yelled, standing up. Rob reached for his arm but was unable to get control. 'It wasn't a man who did that. I don't know who killed her, but I know she wouldn't be dead if it weren't for Catriona Vass, and now we've got to sit here and listen to you say their names in the same breath?'

'Don't you speak ill of my daughter,' Catriona's father joined the fray.

'Oh shit,' I whispered. 'Not good.'

'Your daughter hated my sister when we first got here,' Brandon replied. 'What changed her mind, huh? Or who?'

'Catriona never hurt anyone,' one of the women sitting in the front row replied. 'She was a lamb.'

I thought of Lewis Eggo, of the potion he'd been slipped that had made him sick, and wondered just how much of a lamb Catriona had really been. One with a wild side, to say the least.

Father Christophe began to pray. Lizzy began to cry. Hilda stood her ground. Rob Clark pulled Brandon's fist down from the air. The Vass family bundled themselves up and began to make their way out. One of the men who'd told me I shouldn't have been out after curfew walked into the aisle and grabbed hold of a girl's arm. The facial resemblance screamed 'sister'.

'Let go. You're not in charge of me,' she shouted.

'You little bitch. You'll get home now before you worry our parents sick.'

She spat in his face, and the world turned a little slower for a second. It ended with a slap, brother to sister, then another one, this time thrown by Hilda.

There was a surge of bodies reaching for people, pulling people back, trying to get out, trying to get a better view, words of encouragement and disparagement.

Harris Eggo jumped down from the stage, patted his son on the shoulder and told him to go home. The boy did as his father told him, and only when Lewis was clear of the melee did Harris Eggo let go of his own temper.

'You will stop this right now!' he yelled, no microphone

required. 'Every one of you will get back to your homes. Curfews will only be imposed by the police on this island. Protests must be agreed in advance. We came here today to get answers on behalf of the two girls we've lost. This was never supposed to be about anything else.'

Even Hilda bent her head at that one.

'Now slowly, so no one gets hurt, make your way downstairs and out. Anyone still here five minutes from now gets arrested – I don't care who you are,' Harris said.

A hand tapped me on the shoulder. I turned round.

'Can we talk?' the man asked. It took me a moment amid the confusion to realise that I was staring into the eyes of Flora Kydd's father, absent when I'd gone to visit him.

His daughter had received no mention, but I saw it all in his eyes. The same desperation Rob and Isabella were going through. The same heartbreak as Catriona's father. No less sharp a needle despite the decades that should have blunted it.

'I'll be waiting,' he said.

I headed for Nate.

'See you back at your hotel,' I told him. 'If I can stay with you a bit longer?'

'Of course you can stay with me,' he said. 'Just do me a favour? If you're not coming back with me straight away, stay within the town centre, in properly lit areas, and make sure you're near buildings with lights on so you can call for help.'

I considered telling him to stop worrying, realised that actually I did want Nate to worry about me, gave him the most reassuring smile I could muster, and left.

Taking the stairs down, I realised what had been bugging me about the shell. Specifically that the use of the shell was the detail the police had held back from the public. Which might explain why, as much as my brain protested the possibility, no such violation had been perpetrated against Catriona. A copycat killer could only recreate those aspects of a crime he knew about.

'There can't be two of them,' I reassured myself aloud as I exited the Aros Hall and searched around for Mr Kydd. 'That's too much cruelty for one small island.'

'There's more than enough of it here,' Jasper Kydd said from the shadows behind me. 'Shall we walk?'

Chapter Thirty-Six

We walked away from the harbour front, the better to keep a low profile.

'You were in my house,' Jasper Kydd said.

'I don't want any trouble.' I stopped, bracing myself. He was old, but I was in no fit state to have any sort of fight at all.

'That's not what I'm here for. The point is that you'll have seen the place. No doubt you went up to Flora's bedroom.'

'I did.' We began walking again. Jasper Kydd was a slight man, unthreatening. He kept his hands shoved into his pockets, a flat cap low over his eyes. 'I know it was wrong. For what it's worth, I was visiting you because I was concerned after seeing how upset you were. Also in case there was a tie to Adriana's case. I gather there was a similarity.'

'Have you visited Scotland before, Miss Levesque?' he asked me, his voice carrying so softly on the breeze it was hard to hear him.

'My first time,' I said.

We made our way south and he pointed at the road ahead of him.

'Beautiful, isn't it? I'm guessing some of the scenery is not dissimilar to your home country.'

'Your country's truly awe-inspiring. It's just a shame I'm not seeing it for better reasons. I always wanted to come to Scotland,' I said.

'Aye, well, we get a lot of tourists here. They like to visit Iona Abbey – you should make the time to do that – and Calgary beach in the north-east. They take a cottage for a couple of weeks and visit the distillery. There's peace here. And ice cream, rolling countryside. Everything you see on the adverts.'

'There's a but,' I said.

'Throughout history, the Scottish people have been invaded, used and abused by the lairds and various incoming forces. It's part of what's made us fiercely patriotic and loyal. We build these tight communities, tell our children stories from bygone years, maintain our heritage. For centuries, we fought to wear our history on our shoulders rather than let it slip, irrelevant, into the encroaching brine.'

'I understand that,' I said.

'No, you don't, girl. These aren't just stories to the islanders. The myths you hear, the tales in the tourist guidebooks – we live them still. And legends rise out of a thousand tiny truths. They have power. Do you know what's at the end of this lane?'

I thought about the geography of Tobermory.

'Um, there's the Mull Pottery as you leave town, right?'

'Behind that you'll find the Baliscate Standing Stones. Not a patch on the Lochbuie stones, but these were placed there before Tobermory ever existed. There are ruined castles where witches are supposed to have enchanted those who crossed them. There's a ship at the bottom of the bay where many souls were lost. This whole island, everything you see, exists because of its history and you can't just extract the now from the then.'

'Mr Kydd, I know how you lost Flora. I also know that the passing years will have done nothing to reduce your pain. The last thing I wanted was to drag this all up for you.'

'Drag it up? As if I don't relive it every day?' He took my hand and held it in his warm, rough one. 'Do you think what you witnessed tonight was harmless? Those girls and their rituals, their midnight cavorting and their spells.'

'Hilda explained that it's not really about spells, more about helping the girls get in touch with themselves to feel more empowered.'

'Empowered is one word for it, I suppose. My Flora was scared of them, you know. She was a God-fearing girl, in spite of the fact that her mother and I didn't practise. Hilda's group – led by her mother back then – would meet a few times a month. You've to understand, there's not much to do here for months at a time. So tell a girl she's powerful, that there's magical properties she can harness to have her bidding done, that's as exciting as it gets on a small island. I can see how enticing it would be.'

'Did Flora get dragged into it somehow?' I asked. It had turned bitterly cold, a prying wind finding my face and fingers easy prey, tugging at my clothes. Jasper Kydd hardly seemed to notice the gale whipping up around us.

'No, no. She was very grounded. Others around here, though, were sucked in good and proper. That's all right when it's harmless nonsense. Chanting over a crystal for your future to be revealed to you in a dream, for example. But what happens when the wrong person, someone already suffering serious psychological problems, takes it all too seriously? Believes in the spells and the power?'

'Mr Kydd, I was under the impression that Flora's murderer has never been caught. Are you saying you know who killed your daughter?' I was cold, and it had nothing to do with the wind.

Jasper Kydd stopped at a bench and sat down. Part of me wanted to leave. The expression on his face, the devastation and hopelessness, was so extreme that I wasn't sure I could share it with him. When Lance Proudfoot had recounted the story of covering Flora's death, he said he'd arrived on Mull a boy and gone home a man. I could feel the weight of Lance's experience on my own shoulders as I went to sit at Jasper's side.

'Flora had been invited to join the group. At first she just laughed it off, said it was some of the local girls who liked to drink and party on a Friday night under the guise of something more spiritual. She turned them down gently, but they persisted. The next time she was clearer, citing her own religious beliefs as the reason not to join. Then the carcasses started appearing. A dead crow on our doorstep, a rabbit thrown onto our roof. A dead deer left on the bonnet of our car.

'Flora laughed it off, but she was unhappy. It turned nastier, curses being whispered to her in the local shop, that sort of thing. My daughter was young, and sweet, and she took it to heart. Started burning witch taper marks into the beams of our house. For a while my wife and I let her do it to placate her. Then when she started putting up the herbs so witches wouldn't want to enter, we forbade her to do any more. That's when things went downhill. She rarely went out for a while, spent hours praying in her room. We thought the best thing was to indulge her. Let her do whatever she wanted to feel safe in her own home. There were marks on the walls, the chimney breast, the windowsills. Crosses up in her room. Someone, you see, had really scared her.'

'That's terrible,' I said. 'Poor Flora.'

'She recovered, got back to her old self. Started working at the plant nursery, seemed fine. We forgot about it. My wife got used to the markings. In my own head, it seemed like a silly phase she'd grow out of. Only she never got the chance.'

I could see Flora in my mind, caught up in a bullying circle with a sinister difference. It didn't matter what the mind knew. Logic went out the window when peer pressure and hatefulness were applied.

'When she disappeared, I would sit on her bed for hours, trying to find her with my mind. I wanted to hear her voice, as ridiculous as that sounds. When they identified her body, the only words I could hear her say were, "I told you so, Pa. I tried to warn you."'

'Did she warn you?' I asked.

'Not exactly. It was more what she didn't say. Flora made those burn marks without elaborate tales and drama. Just kept going with it, day after day. There was one girl among them who made her feel especially unsafe. I just thought it was teenager stuff. Honestly, I was more concerned with having enough money to pay the mortgage, and my wife didn't like to bother me with too much of it. I let her take the burden on her shoulders.' He dashed tears away and I swallowed to contain my own. 'And now they're both gone. Mortgage is paid off, and I've no one to share the farm with. It's as quiet as the grave I wish I was in.'

'Jasper, they wouldn't want that for you. None of what happened was your fault.'

'We don't listen to teenagers, Miss Levesque. I don't know what happens to us. We've all been there – felt that confusion, fear and despair – yet when we become adults with teenagers of our own we decide that everything they feel is just a passing fad. Melodrama. Silliness. Why do we do that?'

'To cope,' I said. 'Because parenting is hard.' But he was right. Parenting, not that I'd done it, seemed to me to be like skiing in stilettos. An impossible task that inevitably ended in injury.

'That girl, Lynn, didn't like Flora refusing to join their group. As if Flora had thought she was better than them. Rumour had it she'd been trouble since she was a toddler. Spiteful and two-faced, she was. Then she got a boyfriend from the mainland who came to live with her here. They had a caravan somewhere.'

He broke off the story, staring into the night sky.

'Was it him? The boyfriend?' I asked.

'He was one of several people investigated but they found no evidence against him. He left soon after, saying he was sick of people gossiping. Took Lynn with him. They never once set foot back on Mull again. Her family left not long after.'

'Why do you suspect them?'

'Because they put sand in her mouth,' Jasper said. 'They filled her mouth full of it until she could no longer breathe. Do you know why witches do that when they kill?' I stared at him, unable to speak. 'So you can't name them. If you say what they are, they have no power over you. It's old folklore, from almost every culture and race in the world. Tell the beast its true name and it cannot harm you. For a year after Flora's death I did nothing but read about it. There had been other deaths on Mull, you see. Ancient killings with few records kept. But it's what the witches did here on Mull.' He turned to me, clutched both my hands. 'It's not harmless fun, you see? It distorts and deranges. Makes them feel like they're tapped into some higher power. Certainly some of them are good, and for them it's harmless, but then you get the odd one who uses it as a pathway to something dark and dangerous. Something that can't be controlled.'

'You think a witch killed Adriana?'

'I think a witch persuaded her boyfriend to do something unspeakable to my daughter out of spite and jealousy, and I believe she left her calling card when they did it. I wish I'd listened to Flora. Been home more. Taken her side.'

'I'm so sorry,' I said. A useless feather of a sentiment in a hurricane of grief.

'So am I,' he said. 'You find your girl's killer. You find them and you make sure they're punished for what they did. But don't consign the myths of this island to history or nonsense, because I'm afraid that would be a terrible, terrible mistake.'

Chapter Thirty-Seven

Nate opened the door before I got to it.

'You want a drink?' he asked.

'Not right now.' I stepped inside. 'You said before it would be difficult to conceive of a woman carrying the weight of Adriana's waterlogged body, but what about two women? They could carry her between them, right?'

'Two women, two men, a woman and a man – there are several possibilities. Where's this coming from, Sadie?'

'A place of deep confusion. I don't know why the Clarks are even paying me any more. I'm a total waste of skin right now.'

'Have you taken another blow to the head?' Nate asked. I couldn't blame him for that one. 'That was some show tonight. Feelings are running high. I'm not sure Harris Eggo is going to be able to control the conflict when it really kicks off.'

'What are you going to do?' I asked, flicking on the kettle before pulling off my shoes.

'I'll report back to the Major Investigation Team, ask them to consider permanently stationing additional officers here for as long as it takes to close the investigation. Where did you go after the meeting?'

'Flora Kydd's father, Jasper, wanted to talk. I've only seen him once before at the pub. He was devastated then. Tonight he seemed resigned but concerned. Angry, actually. There was some information he needed me to hear.' I'd grabbed my laptop, logged into the WiFi and was already searching for verification of what Jasper had told me. 'Here it is. *The Law of Names, or True Name, has been embedded in folklore, magic, religion and mysticism since antiquity, and thereafter transferred into popular culture. A true name is the name that most clearly expresses or defines a creature's most basic nature. Calling a creature by its true name will prevent it from exercising any power over its intended victim.*'

Nate carried on where I'd left off and poured boiling water over coffee granules.

'Which is relevant why?' he asked.

'The sand. I've talked this over ad nauseam, and the consensus has been that it's an act of silencing, debasement, or punishment, possibly a very misogynistic act. There are plenty of examples of those in history aimed specifically at women. What Hilda never told me is that filling a mouth with sand on Mull is a more specific reference. It's what witches do to their victims to prevent them from calling out their true name, so that the victim remains powerless to defend themselves. I thought it was just Flora Kydd who'd suffered the same fate, but her father told me it has happened before, in ancient murders on this island. He believes Flora was killed by a disturbed girl who'd got involved with the local pagan group, and her boyfriend. He described the sand as a witch's calling card.' Nate handed me a red-hot mug and I sipped the contents cautiously.

'Which is why you're convinced a woman killed Adriana?'

'Well, if it looks like a duck and swims like a duck . . .'

'Do you think Flora's killer and her boyfriend are back all these years later?' Nate asked.

289

I considered that. 'No,' I concluded. 'They left the island quickly after Flora's death and never returned. They'd have been noticed if they'd come back recently. But that doesn't mean history can't repeat itself.'

'Is that the relevance of the ground cat bones? Was it all part of some spell?'

'No, Hilda just laughed at that. She clearly thought it was ridiculous.' I abandoned the coffee on the bedside table and laid back on the bed, surrendering to the soft duvet and the warmth, closing my eyes.

'Hilda, the same woman who failed to tell you that filling a mouth full of sand was something done by past witches. You're getting a lot of conflicting information.'

'I am, aren't I?' I rolled onto my side. 'Thanks for letting me stay, Nate. It's good to feel safe for the night.'

'No problem. You mind sharing? I can sleep on the floor if it makes you uncomfortable.'

'I'd be insulted,' I told him, shifting across to make sure he had plenty of space, hearing the sounds of him cleaning his teeth and running a shower. In a minute or so, I told myself, I'd get up and do the same.

Nate settled next to me, and soon his breathing slowed. I wanted to sleep. Even after napping the afternoon away, still my body craved rest. But Hilda was on my mind. Her performance at the meeting. Her kindness to me versus the omissions in what she'd told me. Her iron will when protecting the son she hadn't been present to raise, even as she challenged him. Hilda slapping Father Christophe's face at a memorial service to a slain girl.

I had questions for Hilda and there would be no sleeping until I got them. Creeping out of bed as quietly as I could manage, I dressed in the dark, listening for any indication that I'd disturbed Nate. He'd have wanted me to wake him and tell him what I was planning, I knew that, but it would have required persuasion and argument, two things I was in no mood for. Hopefully I could do what I needed to and be back before he was up. He'd be pissed at me, but it didn't seem likely to be anything an apology couldn't fix. To add insult to injury, I pocketed his car keys as I sneaked from his room. It was a hire car, and I wasn't planning on driving it very far anyway.

A few minutes later I arrived back at Loch Peallach, parked at the side of the road and headed into the forest, retracing my steps from that morning as best I could with only my compass and my head torch. At 1 a.m. I saw a glint of light in the distance through the trees.

'Hilda,' I muttered, grateful both that I'd found her place again and that she was obviously home. I picked up my pace, aware that I was cold calling, so shouting out as I went. 'Hello! Hilda, are you awake? It's Sadie. Can we talk?'

The light was deceptive. When she'd walked me from her cabin back to my campsite in the morning, we'd edged around a valley in the woods. Now my pathway was stopped by a steep drop-off, and I had to retrace my steps and head north, approaching the light from a different angle. Spiders had spun their night-time webs, and rodents were busy searching for food. I swiped at my face and jumped away from scurrying paws.

'Hilda, hey Hilda! I know it's late, but it's Sadie and there are some things I have to ask you!'

I was at her door, exhausted, but knowing it was the right thing to have done. The human tendency to wait until morning was often a mistake. The darkness was when more honest conversations took place. If you were going to do a deal with the devil, it wasn't going to be made while the sun was up. Hilda and I were overdue a frank exchange of views.

I reached out to knock on her door, stubbing my toes on a large log at the base.

'What the fuck?' I whispered, knocking anyway and calling out her name again. No reply. I was holding the door handle when I remembered that it opened outward, not inward.

I leaned down, did my best to shift the wood, but it was too heavy and too broad for me to grasp easily.

Giving up on that, I moved along the side of the cabin, peering through the windows. There was a fire still flickering in the grate that had to have been set and fed since the meeting, so she'd returned. It occurred to me that there might be a back door out of the bedroom that I hadn't seen. If she'd had a problem with her lock, perhaps she'd used the log as additional security.

'Is anyone home?' I called, knocking on the windows, embarrassed to be caught sneaking around the back where she might be doing anything, hoping she'd hear me before we made eye contact through the glass. 'It's Sadie, Hilda. Would you let me in?'

There were two windows at the back, smaller than the ones at the front, and I had to stand on my tiptoes to see in. The glass was dirtier where the trees were closer and the leaves had dripped sap onto the panes. There was the blurred outline of movement, something dark and hunched on the floor, shifting slowly, silhouetted against the firelight. A pet, I assumed.

'Hilda, could you open up?' No amount of rubbing cleaned the window. I checked the final side of the cabin. No door. Going back I tried the final window for a better view, standing further back on a tree stump to wave and shout to attract her attention.

That one was cleaner. No movement inside now. Just a dark huddle on the floor. Something slid out from beneath the black mass, slow, creeping, followed by a liquid trail. I strained my neck for a better view, already shrinking back from the pale,

292

withered white flesh that was grabbing, pulling, grabbing, pulling itself along.

'Is that a . . . ? Oh shit. Hilda?' I screamed. 'Hilda, what the fuck?' It was a hand, my eyes finally registered the scrawny, weak movements of the fingers reaching out, moving away from the body. 'No, no, no. Please!' I raced to the front of the house again, frantically dragging my cell from my pocket. No reception so deep in the woods. Nothing at all.

I tried dragging the log away from the front of the door again but it proved useless. Instead I searched in the pathetic light from my headlamp for a rock, ripped off my jacket and wound it around my hand, turned my head away and smashed the rock into a front window. It didn't break cleanly. I don't know why I'd expected a movie-effect shattering. A star shape had formed on the pane with a tiny hole at the centre and my arm was already painful from the ricochet. I slammed the rock into it again, and this time glass flew, leaving jagged splinters in its wake. Using the rock to clear the way, I scraped it around the edge of the pane to minimise the damage as I crawled through. Still my entrance left me with shredded jeans and icy splinters stinging my buttocks.

'Hilda,' I shouted as I jumped down from the windowsill, 'it's Sadie. I'm coming in!'

The only response was a low moan. I raced around the side of the fireplace and into her bedroom, thinking – heart attack, maybe stroke, perhaps a fall. Please let it be one of those.

As I took the corner, the floor became treacle, and each step seemed to take longer than the last. I was aware of my arms reaching out for her, of my own knees buckling at the sight of her fallen body.

She was hunched over the floor, the top of her head resting on the wooden boards, hands reaching out to either side. I took her right in my left, kneeling at her head and turned her face to one side, the shocking cold stiffness of her fingers striking a blow in my mind.

As I turned her head, my hand was filled with the sticky warmth of childhood summer days. Time on the beach, mixing sand with seawater, all the better to create castles that would endure, not crumble. Only this cement was formed of blood and sand, her mouth full of the stuff, the darkness on the floor no shadow from her clothes, but the spread of too much, far too much liquid, and it was still warm, still flowing.

'Oh fuck,' I yelled. My brain, too slowly, realising that a body still bleeding meant a heart still pumping. Shoving unwilling fingers into her mouth, catching the almost imperceptible quiver of her nostrils doing their utmost to drag in oxygen, I clawed out sand, more than I'd ever conceived could fill such a small space. Too late though. Her breath, her last attempt at a breath, exited her body with a tired hiss.

'Don't you give up,' I told her. 'Don't you dare.' I needed to manoeuvre her onto her back to resuscitate her. It was one of those things I'd been trained to do at regular intervals but had only ever used in practice once when a young man had taken a dive off a high bridge. This time I'd be grinding my lips against the bloody sand that a maniac had thrust inside her, and the thought had me gagging even as I slipped my arms around her to shift her onto her back.

It was then that I became aware of the appalling slaughter that had been brought to those peaceful woods. Her slate grey dress was ripped open at the front, one breast left where there should have been two. A bloody, open mess was all that remained, brutally butchered. The wound was jagged edged and clumsy, as if an animal had attacked.

Her fingers jerked, spasmed.

'Oh Hilda,' I said softly, taking her head in my lap, abandoning all thought of CPR. Her lifeblood was a lake on the floor, her body torn in two. Only her eyes were still moving and they slid to lock onto mine, aware, knowing.

I stroked her hair, my tears wetting her cheeks, telling myself she was beyond pain, beyond fear. The last face she saw had to be one filled with kindness.

'It's okay,' I told her. 'I'm going to stay with you.'

I counted the seconds in my head until she passed.

One . . . How would Skittles cope without her, even if they hadn't been close?

Two . . . The log in front of the door hadn't been placed there by Hilda. Someone was either keeping her in or keeping other people out.

Three . . . Where were they? Were they still here? I hadn't even thought to check, and now I was sitting in a pool of blood . . .

Four . . . I had to get out, but I couldn't leave until I knew she was gone. Couldn't leave a dying woman staring into the abyss alone.

Five . . . And after that I still had to make it back to my car. What if they were waiting for me in the woods?

Six . . . Was I better off staying in the cabin until daylight? Staying awake, armed, ready to defend myself?

Seven . . . I saw her severed right breast, a gelatinous lump thrown crudely onto the hearth.

Eight . . . Hilda was gone. Dead in my arms.

The weight of it all, the danger I was in, the fact that she was still alive when I'd found her, the certain knowledge that the person who'd killed her was still in the forest – perhaps running, perhaps lying in wait for me – was a gun to my temple.

Chapter Thirty-Eight

I decided to run. I had to do that without my head torch on for fear of announcing myself like a beacon to anyone lying in wait, but I couldn't risk losing my way. Every part of me was shaking. Armed only with a knife I'd grabbed from a counter in Hilda's kitchen, having failed to anticipate the potential need for a weapon when I'd come, I knew I had one chance only. Sitting on the windowsill, I wanted so badly to retreat. But the outside gave me a fighting chance. The cabin wasn't secure. It could be set alight or entered at any moment.

My legs hated me, resisted at first. I took several deep breaths, frantically gulping oxygen, and I told myself – run or die. Those were the only words I could allow myself to think until I reached the car.

Run or die.

I jumped from that window, bent my knees on landing, prayed that the pale moonlight would be enough to show the way and began to move. Hands out in front, leaping over tree trunks, eyes up to judge the tree layout ahead, eyes down to watch where my feet were falling.

There were noises in the trees behind me. Something larger than small mammals. Twigs were snapping.

Run or die.

The defensive part of my brain wanted to stop, to look, to know for sure what was behind me. My internal fighter ordered me to flee. I'd always been fast. Fast, slight and sure-footed. If ever there'd been a moment to take advantage of those skills it was right then. I didn't stop, picking up speed instead, hoping like hell I could avoid a tree branch through my eye or piercing my suprasternal notch and leaving me gasping for air on the ground.

An owl flew in front of my face and I bit my lip to keep from crying out, flinging my arms up to protect my face, then putting my head down and extending my stride. I lost count of the number of times I nearly tripped, nearly fell, but every time I righted myself, pounded through.

Run or die.

Then the landscape opened up and finally I knew I had to take the precaution of stopping for a moment. I didn't want to. There was danger behind, quite possibly, but also danger ahead if I didn't exercise caution. From here it was clear ground to the loch, and the car was on display at the roadside beyond that. If anyone wanted to take an easy run at me, it was going to be in the next part of my journey. Coming to a halt, in the shadow of the final line of trees, I gave myself no more than five seconds. Focus on the car, key in my right hand, knife in my left. Look right, look left, check for movement or large patches of shadow. Don't look back. Don't get spooked. Just fucking go!

There was movement in my far-right peripheral vision but the ground was uneven. If I looked, there was every chance I'd fall. The car was getting closer but I knew I couldn't hit the unlock button until I was right on top of it. If anyone was waiting on the other side to climb in, then I was in trouble.

Footsteps, I could hear them clearly now. My own breathing was a drum solo in my head. So close. Fifty metres. I was certain someone was right behind me. Head down, arms pumping, I took it at a sprint. Twenty metres. Approaching the car too fast, unable to stop on the damp ground, hitting the side of the car hard enough to wind myself.

I clicked unlock, losing myself in a sickening slo-mo moment when the door handle didn't want to work. Then there was the clunk of the lock springing and the resistance ended. The door opened and I threw myself onto the driver's seat, slamming the door behind me before locking it again. Two seconds to check the rear seat, car in gear, brief glance back to the tree line but the headlights were on and everything else was too dark and too distant.

As I drove, the world began to shake. I tightened my grip on the steering wheel and tried to keep the car steady. It was a full minute later that I realised it was me shaking. Not just my hands, but my whole body, inside and out. I couldn't feel my feet or my fingers. The cold had set in after my frantic dash, and I was awash with freezing sweat that was trickling into my eyes.

The police station had to be my first port of call. I slammed on the brakes outside the front door in Erray Road and began hammering, knowing that while the investigation was ongoing, Eggo had given instructions for the building to be manned 24 hours a day.

'Let me in!' I shouted. 'Help! Please . . .'

The door opened, and a sleepy Simon Bathgate stood there staring at me.

'What the fuck did you do?' he asked.

'You've got to get to Hilda's cabin,' I panted. 'I just found her body. She's been killed, same way Catriona died.' I set my back to the police station wall and allowed my body to slide down until I hit the floor. 'You're going to need scenes of crime, don't touch the log outside the front door – someone put it there. I broke a window to get in.'

Harris Eggo appeared from an internal doorway.

'Jesus Christ, are you injured? Should we call an ambulance?' He knelt at my side.

'No,' I said. 'None of it's my blood. Hilda's been murdered. They butchered her. You've got to get out there to her right now. Call Nate Carlisle too. He should go with you.'

'That's her blood?' Simon Bathgate asked, taking a step back from me. 'All of it?'

'Yes! That's what I've been trying to tell you. She was still alive when I was with her, then she died and I came straight back here.'

'Call the Major Investigation Team, get units out there now,' Harris Eggo instructed. 'I'll follow you. And get Dr Carlisle out of bed.'

'Oh shit, I've got his car. He doesn't know I took it. He'll need a lift there.'

Simon Bathgate was already on the phone organising the response team.

'You stole Dr Carlisle's car tonight?' Eggo asked.

'No! Well, technically yes. He was asleep and I didn't want to wake him.'

'You're sleeping with the pathologist?'

'What? No, I just knew that if I told him where I was going, he'd try to stop me so I left him sleeping . . .'

Harris Eggo shook his head.

'And why were you there, exactly, in the middle of the night, alone?'

'I had some questions for Hilda . . . you know, now really isn't the time to be worrying about this.'

'Miss Levesque, are you sure you're not in need of any medical assistance right now?'

'Yes, I'm shaken but . . .'

'Stand up please.'

I did as I was told, seeing the splash of red I left behind me on the wall, noting the deep scarlet of my hands.

'Hey, I know I look a mess but you don't need to worry about me.'

'I'm not. I'm detaining you, Miss Levesque. You're going to be held in our cells until I can visit the crime scene and return here to interview you under caution. You'll be informed of your full rights and found a lawyer if you want one.'

'You have to be kidding! I just put my life at risk to come here in the dark and notify you. I held her head on my lap as she died, not knowing if I was going to be next.'

'Give me the car keys and your mobile phone please.'

'No, fuck you! You have no right—'

'Fine, I'm arresting you for theft of a motor vehicle and for driving without insurance. That's enough to hold you until I get back. Keys and mobile, now.'

I handed them over.

'Nate Carlisle won't make a complaint against me for the theft. Call him.'

'That's a hire car,' Eggo said. 'You didn't steal it from Dr Carlisle.' He opened the door of a cell and pushed me inside. 'And you're going to wait there without saying one more bloody word until I can get a forensics team to you to take every stitch you're wearing and do a full forensics examination of your hands. What else is in your pockets?'

I patted myself down, pulling the kitchen knife out slowly.

'Well isn't that the thing?' Eggo said. 'Put it on the floor.'

I did what he told me without speaking. He went and fetched an evidence bag, picked it up and labelled it, then he left.

I waited there, shivering in a corner, wondering just what the hell I had done.

Chapter Thirty-Nine

They wouldn't let me see Nate, and that hurt. I'd unwittingly made him a witness which rendered him off-limits to me until they'd either charged me with an offence or released me.

'I don't understand how you can possibly think I did this. I've come to you every time I discovered anything. If I hadn't headed straight here last night, Hilda's body might not have been discovered for days.'

The forensics squad had been in, taken my clothes, cut my nails, swabbed more parts of me than I was comfortable with, and taken a DNA sample and my fingerprints. I'd refused the offer of legal representation but they'd brought a solicitor to the police station anyway.

Harris Eggo sat opposite me drinking black coffee – I'd refused a cup – and looking at me as if I were an alien species. Simon Bathgate was blocking the door, arms crossed, legs parted, clearly on a testosterone high.

'Does it make you feel heroic to have been the one to find Hilda?' Eggo asked.

'Heroic? What the fuck are you talking about?' I fought my rising temper.

'Well, you found Adriana. That must have felt pretty good. Made us look like a bunch of amateurs. Our island, our job, but you turn up and the girl's found straight away.'

'It wasn't straight away. I was searching for four days before I went to Mackinnon's Cave. And I didn't make you look like idiots, I just did my job.'

'Get a taste for the drama after that, did you?' Bathgate asked.

'Simon, I told you, I'm the only one asking questions today,' Eggo told him.

PC Bathgate huffed but shout his mouth.

'Tell me again how you knew where to find Catriona,' Eggo said.

'Gut instinct. Why wouldn't the killer consider using the same location? It obviously had some meaning for him.'

'Except Dr Carlisle has a theory that maybe a different person killed Catriona and Hilda. A theory which I know he shared with you, and which you seemed to agree with.'

'I agreed it was possible, that there were elements that made sense, like the fact that Catriona hadn't been sexually assaulted. So yes, it could be a different killer. Possible but not definitive.'

'Like, maybe the person who killed Catriona then Hilda had a different motivation. Maybe they weren't interested in whatever perverted pleasure the first killer got from what he did with that shell. Perhaps it was a copycat who just wanted the attention.'

There was a giant click inside my head. I stood up.

'No you don't,' I said.

'Want that lawyer now?' Eggo checked.

'No, but if this is going where I think it's going, you're going to need one. I did not kill Catriona and I did not kill Hilda. You have no evidence whatsoever to indicate that I did. You think I got some sort of kick out of finding their bodies? I hate what happened to them and I hate that I had to see them like that. I'm on this island entirely by chance. People don't just decide to start killing for a bit of a thrill.'

'How would you know why people decide to start killing?' Bathgate chipped in.

'Go fuck yourself,' I told him.

'Constable, last warning,' Eggo said. 'Dr Carlisle says those marks on your neck are to do with Rhys Stewart attempting to hang you. Apparently Hilda intervened and took you back to her cabin.'

'Yes,' I said.

'So you knew where she lived. The layout of the place. That she was alone and a long way from any neighbours or passersby.'

'Relevance?' I asked.

'Just sorting out the timeline. Why not report what Skittles did? A man that dangerous and you elected not to notify us in the middle of an investigation when two young women were already dead? That just doesn't ring true.'

I sighed. 'This might not make much sense to you, but Hilda explained the situation with Skittles. How I'd disturbed his father's bones, how he thought I was trying to frame him for the deaths.'

'Weren't you?' Eggo asked.

'I found a skeleton in his cellar, and a missing shell that I believe came from his shop and ended up inside Adriana Clark. My assumptions were justifiable.'

'Rhys Stewart says he was at home above the Emporium at the time you allege he was trying to kill you. Knows nothing about it.'

'What the hell did you expect him to say? Yeah, sure, I hit that woman across the head, tied her up and pushed her off a branch with a noose around her neck. Seriously?'

'You asked about Hilda when you saw her slap Father Christophe outside the church at Catriona's memorial service. What was that about?'

'You ever heard the phrase the enemy of my enemy is my friend?' I growled.

'Oh, so now Father Christophe is your enemy too? How is he wrapped up in all this?'

'It was just a phrase. I only meant that he and I didn't see eye to eye on the way the young women on the island should be conducting themselves. And he knew things about Adriana from confessions that he isn't revealing, things that might help find her killer.'

'So he's doing his job as a priest properly, and you dislike him for that,' Eggo commented.

'You're putting words in my mouth.'

'Dr Carlisle also told us that you found a seaweed crown underneath your pillow at the hotel, and that you contacted him concerned that you might be a target. How was it that someone could have got into your room?'

'Easily. It's a hotel. The maids, the owners, anyone with the master key. I was on the ground floor and the windows were ancient. It's really not that hard to get in somewhere if you're determined enough.'

'I bet,' Bathgate said.

'He leaves or this interview is over,' I said. 'I'm done.'

'This interview is over when I say it is,' Eggo said. 'Bathgate, get out. Send one of the others in.'

'Oh, come on, are you seriously believing a word this bitch says?' Bathgate hissed.

'This is a recorded interview, Constable, and you're jeopardising its future admissibility. Now do as I ordered and get out!'

Bathgate went, and I sat with my arms folded, glaring at the table, until another constable took his place.

'Why didn't you call the police about the seaweed crown? There might have been fingerprints on the window or the door, trace evidence in your room. If you really thought you'd been targeted by Adriana's killer, it was an opportunity to catch him or her.'

'It's a hotel room. Any prints or traces could have come from hundreds of different sources, and the information about the seaweed crown had been released too widely by then. It could as easily have been a prank, or a police officer deciding they didn't want me investigating and trying to scare me off.'

'So it's a conspiracy now, is it?' Eggo asked quietly.

'I haven't exactly been welcomed here with open arms.'

'Have you ever received any treatment for a mental illness or disorder?'

I closed my eyes. What was it that Hilda had asked me? Was I at peace with myself? Nothing left unsaid to those I loved? Had she seen this coming, I wondered? This reframing of the last weeks of my life to suit police purposes? This shaming and reduction of everything I believed in and stood for? My family would be horrified at the thought of me charged with murder. Yes, I had been at each crime scene, and yes, that had been before anyone else. But I sure as hell hadn't imagined Skittles pushing me off that branch, only now there was no one left to back up my version of the story, and I looked like some self-obsessed fantasist.

'No,' I replied calmly. 'I've never received treatment for a mental illness or disorder.'

'You've never self-harmed or committed any other extreme acts to get attention?'

'I think,' I said, leaning forward, 'that you are over-stepping. So let's cut to the chase. Just exactly what is it you're accusing me of, in plain terms?'

'Miss Levesque, you've got to admit it's odd. You found Adriana, then Catriona, now Hilda. The latter in the middle of the night, having left Dr Carlisle asleep in bed. If he hadn't woken up, he'd have provided you with an alibi for several hours.'

'Sergeant, I don't need a goddamned alibi. I came straight here, to you.'

'I want to believe you. Really. But the crime scene is all you. Your footprints in Hilda's blood, your fingerprints everywhere. There's barely a speck of your clothes not covered in her blood. And what, you just sat there with her head in your lap, and watched her die?'

'What should I have done? The front of her was cut apart. She'd lost so much blood already. I could have given her mouth-to-mouth but there was no way her heart was going to start pumping again, there was nothing left in her veins.'

'You're medically qualified now as well then?'

'Enough to know when there's no hope left,' I said.

Eggo opened a file and cast his eyes down some notes.

'You were arrested two years ago and charged with kidnapping, unlawful confinement and assaulting a 16-year-old called Veronique Bell. Those are some serious charges, Miss Levesque. We don't like that sort of thing in Scotland. It sounds an awful lot like what happened to Adriana and Catriona. You've got some explaining to do.'

'This is how desperate you are?'

'Concerned rather than desperate,' he replied.

It was a hijacking, and I had no choice but to explain myself. I didn't want to think about Veronique Bell. I'd hated her, I'd hated myself every minute I'd spent with her, and I hated Harris Eggo for bringing it up.

'All right, if you really want to waste everyone's time. Veronique was a heroin addict who'd run away from her home in Toronto. She was sixteen years old. Took me a while to find her on behalf of her single mother who was looking after her three other children. She'd asked Veronique to leave after drug dealers raided their apartment looking for cash to pay off the girl's drug debts. Mrs Bell became concerned when her daughter hadn't contacted her for several days, and was willing to pay me all her savings to get her daughter home safely. There was information that Veronique was prostituting herself to pay for her fix and accommodation.'

'Sounds grim,' Eggo said.

'Understatement. Anyway, I found her, befriended her, persuaded her to come to my motel room by posing as a fellow user. She hadn't been able to afford any drugs for a while and she started jonesing. Her mother had said do whatever I had to. I made a decision to restrain her, get her through the worst of the symptoms with methadone, then take her home. The confinement charge related to keeping her in the room, the assault was putting a gag in her mouth while she was trying to bite me.'

'Veronique reported you to the police?'

'No, her pimp and drug supplier did that, which is why the information you have is that I was arrested but that there was no subsequent conviction. Her mother persuaded Veronique – a little more rational by then – that giving blow jobs for heroin wasn't exactly a life choice. The drug dealer got put away and I was released.'

'Covered in glory all over again. Some questionable methods used along the way though.'

'Easy to say that when you haven't had to help a young addict covered in needle marks, with two black eyes, self-inflicted cut marks over her thighs and who was recently treated to a home abortion by being kicked in the stomach. I saved her life. I got her home, didn't charge her mother a cent, and I don't regret any of it. Not even the arrest.'

He flicked the file shut.

'We'll have to wait and see what the full police file says when it arrives. I'd like to ask you about the cat bone.'

'No,' I said. 'We're done. I'm finished. Charge me or let me go.'

'I can hold you for twenty-four hours without charge,' Eggo said, looking at his watch. 'There's no rush.'

'I agreed to be interviewed under caution to assist. My assistance is no longer available to you. So put me back in my cell if that's what you want, because I'm done playing nice. You're not interested in the truth. This is bullshit and you know it.'

'Tell me about the knife you had on you last night,' he said. 'No tricks.'

'Fine, but that's your last question. I needed a weapon to get me through the woods and back to my car. I'd clearly turned up only minutes if not seconds before her killer left. He could have been waiting for me right outside her cabin, or anywhere en route to my car. I was exiting through her window. The knife was on the side in her kitchen area. I grabbed it and ran.'

'You didn't do anything else with it?'

'No,' I said. 'I held it in my hand all the way back to the car and put it in my pocket when I started driving off.'

'And the blood on it?'

'All Hilda's, transferred from my hands. Like you said, I was covered in blood.'

'Did you cut yourself on it at all?'

'No,' I shook my head.

'So the tiny snags of skin caught in the blade would be Hilda's too?' he asked.

I felt the blood drain from my face. It was hard to breathe. 'Skin?' I asked.

'Yes, Dr Carlisle has confirmed that the knife with Hilda's blood all over it, and a single set of fingerprints that are a match for yours, also has minute pieces of human skin caught in the blade. Subject to forensic testing, of course, the hypothesis is that the skin is Hilda's. Made all the more likely because Dr Carlisle has already compared the weapon to the marks on her skin and concluded that the knife you handed in was used to cut off her breast. And therefore to kill her.'

Bastard. Eggo had distracted me by asking about Veronique Bell – no doubt knowing there was nothing of substance in the case – to hit me with this. And it had worked. I clutched my stomach to no avail, bending to vomit between my legs as reality hit me.

'I'll have someone clean that,' Harris Eggo said. 'Until then, you'll remain in police custody. Take her back to the cells please, constable.'

That was the moment I made a decision that would affect every day, every hour, of the rest of my life.

Chapter Forty

'Get me the lawyer,' I said.

'She's gone into town to get coffee. Back in fifteen minutes or so.'

'That'll be fine. Call her and tell her I want to talk.'

I sat back down in my cell wearing the charity-shop clothes that had been provided when my own had been taken away, and wondered how long it would be until I'd see my possessions again. Nate would oversee the processing and movement of Hilda's body and then he'd be leaving the island to get on with the postmortem. Meanwhile I'd left everything in his room and I needed it back. A minute later an officer entered the cell area carrying my backpack.

'Yours?' he asked.

'Yes, can I have it? I need to use the bathroom, change my clothes and there are some people I need to contact.'

'I'll go through it and let you know what you can have. Your computer will have to be sent to the mainland for the hard drive to be checked once you're charged.' Once I was charged. Not if. He disappeared again, and I could hear voices through the thick door.

'Nate!' I yelled. 'Nate, please! I have to talk to you.'

Further conversation beyond the door, a raised voice – not Nate's – a door slamming. Quiet. Then the door into the cells opened one more time. Nate appeared, solemn, drawn. My stomach took a dive, and shame enveloped me. I'd screwed up, so very badly that I couldn't find the words to start the conversation.

'When did you last eat?' he asked quietly. I shrugged in reply. 'I gather the lawyer's on her way. You should take whatever advice you're given. This is serious, Sadie.'

'Never mind that. It's you I need to apologise to. I've put you in a dreadful position. Made you a potential witness against me. You've been so kind to me, Nate, more than I deserved.'

'Stop right now and listen to me. The constable has popped out for a cigarette against my medical advice but as a favour to me. You and I can't discuss the cases any more. In fact, we can't talk until the real killer or killers are caught and brought to trial. You and I will potentially both end up being witnesses, and the defence will have a field day with this.'

'So . . . you don't think I killed Hilda?'

'No, but that's irrelevant. The timing, the weapon, your proximity. It's not good, Sadie. They've got grounds to hold you and to charge you.'

'But the same person who killed Hilda must have killed Catriona.'

'For sure. The position of the cut, the wound itself, although made by a different knife, is pretty conclusive that it was the same perpetrator.'

'But the police have nothing to link me to Catriona's killing.'

'You at her father's house, looking in her bedroom, asking questions around the town. PC Bathgate mentioned something about finding you at the Standing Stones, well-hidden but watching Catriona from the bushes. Your number on her call log. And again, you found the body . . .'

'There's no motive.'

'They're going to be asking for you to be evaluated by a psychiatrist. They're building some sort of narcissistic personality disorder theory. They say it fits with your job, you finding the bodies, your previous arrest.' The outside door banged again. 'I'm sorry. I've got to go. I wish you hadn't gone off in the middle of the night like that. If you'd told me—'

'Didn't want to wake you up,' I said. Only that wasn't the truth. 'I guess I knew you'd talk me out of it.'

'I wish you'd given me the opportunity.'

'Nate, if I stay here another woman or girl is going to end up dead. The police are being distracted by me. That's my fault, no one else's. But you know they're going nowhere fast with this investigation.'

'I can't comment on that,' he said. 'I've got to go. I'm leaving the island in an hour.'

'I just meant that I'm sorry. For all the problems I've caused. And for any . . .' I struggled to find a neutral phrase, '. . . for any in the future.'

'Call me when you're in the clear. I'll do all I can to help from my end. I was enjoying getting to know you, Sadie. I wish it had been different.'

He put his warm hand over my cold one and I forced back tears.

'Me too,' I said. 'Hey, listen, I'll be visiting you in Glasgow before you know it. Travel safe.'

I watched his few footsteps from me to the door, saw his steady hand as he pushed it open, the firm line of his jaw as he nodded at whichever officer had done him the favour, and then he was gone. My only wish was that I hadn't cost him too much.

★ ★ ★

I didn't like the decision I'd made. It flew in the face of everything I believed in and everything I'd worked for. Still it seemed the only thing to do.

The lawyer's name was Laura Helm. She was smart, in her thirties, businesslike and had one foot that dragged a little after the other. School would have been cruel. Those teenage years when everyone else got invited to the dance, and you told yourself it didn't matter, you weren't that interested in going anyway. Now she'd drawn the unluckiest straw of them all. Representing a woman who didn't want to talk, who was going to be uncooperative, and then make her life very difficult indeed.

The cells in Mull police station – two of them – were in a small corridor that led to the front desk at one end and the interview room at the other. Ms Helm walked past me, notebook and file in hand, and went to sit in the interview room while I was released from the cell and paraded along to see her. I wasn't handcuffed. It was a small place, I was a known quantity and I hadn't yet been charged with a crime. Plus, it was an island. Where was I going to go?

The lawyer and I sat and talked a while. She explained everything I already knew. What my rights were, what was likely to happen, their grounds for keeping me. Then she asked me to give my version of events. I glazed over. Part acting, part reality.

'Miss Levesque, are you all right? Should I fetch you a glass of water?'

'I have blood pressure issues,' I lied. 'My medication's in the backpack Dr Carlisle brought in, but I'm not sure which pocket. Everything's become very vague. Could you ask the officer to get my things out of the evidence cupboard and go through it?' I rested my head on my arms. Overkill, maybe, but no lawyer was going risk their client passing out in custody with them present and not do something about it.

'Sure, you stay there. It might take a few minutes.' She made her way back up the corridor to the police officer manning the front desk. Harris and Bathgate were both still out at the crime scene.

I picked my head up, exited the interview room, leaned against the wall and stumbled my way up the corridor – plausibility should I have been discovered. Behind the far door I could hear my solicitor arguing with the constable about whether or not a doctor should be called, and if they'd been aware of my medical condition and failed to inform her. I felt sorry for them both.

Taking the only other door off the corridor, I found the tiny kitchen from which officers occasionally appeared carrying mugs or sandwiches. There was a knife there, sharp but not that large, which would have to make do. Summoning a degree of backbone I hadn't previously appreciated I had, I went to the door to the front desk and kicked it open.

There, I had three options. Hold the knife to my own throat, point it at poor Miss Helm or threaten the life of a police officer. The first was preferable in terms of committing fewer criminal offences, but that was also the least likely to have the desired effect.

My lawyer noticed me first, gave a small shriek and a panicked look in the direction of the young police constable who was going through my personal effects.

'Hands up,' I said, feeling bizarrely like a cartoon cowboy. This wasn't me. 'I don't want to hurt either of you.'

The officer began to reach for what was undoubtedly an alarm bell below the counter. If he pressed it, every police unit on the island was going come running.

'You don't want to do that,' I said, stopping him mid-movement.

'Miss Levesque, just put the knife down,' he replied. 'You can't get away with it.'

'Stop talking and do not move another inch towards that alarm,' I said, moving around the counter, keeping my lawyer between him and me.

'It's an island. Where do you think you're going to hide?' He began moving his hand towards the alarm again.

'Do what I'm telling you!' I shouted, lurching forward, waving the knife in the air. He froze.

'Okay, okay!' Miss Helm said. 'We'll do whatever you want.' She was pale and I sucked my guilt down. Enough time later, hopefully, for me to dwell on that.

'Fingers laced behind your heads, make your way into the cells,' I ordered. 'Leave your mobiles on the desk. You'll go first Constable, no heroics.'

They went, more pliant than I'd anticipated, but then I was there on a potential double murder charge. There had been talk of psychiatrists. That wasn't the first knife they'd found me with, and the last one had been covered in a dead woman's blood.

The cells weren't high tech at all. Straightforward key-in-the-lock job.

My instinct was to apologise, but that would have been an expensive luxury. I had things to do that required me to be free. Sooner or later I was going to get caught again, and when I did the fallout from my escape would be phenomenal. If I could claim a sort of temporary psychiatric break caused by finding Hilda's body then my own incarceration, I would get off more lightly, which meant that a rational apology and explanation could only be self-destructive. Better mad than bad.

No time left, I grabbed my effects – the backpack, my cell phone, watch, and the compass that had been in my pocket the previous night – and I went, locking the external doors of the police station behind me. I got moving, switching my phone on as I went, copying my contacts list from the SIM card to the phone itself then dropping the SIM card down a drain. I dumped my sleeping bag with the camping stove into a tractor trailer as it drove past heading out of Tobermory. Wherever it was going, hopefully those items would be discovered later in the day and assumptions about my movements made.

They police would expect me to run for the hills, which is what I should have done, but there was no point escaping from Tobermory when it was clear that was where I needed to be. I took the back path to the home the Clarks had fled, zigzagging as I went, avoiding twitching curtains and vehicles. Over their fence, into their garden, I took the spare kitchen key from its hiding place and entered the house, making it halfway across the kitchen floor before I collapsed.

Nothing I'd done was in character. I should have accepted my fate, sat in the cell, hoped they decided not to charge me and complied with whatever advice my lawyer gave. I wasn't stupid or reckless. I saved lives rather than threatening them. But in the back of my mind, I'd been sitting with Lizzy in the apartment above the pottery shop while her grandmother brought us tea. She'd answered my questions about Catriona, done her best to tell me because she was a good girl even when her friends sometimes led her astray. Her grandmother knew that and had tried to help me too. Now Catriona was dead, and Hilda was dead, and there was a murderer partying across the island looking for women who had dabbled in the pagan arts. Lizzy was one of them, and I couldn't let her be next. Her grandmother shouldn't have to sit in a memorial service for her granddaughter and listen to a lecture on how the young women of Mull had brought death to their own doors as they'd strayed from the paths of perceived righteousness.

There'd been a moment in the night as, muddle-headed and exhausted, I'd slipped in and out of wakefulness, where I'd questioned if I hadn't actually killed those women. In the cave with Catriona, in the cabin with Hilda. I'd begun to doubt myself. Had I slipped a noose around my own neck in the woods, Skittles' presence no more than useful delusion, as I'd let my body slip off that branch? Had Hilda found me there, ranting, and saved my life?

No. No, those were the thoughts that came from seeing too many dead bodies, from standing next door to death and cheating him by only an inch or two, from reading of witches and spells, of sinking galleons and Spanish princesses.

Sleep was all I wanted and the one thing I could not have. I sat on the floor and allowed myself to fantasise about it for a minute: the mattress, duvet, a firm pillow, dark curtains, closed door. Then I picked myself up, raised my chin, and made a decision. I had broken the law to a degree that was going to have the severest of consequences, so I had to make the time available to me count. I had a killer to catch. More than one, I had decided. Nate was right. There was too much separating the first murder from the other two. That was the key. The leap from Adriana to Catriona then Hilda. I had more information than anyone else, and I was close. I knew it. No leads, not so much as a hunch, but I had all the puzzle pieces. I just needed to figure out how to fit them together. Finding the killers wasn't only going to save future victims, it was also the only way to prove my own innocence.

Chapter Forty-One

A man had killed Hilda. Of that one fact, I was certain. The log placed outside her door was so heavy that only the most extraordinary of women could have moved it. As far as the body was concerned, there was none of the posing I'd witnessed with Catriona in the cave. Hilda hadn't even been fully undressed. The scene had been chaotic. No seaweed crown. Just the crudeness of a sanity-defying murder. So he'd killed Catriona, taken his time, thought about how he wanted her to be found, then either run out of time with Hilda because I'd disturbed him, or just grown wilder and lost control. Maybe Hilda had sensed that something was wrong earlier than Catriona had, and put up a fight. In any event, now that Nate had concluded Catriona and Hilda were killed by the same person, all I needed to figure out was that person's motive for killing Catriona.

I knew it wasn't only convenience that had brought me to the empty house. Life and death were simply points on a circle, and for me that circle had begun here. This family had been through so much. The prospect of Rob's incarceration, death threats, fleeing their home and their country. Then attempting to settle on a small island, still scared, keeping their heads down.

318

Except for Addie, desperate to live her life and make friends. She'd found a job, got herself noticed, reached out. Joined a group who performed pagan rituals.

I walked up the stairs slowly, Adriana in my head, needing to get inside her thoughts, her skin. Laying on her bed, I stared at the ceiling she'd once stared at, got comfortable on her duvet, smelled the dying remnants of her perfume on the sheets and watched the delicate autumn sunlight play on her walls.

Catriona had texted Adriana, intending that Adriana should erase the message before meeting that night.

'Scratch that,' I told the ceiling. My brain was still falling prey to that human frailty – filling in the gaps in our knowledge instead of sticking to the facts. A text had been sent from Catriona's cell phone to Adriana's, then Adriana had gone missing. Those were the cold hard facts.

Catriona had been a member of Hilda's group long before Addie had come to the island. Perhaps Catriona was actively recruiting more girls. The theory didn't get me any further. If Catriona had been involved in Addie's murder, why risk leaving text messages on her phone that night? The thought stuck in my head on a loop.

I rolled onto my side to pick up the photo of Adriana with Brandon and Luna from her bedside table, the unpleasant odours of my own body and musty storage rising from the borrowed clothes I was wearing beneath my hoodie.

'Shower,' I muttered, getting off the bed, stripping the clothes away and making for Adriana's en suite. The water as hot as I could bear, with as much lather as the soap could muster, worked its magic. Drying myself, I stared at the clothes on the floor and wondered if I could take a liberty, if only for a short while. I went to Isabella's wardrobe first, but at some point she'd moved all her clothes to the new place. It wasn't ideal, but I tried Adriana's wardrobe next. I was a UK size ten, preferring my clothes on the baggy side given the amount of outdoor exercise I did. Addie, it turned out, didn't share my taste and certainly didn't share my more muscular frame. There was a price to pay for spending all my time skiing, hiking and climbing – I had larger thighs and upper arms than other women my age. Addie had been made of skin and bone. Flicking along the line of clothes searching for something neutral, I was giving up hope among the immaculate size six mini-skirts and crop tops. At the far end, almost hidden by a winter coat, I found what I was looking for: a clean grey hoodie with a white stripe around the waist, and some pale bootleg jeans. Both size ten. I reached for them, then stopped myself.

My heart was beating too fast. I closed my eyes, and when I opened them again all I could see was a photograph in my mind, one I'd seen on the police notice board, constructed from two – maybe more – previous photos of Catriona. Wearing precisely these clothes the day she'd breathed her last breath. Never found.

Until now.

In my mind's eye, I saw her again at the Lochbuie standing stones, dancing, talking to the crowd, arms raised, body on display. Beautiful, curvaceous, her body more mature than her years. I didn't even fight to find a different explanation. These weren't Addie's clothes, many of which still bore American labels and sizing. These had been bought in Scotland, designed for the Scottish weather, to complement a different girl. The clothes had been washed, but not ironed. They weren't torn or damaged. Catriona's captor had persuaded her (forced her, threatened her, my inner voice corrected) to remove the clothes before harming her.

Then brought them back here.

'Why did you do that?' I asked a person not yet present.

The answer was hiding in plain sight. It was a wardrobe,

where clothes were kept. Dump them in the sea and the tide would betray you. A bin, when every pair of eyes on the island was eagle-sharp, would have been an invitation to the police station. In the middle of the island, and fate dictated a hiker or a farmer would happen upon them. They'd needed washing. Remove the blood, the DNA, the evidence trail. Put them somewhere that any leftover DNA could be explained. And as soon as the time came for Adriana's clothes to finally be packed up and sent to recycling or a charity shop, no one would notice these items among so many others. It was clever.

I put my own clothes back on and wandered through to Brandon's room where I wept for his loss. Losing a twin, half of you dying. Had he felt, at some deep psychological level, the pain and terror she'd endured? For a boy who'd thought he'd lost all he had to lose when his school, his home, his friends had been taken from him, he'd subsequently paid a price he could never have anticipated.

His room was a shrine to his sister. Photos pinned inside his wardrobe of them at a concert, in a pool, eating pizza, on a yacht, driving a soft-top through the desert. Arms around each other, their eyes indistinguishable, able to share everything. One another's companion on the strange road they'd been forced to travel.

It was me who'd given him the weapon to justify his revenge. I'd insisted on seeing the cell phone. I'd shown the family the text message and revealed the sender's identity. It was me who'd confirmed that Catriona had lured Addie out in the middle of the night. When I'd found Brandon in Mackinnon's Cave, deranged with grief, I'd had my suspicions about his mental state. The family had kept secrets, and I'd suspected Brandon might have done something awful, criminal even, in America. But then I'd learned the truth about their sudden need to flee, and I'd put everything down to that. I'd been too slow, even having witnessed his rage and frustration. But now it was clear what Brandon had done to Catriona, and given the similarities between Catriona's murder and Hilda's, that must have been his work too. It was Brandon I'd been running from through the woods. Brandon who'd cleaned and left the knife with which I was now suspected of killing Hilda.

I picked up their landline, dialling the number from my phone's contacts file.

'Isabella,' I said. 'I need to see you and Rob at your other house straight away.'

'But we're—'

'Straight away,' I repeated. 'Leave Luna with Brandon until we've had a chance to talk. Don't mention that I'm going to be here.' I put the phone down before she could argue.

I waited in the lounge, expecting them to use the front entrance. The kitchen door opened instead, two pairs of feet, no voices.

'Rob,' I said as he appeared. 'Thank you for coming. Sorry I couldn't explain on the phone. There's a lot to talk about.'

Brandon's face came into view, downcast, scowling. I stabbed my fingernails into my palm, forcing my expression to remain neutral.

'Luna didn't want to be away from Isabella,' Rob explained. 'Brandon offered to come instead.'

'Okay,' I replied slowly. 'I need to tell you what I've—'

'We already know,' Rob said. 'The police came to us after you'd escaped. We said we hadn't seen or heard from you. I'm willing to hear you out before we make any decisions.'

I didn't dare look at Brandon. There was no way of knowing how he was going to react to what I was about to reveal to his father, but he did know that I was about to be charged with a crime he'd committed.

'I didn't kill Hilda,' I said quietly. 'Or Catriona. I think you know that.'

Rob looked me in the eyes, nodded, turned away.

'So who did?' Brandon asked.

His voice wasn't what I'd expected. Today he was calm. The fire and venom that he'd had when he'd shouted his accusations about Catriona the previous night all ebbed away.

I'd already sealed Catriona's clothes in a clean bag and hidden them under Luna's bed until I could direct the police to where they could be found.

The plan had been simpler than the execution was proving. Rob and Isabella were supposed to arrive child-free. I was to explain to them that their son, the only surviving half of a twin, had suffered what I believed to have been an acute psychotic episode caused by extraordinary grief. The fact that I, too, was the subject of a police hunt and a number of allegations of violent offending was a complicating factor I had done my best to ignore. My approach to Brandon's predicament was going to be sympathy with a need for treatment. I was going to propose finding the best lawyer, taking advice, talking to the police with a view to getting a psychiatric report and looking to enter pleas that were reflective of the state of Brandon's mental health. I didn't believe the boy would have killed under any other circumstances. I also didn't believe he was a threat to anyone save those he thought had been responsible for his twin's death. I was hoping to persuade Rob and Isabella that Brandon's confession would, ultimately, be the best thing for their son.

'Rob,' I said. 'This isn't something Brandon should have to deal with. Could we talk alone for a few minutes?'

'I'm not a kid,' Brandon said. 'If this is about Addie then I have every right to know what's going on.'

'It's not about Addie,' I told him.

His eyes widened, something more fearful, less argumentative flickering within him.

'Dad,' he said. 'We'll get in trouble with the police if we stay here. She shouldn't be in our house. You know they told us to call as soon as we heard from her.'

'You can call them the second we've finished our conversation,' I said. 'I'll even call them myself while you're still here if you like.'

'Let's assess that when I've heard what Miss Levesque has to say,' Rob told his son. 'You stay here, we'll go in the kitchen.'

I went first, making sure Rob closed the doors between rooms, walking to the far end and giving Rob no option but to follow me. I liked the proximity to the back door. From there it was only a few strides to the fence and to safety if needed. What I realised was that Brandon was the more known quantity of the two of them. Rob's instinct to protect his son might be less predictable.

'You know I didn't kill those women,' I told him gently. 'But what you don't know is that I now have evidence of the killer's identity.'

Rob shook his head briefly with half a glance to the door we'd just come through. That was when I saw it clearly. He knew what his son had done. Knew, or suspected. Was that why he'd brought Brandon instead of Isabella? To keep the truth from her?

'Say it,' he said. 'Whatever you want to say, get on with it.'

'Listen, this is not a judgement. Losing Addie was devastating for all of you. There's no way of getting through that sort of grief for some people. It destroys them.'

'But you're on the hook now, and you don't want to be charged. What do the police have on you, anyway? Must be compelling for them to be holding you.'

'It was the knife,' I said. 'I picked it up to defend myself when I ran from the scene, not knowing it had been used to kill Hilda.'

'I still don't understand how Addie got drawn into it,' Rob said. 'This whole thing with Hilda and Catriona. It was pointless, childish—'

'Dad,' Brandon said, opening the door behind his father.

I took a step back, hand in my pocket on the bear spray I'd retrieved from my backpack.

'Son, go home. I'm dealing with this.'

'I think we should call Isabella,' I suggested. 'She should be a part of this. Does she . . . suspect anything?'

'What's going on?' Brandon asked.

There was a gun pointed in my face before I could register that Rob had put a hand behind his back to the waistband of his jeans.

'Hey!' I said. 'Wait, I'm not the enemy here—'

'Dad?'

'Brandon, this is not your problem. I'm going to sort it out. Now I need you to leave, go home and look after your mother.'

'I'm not leaving you! What's happening?'

I sighed. 'I know you killed Catriona, Brandon. Hilda too. The pathologist confirmed it was the same killer. You were furious with Catriona, and maybe that was my fault for giving you too much information. We can deal with this, I promise. A good lawyer—'

'What?' Brandon cried.

'Go home!' Rob directed at Brandon, taking a step closer to me.

'What are you going to do to her?' Brandon asked.

'Rob, I found Catriona's clothes in Addie's wardrobe. I've already left a message with the pathologist's office. He'll get it when he exits the helicopter. It can't be undone.'

'We should never have brought you here,' Rob whispered.

'We never asked you to look into anyone's death other than Addie's. When I think that I actually *paid* you to do this to our family.'

'I honestly believe I can help,' I said. 'With treatment, some compromises – I don't think Brandon's ever going to be a danger to anyone else again.'

'I killed them!' Rob screamed, storming into my face, waving the gun like a gavel. 'You stupid, stupid girl!'

'No . . .' Brandon said, staggering back against the wall.

I took two steps forward before Rob pulled me backwards, snaking his arm around my neck, gun to my temple.

'I knew how angry Brandon was, and that if I didn't avenge my daughter's death then he would. Those women got what they deserved. They used Addie like some fucking ritual, they sacrificed her in that cave!'

'You didn't do it,' Brandon sobbed. 'Dad, say you didn't!'

'I did, and it was the right thing to do. The girl was scared. She did everything I told her. I promised if she obeyed me I'd let her go. The old woman was a bitch though, cursing and fighting. You still think their midnight ceremonies are harmless?' he hissed into my ear. 'They wanted Addie from the second they saw her. What they did with that shell . . .'

'But the sand, the seaweed – why go to so much trouble with them?' I asked.

'It had to look like someone from the island had killed them,' he said. 'As for the sand – I just wanted them to experience what Addie had felt.'

'Their right breasts . . . what you did was monstrous.'

'Isn't that what they do to witches here? The hours of research I did to find that and now you've ruined it all,' Rob said.

Brandon sank to the floor.

'You need to look after your son,' I said.

'It's too late,' Rob said. 'It was always too late. From the second I started taking that dirty fucking money. I did my deal with the devil back in Vegas. I always knew he'd come for his pound of flesh. It should've been mine, not Addie's. He sent his witches for her.' His tears were wet on my cheek as he pressed his face to mine. 'I destroyed everything we had. I took everything from my family. My wife couldn't even call her father when he got sick. My kids had to lose their names. Everything. It's my fault we came here.'

'Dad, no!' Brandon sobbed.

I reached out a hand towards Brandon. Rob shoved the pistol into my cheekbone.

'It was my fault Addie died. I saw what that did to Brandon, to Isabella and Luna. I thought if some justice was done, I could make amends.'

'Rob, please, put the gun down. I'm not going to call the police. You've run once, you can run again. Pack up the family and disappear . . .'

'No,' he said. 'No more running. This ends now. I don't want to make them do that again. Close your eyes.'

'Please don't,' Brandon whispered, wide-eyed, a puddle appearing on the floor between his legs.

'I have to. It's for you,' Rob said. 'No choice.'

I thought of Hilda again, finally clearer about her meaning, wondering how she knew what lay in store for me. I shut my eyes.

The gun pulled back an inch from my face. The trigger clicked, and I thought I heard the bullet fly. It hit its target.

Rob's forehead flew backwards as if there were no bones in his neck at all. The sound so loud, so close, I heard it through my skull.

Then his arm falling from my neck, sliding down my back. Blood, warm, coppery, splashing against the cupboards behind us.

Brandon screaming.

Me, silent, open-mouthed.

Reaching out for Brandon who hit my hands away and took his father in his arms. Rob – the back of his skull fragmented – falling to the floor, dead the instant he'd pulled the trigger. I kicked the gun away gently, reeling. Wondering what to do next. Wishing I'd never set foot in Scotland, never heard of Mull.

I would have called the police myself, sooner or later. A neighbour, hearing the gunshot, beat me to it.

They had me on the floor, on my face, restrained, before I could tell them what had happened. I was spared having to explain it to Isabella while I sat in a cell for the following twenty-four hours. Locked up, and glad of it. Whenever I was allowed to roam free on that island, I ended up holding a corpse in my arms.

Chapter Forty-Two

I didn't mind the cell that time. The closeness of it, the safety, not having to see the faces of the bereaved: the best way I can describe it is 'downtime'. Not that I wasn't in trouble, but I wasn't on the hook for a double murder any more. Harris Eggo wouldn't commit to a course of action regarding my escape from custody or the fact that I'd stolen a knife and locked up two people whilst brandishing it. But I'd been operating under exceptional circumstances, and everyone knew it. The procurator fiscal – an almost unintelligible name for the Scottish prosecutor's office – was, according to Eggo, reviewing matters. In the meantime, they had my passport, and if released I'd agreed to a curfew at the bed and breakfast place where Nate had been staying. Just one more hour to go until the maximum period for holding me without charge was up.

The door to the front desk opened, and Simon Bathgate shouted back at me.

'Levesque, visitor for you.'

I stood up. It was Isabella Clark who walked in, sunglasses on, moving slowly, one hand on the wall.

She paused, staring in my direction. I couldn't see through the dark glass to her eyes, but the stillness of her, the intensity, stopped my breath.

'We're going away,' she said. 'I've had our lawyer speak to Sergeant Eggo. They've agreed that we can go to the mainland until the investigation's over. The bodies can be shipped back to the States for burial when they're released.'

'Mrs Clark, I'm so sorry. When you asked me to come here the last thing in the world I wanted was to cause you more pain. I can't even imagine—'

'Rob wanted me to send you back to Canada as soon as I found out Catriona was dead. He tried to persuade me that you were no longer needed. Now I know why. He didn't want you figuring out what he'd done.' She removed her glasses. Beneath them, her eyes were pits of tiredness, but they were dry, with none of the bitter redness that hours of crying would have caused. 'You didn't cause any of this. My children have lost their father because of the things he did. He wasn't a bad man, not when I first met him. He got greedy though, and he changed. It wasn't just the money. He knew perfectly well the sorts of men he was laundering money for, how they operated.'

'If it helps at all, he was destroyed by grief. I think he tried to stay strong for you and for Luna, but when he saw Brandon spiralling downwards he snapped,' I said.

'He blamed himself for all of us being here. And for Addie's death. I'm afraid I blame him for that too. We were doing all right financially, Sadie. He was a good accountant. When he started breaking the rules, he knew the price he'd pay if he got caught. After he gave evidence I only stayed with him because by then our lives were at risk even if we separated. The men he gave evidence against wanted revenge. I figured we were safer staying together as a unit, and I didn't want to put the children through the trauma of being separated from their father. Turned out all the choices I made were wrong.'

I said nothing because there was nothing to say. Isabella had been through too much to be interested in my sympathy, and expressing it was too trivial.

'I've reached out to the men who wanted my husband dead. I still have friends with contacts in Vegas. We've lost Adriana and now Rob. They won't come after us any more. Once this is over, I can go back. Not to Vegas, that wouldn't be tolerated, but we can go live with my family in San Diego. The children will fit in better there.'

'How's Brandon doing?' I asked.

'It may be years before I know the answer to that question,' she said. 'I want to know who killed my daughter. Whether it was one of the dead women, or both of them together, but more than that I want to know why. Whatever the answer is, I need to know. Will you help me?'

Her faith in me, after everything, took my breath away.

'Of course I'll help you,' I said. 'But I can't leave the island, and there are some restrictions on my movements, so are you sure I'm the best person to do this?'

'I'm certain,' she said, slipping her sunglasses back on. 'It's the least Addie deserves.'

She began making her way back up the corridor.

'Isabella,' I called after her. 'I really am just so sorry for everything you've—'

She put one hand on the door and left as I was still speaking. I'd have done the same.

PC Bathgate handed me a plastic bag with my few released belongings in and gave me a twist of a smile. I took a deep breath and exited, no idea what to expect as I walked down through the town. Would I still be mistrusted, was I persona

331

non grata for my connection to the man who had taken two of their community, or could I show my face again now that I'd helped deliver some small portion of justice?

'Miss Levesque?' a man asked as I stood there, gazing along the road.

A stranger standing by a motorbike, in his sixties I guessed, average build, dark grey hair, holding a helmet and smiling at me.

'Should I know you?'

'Lance Proudfoot,' he said, holding up his driving licence. 'We've spoken on the phone.' He held a helmet out to me, his other hand open-palmed towards the bag I was holding.

I ignored both hands, stepped forward and put my arms around his neck, hugging him hard. He responded without a word, wrapping his arms around me and giving a soft laugh.

'How did you know?' I asked.

'There was a news report, fairly vague, of a Canadian woman helping police with their enquiries. I asked my police contact to check on the situation. He seemed to think you'd need to see a friendly face as and when they released you.'

'How long have you been here?'

'A couple of hours,' he said. 'It's no trouble. Any excuse to get the bike out and take the ferry over for a day trip. Mull is beautiful, in spite of the memories it holds for me. So,' he handed me the spare helmet, and this time I took it as he put my bag in a pannier, 'where to?'

It was my stomach that answered first.

'I'm kind of hungry,' I said. 'I've had nothing but an inedible sausage roll today. I thought I'd never want to eat again, but actually I'm starving.'

'Local pub it is then,' he said. 'Hold your head high, drink whisky from the local distillery, and lunch is on me.'

★　★　★

I paused at the doorway of The Blether wondering if I'd be welcome or not, but then Lance pushed me forward, already pulling his wallet from his pocket.

The silence that consumed the bar as we entered was straight out of the movies. I looked around at the familiar faces, trying to find a greeting or an apology to issue – some sort of opener – then Rachel stepped out from behind the bar and took me by the arm.

'Come on in, sweetheart,' she said. 'You two take a seat and I'll bring you whatever you want.' No table in the far corner this time. 'You'll be needing some feeding up after what you've been through.'

'A couple of drams of Ledaig and the menu,' Lance said. 'I haven't set foot in here for decades. They don't make pubs like this any more.'

Rachel patted him on the shoulder, warming to him immediately. It would be hard not to. Lance Proudfoot was old-school and charming.

'We do our best,' she said. 'Now if we could only keep people off their damned mobiles, it really would be like the old days.'

The comment made me reach for my own cell phone. I needed to buy myself a new SIM card, but that wouldn't help me unless it was charged.

'Rachel,' I said. 'Is there somewhere I can charge this? Sorry to ask.'

'No problem at all,' she said. 'They should never have kept you locked up as long as they did. Your people will be wondering if you're okay. Let me put it behind the bar. We keep a fistful of chargers back there.'

I handed it over.

'What you did, finding out who took Catriona and Hilda from us, we're grateful,' Rachel said quietly. 'I know this hasn't been easy on you, but the town is indebted.'

She handed us menus from another table and retreated quietly to the bar.

'Your face tells me you weren't expecting that,' Lance said.

'It was my client who killed their people,' I whispered.

'It was you who discovered that fact, and who stopped any more lives from being lost. It's a best-case scenario for them. There was no monster in their midst. It was an off-islander, an alien. So much better than one of their own, and now – as terrible as this has been – they can start to heal. Catriona and Hilda's bodies can be released for burial. The town can grieve and contemplate a return to normal.'

'You're forgetting Adriana,' I said.

Lewis Eggo appeared, delivering whisky, blushing, and giving me a shy nod. 'You did it,' he said. 'I'm glad you're okay. Rachel says the food is on the house. Will you be leaving now?'

'Not for a little while,' I said. 'There are still some unanswered questions and work to be done.'

'For Adriana?' he asked solemnly. I nodded. 'I'm glad. She deserves justice.'

I put my hand on Lewis's and we stayed like that, quietly, for a few moments. It seemed the island wasn't entirely full of people who disliked me. I needed to rethink my strategy for finding Addie's killer, using honey instead of vinegar maybe.

'You're going to have a bit of a fan club,' Lance noted as Lewis disappeared with our food order. 'Unless you have a theory about Adriana's killer that they don't like.'

'I have no theories at all,' I said, raising my glass. 'Between us, I also didn't figure out who killed Catriona and Hilda. Right family, wrong male.'

Lance stared into his glass for a while.

'I can't even begin to imagine what you've been through,' he said. 'You want to talk about it?'

'Nope. Anything but. You know what I really miss? Poutine.

The Canadian classic – fries with cheese curds, covered in a brown gravy. Best served hot enough to burn your tongue. All the calories to keep you going when there's a couple of feet of snow to get through on your way home. I'll make it for you one day.'

'Sounds like my kind of food,' Lance said. 'Will you head straight back to Canada when things are resolved here?'

'I was hoping to see a bit more of Scotland first, but my sister's baby's due any time now and I need to be there for her. I won't take any cases for a while, maybe go skiing at New Year with friends. Get my priorities straight.'

'Amen to that,' he said. We drained our drinks and Lance waved at Lewis for refills.

'Lance, why did you come? That's not a complaint, by the way – I need all the friends I can get – but you don't know me. It's a lot more than just a kind gesture.'

'I'm semi-retired,' he said. 'Time on my hands, a growing appreciation for my mortality, curiosity about the young woman who phoned me out of the blue and asked for my help.' He paused.

'And?' I asked.

'Flora Kydd. She's haunted me, I think mainly because the case remained open. I was at an impressionable age, and I don't think I'd ever encountered true evil before. It got under my skin. I think helping you is my way of paying some long-overdue respects.'

'I met Flora's father. He explained that the sand was about preventing the victims from speaking their killers' true names. For a mythical creature like a witch, it robs them of their power.'

Lewis put clean glasses down in front of us with the bottle of Ledaig. Lance poured us each a measure and I took a sip. It was peaty and aromatic, straight from the earth.

'The Mull Witches,' Lance said. 'Do you believe the myths then?'

'I believe that certain places have historic means of murder. That patterns emerge over decades, centuries even. In Canada, bodies have occasionally been disposed of by leaving them in remote areas with big bear populations. Great way of getting rid of a corpse, especially just as they come out of hibernation.'

'Like dumping bodies in the Mississippi swamplands?'

'Exactly. Do you think the way murders are committed gives us a sense of geography?'

'Well now I do. You mind if I write a piece about that, if I keep your name out of it and don't reference any of the details you've given me about these killings?'

'Be my guest,' I said. 'You're owed something from this after all you've done.'

Our food arrived, and we ate for a while, listening to the chatter around us. The talk on every side was of the murders, but still no mention of Adriana. Of course, she wasn't just a victim now, she was also the daughter of the man who'd killed their own. Addie was about to lose out yet again.

'Something's been puzzling me,' I said, putting my fork down. 'A text was sent from Catriona's cell phone to Adriana's. Previously I'd thought that maybe Catriona had gotten caught up with someone who persuaded her to help lure Adriana out, then turned on Catriona later and killed her too.'

'But now you know Catriona's murderer was Rob Clark, that no longer makes sense?'

'Exactly. Now, Catriona had security on her phone, facial recognition, so she had to have been present for her phone to be unlocked and used. It's just not possible that she wouldn't have been aware of someone sending those messages, even if she didn't send them herself.'

'I have a friend who's a technical genius. Knows stuff I can't even start to fathom.'

'You think he'd be able to help?'

'If he's not busy hacking some international arms ring or running from the Russian mafia,' Lance grinned. 'I'll ask him and get back to you about it. How does that sound?'

'Perfect. You have some interesting acquaintances for a semi-retired biker from Edinburgh. If this trip has taught me nothing else, it's the value of reaching out and trusting people.'

'Ach, that's Scotland for you. We're not all witches and murderers.'

'I'll drink to that!'

We finished up, thanked Rachel, retrieved my cell and walked back to where Lance had parked his bike.

'I should be getting back to the ferry. Will you be okay?'

'I will,' I assured him, taking my bag from the pannier. 'Better for spending some time with a friend.'

'Go straight to the shop and get a SIM card in that phone of yours then text me your new number, will you?'

I gave him a mock salute as he climbed onto his bike.

'Lance,' I said, walking forward and hugging him, less desperation, more affection this time. 'You have a way of making everything better. Your friends have no idea how lucky they are.'

'Are you not one of them, now?' he smiled, leaning across to kiss me swiftly on the cheek before pulling on his helmet. 'Stay safe, Sadie. I'll be in touch soon.'

I did as he'd instructed me, making my first stop the shop, where I bought a SIM card, some fruit and a sweatshirt with 'Made on Mull' emblazoned on the front – the best I could do until I got to a larger store.

After that, I began the short walk to The Turning Tide Bed & Breakfast, trying not to see Rob Clark's face, trying not to hear Brandon's cries or the shot echoing in my ears. In my head, the question I'd been avoiding for the last full day demanded an answer.

What could I have done differently, so that Rob Clark was still alive now? I came up blank.

I'd been given the same room I'd shared with Nate Carlisle before making the fateful decision to go to Hilda's in the middle of the night. My cell phone rang as I was sinking into a hot bath.

Caller ID told me it was my sister. Delighted as I was to be hearing her voice, I steeled myself against revealing what I'd been through. It had always been my policy to keep the details of my cases from my family. Spreading the misery just wasn't fair.

'Hey Becca,' I smiled as I answered. 'I'm sorry I haven't called for so long! How's that bump—'

'It's started, Sadie,' Becca said. 'I know it's a bit earlier than the due date, but I'm having contractions, proper ones. Mom's coming over now to drive me to the hospital.'

'Oh honey, are you okay? Is anyone with you?'

The enormity of my loss hit me. My failure to be there to hold my sister's hand, comforting her as she made the world a better place by bringing new life into it.

'I'm okay, I just . . . wanted you here so badly. Just to share it all with you. I tried to hold on 'til you got back, I really did. I'm so sorry.'

'Becca, don't. This is all my fault. I'd never have taken this job if I'd known I wouldn't get back to you in time. Listen, I'm coming first thing. I'll get a ferry in the morning, find a flight from Edinburgh or Glasgow. I'll be with you really, really soon.'

'I miss you, Sadie. Your niece misses you. I can't wait for you to come home.'

'Me too. I love you, Becca. You stay strong, get Mom to phone me the second there's news, and kiss that baby from me before anyone else gets the chance.'

A door opened in the background and I heard my mother's voice issuing orders. Becca rang off.

The emptiness inside me was overwhelming. I'd paid too high a price for helping the Clarks. Adriana was dead when I'd arrived and she was still dead now. I hadn't caught her killer. I hadn't kept my promise to my sister. I wasn't where I was most needed in the world. The grief of it consumed me until I made the decision to replace self-pity with action, checking ferries and flights, clearing my departure with Sergeant Eggo, and making things right. After that I texted my new number to Nate, Lance and Isabella Clark, and found my eyes heavy. The commitment I'd made to Isabella – to identify her daughter's killer – was going to have to wait. For once, my own loved ones were going to come first.

It was still only early evening but I was exhausted. I lay down, shut my eyes, imagined myself in a cabin on a mountainside, the snow coming in heavy, the world wrapped in whiteness and silence.

I awoke in the pitch dark to a frantic knocking on my window. 'Sadie, wake up! We need your help.'

Chapter Forty-Three

Ripping back the curtains, I saw Lewis Eggo standing in the rain, palms pressed to the glass. I pulled up the lower pane a few inches.

'Are you okay?'

'The main door to the B&B was locked and I didn't want to hammer.'

'Lewis, how did you find me?'

'My dad gave me instructions. You registered this room number and address for your . . . your curfew while they decide if they're going to charge you. Sorry.' He looked embarrassed for me and I wished I hadn't asked.

'Not a problem. What's going on?'

'I don't know. My dad asked me to give you this straight away.' He pulled an envelope from his pocket, pushed it in through the window and stepped away, rubbing his arms in the cold.

'Miss Levesque' it said on the front in a curling script. I ripped open the seal. *'Forgive the note. Couldn't get through to your mobile. I gather you know Catriona Vass's friend Lizzy, and that you've spoken to her a number of times. Given what I saw when you helped*

340

Brandon Clark and your understanding of distressed teenagers, I wondered if you'd help? Lizzy is at Mackinnon's Cave and threatening suicide. She's asked us not to contact her grandmother yet. If you can come, Lewis can drive you as our other vehicles are already en route there. Please do not discuss the case with Lewis. Lizzy is a friend of his and I don't want him distressed. Harris Eggo.'

'Can you drive me to Mackinnon's Cave, Lewis?'

His face registered shock followed by sadness. He might not have known who was in trouble, but by now the name Mackinnon had become inextricably linked with tragedy.

'All right then,' he said quietly.

'Two minutes.' I threw my Made on Mull sweatshirt over my T-shirt, grabbed jeans, socks and my hiking boots, dressing in under sixty seconds. Exiting through the window, I pushed down hard to secure it, mindful that I could do without any more seaweed under my pillow on my return. Lewis was pale-faced in the moonlight, his eyes red-rimmed. The Tobermory community had suffered too much. Now Lizzy was in peril. I waited until we were in Lewis's car and moving before I began quizzing him.

'So what's going on?' he asked. 'My dad wouldn't tell me anything. He tries to protect me, like I'm still a little kid.'

'He loves you. What father wouldn't want to protect their son? Your dad and I haven't always seen eye-to-eye but I appreciate the fact that you're his priority.'

'I heard him call an ambulance down to the cave. Someone's down there. Did he tell you who?'

'He asked me not to discuss it with you. I'm sorry. It really is for the best as I don't have any details yet.'

'I guess you're the expert on teenagers, right?' He gave a half smile, and I could see the battle going on in his body, boy to man. It was so hard at that age. Hard even when things were normal, but now – defilement and death dropped at their feet like a cat dragging a half-dead mouse – now the island's kids had a different perspective on life.

'I don't regard myself as an expert,' I said. 'I think sometimes it's easier because I'm always a stranger to the teenagers I deal with. You're all so close to one another. Everyone knows everything, people talk, there's not a secret that can be kept. Sometimes strangers are the only people we feel able to trust. How long 'til we get there?'

'From here at this time of night, about twenty minutes. I wouldn't normally go this fast. Dad says a speed limit's a speed limit, irrespective of time or place. But if something else has happened . . .' He broke off, a sob in his throat.

My cell buzzed and I flicked the message open.

'Info about mobile phone security. Call me as soon as you wake up. Lance.'

It was the middle of the night. He hadn't been exaggerating about his lack of regular sleep, but he obviously thought I'd be out of action until a more social time.

'I've got to make a call,' I said.

'Please don't say anything about tonight,' Lewis said. 'Dad wouldn't like it. Some people here are already asking for him to be replaced. I don't want to give them any more reasons to attack him.'

'Got it,' I said, dialling. 'Hey Lance, it's me.'

I pressed the cell to my left ear and leaned into the passenger window to hear properly. The connection was crackly and intermittent.

'Great timing, the hacker friend I told you about came over. I'll put him on.'

There was a general fumbling then another voice, male with an American accent.

'Hey there Sadie, I'm Ben. Lance said you needed to know about breaching security protocols on cell phones, right?'

'Exactly. Can you help?'

'Sure. Do you know what type of phone was breached?'

'Android,' I recalled the information Lizzy had given me.

'Any idea how new the phone is?' Ben asked.

I thought back to Catriona's house and the relative poverty she was living in, her father working all the hours he could, breaking his back on the sea to support them.

'Wouldn't have been new at all. Nothing expensive. Probably second or third hand when she got it.'

'If it was a much older Android cell phone and the software hadn't been updated, the technology could have been fooled by showing the phone a clear facial photo. It's been a security issue with Android for a while. They got it covered in the latest software updates though.'

I stared out of the window into the darkness.

'That's really interesting. Thanks, Ben. You often hang out at Lance's place in the middle of the night?'

'The man's a legend,' he said, and I could hear what I imagined to be beer bottles clinking. 'Never denies access to a friend who needs to borrow his IP address for a night.'

'Legend indeed. Could I just say goodbye to him?'

'Sure, you take care now. Lance, she's all yours.'

'Did that make sense?' Lance asked.

'It did,' I said. 'I won't waste your time telling you how much I owe. You already know.'

'You sound as if you're in a car,' Lance said. 'At 2 a.m.?'

'Off to help out a friend so I'd better go. Have a beer for me.' I ended the call.

Lewis was concentrating on the road so I gazed out of the window, considering Catriona. She must have moved in plenty of different social circles on the island. That meant lots of people with photos of her, particularly given the teenage obsession with posting selfies on social media. Even a complete stranger could have got hold of a photo to cheat her phone security. But then they also needed to get hold of her phone with enough time to send the messages to Adriana, unnoticed.

Her close circle of friends would have been in prime position, the girls with her that night in the Emporium. The ones she conspired with to give the supposed 'love' potion to poor Lewis.

'Who gave you the ginger tea, the potion that made you sick, and told you it was from Catriona?' I asked him.

He shrugged, glanced at me briefly.

'Could it have been Lizzy?'

'I guess it could have been. She was definitely there. It was her who confessed to me what it was all about,' he said. 'Why?'

'Just curious. Did the girls swap phones often? Mess around, take photos with each other's cameras, that sort of thing?'

'Sure,' he said. 'They were with each other every day. Why?'

'Not sure,' I murmured, but there had been a time when Adriana had become friendly with that group of girls. Lizzy would have had access to both girls' cell phones.

'Can we go any faster, Lewis?'

'Of course,' he said. 'I don't want anyone else to die.' He put his foot down.

A conscience is a double-edged sword. An insufficiently well-developed muscle to prevent people from doing things in advance, it often only flexes too late, and then it seizes and cramps until the pain becomes unbearable. All well and good when we've shoplifted candy from the local store or taken your sister's favourite sweater and spilled red wine on it. But murder? How does a conscience deal with that one?

We sped west across the island, close to the cave now, and I looked ahead for the tell-tale swirl of blue lights in the air. I shivered and Lewis reached into the back, handing me a hoodie for an extra layer.

'Here you go, it's big on me so it'll go over the top of yours. I should have warned you to wear a coat. October's turning bitter.'

I put the hoodie on gratefully and looked down at the image on the front, recognising it in spite of the fact that I was around a generation after the U2 cover had been forever ingrained into pop culture.

'I had this on CD,' I said. 'It's called *Boy*, right?'

'Sure,' he smiled. 'My dad gave it to me. He went to one of their first big concerts. Still plays their stuff. Just another minute, but we'll have to park up on the road and walk down to them.'

Still no police lights, and with the dawning lack of official activity came another memory. Luna, saying she thought the boy she'd seen with Adriana had been a daddy. Because he'd had a picture of a little boy 'on him'. Not holding a picture, but literally on him. I stared down at the face now adorning my chest.

What else had Luna said? That they'd seemed to be dancing, that Addie had put a finger over her lips so Luna hadn't alerted her mother. What did dancing look like to a young child? One person reaching out, another pulling away. Addie not wanting to be seen with him.

'I'll park here. We can walk down together. My dad will be trying to keep things low profile,' he said.

'Sure. Could I just use your mobile to phone your dad and make sure I'm properly prepared?' I asked.

'He won't be answering now,' Lewis said. 'Not if he's trying to keep Lizzy calm.'

'I didn't say it was Lizzy.'

Lewis didn't miss a beat. 'I just assumed it was when you started asking about her on the way here,' he said.

The recollections were falling into place fast. Rachel, the

landlady in The Blether, taking my mobile phone, plugging it in behind the bar. Like they did for all the regulars. Lewis behind the bar, with access to Catriona's mobile, not to mention Adriana's things in the pub staffroom.

'There doesn't seem to be anyone here,' I said.

'Maybe they're all in the cave where you found Adriana. It's a bit of a walk. I'm sure we'll meet them down there.'

He took the keys from the ignition and got out, walking round to open my door. I climbed out of the car, keeping a smile on my face.

'It's great that you've helped out like this, but why don't you go back to Tobermory now? Your dad wouldn't want you to see Lizzy in a bad state. I'll ask Simon Bathgate to give me a lift.'

Catriona had been obsessed with Lewis, then Adriana had come along: newer, prettier, an off-islander who could talk about America and casinos and who'd seen all the things teenagers from Mull could only dream of.

'I'll just make sure you get down there safely,' he said. 'It's dark.'

I patted my pockets for my torch and came up wanting. I'd assumed the area would be lit. Cell phone in one pocket, compass in the other. Nothing else.

'I'll be fine. I've been down there before. I think I'd rather go alone.'

We stood still in the darkness, just Lewis Eggo and me, and the sea and the stars.

'What was it your friend told you on the phone?' he asked.

I considered lying, but we were both beyond pretending.

'He said anyone with a photo of Catriona's face could have sent those texts from her mobile to Adriana. That person just needed access to her phone where Catriona wouldn't have seen what he was doing.'

346

Lewis smiled.

'Lots of people had access to Catriona's mobile,' he said. 'She wasn't exactly choosy about who she hung out with.'

'But the only person she wanted to hang out with was you. How long had she waited . . . years? All the time you were growing up together? It must have been close to an obsession for her to have resorted to slipping you potions.'

'She was pathetic,' he said simply. 'When Adriana's father killed her, he did her a favour. She'd have ended up pregnant and squeezing out three or four babies, stuck in this place forever, not a chance of getting out. Honestly, I don't think she even wanted to leave.'

I stuck my hand in my pocket, flicking the side switch on my cell phone upwards to get it in silent mode, and relied on muscle memory to begin the painfully slow task of sending a text as we spoke.

'Adriana, though, she was something else, right? More worldly. More worthy of you and your aspirations. It must have hurt when she rejected you.'

'Fuck you,' he said. Not angry. No emotion at all in his voice. A simple statement, hands relaxed, smiling at me as if we'd just met and were passing the time of day.

'I just want to understand it,' I said. 'Catriona was jealous, right? She hated Adriana for getting all your attention. You were all she'd ever wanted, then this other girl turns up with her American accent and her secrets. Lizzy said Catriona didn't like Addie to start with. Then they got friendly. Friendly enough that Adriana even joined their group, led by Hilda.'

Lewis took a step toward me. I held my ground. He was only eighteen but he was a head taller than me, muscular and undoubtedly stronger. I might have been able to match him for speed over a short distance, but I wasn't going to win running far or in a fist fight. I was vulnerable, and he knew it.

'Catriona manipulated Addie liked she manipulated everyone,' he said. 'If she hadn't poisoned her against me—'

The cat bones. Fake witchcraft props 101. What an idiot I'd been.

'You made it look like Catriona had killed her. In fact you did such a good job of it, of making the Mull Witches seem responsible, that two of them ended up dead.'

'I'm not responsible for that,' he said, an edge to his voice then. 'That was Rob Clark. You fed him the information, you steered him the wrong way. Catriona and Hilda are dead because you came here. Clever you, figuring it all out, getting Lizzy to talk to you.'

'Was I getting too close?' I asked. 'Is that why I'm here now?'

'I tried doing this the nice way when we first met, scaring you off rather than hurting you.' He raised his shoulders and let them fall, slipping his hands into his pockets, sounding as if nothing more were happening than a slight divergence of opinion. Clouds came and went across the moon, the stars dimming.

I remembered Lewis following me from The Blether, nearly back to my hotel, then making an excuse to leave. He'd followed me anyway, apparently.

'It was you who put the seaweed crown under my pillow,' I said. 'Why? To try and get me to leave?'

'Most women would have done,' he said.

'Most women? So this is a gender thing? Is that why you were so angry with Adriana when she didn't fall at your feet the way all the girls from the island always did?'

'You know the thing with Addie? She thought she was better than me. Didn't mind flirting, letting me get close to her, but she was never really interested. Everything about the island was "cute" or "so weird" or "my friends will never believe this!"' Lewis did a passable impression of an American accent and I searched the nearby ground with my eyes for rocks. 'That dumb witches' group was the most exciting thing that happened to her. Late-night ceremonies, worshipping the sea naked on the beaches, hugging trees or whatever the fuck else they do.'

'So you used Catriona's phone to message Addie and get her to sneak out that night, picked her up in your car and pretended you were taking her to meet Catriona,' I said. 'Painted it as if you were doing everyone a favour.'

'She always had a choice,' he said. 'Adriana didn't have to die.'

'What was the choice? Play nice, go skinny dipping, let you indulge your fantasies with her – or drown? Hardly seems fair.'

'I loved her,' he said. 'I hadn't gone with any of the idiot sluts this place had to offer. Why wasn't I good enough for her?'

I could have got back into the car, locked the doors, but then he had the keys.

'You stole the shell from the Emporium, which means you knew in advance that you were going to hurt her. Don't pretend she ever had a choice.'

He smirked.

'I was good though, right? All the witchcraft references. I mean, you fell for it.'

'What about Flora Kydd? How did you find out about her?'

He gave a bitter laugh. 'Did you miss the fact that my father is head of police here? He has all the files in our house. There's a section just for murders, going back decades. Flora wasn't the only one with sand packed in her mouth. It's a much older tradition than that. And honestly, the way you girls talk and bitch and moan, shutting you all up isn't a bad idea.'

I sighed. His car was directly behind me, Lewis in front, not a house for miles. Screaming would be futile. I wondered if Adriana had played along as I was, once she realised there was no Catriona meeting her.

349

'Did she take her clothes off and go swimming with you voluntarily?' I asked.

He tipped his head to one side, lost in the memory. 'I guess she was a little twitchy by then, but she did it. It was cold, but that was part of the fun.'

'Dangerous, night swimming in the dark with so many rocks around. It could as easily have been you who died.'

'I've been swimming these waters my whole life,' he said. 'Let's face it, there's nothing else to do here.'

'Does your dad know? Does he even suspect, just a little?'

'My father is perfectly competent at catching drunk drivers and shoplifters. Anything more complex than that and he's as experienced as a toddler in a science lab. He gets a monthly update with loads of forensics and technological updates. Uses it as a coaster. I, on other hand, actually quite enjoy reading all his files. His handwriting's not as good as mine either. You know, you should never have fallen for that letter. That was sloppy of you.'

'The sealed envelope was a nice touch, as was stepping away to allow me the privacy to read it. Foolish of me though, I admit.' I finished sending the text and took hold of my compass, gripping it hard in my right palm, flexing my calf and thigh muscles to wake them up. 'I do just want to know one thing: did Adriana suffer?'

He closed the gap between us in a single slow, gentle stride. 'Not as much as I could have inflicted on her. More than she wanted to happen.'

I nodded. 'Am I going to?'

'Not if you don't fight me,' he said.

I looked in his eyes. There was nothing there. I'd expected to see cunning or hatred or something resembling panic. His face was skin wrapped around a skull, eyes sitting prettily in their sockets, teeth evenly arranged in a smiling mouth. Nothing at all below the surface. A void worthy of the furthest reaches of space.

'I guess it was a shame for you that Skittles didn't quite kill me on that tree branch. I'm surprised he came up with that idea on his own. Was it you, whispering in his ear that I was trying to frame him for the murders?'

'Now you're crediting me with too much. All I did was tell him I'd seen you heading out of town and in which direction in case he chose to follow. The rope was all his own—'

I punched hard, as hard as I'd ever lashed out in my life, the compass adding to the damage both to Lewis' face and my own fingers. As he went down, I kicked with every ounce of strength I had, aiming for his kidneys. The whomp of air that left him was satisfying, but he was already rolling over and getting his knees underneath him. I wasn't going to land another punch good enough to keep him down.

So I ran.

Lewis was up fast.

I made my decision on the fly.

Follow the road and he'd catch up with me pretty quickly. Stay in the open and he'd spot me. I had to head for shelter and that meant getting down to the water's edge and finding rocks to hide behind. The area was vast, and I'd be able to keep moving from rock to rock in the darkness, evading him. Not down at Mackinnon's Cave, though. That was his territory. He knew how to scramble into the cave mouth, where the best hiding places were. Perhaps that was what he'd wanted all along. Instead of heading down the pathway where the land began its incline towards the sea, I headed upland looking for an alternative path to the shore.

'You can't get away from me!' Lewis shouted.

I kept running, legs pounding, glad of the years of skiing that had made them strong. I could hear him matching my stride from behind. There was no cover on the headland. Nowhere I could stop or conceal myself. No chance of rest.

I gasped oxygen into my lungs to keep going. Stick to the cliff edge, that was the plan. Hug the coastline, try to get just far enough ahead of him that I could climb down unseen. If I could conceal myself and he passed me, it would be almost impossible for him to find me again. My climbing skills were strong. They were the one real advantage I was sure I had over him.

The boulder hit me from nowhere, a combination of sheer bastard luck through the dark and Lewis' determination not to let me get away. It was jagged, slicing into the back of my skull and knocking me to the floor, but I was determined too. Liberty was the prize for Lewis, but mine was life, and sitting on that tree branch, helplessly waiting for Skittles to kill me, had taught me to keep fighting.

I jumped straight back up. Exploring my pain was too expensive a luxury. There was a dip in the path ahead of me, and I could see the spray of water rising up from below the cliffs. The tide was in. That was good. If I could disappear just below the cliff top, Lewis would have no way of seeing me.

'I thought you didn't want to suffer!' he yelled. 'If you stop now, we can talk again. I'll listen to you. Maybe we can find a compromise.'

There was a new desperation in his voice which was all I needed to keep going. Him thinking my escape was a possibility. Him offering compromise. His weakness on display. Gritting my teeth I extended my stride and kept sprinting, head low, arms pumping.

It was the driftwood, not Lewis, that took me down. A large branch someone must have found on the beach and brought up as a souvenir, straight across my path, catching my toes. I flew forward, crashed down hard, the breath knocked from my lungs, crying out as I landed.

Lewis didn't wait to be tripped, launching himself in my direction, landing full on my back and wrapping an arm around my throat, tightening his grip.

I flailed uselessly, my throat still weak and bruised from the near-hanging – but then Lewis was all too aware of that.

Reaching out my hand, I found the branch that had been my downfall, dragging it closer until I could control the length of it, then I jabbed it upwards, over my shoulder, into his face.

His wounded-animal cry was a symphony. His arm released my neck. The pressure left my back and I turned my upper body enough to stab his face with the stick a second time, hearing and feeling the gelatinous popping.

Lewis screamed and the air was on fire with pain and fury. He struck out but his aim was off, blood dripping from his face onto my lower body as he covered his injured eye with one hand.

I shoved him off me, him yelling, crying. Me screeching, cursing.

Getting to my feet, I kept the stick in my hand, needing only to get far enough away that I could hide until daylight.

Lewis was going to need medical attention immediately. He had no choice, not if he wanted to keep that eye.

More slowly, I made my way to the cliff edge, feeling my way with my feet, nervous of more branches in my path. Heading south, knowing that sooner or later there would be a place to hide or a house in the distance. One or the other. That was the beauty of an island. Sooner or later the circle of land meant I would find life.

'Help me!' Lewis screamed from behind me. 'My eye. My fucking eye is out of its socket!'

'Fuck you,' I rasped. 'That's for Addie.'

I heard eight noises – thumps in rapid succession. He was never as far behind me as I'd thought, or perhaps I hadn't staggered away from him in a straight line.

Lewis's hands on my back, me flying through the air, getting one foot down but tripping forward again, too much force behind me to stop, then an icy breeze beneath me, salt in my eyes.

Forward momentum for another millisecond. Then down I went.

My hands reaching out, scrabbling for the cliff edge, grass slipping through my fingers, my nails flying off as I tried to dig them into solid rock.

Down.

My knee crashing into the cliff face, hip following on a sliver of an outcrop, my left hand finding an ancient tree root. Stopping, sliding, clutching hold.

Not daring to breathe, hardly daring to open my eyes.

Then a whooping from above. A celebration. Lewis at the top of the cliff, believing I was gone, no idea I was just feet below him, hanging on for dear life.

I bit my tongue to keep the dark silent, the cacophony of waves beneath me providing the cover I needed for my harsh breathing.

The outcrop was maybe half a foot wide. I just needed to wait it out until daylight, or until I could climb down. Lewis, wherever he was, now quiet. I turned my body so I was side on to the cliff face.

'Thank you,' I told the tree root, leaning my head against it. 'Thank you,' I said to the outcrop, pressing my palm into the solid land I was perched on.

I leaned over to get my cell phone from my pocket, praying I hadn't dropped it on the cliffs above, joyful when I felt its solid mass. With my left hand, I began to tap in an SOS, hoping against hope that the message would be read, still clutching the tree root with my right hand.

As I turned to punch the letters onto the screen, my compass clattered beneath my leg. I hadn't even realised I'd still been holding it as I'd fallen, nor that it could possibly have landed safely next to me. I reached for it instinctively. I was never without a compass, knowing I could always get home with that simple guide, an emotional comforter more than a tool.

It was the too-long arm of Lewis's U2 hoodie that swept it off the rock shelf before I could grasp it.

It was a simple reaction to reach for it, twist my body, lean too far.

It was gravity that pulled me from my safe haven into the air, onto the crest of the waves, through the depths below.

It was the tide that took me down.

And it was the blow to my head that Lewis had dealt me earlier that disoriented me in the churning, turning, cold-boiling waters.

Hilda's face was what I saw as my body spun and whirled and pirouetted.

'Are you at peace with yourself, Sadie?' she asked me once more. 'Truly? Nothing left unsaid to those you love?'

Too much, I thought. I was wrong the first time.

It was as if I'd never said a single word to those I loved.

It was the weight of that regret that pulled me down. The knowledge that I'd never hold my baby niece, never rock her to sleep or watch her graduate. That I'd never see my own mother again, or tell Adriana's mother who had taken her daughter's life. That I would never kiss Nate Carlisle the way I'd imagined myself kissing him or explain how brilliant I thought he was, how kind, how strong and compassionate. That I'd never see my life unfold.

My body hit rocks as the tide came and went, and I felt nothing. My hair finally met its seaweed crown, fashioned by the sea itself. A car engine on the road above roared into life and sped away.

There was only momentary grief, then a distancing; the relaxing of my grip on the world above and beyond the sea.

And the endless grey-blue-green from inside the waves as I stared up at the moon from my grave.

Chapter Forty-Four

The Island

Sadie Levesque bobbed along on the tide. The threat to her life had begun the moment she set foot on the island. Eyes crawled over every surface of her being. Bets were made, man to man. Gossip slithered from tongue to tongue. Who is she? Where has she come from? How long will she stay?

Had those same curious people looked inward at their own, they would have noticed the boy who couldn't keep his eyes off the beautiful American-Latina girl at his side behind the bar. They'd have heard her turn him down, always with a smile, lightening the rejection with a joke. Someone would have noticed them in the alley at the back of The Blether, as he pulled her towards him and she pulled away. The timeless dance of the keen with the less-so. Witnessed only by one little girl who could not possibly have understood the importance of what she'd seen.

Had those curious people looked inwards, they'd have seen in Catriona Vass not some showy, attention-grabbing teenager, but a girl left alone too often, whose father still mourned his dead wife and who put out to sea every day not to fish, but to lose his grief among the tides. Catriona, whose absent father made it all too easy for Rob Clark to tempt her into his car, asking to talk about Adriana, saying he just wanted to get a sense of how her life had been on the island. Catriona, once so jealous of Adriana, who had cried out for her own father as she'd bled her last drop in a freezing cave, protesting her innocence to a man too deranged with grief to believe her.

Tobermory's townsfolk, had they been inclined to look with unblinkered eyes, would have seen that Hilda was the truest form of their ancestor, embodying the pride and the fight of the Scots island dwellers. The unsentimental mother who does not dote or coddle, but whose offspring always survive.

It was those curious people's refusal to look inward that cost Sadie her life. In that same, swift moment, Nate Carlisle's heart was broken from the loss of a lover he never even held. Lance Proudfoot would be left to wonder when he would learn to listen to his gut, and if he couldn't have saved Sadie's life had he done so.

But the island knows more deaths in a single day than you will encounter in your lifetime. Sadie was but one. Deer fell, foxes were shot, rabbits were trapped, rats poisoned, mice snared, ants trampled, birds, fish, snakes, insects – all life, millions upon millions of souls ending their journeys. The island felt it all.

The people of Tobermory went to their beds that night wearing robes of guilt. They cringed at the memory of the cruel words they'd whispered about Sadie. They papered over the cracks of the lies they'd spread about her. Harris Eggo would find himself with a drink in his hand every time he recalled Sadie's face, and his son's evil.

The dead do not suffer. That is reserved for the living. Sadie's memory lives on. Pictures of her will be framed and hung after her body becomes an empty vessel. And the good she did remains. It rests undiminished in the atmosphere alongside the joy Adriana brought her friends and family, and the light Catriona brought to Tobermory's dullest days. It fuses with Flora Kydd's sweetness and becomes tangible, positively charged energy that visitors will comment on when they first set foot on the Isle of Mull. A sense of peace. An extraordinary sanctuary in a chaotic world. An oasis.

The island welcomed Sadie home.

Chapter Forty-Five

I drifted for a while, ebbing and flowing within my body, then I used it as a raft until I learned to let go, and could finally float above it. The waves were unkind to my corpse. Rocks cut it and bashed it until even Nate would struggle to identify my face.

That first night was long and dark. The sunrise brought some measure of relief, but the real peace came as my body swept ashore, the hood of Lewis's U2 hoodie snagging on an old, wedged lobster pot, tethering me until a fisherman saw my swollen body alive with crabs and flies. Harris Eggo was the first to arrive.

I felt his distress as he recognised the borrowed item of clothing I was found in. And some other emotion – turmoil, I think. He sat there next to what had been me for some minutes, looking at me, looking away. He had a chance, I realised, to take the hoodie from my body. To destroy it. An opportunity to believe the story his son had told him about a drunken night in the woods that had gone horribly wrong as he'd fallen into a tree, unable to see the incoming branch before it had violated his eye. Lewis – already at a hospital on the mainland and drifting away in a fog of anaesthesia – had known his father didn't believe him. But they'd played their roles – concerned dad and injured child – and waited to see what else fate had in store for them.

It arrived that morning in the form of Lance Proudfoot. The message I'd texted blind from my pocket had reached him, making little sense initially.

'Lews egg kill add,' was how my message had arrived on Lance's screen. It had taken him an hour to fill in the missing letters from our previous conversations, and by then he was already trying, uselessly, to call me. Cell phone stuck on a ledge below a cliff, me floating in the sea. His policeman friend had triangulated the phone signal three hours later. They found my phone at 10 a.m.

By lunchtime, Harris Eggo had relinquished control of the case and Dr Nate Carlisle had asked another pathologist to take over. Both of them attached in their own way, fearing an inability to be rational. Lance Proudfoot arrived on Mull once more that afternoon, driving directly to the cliffs above Mackinnon's Cave, weeping for me, quietly and with dignified grief – the sadness when what is lost isn't the years that build deep friendships, but the brief burst of mutual understanding that promises a friendship to come. He wept for the loss of me, for the grief my passing would cause those who loved me, and for all those other women taken from Mull too soon, too cruelly.

Lance Proudfoot opened a bottle of Ledaig on that clifftop, two shot glasses at his side: one for him, one for me. He raised his glass and smiled to the woman he imagined next to him. He told me how brave I'd been, how steadfast and committed. He told me that I could rest. And we cried together, although he couldn't see me smiling back at him, or feel the weight of me leaning against him. I told him I would watch over him, for what it was worth, not even really knowing what that could mean to either of us.

Police Scotland's Major Investigation Team relieved every officer on Mull of any connection with the case. Lewis, who survived surgery but awoke from the anaesthetic handcuffed by his left wrist to a bed, would be known in prison as one-eye. Proper procedure was followed at every turn. No interviews were conducted until Lewis was fit, and then a lawyer was present throughout. Harris Eggo resigned from the police to stand by his son and see him through the trial, in spite of his broken heart and the desire every night to drown himself in a vat of single malt and avoid the painful dawning of each new day. The Eggo family left Mull quietly, without conflict, and never returned. Lewis, convicted at trial, never expressed any remorse for what he'd done, but he did ask his lawyer to petition the police for the return of the U2 hoodie that his father had given him. The favour was not granted.

I saw it all not as a movie, but in short bursts of knowledge. There is no chronology after death. No heavenly bodies, no blissful reunions, but there is a gradual unburdening of emotions, the further we drift from our corporeal life.

I could see Isabella, Brandon and Luna as they settled in San Diego, and soaked up their long sunsets and walks on beaches. I watched Catriona Vass's father pass and knew that he felt nothing but relief as his heart beat its last. There is, after all, only so much pain any one human can bear. Mull returned to normal on its streets first of all, but the townsfolk still double-checked their locks at night, and the teenagers stayed awake whispering to one another on their phones, as if the horrors that had invaded might still be lurking.

A memorial service was held for me on the island, curiously, as unwelcome as I had been. Perhaps it was a salving of the collective conscience that I'd met my end so far away from my own home. The people gathered at Calgary Beach on the north-west coast – a place I'd heard about but never visited – with a sense that it could be a bridge between my Canadian home and the place where I'd perished. Nate gave a eulogy so sweet that I barely recognised myself. He fought back tears and squashed his own hopes and dreams down to that low place we all have inside us.

That, of course, is what death does. It washes clean our faults, our failings and foibles, to leave only good wishes and kind memories. He didn't stay the night on the island where we'd met and I'd first felt the lure of his intelligence and stillness. He left the memory of our chaste night together behind him, regretting – as I had in the seconds between knowing I was dying and passing into death – the fact that we hadn't had the time to see what more there might have been.

I saw the truths behind my suspicions. Father Christophe's upbringing, and the prostitutes his own father sneaked into their home, leaving the boy with a desire to transform all women into virtuous homemakers. The burn mark on Simon Bathgate's hand, caused by a bully of a foster carer who had rendered a child powerless and seeking to assert himself as an adult. I felt Rhys Stewart's fear, a child in an adult's body only partially equipped to deal with the world. The void inside Lewis Eggo. The consuming, echoing, terrible void, that he'd wanted to fill with the perfect relationship with the most perfect girl he had ever seen. If only she had wanted him in return. Flora Kydd's dreadful death at the hands of a girl who'd been told she was powerful, and who had decided that power was destruction. She hadn't stopped killing since.

★　★　★

My mother flew to Scotland to accompany my body home once it was released after the guilty verdict and Lewis's sentencing. I was cremated, my ashes scattered on the ski slopes at Banff, flying through the crystal air, soaking into the snow and joining the land that I loved. My sister held her beautiful, perfect, heavenly girl – Sadie – and wept as the baby slept peacefully in her arms. If my father was able to absorb the information that I was dead, he showed no sign of it. Small mercies.

But my soul, the single cell of me that retained my consciousness, remains above Mull and I finally know what Hilda knew. The pulse of the living, breathing land. The bloodrush of the timeless, unceasing sea. The thriving and failing of the men and women who come and go on the island. The circling truths of centuries: that the witches have been scapegoated once more, and will be again.

Some have suggested that we burn our history books. Remove them from our precious libraries. Prevent myths and folklore from being taught in schools. We blame the retelling, not those who abuse, twist and contort those tales for their own purposes, missing the crucial point: that the women and girls suffered unspeakable deaths not because of Mull's history, but because we, as ever, failed to learn from it.

I wait there and I watch for the next girl whose life will be stolen on that small isle, ready to catch her as she falls, to soothe her cries, to ease her pain. To scoop the sand from her mouth, to heal her cut breast. Knowing the truth. That all women are witches. And that Mull will never allow its myths to be consigned to its past.

Author Note

It goes without saying that *The Last Girl to Die* is a work of fiction. It's nothing more than a story dredged from the depths of my mind. The Isle of Mull, on the other hand, is very real and – other than geographically and mythically – bears no resemblance to the Mull of my novel.

Mull's actual people are warm-hearted, kind, welcoming and forward-thinking. I hope they will allow me to borrow their legends and their history, which lend themselves so perfectly to setting a story there. The island is a magical place. The Spanish galleon sunk in the bay is real. The folklore of the Mull witches is firmly established.

Take my advice; visit Mull. Wander through Tobermory. Go to the standing stones. Take the time to sit where proud castles once stood, and imagine a life where you fought for absolutely everything. Hike the lesser-trodden trails and skim stones on the lochs. Don't miss Mackinnon's Cave whose history is long and fascinating. Sample the whisky. And don't expect any murders – the Isle of Mull is the opposite of its alternate reality in my book.

Scotland is the most intriguing country. It strides fearlessly into the future as it carries its past in its arms, ever present, ever loved. This is why it's such an ideal setting for novels, particularly for exploring the darker side of human nature. Every time I leave Scotland, I leave my heart behind. You won't meet strangers who make better company in any other country in the world. So here's my apology to the Mull islanders – you are not the people in this book. Your breath-taking scenery I have unashamedly stolen, likewise your amazing tales of past times and the relentless, unforgiving sea. Everything and everyone else herein is fantasy.

Helen Fields

**Read on for a sneak peek of
Helen Fields's new novel, *The Institution*
coming spring 2023 . . .**

Chapter 1

MONDAY

The dead often made more compelling company than the living.
That had been Connie's experience. They told their story plainly,
without subterfuge or hyperbole, and they asked for remarkably
little in return. Justice, perhaps, or to protect others who might
follow the same path, though this particular body was going
to make greater demands on her, and rightly so.

Dr Connie Woolwine gripped the corpse's hand with her
own. In life, the two of them might have been friends, bonded
through a mutual love of medicine and helping the hopeless.
In death, the common denominator was the baby one of them
had carried and whom the other had been engaged to find.

'Who took her from you, Tara?' Connie asked. 'How could
they have been so cruel?' She ran gloved fingers over the dead
woman's hair, admiring the silken mass, bobby pins still stuck

randomly here and there, where a struggle had loosened her bun. 'Do you mind if I look at what they did to you? I'll be gentle. You can trust me.'

Connie gave it a moment before folding down a section of the sheet that covered nurse Tara Cameron's body, and was reminded of a childhood game played in a group. Each player had a piece of paper and a pencil. Every person drew feet, folded the paper over and passed it on, the next drew the legs and folded it again and so on until there was a whole body waiting to be revealed in all its ridiculous, hilarious jollity. Not so the picture unfolding before her eyes now. Connie let the injuries – the brush-strokes of murder – tell their story.

Tara's face was relatively unmarked, unless you counted the mascara that had bled down from her eyes, the wet blackness dripping outwards to leave sad trails across each temple. The young woman had been on her back as she'd died and she'd been conscious for most of it, crying both for the loss of her child and for her own impending end. She would have had more than enough medical knowledge to understand there was no way of surviving what was happening to her.

Almost invisible, mistakable to the untrained eye as faint lipstick smudges, was the reddening that extended from each corner of her mouth.

'Was that the first thing they did, gag you?' Connie asked her, running a fingernail over the minuscule abrasions the material had left. 'It must have been, or you'd have called for help.'

A tiny, dark stud sat in her left earlobe. Connie ran her thumb over it, wondering who had given Tara the earrings, and when. The surface came away as the glove left the jewellery, and suddenly it was a diamond stained with a droplet of blood. There was no such stud in the right ear, and the possible explanations for that were many, but Connie could almost see the gag being pulled roughly off and catching on the jewel, popping it from the butterfly clip that held it in place.

Neck and shoulders next. The clear, bloody circle shapes of

two fingertips sat at the side of Tara's neck, a moment frozen in time as her attacker felt for a pulse. Connie already knew they would find no prints in the blood. Whoever committed the atrocity had worn gloves. Nothing had been left to chance. Only the smallest detail, unforeseeable, had left Tara's corpse recoverable in the way it had been.

Her shoulders, undamaged, unblemished, spoke volumes about Tara's life. At 30 years of age, her skin tone was healthy, her flesh firm and unmarked. Thin white lines from shoulder to breast evidenced a bikini worn somewhere hot. She'd liked being outside, enjoyed the feel of heat on her body. It was a hopeful thing, to holiday. A passing of time in the belief that you had enough of it left to simply enjoy, to forget yourself for a while and be frivolous. Connie wondered what Tara would have done with that vacation time if she'd known what fate had in store for her. Spent it with family or putting her affairs in order? Written letters from the woman she would never have the chance to grow into, to help those she loved through the coming darkness?

Another downward fold of the sheet. Breasts, unharmed, just starting to swell with first milk. Speckled with blood that had dried to minuscule, blackening flakes and left her smooth skin roughly textured. To the sides, her upper arms reflected cruel fingers that had clenched hard enough to leave bruises, the ghosts of a man who had been swift and merciless in restraining her. Thumb marks on the inside of her arms, fingers on the outer flesh. Tara had to have looked him in the face then, known the man who would go on to kill her. His face would have been as close as Connie's was to Tara now.

There would almost certainly be some clue on the body. Trace DNA from skin cells, a drop of sweat, a fleck of saliva shed in the physicality of the attack. Technological advancements had rendered every body a forensic map waiting to be discovered, a trail of touches, kisses, slaps and scrapes. One big chemical party. If only there were time for such discoveries to be made.

But there wasn't. Connie checked the clock that ticked away at her from the cream tiled wall, and forced herself to hurry along. She was short on minutes. Next fold. Lower arms, rib cage, stomach, abdomen. She steeled herself. The further down she looked, the bloodier the residue. Tara's loose skin flopped and sagged around her belly, crinkling where it had been suddenly spared its former swell. It wasn't a beating. There was no evidence of blunt force. This was something altogether worse.

At the base of Tara's abdomen a single slash had been made, roughly 7 inches long, just deep enough to part the skin and reach the muscles. Tiny, regular wounds around the edge showed where clamps had been applied to hold the skin back and facilitate internal access. From there, the cuts were layered until the womb was accessible. And that was most of the story. Not all of it, but most.

Tara's body had been violated, her baby taken. The womb that for 36 weeks had been the ideal nest and transportation system as the baby readied itself for the outside world, had been vandalised and robbed. It was by no means a professional job but it wasn't a bad effort. Someone had done their homework. A teacher grading their work would have given them a B for effort and a C+ for the final product, and that was enough to perform a non-consensual caesarian section.

It was called foetal abduction, and it was possibly the worst crime imaginable as far as Connie was concerned. No small claim given how high her professional experiences had set the bar. It was murder, too, but that hadn't been the attacker's primary motivation.

The corpse was little more than collateral damage from the main event.

No effort had been made to close Tara's wounds. She'd bled to death as the baby had been prepared for removal from the building. Silenced, bound by the wrists with something thin and hard, held down, Tara had been far too awake as the most precious thing in the world had been stolen from her.

Connie put one gentle hand over the wound as if wishing

she could turn back time, tempted to grab the lips of it and close the gaping hole. As if closing it could return the baby to its loving mother's body.

Tara's hands were swollen. The surgery, for anyone sick enough to call it that, had taken some time. Connie walked her own fingertips, centimetre by centimetre, down Tara's left hand, probing the bones gently. Only a full post-mortem with X-rays would be conclusive, but she felt sure there were fractures beneath the crimson blooms on the skin. The narrative of those injuries was expanded by her nails, snapped and split, bloody and blackening.

'You fought so hard,' she soothed. 'I hope you know that you did all you could for your baby. Some fights are unwinnable. Your attacker was too well prepared.' Connie patted the corpse's hand as her own grandmother had patted hers when she'd needed comforting. You learned how to love early if you were lucky, and those skills either stayed with you for life or eluded you forever. Connie wondered what Tara's baby was seeing and learning in the first few tender, precarious hours of life. Nothing good.

From there on down, little new information presented itself. There was some bruising on Tara's legs, again around the ankles which also appeared to have been bound. Tara's body hadn't yet reached the extremes of discoloration that the days after death would bring, so soon had Connie been called in following the discovery. Time being of the essence was a grotesque under-statement.

The mortuary suite door creaked, jammed, was thumped and finally gave way. It had hardly been used in years and the fabric of the building would clearly have preferred the area to remain sealed, but needs must.

'Dr Woolwine, I'm Kenneth Le Fay. We were wondering if you were nearly finished?' a man asked.

'Nearly,' Connie said.

'So . . . how long? Only the family is waiting in my office. I don't know if you were made aware but the consultant pediatrician takes the view that the baby cannot survive more than 7 days, having been removed in such a traumatic manner.'

'A week is what I figured,' she said. 'After that the trail will have gone cold anyway.'

His voice was harsh in his throat and she was reminded of the sound of an insect rubbing its back legs together. Mr Le Fay's gaze lingered where Connie was holding the dead woman's hand. He was unable to keep the surprised distaste from his face.

'I'll be right out,' she said. He forced the door opened a few degrees wider and extended his arm to encourage Connie to leave. 'Privacy would be best,' she added.

He sighed, but left her alone without an argument. Connie didn't hold it against him. Kenneth Le Fay was the head of a busy, specialised mental health hospital that housed high security patients. This wasn't the first death on his watch, nor would it be his last, but it was certainly the one that was going to cause him the most sleepless nights.

'I've got to go,' Connie told Tara, folding the sheet section by section back over her cold flesh. 'I'm going to do what I can. No promises, it wouldn't be fair to make any, but I'll get started today and I'm going to give it everything I've got. For what it's worth, I believe your baby's still alive right now. I'm so fucking sorry this happened to you.'

She stroked Tara's hair once more and leaned over her forehead, tempted to kiss the smooth skin and wish the poor young woman into a sounder sleep. The inevitable transfer of DNA prevented her from being so careless.

'I'll come see you again when all this is over, and I'll have more time to spend with you then. Don't give up hope.'

Already hooked? Order your copy of *The Institution* in store or online now.

**If you loved *The Last Girl to Die*,
then why not try Helen Fields's iconic
DI Callanach series?**

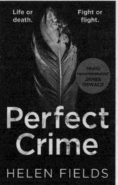

Available from all good bookstores now.

And don't miss these fantastically twisty crime thrillers . . .

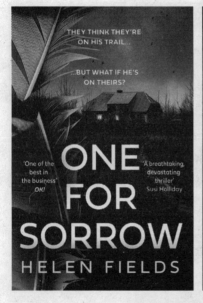

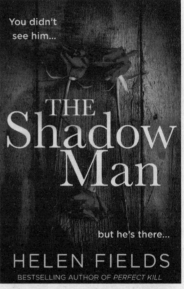

Available from all good bookstores now.